Publisher
Crime Time
7a King Henry's Walk
Islington
London N1 4NX
Fax: 020 7249 5940
e-mail: editor@crimetime.co.uk
Website:www.crimetime.co.uk

Distribution
Turnaround

Printing
Omnia, Glasgow

Editor
Barry Forshaw

Production Editor
Paul Brazier

Film Editor
Michael Carlson

TV & Music Editor
Charles Waring

Advertising
Philomena Muinzer
Tel: 020 8964 9106
Fax: 020 8881 5088

Subscriptions
£20 for 4 issues to
Crime Time Subscriptions,
18 Coleswood Road, Harpenden,
Herts AL5 1EQ
Fax: 01582 712244
www.crimetime.co.uk

Legal
Crime Time is copyright © 2001
Crime Time ISBN 1-84243-019-X

Crime Time on the web
Looking for that particular review
or feature? Visit our website on
www.crimetime.co.uk: up-dated
weekly, and easier than looking
in your cherished back issues!

2001

THE DESK

Writing these words just before setting out for the annual beanfeast that is Dead on Deansgate (organised by Waterstones and the CWA), I find myself wondering how useful such junkets are. Heavily supported by almost any crime writer you can shake a stick at, there is great pressure on anyone involved with the crime writing fraternity to attend. I didn't make it last year, relying on several writers who contribute to this magazine (notably Natasha Cooper, Mark Timlin and Adrian Muller) to fill me in on all the gossip. But I certainly paid a price, not least in nagging from these worthies, but from every publicist, publisher and author I encountered in the process of putting out Crime Time. But you should have been there! How could you miss it? You really needed to have been there to see X lay into Y, and so on. Facetiousness aside, there is absolutely nothing wrong with authors celebrating the craft, and if the events help push a few more books, all the better. Perhaps some of us are better suited to the solitary pursuits of crime reading than the elbow bending of such events as this. But just in case this comes across as a rather negative piece, there is one important point to be made. The other hat I wear when not editing CT is that of the writer for various papers and magazines on SF, and a relationship between SF writers and their readers could not be more different from that of crime writers and readers. In SF, a barely disguised contempt is the watchword of most writers for their readers, whereas the camaraderie between crime writers and readers is much more pronounced, with a genuine sense of an adult interchange taking place. Of course, there are embarrassing crime fans, but most aficionados do not seem to play into the hands of the press by presenting themselves in the spectacularly embarrassing style of many SF fans. Still, it is often salutary for writers to come up against their readers: the ivory tower approach may work if your concerns are exclusively literary, but crime writing is a popular form and needs the energy that comes from the interplay between writers and readers.

This issue is devoted to the Pulps, in all their garish splendour. Perhaps nowadays most of us only read this material when it has acquired the patina of respectability (Chandler, Hammett et al.), but there's no denying the seductive charm of those exploitative illustrations. The craftsmen who turned them out – writers and illustrators – have long been underrated, and I thought it was time to ask CT writers such as Mike Ashley to celebrate their skills in modest fashion. The theme for the next CT will be women and crime, with the largest ever survey of female crime writers undertaken by any magazine. As soon as I get back from Deansgate, I have to start copy-editing the thousands of words already received, but I'm sure that the musings of everyone from Minette Walters to Lindsey Davies will keep it from being too arduous a task.

Our website (www.crimetime.co.uk) adds articles, news and reviews on a weekly basis – so finding that half-remembered piece on Dorothy L. Sayers or James M. Cain might be a little easier online than thumbing through your yellowing issues of the magazine. Steve Kelly, who handles our website (along with his own Richmond Review), has also inaugurated buying links for those items you might be tempted by. And don't miss the new site book2book (http://www.book2book.co.uk), fascinating for anyone interested or involved in the world of books.

Barry Forshaw

THRILL-MAD PUSSYCATS

Mike Ashley

Who better than our resident pulp maven, Mike Ashley, to kick off our pulp celebration – with a look at the book that furnished several of our illustrations this issue?

*T*hrill-Mad Pussycats, eh? A book about a tom cat's holiday, maybe? Nope. Not when you consider in the same series is *Hellcat Amazons* and *Teen-Rebel Dopefiends*. And when I say these are postcards, you may still be wondering. What the hell am I doing reviewing postcards?

Ah, well, these are rather special. Prion Books have started to issue a series of what they call 'Pulp Postcards'. Now, to the pedants amongst us (yep, here I am), pulp means the wonderfully fragile pulp magazines of yesteryear and you might expect therefore to see the lurid covers of *Dime Mystery* or *Spicy Adventure Stories*. But no. Thanks to Quentin Tarantino, pulp these days has come to be associated with sleaze and hard-boiled crime, stuff that was once thought more trash than treasure, but which is now a collector's heaven.

This pad, and its two partners, is a collection of thirty-one cover reproductions of good-girl art from crime and sleaze paperbacks of the late forties to the early sixties. Books with such wonderful titles as *Sin on*

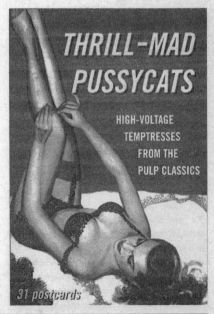

THRILL-MAD PUSSYCATS

HIGH-VOLTAGE
TEMPTRESSES
FROM THE
PULP CLASSICS

31 postcards

Wheels, Tomcat in Tights, Pit Stop Nympho and *Nautipuss* and from such publishers as Beacon, Midwood, Quarter and Rainbow.

The reproductions are excellent. I suspect they've been computer enhanced, as there's not a crease or a blotch in sight. If the original paperbacks were in this same mint condition they'd be worth £10, £15, £20 or more. There are some real gems in this lot. I've seen David Charlson's *No Time for Marriage* from Venus Books listed at $100 (around £70), though a more sensible price for it is around £20. Even so, if you had all thirty-one books represented in this one pad, I reckon you'd have around £400 worth of tat.

There are examples here of several of the collectable sleaze authors – Orrie Hitt, Florence Stonebraker (also under her alias Thomas Stone), Norman Bligh, Jack Hanley – all treasures. There are also examples

of more mainstream authors who drifted in and out of this scene in the fifties, such as Edwin Gilbert and Charles Gorham.

All of the covers are delightful. All depict lusting and voluptuous temptresses leaving little to the imagination — just like the titles: *Quickie* or *Pushover* or *Man Bait*! I love the cover blurbs like this from *Loves of a Girl Wrestler* – 'Mauled, Manhandled, Exhibited Before Lusting Eyes _ This Lovely Creature Fought for Depravity and Disgrace at the hands of bone-crushing men and passionate amazons.' Beat that, Jackie Collins!

If I have one beef with Prion, it's that no attempt has been made to identify the cover artists themselves. It's their work that sold these books and will sell these cards, yet they're the unsung heroes in all of this. I confess I don't know most of them. There are two examples of the brilliance of British artist Reginald Heade, whose work is highly collectable, and who is represented here with *Coffin for a Cutie* by Spike Morelli and *Plaything of Passion* by Jeanette Revere. But I'd love to know who did the artwork for *Marriage Can Wait* or *Fast, Loose and Lovely* or *Tomcat in Tights*.

They're wonderful cards (though a bit expensive at the equivalent of 25p a card), and they're the kind of thing you're likely to keep as they are, not actually send them to anyone. Maybe they'll even start a passion for collecting the real books – and there are a helluva lot of them out there.

Maybe Prion will turn to the real pulps next – and credit the artists.

Thrill-Mad Pussycats – High Voltage Temptresses from the Pulp Classics (£7.99, Prion Books, 1-85375-394-7)

THE PULPS

Peter Haining

Peter Haining's The Classic Era of American Pulp Magazines *is a loving celebration of something dear to his (and our) heart. We asked Peter how it all started for him*

I saw my first pulp magazines heaped up on a counter in the UK chain store Woolworths in the early 1950s. The brilliant red and yellow covers, with their illustrations of violent action and beautiful girls in various stages of disarray, immediately caught my schoolboy imagination. So, instead of spending my weekly pocket money on sweets and the usual comic, I purchased a copy of a magazine called *Weird Tales*. I walked home, my head lost in worlds of fantasy and horror, and somehow knew I would never be quite the same again. It would, in fact, be a while before I came to appreciate the uniqueness of these American magazines, shipped across the Atlantic and sold cut price in various out-

The Classic Era of
AMERICAN PULP MAGAZINES
PETER HAINING

lets such as Woolworths – and a lot longer before I learned about their history. I did soon discover, though, that they were not approved reading by my parents, and any copies of *Weird Tales* – and another favourite, *Black Mask* – that I could afford, had to be secreted away for reading by flashlight under the bedclothes. Little did I realise then that there had been teenagers just like me doing exactly the same thing in the United States, a generation earlier.

In the fifty years since then, I have constantly been on the lookout for copies of these remarkable magazines – becoming ever rarer by the year – and now own a quite substantial archive, which has helped to make this book possible. Sadly, my first copy of *Weird Tales* has long since disappeared (left behind in the loft of one of the family houses when we moved, I believe) but the memory of the magazine, the words, and the pictures, linger on. It was a

purchase of the purest chance that opened the doors into the unique world of the pulps. There were hundreds of pulp magazines – gaudy, sensation-packed fiction titles that sold at between five cents and a quarter. Their classic era was from the 1920s to the 1940s, and they catered to basic needs in the male psyche because their market was almost solely focused on the US male: his aspirations to be 'redblooded' and a 'he-man', and to have a life of action and adventure in which beautiful women fell easily into his arms, and even into his bed. Such dreams came true only for the few, so the pulps catered to fantasies – providing armchair action and masturbatory ideals. As Tony Goodstone, one of the first pulp historians, put it: every month during the 20s, 30s, and 40s, millions of redblooded American males barricaded themselves behind the bathroom doors of the nation with the latest offerings of their favourite pulp magazine. Proscribed by par-

ents, condemned by educators, and ignored by critics, the pulps were the development of a fiction form rooted in the early nineteenth century, and were, according to the magazine *Playboy*, "Those likeable lurid novels for which whole forests were levelled and upon which a whole generation of American youth was hair-raised."

The pulps were the young men's magazines of their time – a period of time in the US that was more puritanical, more troubled, and more repressed than it is possible to believe of a nation that so prides itself on its freedoms. Some women did read these magazines – the columns of readers' letters in quite a few provide evidence of an open-minded minority who wanted more equality with the men in their lives – but the rights that women enjoy today were a long way off.

It has been said that the pulps, with their bluntly provocative titles and lurid covers, were a "cradle of sensationalism". But that ignores the fact that they were the medium through which some excellent and sometimes experimental writing was published. They were also the place where some memorable art appeared, as the pages of this book will bear convincing witness. Although the magazines were mass-produced and largely stereotyped in their genres, they were read as eagerly then as television programmes are watched by people today. The constant need to fill pages, month after month, gave the more adventurous editors and art directors the excuse to publish whatever took their fancy, and they were safe in the knowledge that they could lay their hands on plenty of more traditional fare for any nit-picking readers who complained.

It is important to know a little of the history of those times in order to put the magazines into the context of the events that shaped the major genres that are the focus of this book. In January 1920, for instance, the Eighteenth Amendment to the US Constitution came into force, banning the production and sale of alcohol. Prohibition had, of course, been operating in some States since the middle of the previous century, because alcohol was viewed there as a sin, and a lot of married women were convinced that bars would ruin family life. Only the mayor of New York foresaw the biggest problem – he reckoned he would need an extra 250,000 police officers to keep the city dry. Indeed, the harder the authorities tried, the harder the people, especially the young, rebelled. Scott Fitzgerald chronicled as much in his novels, such as *This Side of Paradise* (1920), in which he caught the spirit of fast-living

youth and coined the term the Jazz Age.

In the world of fashion, too, skirts were getting higher and higher, in a trend toward minimum clothes and maximum cosmetics, as one writer described these 'shocking' sights. Corsets were also on the way out and sexy underwear was very much in – although in a handful of States the authorities became so alarmed about this that they seriously suggested that 'inappropriately dressed women' should be locked up. Along with drinking, which took place surreptitiously, of course, and at a quarter a shot was an expensive pursuit, smoking was frowned upon, as well as shaking about to the latest dance crazes, especially the Charleston. One group of churchmen was so incensed by the playing of jazz that they described it as 'a return to the jungle', and in 1927 the blonde bombshell Mae West pushed the boundaries of propriety even further with her play *Sex*, which

mocked the conventions of virtue and decency. Evidence was given against her by some police officers who sneaked into a performance, and Mae was found guilty of indecent behaviour, fined $500, and sent to prison for ten days. The sexual revolution had arrived, even if it was not quite under way yet.

On the other hand, the impact of crime and gangsterism upon the fabric of US society was growing increasingly worse as the decade progressed – culminating in the infamous Valentine's Day Massacre in Chicago on February 14, 1929, when seven mobsters were lined up against a beer-house wall and mown down with sub-machine guns. The killers were all in the employ of Al Capone and were 'protecting' his monopoly in the city in the supplying of bootleg liquor, extortion, and prostitution. Worse still was to come on October 24, 1929, when Wall Street crashed and 13 million shares were traded on a panic-stricken New York stock exchange. This 'Black Thursday' marked the start of the Depression, which would affect the whole of the US during the next few years. It would take the steadying hand of the new president, Franklin D. Roosevelt, to put the country back to work, end Prohibition (in 1933), and wage war against organised crime. For most folk there was little relief from this gloom apart from the escapism of radio, the movies (where the talkies had just arrived) and, as it transpired, the pulps – tickets to cheap thrills and gaudy pictures for the price of small change. Few publishing phenomena were better timed than that of the pulp magazines.

The pulp magazine was the idea of a former telegraph operator from Augusta,

sell his 'pulps' at ten cents – less than half the price of a typical slick. It was a decision that would make his fortune and revolutionise publishing. The resulting pulp magazines measured, on average, ten inches by seven inches. The number of pages was normally 128 – containing something like 120,000 words of fiction – all stapled together through the cover, close to the spine. The paper, on which the text was printed in double columns, was thick and porous, and the edges were left uncut. The magazines gave off an unmistakable smell, which is still detectable in surviving copies today, and the pages usually turned yellow within months. But such factors failed to discourage the millions of potential readers who earned only meagre wages. The average earnings of a factory hand, for example, were about $7 for a ten to twelve hour day. Such people just wanted entertainment and escapist fare: simple, fast, and graphically

Maine, named Frank Andrew Munsey. He came to New York in 1882 determined to become a publisher. He had a simple maxim: The story is more important than the paper it is printed on, and he knew that, thanks to the advent of the new high-speed printing presses, it was possible to mass produce magazines in a way that had never been possible before. Munsey was well aware that the other popular publications of the time, such as *Harper's*, *Scribner's*, and *The Century* were printed on glossy or 'slick' paper made of rag-content stock. But he decided that if he used the much cheaper pulp paper, which was derived from a wood-fibre base and referred to as 'newsprint', he would be able to offer a much cheaper product. He would give readers a suggestion of value for money by giving the magazines a four-colour cover printed on art paper. The saving in costs, Munsey reckoned, would enable him to

illustrated. The pulps came into being as rivals to the slicks, which catered to the better-off sections of the US, and they quickly earned a reputation for being exploitative, unsophisticated, violent, and sexist. While this was true to a degree, they were also the proving grounds in which some great writers first made their mark – men such as Edgar Rice Burroughs, Max Brand, Zane Grey, Dashiell Hammett, Raymond Chandler, Erle Stanley Gardner, Howard Phillips Lovecraft, Clark Ashton Smith, Abraham Merritt, Robert E. Howard, Robert E. Heinlein, John D. MacDonald, Isaac Asimov, Ray Bradbury, and many others whose names will crop up in these pages. As more than one historian of the era has noted, there has not been a time, before or since, when so much entertaining fiction was available to so many so cheaply – albeit with a fair helping of trash thrown in too. The quality of the cover art

and interior illustrations of the pulps has similarly been unfairly ridiculed without due study being made. In the early days, there were generally very few pictures inside the magazines, and those that there were had to be drawn in simple, bold strokes to avoid being over-inked or smudged into unrecognisable blurs when printed on the pulp paper. With the passage of time, however, a whole school of artists, some now deservedly famous and others long overdue for recognition, provided colourful, action-packed pictures of every conceivable situation, all intended to part customers from their hard-earned cash. At its best, the artwork had the same come-on effect as contemporary graphic art elsewhere, such as a poster advertising a new feature film or the next episode of a serial. These pictures may not always have been an accurate reflection of the contents, but their impact on sales was undeniable. Writing about this element of pulp magazine history in his *Handbook of American Culture* (1977), Bill Blackbeard has said: "Illustrating the pulps was nearly as important for sales in the 1930s as the lurid covers of nickel thrillers had been for their prosperity at the turn of the century [...] Supplying the considerable quantity of artwork was the task of a few dozen well-worked, professional ink, watercolour and oil artists, who varied in quality and reputation from the dreariest kind of scrawlers and daubers who worked for Desperation Row (as the skin-of-their-teeth pulp houses were called) to a number of fine artists of international fame who did occasional or regular pulp magazine illustrations for bread-and-butter money. Most, of course, were artists of reasonable competence and occasional flairs of real genius."

Among the role call of these artists are names such as Paul Stahr, Hubert Rogers, John Newton Howitt, Walter M. Baumhofer, Max Plaisted, Harold S. Delay, Earle Bergey, Peter Driben, Enoch Bolles, Amos Sewell, Tom Greiner, Hans Waldemar Wessolowski, Howard V. Brown, Fred Craft, Rudolph Belarski, Rafael De Soto, Tom Lovell, Norman Saunders, J. E. Allen, Lyman Anderson, H. V. Parkhurst, Rudolph W. Zirm, Frank R. Paul, H. J. Ward, Monroe Eisenberg, Marvin Singer, Robert Gibson Jones, Virgil Finlay, Peter Poulton, Alexander Leydenfrost, Paul Orban, John Fleming Gould, Hannes Bok, Leo Morey, Alex Schomberg, Wynne W. Davis, Edd Cartier, Frank Kelly Freas, not forgetting a trio of outstanding women, Margaret Brundage, Irene Zimmerman, and Pauline Drappier. It is the artists' work especially that is being celebrated in this book. Without it the pulps might have amounted to only a chapter or two in publishing history rather than a gloriously colourful era packed with compelling – occasionally notorious – images that today provoke feelings of nostalgia among those old enough to remember, and a nod of admiration from younger generations seeing them for the first time. It has to be admitted that there were cheap publications for the masses long before Frank Munsey initiated the 'rag-paper to pulp-riches' era from his offices at 280 Broadway, New York. Almost a century earlier, a London entrepreneur, Edward Lloyd, had been at the forefront of a group of publishers in the city issuing Penny Dreadfuls, which enthralled the British public with serial stories of action, adventure, and plenty of lust (nothing new, you see). *Varney the*

Vampyre, The Feast of Blood (1847), the daring exploits of *The Smuggler King* (1849), and the semi-pornographic liaisons of *The Merry Wives of London* (1850) all had lurid front-cover illustrations of gory encounters and terrified maidens. A little later, the firm of Beadle and Adams was the first to catch the US public's fancy with Dime Novels. These weekly publications recounted the exploits of men like the backwoods hero Deadwood Dick, the sporting champion Frank Merriwell, the ingenious boy inventor Frank Reade, and, perhaps most popular of all, the enduring young sleuth Nick Carter. Frank Munsey launched the pulp era in 1896 with a short story magazine of action and adventure tales, the *Argosy*. The magazine recruited its writers from everywhere – some, like Borden Chase, from the most unlikely backgrounds. Chase, whose real name was Frank Fowler, had worked in Chicago as a driver for Frankie Yale, a

well-known bootlegger, until the day the mobster was shot by Al Capone. Fearing for his life, Fowler moved to New York, changed his name, and took to pulp writing with gusto. He remembered the experiences of those days well when he later moved again to Hollywood, where he soon became a script writer: "I was like a lot of other guys who got into writing for the pulps because they were there. They were looking for people with imagination – it didn't matter if you hadn't been to some of the places you wrote about as long as you could tell a good story. The crime stuff came easy to me so that's what I did. The editors at Munsey's always needed copy fast and you could get a cheque as soon as the story was accepted and they signed a voucher. They paid a dollar a thousand words. I once heard a story that Frank Munsey would evaluate the worth of a story by how heavy the manuscript felt in his hand, but that never happened to me!"

The success of *Argosy* inspired several more titles, including *All Story Magazine*, *The Cavalier*, and *The Scrap Book*, all masterminded by Munsey's brilliant editor, Robert H. Davis – the man who discovered Edgar Rice Burroughs and Max Brand to name just two writers. Within a few years, the Munsey quarter had spawned an industry that would ultimately generate in excess of 300 titles. Their rivals were numerous, and all of them were anxious to get a piece of the pulp action: Street & Smith, Clayton Magazines, Popular Publications, Thrilling Publications, Culture Publications, the A. A. Wyn Group, and many more who will all feature in the following pages. Although the pulps were sold predominantly in the US, some were exported to Europe – often as ballast in merchant vessels – where they were sold off cheaply in chain stores like Woolworths. In time, Britain would produce its own range of pulps in what became known as the 'Mushroom Jungle'. The story of these 'Yankee Mags', as they were called, is dealt with in the final chapter. The variety of the pulps produced in the US during their heyday was truly incredible. Jostling alongside each other on the news-stands could be found *Adventure*, *Amazing Stories*, *Black Mask*, *Famous Fantastic Mysteries*, *Detective Story Magazine*, *Ghost Stories*, *Golden Fleece*, *Horror Stories*, *Marvel Science Stories*, *New York Nights*, *Oriental Stories*, *Private Detective*, *Spicy Mystery Stories*, *Stolen Sweets*, *Terror Tales*, *War Stories*, and *Weird Tales* to name just a few. Also fighting for space were the solo titles *The Shadow*, *Doc Savage*, *Dusty Ayres and his Battle Birds*, *Secret Agent X*, *Doctor Death*, *Captain Satan*, *Sheena, Queen of the Jungle*, and a number of others that survived beyond the pulp era as paperbacks or comics, and have been fully dealt with elsewhere. This list of titles merely hints at the dozens of similar magazines, catering for every possible taste, that poured from the presses in the US during the years between the two world wars. Some would prove very successful, but others would disappear after only a single issue. The hard-nosed pulp magnates and quick-buck publishers who worked side-by-side in this pulp jungle were united only in one simple factor – their attitude toward every title they issued. If the public didn't buy it in sufficient quantities, they ceased its publication immediately. In this context, the *Dictionary of American Biography* has some rather unflattering things to say about the 'founding father', Frank Munsey, which are no doubt just as true of many of his rivals: "He was not a reformer, nor an idealist, nor was he deeply interested in any causes. His passion was to found or purchase magazines and, later, newspapers. If one of his magazines failed to earn well he killed it and began another; if public taste passed from one of his productions he dropped it to develop another."

All the major pulp publishers were quick to seize on any new interest or trend, often following one another slavishly until the genre had become saturated with identical titles and sales dropped. It is perhaps pertinent to note that the rise of the superheroes like The Shadow, Doc Savage, Spider and the others coincided with the downfall of public figures during the Depression. The rise of crime in the US and the emergence of dictators in Europe were also regarded by the pulp publishers and their writers as forces that could be combated only by men

of supernormal powers. The pulps were not just intended to entertain the reader – they were also meant to make him feel better about himself, his prospects, and especially his sex life. With this in mind, companies did not use the magazines to sell ordinary things like clothes or food, but instead tried to sell any number of do-it-yourself fitness courses, cures for bad breath, sex aids, 'home' movies, quack medicines, peek-a-boo nighties, and – because the magazines were full of unclothed girls – even courses in learning how to draw. Charles Atlas, who offered to help scrawny young men to keep their girls, rather than lose them to sand-kicking bullies, was one of the most prolific advertisers. And several less reputable companies pandered to every fad and fancy imaginable in the magazine's personal columns at the back. On offer were 'unretouched' photographs of French models, methods for curing weak bladders, ruptures, and piles, potions and lotions to

restore energy and 'pep', instructions on how to hypnotise people (the illustration showing a beautiful girl, of course), pen-pals for lonely hearts, and a whole range of illustrated booklets and novelties – 'The Kind Men Like!' And because this was the Depression, there were courses in how to become an electrician, a salesman, even a detective, plus any number of ways to 'Earn Money At Home!'

The eventual death knell for the pulps began to sound during and after the end of the Second World War. Paper fell into short supply and became more costly – as did the metal required for the staples. These became so expensive that some publishers were forced to use just one through the spine. Tastes were also changing. A new sophistication was evident among readers, and suddenly the pulps were being regarded as 'something from the old days'. On the literary scene, a whole new generation of writers was starting to emerge who aspired to more permanent – and better paid – markets than the ephemeral, penny-a-line pulps. A few of the more popular pulp titles were downsized to digest format by their proprietors, as if to deny their heritage. At the same time, the frantic pace of the storytelling disappeared, along with the unashamed gaudiness of the art, which had been essential ingredients of the pulps. As sales of the rest fell and the frequency of publication stumbled from monthly to quarterly, the major distributors servicing the nation's news-stands drove the final nail in the coffin by cancelling their orders in favour of the exploding new market for comic books and original paperback fiction. Television, which was rapidly becoming a feature in every household, also cut savage-

ly into the reading habits of the nation. Ironically, at this very time, *Argosy* and *Blue Book*, which had pioneered the pulp legend, were revamped, and reappeared on the news-stands as slick magazines! Some people felt that Frank Munsey would have turned in his grave, but others believed that the old pulp-meister would have already acted before the writing was on the wall. Whatever the case, the pulp magazine legend was secure. But the telling of it has required the passage of time and an end to the prejudice and snobbery directed against a very special era – when cheap thrills and big shots were the stuff of dreams for millions of ordinary people.

A golden era: I believe *Crime Time* readers will agree.

The Classic Era of American Pulp Magazines is published by Prion.

JIM SALLIS: DISSONANT CHORDS

Eve Tan Gee talks to the man; **Woody Haut** looks at his major new study of Chester Himes.

Can we talk about your new books?
Since you're buying the coffee, of course we can. The latest major work to be published is the Chester Himes biography, two years of my life packed into 400+ pages, commissioned and brought out by Canongate Books in Edinburgh. The man to blame is Jamie Byng. It's quite a fine book, I think, though I remember partway into it complaining to a friend that, whereas writing novels was like building a treehouse or sundeck, all light and air, doing biography more closely resembles remodelling your bathroom: broken tiles and stinky pipes everywhere, floor torn up, nothing fits anything else… Also recently out, from Toxic, is a volume of my collected stories, *Time's Hammers*. And from No Exit, an 'ace double' edition of the first two Lew Griffin novels, *The Long-Legged Fly* and *Moth*. In the States there's also an essay collection, *Gently into the Land of the Meateaters*, and one of two scheduled poetry collections, *Sorrow's*

Kitchen. The final Lew Griffin novel, *Ghost of a Flea*, should be out next Fall.

Favourite writers?
It would prove a very long list. The first to influence me strongly were science fiction writers. I grew up pretty much reading everything: Dickens and Hemingway, Faulkner, Steinbeck, alongside Sturgeon, Jerry Sohl, Richard Matheson, not recognizing much difference. (I still don't.) But it was the science fiction writers I learned the most from, at first, and from whom I took inspiration. *Time's Hammers* divides rather neatly into two volumes, one of them science fiction and fantasy stories, the other mystery and suspense stories. A third collection, *Beautiful White Ruins of America*, as yet unplaced, comprises more directly 'literary' or 'experimental' stories.

When I first began writing seriously, or trying to, I thought of myself as a poet and was strongly in thrall to Frost, Creeley, Lowell, Stevens – that whole range of modernist poets. I'd also discovered Joyce and Pynchon and begun groping my way towards Apollinaire and Cendrars, which led to what may be the most urgent single influence on my work, certainly on my poetry, and which to some considerable extent defines that work's difference from most contemporary Stateside writing: French literature.

But favourites in your field?

Well, I'm not sure what you mean by 'my field'. I have peers among mystery writers, another set among science fiction folk, a cadre of poets, critics and 'literary' people who are friends. Sadly, they're rarely seen at the same parties, and rarely intermarry. If *I* ran the zoo...

Of working writers, I read everything by Thomas Pynchon, George Pelecanos, Iain Sinclair, Daniel Woodrell. I try my best to keep up with Larry Block, Don Westlake, K. C. Constantine, Jim Burke. As columnist for *The Magazine of Fantasy & Science Fiction*, and earlier as SF critic for the LA Times, I've kept up with all that. And I reread, regularly, *Ulysses*, Chandler, *Candide*, Nathanael West, *Gravity's Rainbow*, Auden and Yeats, *The Recognitions*, much of Queneau, favourite Sturgeon, Guillevic, *L'Ecume des Jours*. I subscribe to various literary journals, different ones each year – *High Plains Literary Review*, *Field*, *The Georgia Review* – and read those closely, along with issues of many others in which my own work appears.

How important is your privacy?

Let us always have a condom, Flaubert wrote to mistress Louise Colet, to protect the health of our soul amid the filth into which it is plunged – Flaubert remarking in particular the breakdown of language under the degrading impact of journalism, advertisement and political slogans in a culture over-inflated with unassimilable data. In a culture where even simple civility has come under attack, where constantly we are urged to 'share' our every untoward thought and to 'express our feelings' under peril of isolation, social ill, or madness, it's not too surprising that values such as privacy and discretion should come to be thought of as suspicious, even aberrant.

An oblique, discursive answer to your question – if an answer at all – for which I apologise. But it is a very complicated question. Stephen Daedalus fears those big words that make us so unhappy. Lew and my other characters, I think, tend to fear the word 'should' more than most others.

With either Bush or Gore as the next president, can you remain apolitical?

I'm not sure it's possible to write seriously – as opposed to scarecrow writing, when you just stuff old clothes with straw, excelsior, styrofoam peanuts or old copies of TV Guide and set them out in a field – *without* being political. This is rather a different thing from taking a political stance. But whenever one writes from the centre of self, alternately struggling and dancing with the material, the writing has to be imbued with one's personality, and that in itself – personality, speaking up – is political. Remember that crime and mystery fiction (virtually all American literature, some would insist) developed not from the novel, which concerns itself with man making his way in society, but from the romance, which typically concerns itself with an individual opposed to that society.

One of the things that drew me to crime fiction was the prolapse into it, in the late 1970s and early 80s, of writers like Roger Simon and Stephen Greenleaf, writers who clearly in earlier times would have been 'mainstream', liberals seeking new ways to grapple with all they were seeing about them in a radically transfigured society. It was the same thing that drew me to science fiction a couple of decades earlier. Someone said of Voltaire that he wished to express himself freely yet avoid the Bastille. These writers hunted that same elusive rabbit. They wished to write freely, fully, yet still have readers.

Wallace Stegner among others (including Chester Himes in his great speech at the University of Chicago) noted that many if not all our most serious problems derive from the fact that we here in the States comprise a nation of highly stimulated appetites. There's this constant stimulation of appetites for things – from the brimming cornucopia promised us by our Constitution, to everything the movies, television, magazines and shop windows dangle before us – without provision of economic and other means of gratifying them. The writer, it seems to me, has to remind us to step back from all that, from the deluge of messages, the reductive news, the virtual instruction manual our media have become: buy this, desire that, behave in this socially-approved manner. Our reading of the world is formed by the language through which we experience it, by the language *available* to us.

So: on the one hand, more and more information coming at us all the time; and on the other, ever-diminishing content.

Can we put the genie back in the bottle once it's uncorked? Probably not. We can follow Flaubert's advice to have always at hand a condom, though. Lash yourself to the mast and sail past those cheesy sirens!

Are you a dutiful writer – or do you need a rocket to get started?

Well, I tend to be a binge worker, throwing myself overboard and swimming like hell till I've reached shore. *The Long-Legged Fly* was written in a month, most of the other novels in four to six months. Working on the Himes bio, I went down in a kind of intellectual bathysphere and didn't come up till, eighteen months later, it was done. The bends are an amazing experience. That having been said, I have to add that I sit down here every morning about six o'clock and begin work. And I keep at it most of the day, with time out to read a bit, walk up Park Slope or down Third to the library, munch on bagels at Einstein Brothers' across the street here in Phoenix, Brooklyn's Bagels by the Park, La Madeleine in Fort Worth, to sit on the porch with Karyn watching hummingbirds dart to and from the feeder there, geckos emerge in their saucer-toe gravity boots, bats drop by the dozen from the hula skirts of palm trees, while violent pink-and-charcoal sunsets open like parachutes above us.

As time goes on, too, there's more and more busy work – reading proofs, overseeing new editions and vetting translations, checking text for reissues, interviews, correspondence. Work hard at what you're called to do, my brother (also a writer) says, and that's the bird you wind up holding. All the sludge conspires to keep you from the very work that made it all possible, and gave you reason in the first place.

The cinema?

I wonder sometimes if the foreign films upon which I gorged as a young man (because I could find what was in there nowhere else) may not be the most important early influence on my work, on the way I perceive and elect to adumbrate the world. More than once I've compared this to specific hunger in pregnant women who, sensing somehow that it contains elements they need, will peel paint off the wall and consume it. Bergman, Fellini, Antonioni, many obscure and often forgotten films.

Music. Ah, well_ I'd suppose that three books having to do with music, dozens of articles and hundreds of record reviews and the like address the importance of music to me better than I, prattling on here, ever could. Not to mention music as a constant theme in the Lew Griffin books. Or that the title of *Black Night's Gonna Catch Me Here: Selected Poems 1968-1998*, this sometimes arcane collection of poems, derives from a standard blues line.

Is the book still relevant?

Perhaps more like hanging by a single toenail, and that nail pulling free... No one who's spoken with young folk these days can sustain much illusion that books, literature, have anything to do with life as most of us live it now. Alas. Whereas religion still has a hold_but I'm bound to be unhappy with that.:. I have not a religious bone in my body. In fact, having been raised in Baptist churches and with Southern assumptions, I have, if anything, a decided anti-religious bias. Basically, though, I just don't get it.

Any new Lew Griffins due?

The next *published* book will be the last, the sixth, Lew Griffin novel, weighing in at about 150 pages just now and, as I mentioned back at the beginning, due next Fall. Past that, I can't say much. We'll take up position on opposite banks, burn fires to convince the other we have more troops than we do. Then one morning one or the other of us will attack...

And Woody Haut on –
Chester Himes: A Life by James Sallis
(£18.99, Payback Press, ISBN 0-86241-954-9)

The ghost of Chester Himes has long-haunted James Sallis' fiction. Though the latter's Lew Griffin might not be as angry nor as pathological as Himes' protagonists, he, no less than Bob Jones in *If He Hollers* or Jesse Robinson in *The End of the Primitive*, has been tattooed by the culture. Given that, and the fact that Sallis has been writing about Himes since *Difficult Lives,* an excellent, if small and source-cribbing 1993 study of Himes, Jim Thompson and David Goodis, it's not surprising that Sallis should have taken his investigation a step further. Or that *Chester Himes: A Life* should be as perceptive and well-written as it is.

It's Sallis' opinion that Himes, the author of such diverse narratives as *If He Hollers Let Him Go, The End of a Primitive* and *Blind Man With a Pistol*, is not only a great crime novelist, but a major twentieth century American writer, as well as the most perceptive of African-American storytellers. Certainly, Himes was more than *just* the author of those darkly humorous, surreal and violent Harlem-set detective novels featuring Gravedigger and Coffin Ed. Equally, one could say that, forged from racism and the inequalities of everyday American life, every Himes story is, in effect, a crime narrative.

Because there is not a great deal of first-hand information about Himes that hasn't seen the light of day, Sallis seeks his subject in the stories themselves. In lesser hands this might be a bit dodgy. But, maintaining that Himes' stories are often more autobiographical than his two volumes of autobiography, Sallis' literary acumen successfully locates Himes' life in his fiction, from his rebellious youth to his seven-year prison stretch, from his forty-foot fall down an elevator shaft to his psychosexual obsessions and literary disappointments. Likewise, Sallis neither skimps when it comes to Himes' selfishness, his inflated notion of art, his misuse of women, and his paranoia, nor short-changes us regarding Himes' often-unappreciated literary genius.

It was his fear of, and loathing for, a cruelly divided society that energised Himes' writing. When the 1965 Watts riots broke, Himes merely wondered why it hadn't happened earlier, while in an unpublished short story, *Daydream*, the black protagonist dreams of wreaking vengeance on white southerners. Alone in his New York hotel room, he looks in the mirror, saying, "You are sick, son... But that isn't anything to worry about. We are all sick. Sicker than we know." But Himes often found himself caught between white critics who considered his work unnecessarily angry, and black critics who accused him of saying things about which white folks should remain ignorant. Having finished his tour-de-force *The End of a Primitive*, a book he sold outright for a mere thousand dollars, he boasted that the novel would at least be 'something to hate me for'. Soon Himes had burnt his literary and personal bridges. By the mid-1950s, he was already exiled in Europe. It was in France, with the publication of his Gravedigger and Coffin Ed novels, that he achieved a degree of noto-riety. Though they were written quickly – Serie Noire had originally contracted him to produce a novel every two months – and for subsistence money, these freewheeling books with their nightmare scenarios were to take the mystery genre into uncharted territory. As Sallis points out, Himes' work transcends genres, while his literary output constitutes a microcosm of American social history from World War II through the days of black urban rebellions of the 1960s. No one seriously interested in crime fiction should be without his novels. And no one seriously interested in his novels should be without this book.

And from Jim –

So far this year, a trade paperback of one of my novels, new editions of my translation of Raymond Queneau's *Saint Glinglin* and of my book on noir writers, *Difficult Lives*, a collection of essays, *Gently into the Land of the Meateaters*, a collected stories, and a biography of Chester Himes have appeared. Now, from Michigan State University Press, comes *Sorrow's Kitchen*, a major collection of poems.

It's been a landmark year, highlighted by last month's UK tour: many fine interviews, much fine conversation, discussions over *Death Will Have Your Eyes* becoming a movie, even plans for (no one is safe!) a record. There was tremendous interest all over in the Himes biography.

My essay on Guillevic is due shortly in the *Boston Review*, my column on Neal Barrett and Terry Bisson up any day now in *The Magazine of Fantasy & Science Fiction*. Other pieces on Gerald Kersh and Boris Vian are underway. Next year sees *Black Night's Gonna Catch Me Here: Selected Poems 1968-1998* from Salmon Publishing in County Clare, Ireland, and the final Lew Griffin novel, *Ghost of a Flea*.

JIM SALLIS: AN OVERVIEW

Woody Haut

James Sallis' 1992 *The Long-Legged Fly* is the first in a series of highly original private eye novels featuring African-American New Orleans freelancer Lew Griffin. With a poet's heart, Sallis' investigator deploys his knowledge of these meaningful streets to become not only a debt collector and private eye, but, fluent in Louisiana French, a part-time university lecturer in French literature, and, finally, a writer of detective fiction. Far-fetched, perhaps, but Sallis, a former science fiction writer from Helena, Arkansas (RIP Sonny Boy Williamson), portrays Griffin's transformation and multi-faceted existence with skill and subtlety.

True to Sallis' aesthetics, a chance meeting or thought might result in a previously unforeseen narrative diversion. *The Long-Legged Fly* begins in 1964, with Griffin's infamous crime, moves to 1970 and 1984 before ending in 1990 with the disappearance of Griffin's son. It's only in *Eye of the Cricket,* three novels later, that his son's disappearance is resolved. Playing with the ambiguity existing between author and protagonist, Sallis, in the latter novel, places Lew in hospital where he must identify a young man, apparently homeless, whose sole possession is a well worn, notated copy of one of Griffin's out-of-print novels bearing an inscription from the author to his son. When the young man comes to, he claims to be Lew Griffin, and, in a notebook, says he has begun work on a new novel. Griffin, suffering from writer's block, can only kick-start his next book, which may or may not be the one the young man has claimed as his own, and reacquaint himself with his son, after visiting a host of displaced souls who inhabit the outer limits of a dog-eat-dog culture.

Seeking to subvert the expectations of genre fiction, Sallis will invariably set out, in the opening pages, the shell of his novel, only for it to open up to reveal other narrative possibilities. For here fiction, as a form, can create as much as replicate reality. Nevertheless, things can get complicated. A white man writing about a black protagonist, Sallis intentionally crosses cultures and blurs boundaries. He ends *The Long-Legged Fly* with Lew Griffin, suffering from a concussion and cracked ribs, having written his first novel, *Skull Meat,* about a Cajun detective, and is eighty pages into his second novel, *The Severed Hand*. The reader now knows nothing in a Sallis novel can be taken at face value. Griffin has even written a novel called *The Long-Legged Fly*, which ends with the author forsaking his Cajun investigator for another fictional private eye, named Lew Griffin. While Sallis' next novel is *Moth,* Griffin, in *The Long-Legged Fly*, insists *his* next novel will be *Black Hornet,* which, in reality, will be Sallis' third novel. Establishing the artifice of the narrative, Sallis' *Moth* begins with the same sentences with which Griffin ends *The Long-Legged Fly*: "It is midnight. It is not raining." Suddenly, it's apparent that Lew Griffin has made up the entire narrative. Then again, perhaps he hasn't.

By the publication of *Black Hornet*, Griffin has become, like Sallis, an established writer of detective fiction. Delving into the world of African-American politics, Griffin recalls meeting Chester Himes, whose spirit permeates the book. Here Griffin explains the direction of his fiction: "Every day you head out in a dozen different directions, become a dozen different people; some of them make it back home that night, others don't."

Caught between entertaining readers and conveying the notion that they are involved in a literary act, Sallis, well-versed in the history of pulp literature and the author of a study of Goodis, Thompson and Himes, must, if his novels are to work, distance himself from the novel-as-literary-product, yet sustain the narrative by maintaining its element of suspense. Not an easy task in a genre known for its structural demands. Nevertheless, Sallis remains true to his investigatory techniques. One can only admire his seriousness as much as his playfulness, as he alters the genre, stretching its boundaries as few have done.

James Sallis Bibliography – page 22

JAMES SALLIS BIBLIOGRAPHY

Lew Griffin Books:

The Long Legged Fly (Carroll & Graf, New York, 1992; No Exit, Harpenden, 1996)

Moth (Carroll & Graf, New York, 1993; No Exit, Harpenden, 1996)

Black Hornet (Carroll & Graf, New York, 1994; No Exit, Harpenden, 1997)

Eye of the Cricket (Walker & Co., New York, 1997; No Exit, Harpenden, 1998)

Blue Bottle (Walker & Co., New York, 1999; No Exit, Harpenden, 1998)

The Long-Legged Fly/Moth (omnibus edition) (New Exit, Harpenden, 2000)

Ghost of a Flea (forthcoming in the US from Walker & Co., 2001, in UK from No Exit, 2001)

Other Novels:

Renderings (Black Heron Press, Seattle, 1995)

Death Will Have Your Eyes (St Martin's Press, New York, 1997; No Exit, Harpenden, 1997

Short Stories and Poetry:

A Few Last Words (Macmillan, New York, 1970)

Limits of the Sensible World (Host, Austin, 1994)

Time's Hammers: Collected Stories Volume 1 (short story collection, Toxic, 2000)

Black Night Gonna Catch Me – Selected Poetry, 1968-1998 (Salem, USA, 2001)

Sorrow's Kitchen (poetry) (Michigan State University, USA, 2000)

Criticism:

Difficult Lives – Jim Thompson, David Goodis, Chester Himes (Gryphon, New York, 1993, revised edition forthcoming from Gryphon in 2000)

Ash of Stars: On the Writings of Samuel R. Delaney (University of Mississippi, Jackson, 1996)

Gently into the Land of the Meateaters (Black Heron, Seattle, 2000)

Chester Himes: A Life (Payback, Edinburgh, 2000; Walker & Co., New York, 2000)

Musicology:

The Guitar Players: One Instrument and Its Masters in American Music (William Morrow, New York, 1982; revised edition University of Nebraska, Lincoln and London, 1994)

Jazz Guitars: An Anthology (edited by James Sallis) (William Morrow, New York, 1984)

The Guitar in Jazz (edited by James Sallis) (University of Nebraska, Lincoln, 1996)

SARA PARETSKY

talks to Barry Forshaw

Amazingly, we haven't done it before: Crime Time *has never talked to one of the most distinctive and original voices in the genre. The appearance of* Hard Time *(Penguin) was the perfect occasion for us to catch up with the creator of V. I. Warshawski*

You have a particularly dedicated British following
I'm very pleased by that. And actually, Livia Gollancz, who bought my very first book, initiated that. It was a great feeling to become part of such a prestigious list – a really enviable place to be.

You seem to be at pains in your books to avoid stultifying. Do you make a conscious effort to rigorously avoid repetition?
Well, I'm glad you feel that. It's just a constant struggle when you're writing about a series character, it's hard to keep that character alive. When I felt that I needed a break from V. I., I wrote *Ghost Country*, which was a very different kind of book. And I'm glad that I did, as I was able to come back to her in *Hard Time* with a better way of writing about her.

The new book tackles a lot of topical issues.
I'm concerned about issues such as globalisation of the media. It seems to me that

for any government to function properly – and I suppose I'm principally talking about the States – it requires a diligent, independent press. And when the big movie companies own all the media outlets and the publishing companies, that's not a healthy

state of affairs. So when I was writing *Hard Time*, I was thinking how all these global conglomerates run things with their own particular agendas in mind, and I thought about those disenfranchised people who don't have a voice or a defence.

Would that describe V. I. in this book? She expresses some trenchant views on these matters.

She's someone who's not prepared to compromise, and that makes her very lonely and very vulnerable.

Isn't it a problem, when dealing with issues as big as this, to keep a single individual at the very centre of the narrative? Or is there a danger that her concerns will be eclipsed?

Yes, there is. But hopefully the situations I put her in are strong enough to make the reader care. I start the book by having her nearly run over this woman who's been left in the road. Now, because it's a novel, and things have to happen in a somewhat more ordered way than they might in real life, I made this a thread that ultimately connects her to these global conglomerates. Some of her concerns are idiosyncratic: can one person continue to be true to his or her own principles in a world of compromise?

Is V. I. brave or foolhardy?

That's an interesting question. I try to make her brave, but not in any simplistic way. Actually, that's an issue that greatly concerns me personally. When I think of Hitler and the Nazi period, I think of those people who behaved with tremendous courage in the face of this appalling threat, and think: would I do that? There's part of me that

thinks: no, I wouldn't, more's the pity.

So is your protagonist your surrogate in that respect?

Yes, but I think of her as a person who speaks more than a person who acts. It's what she says that matters most to me.

Are you bored with the endless comparisons with Sue Grafton?

Well, it's had one effect: I used to read her and enjoy her, when it was just a question of the fact that we had both started at roughly the same time, and happened to hit on several similar ideas, such as an older male confidant for our heroines. But now I feel that I can't read her for that very reason – I have to fight any inadvertent influence. And I guess she feels the same.

'*Hard Time* is a compulsive read, revealing its author at her most passionate and most page-turning' *Express on Sunday*

HARD TIME

SARA PARETSKY

CRIME, REDEMPTION AND VIDEOTAPE: JAMES LEE BURKE

Charles Waring

To mark the auspicious occasion of the publication of James Lee Burke's new hardback opus, *Purple Cane Road*, Orion's press department has gone into overdrive (or should that be overkill?) and put together an attractive promotional package for prospective book reviewers – it includes a signed proof copy of the new novel (a collectors item indeed!) plus an explanatory 'letter' from the author himself and, perhaps most significantly of all, a forty-eight-minute video which finds Burke discussing his life, philosophy and work. We'll get to the book later, but first, let's briefly examine those other items.

In the printed letter (you didn't think it would be handwritten did you?), Burke addresses the reader and talks nebulously about concepts like a writer's artistic

vision and the mysterious act of creation, concluding somewhat pretentiously, "I think *Purple Cane Road* is a song, my best

work certainly and a novel that I will always love, in the same way you love your child." Hmm. However, the promotional video, entitled *James Lee Burke's Crime and Forgiveness*, offers a candid and insightful portrait of the author that for me, at least, dispelled any cynicism in my mind that the letter had engendered. The video is obviously tailor-made for commercial television, evidenced by the fact that it is divided into four, advertisement-friendly, segments of equal duration. Visually, it offers a clichéd perspective of the Bayou territory covered by Burke's Dave Robicheaux books. You get a music soundtrack consisting of a bluesy, lonesome harmonica competing with the sibilant noise of chirruping cicadas against a visual backcloth of sultry southern swampland. The film is heavy on atmosphere but also, surprisingly, offers substantial insight *à propos* of Burke's authorial *raison d'être* and personal philosophy. Less effective, however, are the melodramatic visual recreations of scenes from Burke's books (with the novelist narrating) which punctuate the author's confessions to camera.

Burke himself is not the intense, saturnine figure you might imagine from reading his work. Sporting a mandatory cowboy hat and speaking in a soft tone with an elongated southern vowel sound, the novelist is relaxed and amiable. Although middle-aged with a creased, well-worn visage and yellowing, uneven teeth, Burke exhibits an almost boyish demeanour that doesn't come across on his more sober publicity photos. He expatiates on various topics, ventilating his thoughts in the kind of cogent, articulate manner that you'd expect from such an eloquent prose writer. Like so many Americans, James Lee Burke has a clear sense of his own roots and takes pride in his heritage. In the video, he visits a Methodist churchyard in New Iberia, Louisiana, where many of his forbears are buried. He can trace his ancestral history back to the period of the Texas Revolution in the early part of the nineteenth century when William Burke, an Irish immigrant hailing from Waterford, joined Sam Houston's army and fought against the Mexican forces led by Santa Anna. William Burke miraculously managed to escape a massacre inflicted on his fellow Texans only to succumb to scarlet fever two years later at the age of thirty. As for the writer himself, we learn that he was a social worker in the mid 1960s working in South Central Los Angeles and that his experiences there laid the foundations for the moral perspective that informs his crime fiction.

Burke's detective protagonist, Dave Robicheaux, inevitably comes under scrutiny. He talks at length about Robicheaux's virtues and foibles and also attempts to shed light on the defining 'Garden of Gethsemane' moment, which has helped shape the Cajun detective's life. What Burke is describing is essentially a kind of religious epiphany, a moment of transfiguration: "Dave Robicheaux in the novels talks about experiencing the Garden of Gethsemane. He doesn't coin the term – a psychologist gives it to him in a therapy session. But it's a term that psychologists use to describe an event which St John of the Cross called 'the long night of the soul.' Only a small percentage of the human population ever experience it, but the person who goes through that rite of passage, that keyhole in the dimension, is forever changed by it.

The people who experience it eventually have what the layperson or even a theologian might call a religious moment, where they make a decision about their lives that they never share with another: they never tell anybody about it but they're forever changed and they turn into good people. But they literally sweat blood."

Morality and the eternal conflict between good and evil are the main focus of Burke's cogitations regarding his own work. "The evil we find in my books is of two kinds: we meet some sociopaths who are obvious – they're the kind of guys who end up on death row and in penitentiaries. They're recognisable because they're usually ugly and stupid and they break into jails rather than out of them. But Dave Robicheaux is always more concerned, as Billy Bob Holland is, with those who insinuate their way into the mainstream of society. These are sociopaths who are far more cunning. They have the appearance of normalcy but they're totally devoid of conscience. They're out of Machiavelli's *The Prince* – nobody refers to The Prince as a sociopath but that's exactly what he is. Virtually all political leaders who have large influence are students of Machiavelli, not St Francis of Assisi." Quite.

Burke describes himself as a traditional liberal but has views on the nature of evil, which, with their sense of Biblical transgression from righteousness, go against the grain of orthodox social work training. Burke's viewpoint is reflected in Dave Robicheaux's own perceptions. "He [Dave Robicheaux] says maybe there are those who are made different through environment or genetics but there's a third, more disturbing theory, that perhaps there are those who make a conscious choice for evil. They step of their own volition across the line and deliberately murder all light in their souls and, he says, that's the group that causes the real problem. It's not something they evolved into. There's a moment that comes – like the Garden of Gethsemane experience – when they choose evil rather than good as a world that will define their lives. I believe that." Robicheaux himself, with his alcohol dependency and propensity to use violence, is a seriously flawed man, a person who has been tainted by the evil he encounters and as a result bears both physical and psychological scars. It's a burden, though, that the police, with their close proximity to those who commit heinous acts, have to shoulder – but the consequences can be catastrophic: "That kind of life [Dave Robicheaux's] exposes a person to cynicism and a dark view of humanity that has an obviously injurious effect on the psyche: alcoholism,

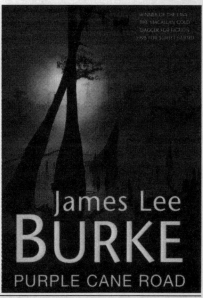

James Lee
BURKE
PURPLE CANE ROAD

divorce rates, suicide rates are all high among police officers." Burke also acknowledges that the police and criminals 'share commonalities', which results in an almost symbiotic understanding of one another's rationales.

Regarding the liberal sprinkling of violence that characterises his books, Burke has this to say: "When we see violence used, either by Billy Bob Holland or Dave Robicheaux, it is always in defence of another. Both narrators always indicate that it is not a victory but a defeat because violence always dehumanises. It debases the perpetrator as well as the victim, even when it absolutely necessary." Finally, Burke claims that the most rewarding aspect of being a writer is meeting readers who confess to him that his books have prompted them, like hero Dave Robicheaux, to confront their alcoholism and adopt positive measures to begin a new life.

From the video evidence, James Lee Burke, appears to be almost as interesting a character as those found in his novels. However, I believe that the real key that unlocks the door to a writer's psyche is found in the books they write rather than the interviews they give. James Lee Burke has two new books out at the moment and here's the CT verdict on both.

Purple Cane Road by James Lee Burke, Orion, £12.99, 0-7528-2557-7

Let's face it, Dave Robicheaux wouldn't know happiness if it pistol-whipped him across the head. If truth be told, the Cajun copper is something of a miserable bastard, whose unrelenting trials and tribulations in eleven of James Lee Burke's crime novels would give even Job a run for his money. While

Robicheaux's soul has not yet been totally possessed by the twin demons of booze and violence, he is unequivocally a man haunted by ghosts from the past – his experiences in Vietnam while in the army, and subsequently on the mean streets of New Orleans as a cop, brought him face to face with his own moral fragility in a world which thrives on cruelty, pain, violence and senseless death. Furthermore, he has been tainted by his proximity to evil. But it has become the oxygen he breathes. This is not to say that Robicheaux is nefarious or corrupt – in order to combat the evil he encounters he has to adopt a similar mindset. He has become as predatory as the wrongdoers he pursues. Consequently, Robicheaux, finds it hard to live with himself and reconcile his work as a cop with family life. Aware of his own failings, he tries desperately to redeem himself by quitting the bottle and curbing his violent disposition. But those two aspects of his personality are far too deeply rooted in his own psyche for him to renounce them altogether.

Each new Robicheaux novel by James Lee Burke achieves much more than the presentation of a new episode in the detective's life – it adds additional layers to an ever-evolving, complex portrait of his personality. *Purple Cane Road* is James Lee Burke's eleventh mystery novel featuring the so-called 'gumbo gumshoe'. The charismatic Cajun detective investigates the brutal slaying of an elderly man, Vachel Carmouche, the former State executioner, who is found hacked to death in his kitchen. Suspicion falls upon the Creole twins, Letty and Passion Labiche, both of whom claim to have been sexually abused as children by Carmouche. While Robicheaux attempts to get to the bottom of this seemingly straightforward case, he is shaken by a revelation from a pimp regarding his own mother, who was murdered in the 1960s: apparently, two bent cops who were moonlighting for the mob were responsible for her death. Add to this equation a corrupt attorney general and a bizarre contract killer who is stalking Robicheaux's daughter and you have an inventive book whose plot lines intersect with a compelling complexity. Both the book's primary and secondary characters are substantive and memorable while the action travels at a brisk pace. But it is Burke's narrative that commands most attention – the prose he uses to evoke atmosphere achieves a lyricism that almost achieves the sonorities associated with poetry.

Although the novel's tone is elegiac and aches with an excruciating sense of despair, it's Robicheaux's humanity which shines a light through the gloom and invests the book with a life-affirming quality. *Purple Cane Road* is undoubtedly Burke's best novel yet, an ambitious work which blurs the boundaries between so-called 'serious' literature and crime fiction.

Heartwood by James Lee Burke, Orion, £5.99, 0-7528-3419-3
New out in paperback is Burke's second novel featuring the former Texas Ranger turned small town lawyer, Billy Bob Holland (he previously appeared in *Cimarron Rose*). Set in the small Texan community of Deaf Smith, *Heartwood* begins with local business tycoon and professional arsehole, Earl Dietrich, accusing a former rodeo champion down on his luck, Wilbur Pickett, of purloining a valuable watch from his safe. However, Billy Bob's acceptance as Pickett's defence lawyer and his subsequent examination of the evidence opens a proverbial can of worms involving oil prospecting, insurance scams, murder, racism, homophobia, mercenaries, clairvoyant Native Americans, corrupt small town cops and Latino gang bangers. And while all this is going on, Billy Bob nurtures a smouldering, latent passion for the Amazonian private eye, Temple Carroll.

Like James Lee Burke's other alter ego, Dave Robicheaux, Billy Bob Holland is a haunted man – he is accompanied by the spectre of LQ Navarro, a former Texas Ranger colleague whom Billy Bob accidentally shot dead on a drug raid in Mexico. Navarro appears at intermittent intervals throughout the novel to impart nuggets of wisdom to the lawyer. Burke handles this potentially risible supernatural element of the book with aplomb, preventing the relationship between these two characters descending into Randall-and-Hopkirk-like absurdity. An immensely satisfying read.

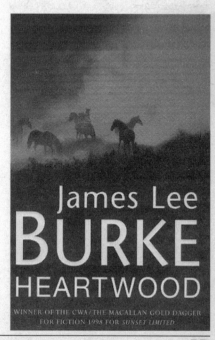

James Lee
BURKE
HEARTWOOD

WINNER OF THE CWA/THE MACALLAN GOLD DAGGER
FOR FICTION 1998 FOR *SUNSET LIMITED*

FACE OF A STRANGER: ANNE PERRY

Adrian Muller

In 1979 Anne Perry's first novel, The Cater Street Hangman, *introduced Thomas and Charlotte Pitt. They were the protagonists of one of two sets of Victorian crime novels to be written by the British author. Ten books later, the second series debuted with investigator William Monk and nurse Hester Latterly in* The Face of a Stranger. *Two years ago the author briefly jumped genre with* Tathea, *the first in a planned fantasy trilogy, and this year a third historical crime series is launched.* The One Thing More *is set during the French Revolution and introduces Celie, Perry's new heroine. In the following interview Adrian Muller looks at Anne Perry's exceptional life and her career as a novelist.*

Anne Perry came to crime writing after numerous career changes, all the while writing manuscripts in different genres. "Writing is the only thing I ever really wanted to do," she remarks when asked about her perseverance. It was only when Perry wrote a crime novel that success finally struck. In *The Cater Street Hangman* it is the death of a servant that brings policeman Thomas Pitt to the Ellison household. Then, gradually, as the investigation progresses, a romance develops between Pitt and Charlotte Ellison, the middle daughter of the family. The subsequent marriage between the upper- and working-class protagonists allowed for the diversity of Victorian norms and values to be covered in the books that followed.

Explaining the origin of the plot for the first instalment she says, "My stepfather had an idea for a book about who Jack the Ripper might have been. I wasn't curious about who the Ripper was, and I hope they never find out – it is much better as a mystery – but," Perry continues, "through that suggestion I became interested as to what might happen to a group of people when they find themselves under an enormous pressure by the threat of murder. It comes closer and closer to home, and then they suddenly realise it could be somebody they know, even somebody they care about in their own family. That is when the relationships start to fracture," the author says, "and everything has to be re-assessed. That is how I came to write *The Cater Street Hangman*."

As fond as Anne Perry is of the early

Pitts, the author feels she didn't hit her stride until she changed publishers in 1990. "My first American publisher only took things after I had written them", the author explains, "they never commissioned anything in advance. Consequently you will find that in my first ten books I played things fairly safe. Then I moved to Ballantine, who really allowed me to know that they believed in me. They commissioned books in advance which allowed me to feel that I could break out and put more of myself into my work, to start packing the punches. That is when I started the Monk series. You'll find, I think, quite a jump in quality when I changed publishers," Perry concludes.

The Face of a Stranger was published in 1990. In it a man awakens in a mid-nineteenth century London hospital to find that an accident has robbed him of his memory. He soon discovers that his name is William Monk, and that he is a policeman by profession. Gradually, throughout this book and its sequels, he regains bits of his past, not always liking what he finds. "All I wanted to do was to write a book allowing me to speak with a different voice", Perry says. "I didn't know it was going to be a series. In fact," she adds, "in my first draft Monk was guilty, but the publishers wouldn't have that because they wanted more Monk books." It is also in The Face of a Stranger that William Monk first meets Hester Lat-

terly, a fiercely independent nurse. Together with Oliver Rathbone, a barrister who made his entrance in Defend and Betray, the three became the leading characters in the Monk novels.

There has been speculation that Monk's history – memory loss and his ensuing discovery that he had not been a pleasant person – was Anne Perry's attempt to allow herself to examine some traumatic experiences that were the basis for a film called Heavenly Creatures. Following the release of this stylised account of the murder by Juliet Hulme and Pauline Parker of Pauline's mother, a journalist discovered that Anne Perry was in fact Juliet Hulme. Not unexpectedly a wave of media coverage followed. Born in London in 1938, at the age of six Juliet Hulme was sent to stay with family friends in the Bahamas. She had been suffering from a particularly bad case of pneumonia, and her parents were told their daughter would not survive another British winter. It was not until 1948 that she rejoined her parents in New Zealand, where her father had been appointed rector of Canterbury University College in Christchurch. When she was thirteen Juliet met Pauline Parker at Christchurch Girls High School, and a close friendship developed between the youngsters. The threat to this friendship ultimately led to Juliet and Pauline's convictions for murder, and the adolescent girls were sent to separate prisons, never to see each other again. Upon her release, shortly after her twenty-first birthday, Juliet Hulme was given a passport in the name of Anne Stuart – Stuart being the name of her maternal grandmother – and was put on a plane to Britain. Back in England she went to live with her mother, who by then had married her stepfather, Bill Perry. It was when she decided to take on her stepfather's name that the future author became Anne Perry.

When asked if her experiences as a child had been an influence on the Monk novels, Perry denies that this is the case. "It was not in order to examine myself," she says, "it was in order to examine others looking for 'monsters', and then allowing them to discover that there are no monsters, there are only people." She adds, "We don't necessarily like all of ourselves, but bit by bit we learn to understand and then, when you understand yourself, one hopes you can transfer that understanding to other people." To clarify her explanation further she refers to a comment a reader made. "Somebody said to me that one of the reasons she enjoys reading the Monks is because, as Monk discovers a little more of himself in each story, she feels she discovers a little more of herself as well. That reader has caught what I'm really trying to say. You discover yourself through discovering others. Then perhaps you reverse the process and discover others by discovering yourself."

Perry is less certain how her culpability in the death of Mrs Parker influenced her writing. "I don't know," she says. "Everything in life influences who you are and probably I'm a much more thoughtful person because of it. I probably leap to judgement on others a great deal less because of it, but it's not something I think about very often. I have come to terms with it, but obviously you can't have something like

that happen in your life without it affecting you unless you're totally mentally out of it." She pauses momentarily to consider her words. "It informs who I am, and who I am informs my writing."

Feedback from her readers is important to Anne Perry, and she finds her trips to the United States very rewarding. "My American publishers are very good and bring me over every year for a promotional tour of four to six weeks. I don't visit every State in the Union," she says with a smile, "but certainly quite a few of them." While she is there to publicise her latest novel, the trips are also of great value to the author because they give her the most direct contact with her readers. "I hear what people think, and what they read in what I write. It's very, very encouraging." It was on such an occasion that the author was paid a memorable compliment. "A man in San Diego told me that he taught at a high school and that my books were required reading for his course. I thought, "Oh that's nice", and I asked him whether he taught History or Literature. He answered, "Ethics". Now that's the pay off!"

Although the two series share Victorian England as a setting, there are numerous distinctions between them. The Monk books take place around the middle of the nineteenth century, and the Pitts some forty years later. There is a difference in tone as well. "The Pitt books are set in a slightly lighter period. There was a lot more glamour and fun in the nineties, and the stories are socially and politically orientated. The Monks are darker, and tend to have legal, medical and military backgrounds. They nearly always have a trial in them, and they also have this edgy relationship between

Monk, Latterly, and Rathbone." It is unlikely that Anne Perry will ever let the main characters from her two series cross each other's paths because the author is not willing to pre-determine the futures of Monk, Latterly and Rathbone. She does not rule out, however, that older cast members from the Pitt novels may make an appearance in the Monk series.

For a long time Perry was undecided as to how the relationships between Monk, Latterly and Rathbone would develop. Anxious that the Monk books did not take on too many aspects of the Pitt series, she had her doubts whether Hester Latterly would ever marry either of the two men in her life. "I brought Oliver to the brink of asking Hester to marry him," the author says, "but when she realised what he was going to say she steered the conversation in a different direction. The shadow of Monk would have been too heavy between them." As for Monk, Perry felt that he could never marry anyone but Latterly. The author played with the idea of William asking Hester to marry him, only to break off the engagement because he discovers something appalling in his past. "He would have decided she shouldn't be saddled with him, and Hester would be absolutely livid. "How dare you decide for me!", Hester would have responded." Of course loyal fans will know what ultimately did happen.

One of the other common elements of the two series is strong female characters, and the author disagrees that her women and their relationships with men are ahead of their time. "I write about strong women because it would be anachronistic not to," she says. According to the author, the cause

of women's rights saw significant activism and progress during the nineteenth century. Perry uses her grandmother as an example that progressive attitudes existed in Charlotte's era. "My father was born in 1908, and his mother worked like the blazes and put both him and his sisters through university," Perry states. Her father studied Mathematics, Physics, and Astronomy; her aunts studied Politics, Philosophy, and Law rather than Humanities, the usual subject for those few women who attended university at that time. "This for a family from an ordinary working class background in Salford," adding, "and my paternal grandmother would not have been much younger than Charlotte."

The author's decision to make Hester Latterly one of Florence Nightingale's Crimean War nurses was again very specific. "I wanted Hester to be a woman with courage," she says, "and she needed a reason to have the courage, experience and independence that she has. She'd be completely out of her time if there was no explanation for it, if she were this extraordinary woman having grown up in ordinary circumstances. Being a nurse in the Crimea, she would have gained this independence and experience of exercising judgement, authority and decision. She would have been through more than enough to prompt her to act contrary to her earlier upbringing. Yet without that background she would be quite unbelievable."

Anne Perry had always intended to have male and female protagonists in both of her series, but the inclusion of both sexes also had specific purposes, practicality not being the least of them. "The reason was to get more than one point of view," she explains. "If I limited myself to the female role there would have been so many places I couldn't have gone. It would be very restricting, especially in Victorian times when male and female roles are so different. Also, because I am a woman I wanted a woman's point of view. I think women observe things differently from men. They particularly notice body language more than men do. We can hold a trivial conversation about the weather, but what we are really communicating can be a lot more important. Men are a lot more literal, I think, and in the past they didn't have to pay as much attention to body language because they had all the power, be it physical or financial." Relying on two kinds of research, the author's historical investigation mostly comes from reference books. "However," Anne Perry says, "they aren't a great deal of use when it comes to what a person was thinking or feeling, and that is far more important." When it comes to human behaviour, she counts on her experience of relating to people. "If you know only people who are roughly similar to yourself, with the same sort of interests, that narrows your world a great deal. So, being interested in, and knowing as wide a variety of people as possible is one of the best ways of research I know," she says, "and I would say the key thing is to like them."

Whilst she was living in the United States in the late 1960s, Anne Perry came across what has been a major influence on her life and work ever since. "I didn't encounter the Church until I was about twenty-seven, some twelve years after I'd come to terms with what had happened in New Zealand," Perry says. "I'd gone to a lot of the different Christian churches that had crossed my path, and each one had offered a lot, but there was always something I couldn't agree with. So therefore I decided I was going to walk my own path, be a religious person but not attached to any church." This changed when she learned about the Church of Jesus Christ of Latter-Day Saints, also known as the Mormon Church. Recalling her feelings at the time Perry says, "I thought "Just a minute, this is what I believe!" It was what I had worked out myself plus a whole lot more I hadn't even thought of." While she is observant of her religion, Perry is not fanatical about her faith. However it is significant to know why the Mormon religion appealed to Perry because its teachings find their way into the author's books, not as dogma, but as a strong guiding philosophy. Unlike most Christian religions, the Mormon faith does not see the human banishment from Eden as a punishment. For them it is the first step in a process of progressing and growing into becoming a full individual. Being able to make the right choices and distinctions, and making the necessary mistakes along the way, is part of this process. Ultimately people will progress to knowledge where they can choose good because they understand what it is, and they realise it is what they want. "It is the idea that you continue to learn and to grow until you become braver, wiser, more generous, more compassionate," Perry explains. "A purity of heart is not being unblemished, it's learning to understand your faults, so that you can erase them yourself. It's purity of intent."

Perry feels forgiveness is an important part of erasing one's faults. "If God will forgive after a certain period of appropriate understanding and repentance, then you cannot be self-indulgent, and you've got to forgive yourself as well. Self-castigation really is pretty selfish. You have the responsibility to say, "I did something I shouldn't have done. I understand that it was wrong and why it was wrong, and if I can put it right I will. If I can't, then I will absorb myself in becoming as good a person as I can. I will forgive myself and I will jolly well forgive others as well," because another part of Christianity is that you will be forgiven as you forgive. If you cannot forgive others, you cannot expect to be forgiven, and if you truly wish to be forgiven you will want to forgive others because you will know what it is like to need to be forgiven. That again is very basic Christianity, it's love of other people." A further important point is that whilst Anne Perry's work is morally

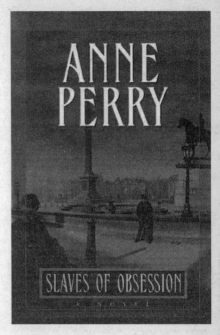

grounded, it is also infused with humour, and it is never moralistic. "I don't go to the Scriptures with the idea of finding a theme," she says. "If you are true to your religion it's got to be a way of life that informs everything you do, otherwise it's simply a Sunday observance." Having said this, Perry also stresses that, "It is never "What does the Church teach?", that I want to write about, it's "What do I believe? What do I care about?"" She presumes that all writers feel the same way and base their work on their own ethical beliefs, whether they are religious or not. "If you're not writing what you care about or what you believe in, then I suggest you do something else."

For some years now, Anne Perry has been living in Ross-shire, Scotland. Her beautiful home has a stunning view over the Dornoch Firth, and the house is situated on what can only be described as a miniature estate. Most days there are at least two people working on the property, and the author also has two part-time secretaries to assist with her writing one Pitt and one Monk novel a year. Perry explains that she is able to keep up a consistent output because she enjoys what she does and that she usually works six days a week. "I normally start about nine in the morning, pause for a little while at five, before going back at maybe ten, often working till after midnight." Invaluable to Anne Perry's work is friend and next-door neighbour Meg MacDonald. "Not only is she a good constructive critic," the author says, "she is very good for brainstorming and helps with the creative side of things. We work two mornings a week together." It was MacDonald who 'saved' one of the supporting cast members from a very nasty death. "The character is gang-raped," the author explains, "and he was going be so badly wounded, psychologically as well as physically, that he was going to die. Meg said, "Do we have to kill him off?" I thought, "Well, no, it really isn't necessary." So I changed my mind on that. I – and I hope the readers too – have got fonder and fonder of him as time has gone by. It would just make the book too dark if I had let him go. The whole story's pretty tragic in a lot of other respects, so I hope I've balanced it out."

It would not have been the first time that Perry had disposed of one of the figures who previously had played a prominent supporting part in her books. Yet, as long as the reaction of both the surviving characters and her readers is strong enough, she has no great difficulty in killing them off. When writing about death in her books, it is not the corpses that concerns the author so much, "It's the pain and the fear involved that bothers me," she says, adding, "The deaths in my books are intended to leave you shaken." Such traumas also have a lasting influence on the remaining characters in her books. "Some authors do not change their principal character. I don't mean make them a different person," Perry explains, "I mean the protagonist is not altered by what happens. Do you think that anybody could experience those things and be worth a damn and not be altered?!"

Before she begins to write, Anne Perry has plotted and planned her novel thoroughly. She has summarised each chapter, scene by scene, explaining that, "I need a pretty good structure or it's going to be a lousy book." Early on she has already established the nature and the reason for the crime. More importantly Perry will have asked herself why the perpetrators would have felt that committing it was the only course open to them. "If there's another, easier way, they're going to take it," she says. "I don't want to write about somebody who kills because it amuses them, and I also don't find financial gain is a very interesting motive." What is a frequent motive in Perry's books, however, is the human desire for power, and this desire is most strongly represented by the Inner Circle in the Pitt novels. Thomas Pitt, who is identified by Perry as most often voicing her own convictions, has frequently been offered membership in this organisation, which very much resembles the secret Freemason institutions of the time. He has always refused to join what he sees as a faceless entity, on the grounds that he would be relinquishing his right to heed his own conscience. The latter is again inspired by Perry's personal convictions. "I believe the one thing you must hang onto for eternity is your free agency, it's basic Mormon philosophy. Free agency means your right to follow your own conscience, and you never ever give up your individual freedom of conscience. Obviously if you are going to do something that is outside the law of the land, you are going to have to pay the consequences for it, but our articles of faith state that you must obey the law of the land in which you live." Realising that there are situations where this might contravene basic human rights, Perry admits that in those instances fighting for change is permissible, "but," she stresses again, "you would accept the consequences."

These thought processes go a long way to explaining the depth of the author's characters, including her villains. On numerous occasions even the latter earn the reader's sympathy, perhaps due to the fact that they are often victims themselves of the oppressive Victorian society in which they live. Perry will only partially accept this reasoning. "I don't think society can be blamed for everything," she says. "I like to think we are responsible for our own actions to a considerable degree, varying with the person and the circumstances. In one of my books two girls, who were sold into prostitution at the ages of eight and ten, go on to kill men making a profit from child prostitution. In that book especially I would say society was to blame and, whilst I don't advocate murder, those men certainly had it coming. I can understand people having compulsions, but

to use other people's compulsions and to feed it for profit..." Yet despite her understanding of people with addictions of various natures, she dislikes the 'victim' mentality. "It means you are helpless," she says. "I would far rather think that most of my problems are my own fault, because then that means I can fix them. I can stop being that way and do something about it."

After many years, the first dramatisation of one of Anne Perry's books finally made it to the small screen last year. The BBC had the initial option to the rights of the Charlotte and Thomas Pitt books, but let their contract lapse after numerous scriptwriters were unable to produce satisfactory adaptations. Other production companies were interested in optioning the Pitt novels, but

Perry chose to sell the rights to Ardent, a company owned by Prince Edward. "Ardent already had the option on the Monks through an actress-turned-producer called Jane Merrow," the author explains. "So I chose Ardent partly because I wanted to keep the books with the same people rather than have them conflicting with each other. I also went with Ardent because I already knew the people there. I trusted that they would do adaptations in line with what I would feel happy with." Despite alterations to the structure of *The Cater Street Hangman*, Perry was happy with the direction of the adaptation. "I think they improved it in every sense. *The Cater Street Hangman* was my first book, and it was a bit raw. Obviously for a two-hour drama the plot had to be condensed quite a lot and they played up the love story. I think that they were correct in that and, if I were to write it again now, I would have the nerve to make the love story stronger as well. At the time I thought, "No, you're writing a mystery, don't dare do this. It isn't done"." Though Anne Perry remains hopeful, there sadly is no prospect of further adaptations for either the big or small screen in the immediate future.

Tathea, Anne Perry's fantasy published in 1998, is a book close to her heart. When she talks about fantasy novels she does not mean "dungeons and dragons" as she puts it, but stories that have a profound moral suggestion. "The best fantasies are explorations of perhaps not so much good and evil, but right and wrong," she says. "I don't think there's anything in the world that interests me quite as much as what we should do and what we sometimes do do that's not right." Surprising herself, Perry suddenly formulates a defini-tion for the genre. "I have never said this before, but this is what I think a fantasy should be: a spiritual truth or reality, illustrated in some dramatic yet concrete form." The title of the book is the name of the protagonist, a woman who asks the universal questions "Who am I, and why do I exist?" Tathea finds her answers in spiritual truth which she brings back to earth, but truth has many consequences. "Truth forces people to grow," Perry says. "The experiences which are most profound, offering growth, are also those which are most painful, and therefore we often decline them. They force people out of what the Americans call 'the comfort zone', but when you are in the comfort zone you are not growing, and growing hurts! What we're scared of is that we'll be alone, that we'll be hurt, and that we'll fail and make fools of ourselves, but if you don't go out there and try you'll certainly fail."

The author's most recent book is *Half Moon Street*, published in April and the latest in the Pitt series; *Slaves and Obsession*, the new Monk, is out in December. The most imminent title is *The One More Thing*, Anne Perry's mystery set during the French Revolution. She developed the characters and plot whilst she was writing a short story for an anthology by different writers for publishing company Orion. "I liked the protagonists," she says, "so I want to carry on with them. The novella finishes with the September massacres in 1792, and I'm going to pick up the story in October, taking it through to the execution of King Louis XVI in January 1793." The author concludes, "Maybe, if somebody believes I can do a French Revolution crime novel, they might take my straight novel of the same period as well."

ANNE PERRY

Anne Perry lives in Scotland. As well as the highly praised William Monk, she writes the equally highly praised and bestselling Inspector Pitt series, one of which was recently adapted for television as *The Cater Street Hangman*. Over 10 million of her books have been sold worldwide, one million of them in the UK. She has worked as an airline stewardess and a ship-to-shore bursar, and managed a furniture store in Beverley Hills before becoming a full-time writer. She is hugely popular in the US where she recently won an Edgar for her short story *Heroes*. She is equally popular in France where six

of her books have reached the top ten bestseller list. *The One Thing More* (Headline) represents Anne Perry's intriguing departure from her Inspector Pitt and William Monk series to bring the terrors of the French Revolution to life. In January 1793 Celie watches as Louis XVI is sentenced to death. She is one of a small group of people afraid that, once throneless, France will quickly be conquered by its neighbouring countries. They are determined to rescue the king, but when their secret leader is murdered, Celie and her fugitive lover must piece together the plan to act before the execution takes place.

BIBLIOGRAPHY

Pitt series:
Cater Street Hangman (1979)
Callander Square (1980)
Paragon Walk (1981)
Resurrection Row (1981)
Rutland Place (1983)
Bluegate Fields (1984)
Death in the Devil's Acre
(1980)
Cardington Crescent (1987)
Silence in Hanover Close (1989)
Bethlehem Row (1990)
Highgate Rise (1991)
Belgrave Square (1992)
Farrier's Lane (1993)

The Hyde Park Headsman
(1994)
Traitors Gate (1994)
Pentecote Alley (1996)
Ashworth Hall (1997)
Brunswick Gardens (1998)
Bedford Square (1999)
Half Moon Street (2000)
The Whitechapel Conspiracy
(2001)

Monk series:
The Face of a Stranger (1990)
A Dangerous Morning (1991)
Defend and Betray (1992)

A Sudden Fearful Death (1993)
The Sins of the Wolf (1994)
Cain His Brother (1995)
Weighed in the Balance (1996)
The Silent Cry (1997)
The Whited Sepulchres (1998)
The Twisted Root (1999)
Slaves and Obsession (2000)

Non-series books:
Tathea (1999)
The One Thing More (2000)

Publisher: Headline

STEPHEN AMIDON: APOCALYPTIC TIMES

Mark Campbell

The New City is the fourth of Stephen Amidon's novels, a novel of crime and retribution that should lift him from the relative obscurity of art-house literature and into the spotlight of mainstream success. An epic book on many levels, Amidon's deceptively easy prose comes from the autobiographical nature of the subject matter itself. He spent his formative years in Columbia, Maryland, a new city that mirrors the Newton of the book. He witnessed firsthand the uneasy mix of rich, poor, black and white that formed the brave but flawed social experiment. The New City takes place in the summer of 1973 – the year Amidon turned fourteen – and it's a story that's clearly close to his heart. It's one he says he wanted to write for twenty years.

As we settle down to talk, it's immediately obvious that Amidon is an intense man, confident and surefooted. Unfazed by my dubious reference to The Towering Inferno, *he reveals the same intelligence and precision of thought he displays so eloquently in his prose.*

First off, how do you respond to the alleged quote from a reader, "Like Tom Wolfe with an editor"?

You know, I haven't read *A Man in Full* yet, though I certainly plan to. But *Bonfire of the Vanities* is one of my all-time favourite books, so any comparisons to it are most welcome. I think Wolfe is right to think that American writers have become too inward-directed and modest in their vision. We need novels that engage contemporary society. But, for obvious reasons, the person most chuffed by the quote was Gerry Howard, my editor at Doubleday!

According to the blurb you wrote in the press release, this is very autobiographical. So where does fact stop and fiction begin?

Well, the general setting is quite factual. In the late 1960s a visionary urban planner built this new city in central Maryland called Columbia. It incorporated lots of the stuff I used to 'build' Newton – bike paths, ergonomic architecture, etc. But having used this as a jumping off point, I then began to add my own elements. The layout of Newton is not the same as Columbia, for instance, and I've made up a lot of street and village names. The main reason for this was that my city had to serve a fictional agenda rather than an historical one. Also, I didn't want to get into a situation where denizens of Columbia accused me of getting it wrong – though they have anyway.

The new city seems like a metaphor for a new country, like America. Is it?
That's right. America is called a new city by the early Puritan writers. With the exception of Indians and slaves, just about everybody, from the pilgrims to poor Elian Gonzalez's mother, came here for a new start, just as the Swopes and Wootens and Truaxes come to Newton.

Are you saying that even if you try to make a fresh start, the result will always be failure?
I suppose I am saying that such a utopian project is doomed, yes. But only because we are trying to be better than we are.

The unresolved ending – part of the grand plan, or the only way you could see to finish the novel?
It certainly wasn't part of the grand plan – I didn't have one! No, it was more that I reached that point and thought, "Okay, that's it". I like the idea that the book ends with the word 'future'. I mean, without being too didactic, I guess I'm saying the city

is still being built, that the battle between Swope and Wooten is still ongoing.

For some reason I'm reminded of that 1974 disaster epic *The Towering Inferno* – this vast, man-made edifice, a population in miniature, two strong characters from different classes working together, the spread of fire at the end... Was this an influence, or am I seeing connections that aren't there?
That's my kids' favourite movie and definitely makes my list. It's funny, in an early draft I had a sentence about Swope and his wife watching the film, but had to take it out because the timing was wrong – the book is set in '73. You're probably too young to recall, but Irwin Allen's apocalyptic movies were very big back then, and I don't think it was an accident. I mean, they were apocalyptic times, when the world's whole bloody infrastructure was coming down. But in terms of being a specific influence, not that I'm aware of.

In the best possible way, the tangled human relationships are rather like a good soap opera – passion, envy, vengeance etc... Were classy soaps like *ER* an influence?
Well, I know what you mean. I love *ER* and more so *Homicide* and *NYPD Blue*. Even more, I love Altman films like *M*A*S*H*, *The Player* and *Short Cuts*, as well as the work of Richard Linklater who did *Dazed and Confused*, P T Anderson (*Boogie Nights*) and the great Todd Solenz (*Happiness*). What these works share with soaps and hopefully my own stuff is that they assign equal weight to a cast of characters rather than choosing out a protago-

nist. They follow a series of linked stories rather than one narrative. I think this adds breadth and depth to the story, making it seem like it's capturing a community.

Why did you use just a handful of characters in this vast, new cityscape?
They didn't seem like a handful to me at the time! But looking back, I see what you mean. I guess since the ones I do use represent different parts of the city I felt like I had it covered.

None of the characters seem wholly likeable.
Well, with the exception of my own wife and children, I don't know anyone who is wholly likeable – myself included. So it would be hard to make warm and cuddly characters and at the same time be honest. With the exception of Diggory Venn (and he has red shit all over him), who's totally likeable in Hardy? I think that explicitly likeable characters are the curse of modern fiction.

Did you plot very carefully the escalating violence in the latter half of the book?
I did and I didn't. I wanted there to be an apocalyptic ending, but the actual choreography of the violence didn't suggest itself until after the characters and their conflicts had been fully developed. I must confess that near the end of the writing the story was sort of rampaging at its own pace and logic.

The theme of jealousy comes over strongly – especially between the two main characters and their sons. And like *Othello*, most of it would have

been resolved by a casual remark early on.
Yes. I'm always fascinated by stories of siblings who haven't spoken for twenty years because of an imagined insult, or of couples who break up over a tiny misunderstanding. So much human conflict boils up from nothing. Have you seen Michael Mann's brilliant *The Insider*? What's amazing is that it details this huge event – the uncovering of a massive conspiracy by Big Tobacco – and yet the whole thing derives from the fact the tobacco company chairman needlessly insulted his researcher, and then got the FBI to pettily harass the man, which piqued the curiosity of a CBS producer. And look at WWI, for God's sake! But in *The New City* I also wanted to show how the veneer of civility that exists between the races in America is very thin and fragile, and can be shredded by only the slightest of disturbances.

There are some memorable flashbacks in the novel, such as when Vietnam vet John Truax discovers a maggot-filled cave, and Earl Wooten starves almost to death because of a simple oversight – were these based on truth?
Both were fictitious. But hopefully plausible.

I'm very impressed with your clear, unmuddied prose – are you a self-taught writer?
Yes – I'm not a big believer in writing schools.

How did you get started on the rocky road to journalism?
By serving as a theatre critic in a small North Carolina city, which is a form of tor-

ture the North Koreans would do well to study. After I moved to London I got my real start by writing a bunch of letters, the only one of which was answered was by Auberon Waugh at the *Literary Review*.

As well as writing fiction, you've been involved in some radio work, haven't you?
Yes, I've been on the BBC World Service reviewing books, and also on Radio 4, most notably doing a feature about Huck Finn for Kaleidoscope Extra

Until recently, you lived in an 'old city' – London. Did you enjoy the experience?
I loved living in London; it's my favourite city in the world by a wide margin. Unfortunately, it is not part of the United States and therefore it's an untenable place for an American writer concerned with American themes to spend his entire life!

Who are your literary heroes?
Just one – Thomas Hardy.

Which of your previous three novels are you most happy with?
I think it has to be *Thirst,* but don't ask me why. I guess I just think about it more than the others. The reason may be that I wrote it very quickly and unconsciously. Not that I think it couldn't have been better; it's just that it was very deeply felt.

Tell me about your working day – do you have a routine?
Well, I work on fiction in the morning then spend the afternoon doing freelance work, if there is any. But it's not like I spend eight hours a day at the computer. I'm a compulsive break-taker and school-runner.

What are your feelings about a possible film version of *The New City*? I understand film rights are currently under negotiation.
I suppose it would be interesting to see, though I don't imagine anyone would spend all that money without lightening the book's dark cynicism.

Would you want to be involved?
I'd love to be, although I've been around long enough to know that my input wouldn't be quite as venerated as I'd wish. But, hey, money's money.

What are your favourite books and films? (Apart from *The Towering Inferno*!)
That's easy. Starting with books, it has to be *Return of the Native* (Thomas Hardy), *Crime and Punishment* (Fyodor Dostoyevsky), *White Noise* (Don DeLillo) and *The Moviegoer* (Walker Percy). As for movies, well they tend to be crime orientated – *The Godfather I* and *II*, *To Live and Die in LA*, *Wages of Fear* and *Goodfellas* would be my favourites.

How did your publicity tour go?
It was good and bad. I like talking about the book on radio, but I hate reading in public. And hotel rooms are fun in a weird sort of way.

Do you enjoy self-publicity?
Well, it beats self-anonymity.

And what are you planning next?
I'm working on another big novel.

ATOM BY ATOM

Steve Aylett

Wouldn't fictional detectives get to the truth quicker if they immediately shadowed their clients home? Readers familiar with the genre know the clients always turn out to be knee-deep in their own corruption, so why not go at once to the heart of the matter? *Atom* is the third of my books set in Beerlight, a city where crime has been perfected to an art form. Taffy Atom is a trickster detective who harasses anyone who tries to hire him. The story proceeds like a road that you're following, only to find that the main character is taking a different route, or is simply stopping at home and drinking tea, snuggling up with a good book. When cornered into conversation, he will use it for his own amusement. There are few things more disconcerting to people during a deadly serious discussion than to hear you extend the last syllable of your sentence for a minute and a half, phasing it in and out with an open face.

Atom is also a Maltese Falcon parody – everybody does one, here's mine, by reference to the movie, Hammett's book and the Picador Film Classic Library photo script published in 1974. The thing I never understood in the movie of *The Maltese Falcon* is Spade's attraction to Brigid O'Shaughnessy as played by Mary Astor, this twitchy little thing, totally pinched and dishonest. I don't really believe that part. A character like that

appeared with Atom briefly in the short story *Tail*, collected in *Toxicology*. There was a line that went: "If she found a spider in the bath she'd flirt with it." Any sane man prefers a woman who won't strain to prove anything, there's none of that fronting-off which is so irritating and exhausting. In *Atom*, the nearest to that we get is a bland girl called Kitty Stickler, a woman who's been suckered into making herself as standard-issue as possible, removing all distinguishing features and airbrushing herself almost out of existence – that's supposed to be attractive. In fact she's physically invisible to most people, she has to stamp her foot or knock something over to make people see her. Atom's girlfriend Madison Drowner is based on Lauren Bacall as she was in *The Big Sleep* or *To Have and Have Not*. She's got texture. There's a great line –

Henry Blince says, "You're breaking my heart here", and she replies, walking out, "Break your own heart – I'm busy." I love that one. I know I wrote it, but I love it. Then there's the thug called Joanna. In movies like Falcon there was always a gun-toting errand boy with a girl's name like Wilmer or Carol or whatever, so here there's one called Joanna. Falcon consists almost entirely of people in rooms talking, and talking well. A series of beautiful stand-offs: the pop-eyed Cairo getting impotently over-wrought and the great Gutman, speaking 'candidly'. I like to think that they're all still gathered in that hotel room, talking in endless candour about the black bird.

A short way through the writing of *Atom* I did a short story called *The Siri Gun* which featured Atom, told in the first person and giving a version of what happens after the events in *Atom*. That story was

"Manic . . . neo-noir."
- Publishers Weekly

first published here in *Crime Time* (Issue 2.2) and later collected in *Toxicology* (Four Walls Eight Windows, New York). *Tail* also appears in that collection along with some Henry Blince stories. As most readers of Slaughtermatic and The Crime Studio immediately recognised, Blince is basically Orson Welles' Quinlan in *Touch of Evil*. He turns up again in *Atom*, with a cigar the size of a chair-leg. A cop "flushed down the pan and grown huge in the sewers", he's a terrible character, but juicy to write.

Somewhere along the way the notion of a Taffy Atom radio show came up, directed by Josh Halil: a fifteen minute segment was recorded with the actors Kerry Shale and Lorelei King. It was a real sensurround production, but the networks made it clear that as a radio play it was missing five vital elements: 1) middle-class dinner parties; 2) middle-class affairs; 3) middle-class divorces; 4) crunching leaves; 5) cows. So back to the book.

I went into the Beerlight mob stuff a lot more with Eddie Thermidor and his boys, and the whole argument between old-style guns and computerised smart guns or fire-by-wires. I got bored a long time ago with the empty noise of normal gunfights, so now most of the firearms represent a mental stance. In *Atom* there's a new line in mood guns, metabolics, vogues, voyeurs, fuzzies, carnatics, diagnostics, penrose rifles and tantrum guns. (I've noticed that in response to all the shootings in the States they're now designing smart guns with an ID recognition grip, to ensure that people use their own guns to shoot each other.) There's also a thing called a syndication bomb which strips the subtext from whatever situation it's tripped in, leaving everything flat and

'A terrific read'
THE FACE

meaningless for up to three hours. Another element of the title is the theme of nuclear war and the survival of bugs after the event. I was confused for a while by the strange complacency that came about a few years ago when the number of nuclear weapons was reduced just a little bit, so that humanity can now be destroyed merely dozens of times over, rather than hundreds of times over. People grasp frantically at any resource for denial and in a position of total powerlessness it's understandable.

Lining up some of the chapter headings with those in Hammett's book, I then bunged in all the usual codes and references and backward messages I do for my own amusement and which no-one notices. I don't think in words but in shapes, and each book presents itself to me as a coloured and textured shape floating in headspace. The writing of the book is just the filling-in of the

DNA detail to create this thing. Suck it up.

Ideally I'd like to make a reader's head explode by affecting the chemical nature of their body. This could be done by making a book which is disguised anti-matter, and which only reveals itself after the reader has ingested it. I like the idea of re-wiring something so much, changing something atom by atom, that it may look normal, it'll have the shape of something everyday but it's actually pure hypertoxicity, something totally different at the raw level. It's got alien insides. You get a shock at first when it feels and weighs different than you think – you've totally misjudged what it's made of, what it is. But it's already inside you. Now you are dangerous.

Atom is published by Phoenix House

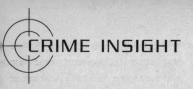

A DEADLY HUSH

Carol Anne Davis

What would you do if the neighbours were ruining your life with their relentless noise? You'd politely ask them to tone it down, and if that failed you'd ask the authorities to deal with it. What if the law failed you and every legal means of escape was blocked? You might plan to permanently silence your persecutors by yourself…

I found myself in just this situation several years ago when I was living in a residential street in central Edinburgh. I loved the area, and had lived there for about five years when three young male graduates moved into the flat upstairs, bringing half of the rave scene with them. Thereafter, I didn't have an unbroken night's sleep. The days were equally bad. I worked from home and so did one of the young professionals upstairs – the only difference being that he worked to the sound of music. And being a generous sort, he was determined to share it with me.

Like most polite people, I suffered in silence at first and tried writing in different parts of the house but I could hear  his music in every room. It was aural torture. Eventually I went upstairs and asked him nicely to tone it down. He gave me an insolent stare and said he'd see what he could do. He turned it down a few decibels but an hour or two later his flatmates came in and turned it back up again. They also did various other anti-social things that caused damage to my property. These acts are all faithfully reproduced in *Noise Abatement*. If it reads like a living nightmare, that's because it was.

Until then, I'd thought that educated people should be able to talk to each other, reach a compromise. I even offered to buy them carpets as insulation to cover their bare polished wooden floor, but they refused. Image, it seemed, was everything. Like the characters in the book, I tried various legal channels to silence the quartet. It was then that I found out the difference between the 'crack down on noisy neighbours' hype and the reality. None of the organisations I contacted had the time or the resources to really make a difference. Yes, the police did come out eventually and tell the guilty party to turn it down – but they weren't there half an hour later when they put the sound right back up again. And they'd already told me that it wasn't a police problem and they wouldn't come out a second time.

That's where the crime element started to creep in. I'd be catapulted from sleep several nights a week by the all singing, all dancing arseholes. I'd lie there with my heart beating fast and fantasise about beating the hell out of them. If someone could have guaranteed that I wouldn't get caught, then there would already be four less people in the world. I remember one night two of the men started fighting and I saw my ceiling shake as they battered into their window alcove. I started hoping that they'd crash right through it and plunge several storeys to the ungiving pavement below. I didn't want them to die immediately but to suffer greatly and expire just as the ambulance arrived.

I started to wonder if it was just me that had these thoughts. Then I got into conversation with this girl I knew – a vegetarian pacifist who had brought up her own child without ever hitting him. And she told me that she'd had noisy neighbours and had lain awake thinking about stabbing them and dumping their bodies in the canal. And I started reading of other mild people who had killed their neighbours because they couldn't cope with the acoustic agony. The seeds of *Noise Abatement's* increasingly gruesome and murderous plot was born.

Living with other people's noise makes you unable to control your own life. You can't rent a video – because they may decide to put on their stereo and you won't be able to hear your movie. You can't invite people home with you for a relaxing drink because they can't stand the constant thumping above and they leave. You can't have sex or sleep or enjoy a meal because at any moment the party animals may swing into action. You can't even go on holiday to escape them because they may forget that they'd started running a bath and go out for the night, seriously damaging your property.

Like Caroline in *Noise Abatement* I became physically ill in the end. Most people do. I collapsed and was subjected to a barrage of hospital tests. At one stage I was so ill that I could hardly walk. Many sufferers choose to permanently end their own torment – the suicide rate amongst people with such antisocial neighbours is very high. Although it involved a colossal amount of effort, I eventually managed to escape. On my last week in the old flat, I was exhaustedly carrying some empty packing crates upstairs when one of my neighbours came up behind me. He asked if I was looking forward to the move. "No," I said, "I'd planned to stay here for several years and really can't afford this, but you've driven me to it." I also reminded him that I worked freelance and that all the editors I'd ever worked for knew to phone me at this telephone number, which I couldn't take with me. I'd lose lots of casual work through this.

There was a pause and I stared up at him, hoping he'd realise that he'd taken a contented young woman and reduced her to a physical and emotional wreck. "Still," he said, "It's nice to have a change of scene."

Noise Abatement by Carol Anne Davis is published by The Do-Not Press. Hardback £15, paperback £7.50.

NATASHA COOPER

Natasha Cooper, who was born in London, worked in publishing for ten years before leaving to write full time in 1986. Her first crime novel, *Festering Lilies*, was published in 1990, the year she joined the Crime Writers' Association. This year sees her taking the chair of the CWA and publishing *Prey to All*, her tenth crime novel. Her first six crime novels form the tongue-in-cheek series that stars Willow King, a severe civil servant with a secret double life as glamorous romantic novelist, Cressida Woodruffe. They allowed Cooper to take a frivolously irreverent look at various institutions that affect life in Britain, and to challenge the lazy habits of those who make judgements about people on the basis of their appearance.

Creeping Ivy was something of a turning point, with Willow/Cressida taking only a walk-on role. That novel belongs to Trish Maguire, Cooper's new heroine, who features in novels that are grittier and more realistic than the earlier series. Trish is a thirty-something barrister, specialising in family law. Reviews of *Prey to All* include: "Trish is an engaging character, warm and human, and well drawn" (Donna Leon, *The Sunday Times*); "Natasha Cooper possesses the ability to write some of the most dark and realistic crime novels around" (*Birmingham Post*); "Cooper's novels are a welcome alternative [to the violence of much recent crime fiction]: convincing and hard-hitting, they explore how ordinary people get caught up in appalling events" (*The Times*); "Natasha Cooper is another writer who deals with real life. Trish Maguire, a lawyer, is a flesh and blood character with a likeable per-

BIBLIOGRAPHY

As Natasha Cooper:
Festering Lilies (1990)
Poison Flowers (1991)
Bloody Roses (1992)
Bitter Herbs (1993)

Rotten Apples (1994)
Fruiting Bodies (1995)
Sour Grapes (1996)
Creeping Ivy (1997)
Fault Lines (1998)

Prey to All (1999)
Publisher: Simon & Schuster
As Clare Layton:
Clutch of Phantoms (2000)
Publisher: HarperCollins

sonality. The ending of this accomplished novel is both bitter and believable" (Susanna Yager, *Sunday Telegraph*).

In the late 1990s, Cooper decided to add an extra dimension to her writing life, looking not so much at current crime and investigation as at the longterm effects of violence on perpetrators, sufferers, and their friends and family. In order to distinguish these novels from her others, she writes them as Clare Layton. The first, *Clutch of Phantoms*, is a two-hander. One of the principal characters is seventy-four year old Livia Claughton, just out of prison after an extended life sentence for the murder of her husband and his mistress. The other, Cass, is her granddaughter, a twenty-seven year old hotshot City trader, who believes her grandparents died in a car crash. Their developing relationship, as well as the friendship Livia makes with an eleven year old arsonist, and Cass's dealings with Christopher Bromyard, make this novel warm as well as hard-hitting. Cooper/Layton is now at work on the second, which is about rape and the crisis in masculinity. It is due to be published in 2001.

In addition to her two novel-writing personae, Cooper also reviews for a variety of newspapers and journals, including *Crime Time*, *The Times Literary Supplement*, and the *Express*. She regularly speaks at crime-writing conferences and on the radio. Her main interests outside work lie, as readers of her Willow King novels may guess, in food and wine. She is a good cook and an even better eater, and she believes that one of the greatest pleasures in life is to sit over a leisurely meal with friends, talking – a lot.

HARDBOILED DYSFUNCTIONALITY

Gary Lovisi

My first Vic Powers' novel is a hard-boiled crime thriller called *Blood in Brooklyn* (out now from Do Not Press). The first Vic short story collection, *Dirty Dogs*, came out some time ago. Vic is a former cop, thrown off the force, a killer for hire, a louse and a bad guy who tries to do the right thing but, like a lot of us, is a dysfunctional person who always seems to screw it up. Usually in the worst way. He's a bad guy, but not an evil one, and that's the rub: he goes up against the evil ones and beats them at their own game. I've been writing hardboiled crime for a long time but the Vic stories, and especially this novel, is unrelentingly hard-boiled, brutal, and yet I think it has so much heart, you see, the one thing in his miserable life Vic loves is his wife and now he's being haunted by a memory from his long-lost past and his wife is in danger.

Writers who inspired me: in some ways there are too many to mention. I also have been collecting and reading SF and crime for a long time. The classics: Edgar Rice Burroughs, Robert E. Howard, Dashiell Hammett, Raoul Whitfield, and a lot of newer people, James Crumley, James Ellroy, and especially Andrew Vachss. Since I write a lot of diverse material, and read a lot, and I also edit and publish two magazines, Paperback Parade and Hardboiled, there's a lot of influences, but they are all transmogrified by my life experiences.

Of current writers, there are some people I like, some I don't, some whose work I like, some whose work I don't. But I don't worry about any of that, I'm too busy for in-fighting and back-stabbing games. Are there writers whose work I never miss? Absolutely! The prime one is Andrew Vachss. His work is stunning and so hardboiled, but not cruel or gratuitous, he's like a lighthouse in a gale showing the way to safety and security for us all in his work. When I read Andrew's work I read it one page at a time, I stop, I think, then continue. His work, sometimes even each sentence, is so full of implications, ideas, possibilities, and truth. There are others who never try to miss: in the UK I really like Ken Bruen's work, Russell James, Mark Timlin and others.

I like lean, hard, fast, focused stories: they have a beginning, middle, end, and good characters, make a point, have a real story, and surprise you or shock you by the time you get to the end. Sex can shock, so can a lot of other things, but it's just one ingredient on the shelf of a good writer and like anything else it depends on how you use it.

There are plenty of writers that are apolitical, plenty that are honestly politically left and a few honestly politically to the right. And a ton of politically correct. I prefer to read the honest ones. Then I can decide. I try to make my work the same way and let the reader decide. There's no political stance unless you have been so politically co-opted or intimidated by politically correct coward storm troopers that you don't know which way is up anymore. Which, is what all totalitarians seek. And if no one publishes you, so be it. Be brave, struggle, fight. You will win. And if you don't get published, you will still win. And then… well, who knows. Never give up!

Because I have a full-time job, and in my spare time publish two magazines and books under my Gryphon Books imprint (for more info see my website at: www.Gryphonbooks.com) I don't have as much time as I would like to write, but, I've been doing it a loooong time. I've written a LOT of stories and continually revise, update, expand. I also write non-fiction, articles, bibliographies, etc., so I keep busy. I'm too busy even to get writer's block, if I encounter resistance or delay in one area I move to another. I often work on four or five projects at the same time. I have to. I have no choice and don't have the luxury some people do. But I thoroughly enjoy everything I do and I am very proud of this latest, *Blood in Brooklyn.*

I write a kind of hardboiled that, to me, is more realistic because it is often so strange, so brutal, maybe even crazy, it mirrors the dysfunctionality in our world and where our society (schools, government, etc.) make things even worse. Though they are there to help, to make things better. Don't believe it. I also write stuff that is so hardboiled it can be very funny, like real life, if you've ever been knee-deep in the

shit you know exactly what I mean. It's not for everyone, but then again, I'm writing for myself, writing what I want to write, you can come along and take a ride, or pass it by. What matters to me is not the people that pass it by, but the brave ones who climb onboard, I want to write my heart out for them. Doesn't matter if it's ten people or ten million. I write what I want and if no one will publish it, so be it, and if I believe in it enough, I will publish it myself. Like I did with my first short story collection *Extreme Measures* or the Vic Powers collection, *Dirty Dogs*. It's next to impossible even for a big name author to sell a short story collection to a major publisher these days, and totally impossible for a less known author like myself. So be it. I believe very strongly in artists controlling the ways and means of production of their work. Writers, painters, musicians – think about it. Edgar Rice Burroughs began his own publishing company, every successful musical group starts up its own label, writers should have that same option and that same control over their own work.

I love New York City, where I've lived now for a long time, but, like Vic, I'm haunted by Norfolk, Virginia, and that comes through in a lot of my work. Though places offer mood, it's characters that get the juices flowing. Griff and Fats work in a city that Griff calls Bay City, but it ain't. Even so many years later (the novel and three stories take place in 1962 so far), Griff can't talk about it. The mood there is not so much 'Bay City', but the fact that thirty years later even this toughest copper can't tell you the name of the real city. What's that tell you? You want implications…

My present publisher is Jim Driver of the Do Not Press, and Jim is fighting the good fight bringing out new and gutsy fiction that the bigger houses are scared shitless to touch. Bravo! Jim's a good guy, and I'm the only American writer he publishes, I'm kind of an American expatriate writer – and I didn't even have to leave home to do it! Truth is, American publishers are generally a waste. Real publishing is a business run by crazy individuals who love books, not mega-conglomerates that only want to publish one book – or the same book over and over. Jim's a hero. All in all I've been treated pretty well by the editors and publishers I've worked with – or I don't work with them.

A writer should control his or her own work. That includes writers publishing their own work. If you are a real writer, not some damn dilettante, and believe in your work, because it is your life's work, then you should have control over it. I just read where Joe Lansdale, who is someone I admire and whose work I really enjoy, did something else I admire: he began his own publishing company Mojo Press. Now that's cool!

Jim is looking at my new book now. It's called *Mars Needs Books*. It's something new and different, a mix of hardboiled and SF, a novel that has aspects of the totalitarianism of 1984 with the surreal work of Philip K. Dick with, of all things, paperback collectors on Mars. Unique, but really cool. But there is reason behind the apparent madness. It's surreal and tough, but not violent at all. In fact, it's a very interior novel, a lot of narration, dialogue, and ideas. It's fun and says some things about our future and our present. I think it's the best damn thing I've written so far and is an important book.

RHYME RHYMES WITH CRIME
(AND SOMETHING MORE)

H. R. F. Keating

As the last Inspector Ghote book is published, I find myself going back to his genesis. After having written fiction ever since 1959 (or earlier with, still preserved if unfinished, my first story typed out at age eight), I have discovered, with a new millennium, a new way of doing it. And one which, with reservations, I recommend to my fellow novelists as having some unexpected advantages. It is the novel in verse.

I was led to it because my interest in Inspector Ghote's India drew me to a book, *The Golden Gate*, written by Vikram Seth before he went on to produce that wonderful and wonderfully readable story of love, politics and poetry, *A Suitable Boy*. In fact I had my doubts about *The Golden Gate*, not because I knew it was not about India – it depicts the pleasure-loving life of San Francisco – but because it was written in verse. Knowing this about it was nearly enough to make me keep my pennies in my pocket in the bookshop. But I plunged. And discovered that writing in verse, far from being an obstacle to easy reading, is a positive inducement to continue turning the pages.

So I said to myself, "If Vikram Seth can write an attractive novel in verse, could I possibly write a crime novel in the same way?" I knew, if I tried, it would be a tough task. *The Golden Gate*, I believe, owes much of its success to being written in a complicated verse-form taken from Charles Johnston's translation of Pushkin's *Eugene Onegin*. It is in stanzas of fourteen lines in what is technically known as tetrameter, that is with four feet to each line rather than the five of most metrical poetry in English. But Pushkin, Charles Johnston and Vikram Seth also used a quite complicated rhyme scheme, one best described as ABAB CCDD EFFE GG. Trouble ahead. However, the pattern of the verse, I found, is what keeps you subconsciously head-down in the story while avoiding the monotony that is the danger of rhymed couplets. The shortness of the lines, too, makes them extremely swift moving, and so, as I discovered, swift reading.

I thought therefore that I should use the same metre, the same rhyme scheme. Or try to. I began with almost trembling caution, picking my way with a single test stanza describing the form of the classical detective story which I then saw my book as being. "Snow", I wrote. And then, bit by bit, the words came.

> Snow, a carpet of pure white
> with every little footmark showing.
> The mystery story at its height
> could count on every reader knowing...

It was, if not a doddle, at least something that could be done. What you need is a reasonably large vocabulary, a willingness to try every variation of grammar and syntax and a rhyming dictionary for when things get temporarily difficult. No need to be ashamed of the rhyming aid, although it must be an advantage to be like Vikram Seth

and in his English-speaking household to have started to spout rhymes – cat, mat, sat – at the age of three. But the thing to remember is that what one is writing is not poetry, the delving of the imagination: it is verse, the use of a different type of language.

And, curiously enough, those moments of obstruction, when it seems to be impossible to find the right rhyme or the right metrical pattern for what you want to say, can be turned to good account. As long ago as 1602 Thomas Campion wrote of a fault in rhyming which he said was "almost intolerable", that "it enforceth a man oftentimes to abjure his matter and extend a short conceit beyond all bounds of art; for in the quatorzains, methinks, the poet handles his subject as tyrannically as Procrustes the thief his prisoners [...] too short [...] he would stretch them longer, if too long, he would cut them shorter." All true enough. But, I came to learn, in the stretching (the working round to setting down your original thought by putting another in first) you sometimes drag up from the subconscious something that adds materially to what you think you are saying. In this way you often find you have dug that much deeper, hit on a new, unexpected and revealing truth. Or, in other words, you have written a better novel. In my case, this turned out to mean I produced, instead of the say-little Agatha Christie-type detective story, what you might call a detective novel.

Of course, there is one sort of reader that refuses to believe that Thomas Campion was not right, and this despite such fine examples of verse novels from the past as Byron's *Don Juan* or Elizabeth Barrett Browning's *Aurora Leigh*. These doubting

Thomases tend to lurk in publishers' sales departments. "Can't be read: won't sell: don't publish." So I was lucky that my book eventually came into the hands of a two-person firm of daring called the Flambard Press (mercifully, computer-connected to almost every bookshop in the land). So in September *Jack, the Lady Killer* is coming out from them, and in America from another small publisher, the Poisoned Pen Press. However, if some of you out there take up the line that has run from Pushkin through the translator Charles Johnston, through Vikram Seth and at last to me, then perhaps more people in publishing will be ready to acknowledge the novel in verse as still having distinct and useful advantages. Let's see.

There is yet one other bonus to verse, besides that unearthing of thoughts you never supposed you had and finding out that our chosen form is, oddly enough, every bit as readable as prose fiction. It is this: that a thought or an idea, which in a straightforward novel would seem absurdly banal, put into verse takes on a more emphatic, weightier meaning without, I like to think, seeming portentous. I offer, with diffidence, as an example the last two lines of *Jack, the Lady Killer*, a book which came to tell eventually of the moral development of a young man arriving in the British Raj of the 1930s. I don't think I would have ever dared to write them as the final words of a straight crime story. But I like to think that as the last lines of a detective novel in verse they have a true reverberation they would not otherwise have possessed:

H.R.F. KEATING

Jack
the
LADY KILLER

FLAMBARD

Jack Steele, a boy a week ago,
    is now a man. Thus do we grow.

DEEP DECEPTION

Hilary Bonner

My latest is *A Deep Deceit* (Heinemann). It's set partly in the West Country, as are all my novels – this time Cornwall – and also in America, in the Florida Keys. It's about doubt and deception, passion and betrayal, and is the story of a couple living in St Ives who share a dreadful secret and are trying to hide from their pasts. It's intensely psychological and moody and was by far the most difficult to write of my five novels so far. I just hope it wasn't too difficult for me and that I succeeded in the end – my publishers think that I did, which is encouraging!

I have been very lucky. I do not have any unpublished work. The very first novel I wrote was published. And as for any other writing – well, I have made a living as a journalist or writer of some kind since I was eighteen and my first novel, *The Cruelty of Morning* remains the only thing I have ever written on spec without a fee of some kind – an advance, a commission or being on salary. I do know how fortunate I was to be taken on immediately by the first agent who read *Cruelty*, who then sold the book within just a few weeks.

Ruth Rendell is my hero. I think she just gets better and better. She could be lazy now, anything she writes is going to sell, but she isn't. Each one of her books seems new and fresh and they're always meticulously researched. Val McDermid is a favourite among the newer group of crime writers. I read her avidly and as I meet more and more contemporary crime writers I always want to read their books to see what their work is like. Switching to America, I am a great James Ellroy fan, but I don't necessarily read more crime fiction than anything else. Like so many writers I read everything I can get my hands on. A favourite discovery over the last couple of years has been the American writer Mark Childress. He really is an original. You cannot put his books into a genre, he has invented his own, funny, sometimes tragic, and completely off the wall. His novel *Crazy in Alabama*, which has recently been made into a not terribly well reviewed film starring Melanie Griffiths, is possibly my favourite contemporary novel. I have also, I must admit, only recently discovered Gabriel Garcia Marquez, and he is of course, sheer magic.

I do write explicit sex scenes. My first novel in particular was overtly sexual, but then so was it's whole theme. It always intrigues me that sex and violence are so often talked about in one breath. After all sex is a joyful thing which is a part of almost everyone's life to some degree or other, whereas violence, thankfully, is horrific and repulsive to the vast majority of us, and we hope never to have to confront it. It therefore does not fail to surprise me that far more people seem to be shocked by sex in fiction than by violence. As for what other writers do – well again, I think the key is that you can only write what you are comfortable with. Some writers are thoroughly uncomfortable with sex scenes, and if they are persuaded by their publishers to include sex scenes then that usually shows. For myself I apparently bare the dubious distinction of being the only first time author Heinemann have ever asked to tone down the sex!

I always write an outline for my books and I always immerse myself in research. For me a story comes to life when I visit the places where it is going to happen, and talk to the kind of people I am going to focus on, like police officers and doctors. I spent time both in Cornwall and the Florida Keys while writing *A Deep Deceit*, and one of my many kind policemen friends took me on a tour of the relevant police stations of Cornwall, and showed me around Penzance Magistrates Court and so on. I have an escape scene from the cells there, and when I was taken around them I could immediately visualise how my character could get away (through an external door with an ordinary Yale lock) and make a dash for it across the car park! I do research from books and from the internet, but my first instinct is always to do so first hand from life. Apart from anything else, at least that way you're making your own mistakes and not copying any-

one else's.

As for actually writing – I wish I was one of those wonderful organised people who sit down promptly at 9am every morning, pencils sharpened etc., and write for x number of allocated hours. I'm not. On a good day I never fail to be amazed at how much I can do – I think my record is 7,000 (very un-edited) words. On a bad day I never fail to be amazed by my ability to produce so little. Sometimes nothing at all. I don't believe in writer's block, just bone idleness, upon which I am an expert. I specialise in displacement activities and I can idle for Britain. Every time I finish a book I consider it a miracle. However my production rate always increases dramatically as a deadline approaches. I am a journalist after all. And that's my saving grace, I suppose. Somehow or other I manage

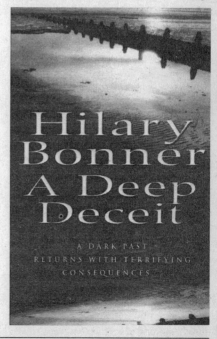

Hilary
Bonner
A Deep
Deceit

A DARK PAST
RETURNS WITH TERRIFYING
CONSEQUENCES

never to miss deadlines – or I haven't yet, anyway.

I was extraordinarily lucky with my third year primary school teacher. Her name was Miss Pollock and she may still be the only teacher in the world to have contrived daily to get a class of seven year olds to beg for more Shakespeare. I was brought up in the North Devon town of Bideford. There was no theatre nearby and few of us had television in our homes. Miss Pollock used to bring to school those wonderful old LPs of Shakespearean plays featuring legends like Gielgud and Olivier. I can still remember the impact of hearing those extraordinary voices for the first time. She was a very clever woman and we only got to listen if we were good (how about that – Shakespeare as a reward for seven year olds), and then only for a few minutes each day, so we were always left wanting more. Miss Pollock was a traditional old fashioned English schoolmistress. Her hair was cut no-nonsense short and she invariably wore a brown raincoat. She used to ride her bicycle the two miles or so from the village of Northam every day. I lived at the bottom of the long steep hill which led up to my school and each morning I used to run down to the corner and wait for her. Then while we walked up the hill together, her pushing her bike, she would talk to me about books and writers, something I did not experience at home because my parents were not readers and there were virtually no books in our house. Miss Pollock introduced me to the wonders of modern poetry, particularly Ted Hughes and T. S. Elliot, and I still have an early edition of Ted Hugh's *The Hawk in the Rain*, which I

bought with my own pocket money when I was eight, my name written proudly inside it in childish handwriting. Goodness knows what I really understood about any of the great writers to whom she introduced me, but she encouraged me to appreciate their worth and above all else to thoroughly enjoy them at my own level. She instilled in me a love of language which has never left me and I will always be grateful to her.

I would describe my relationship with my publishers as, touch wood, cross all my fingers and toes, excellent. My editor Lynne Drew has, I hope, also become a friend, but more than anything she is a complete professional. I have tremendous respect for her. And that is vitally important. I do know that I need editing, though. I think probably all writers do, but I understand they don't all know it! I think my journalistic background has probably helped with my relationship with book editors, because I am used to the editing process and I don't resent it. If my books can be made a little better, then that's all that matters.

I am totally against all organised religions on the ground of the endless unspeakable evils for which they have been responsible over the centuries. So I don't have any religious sense.

I have only just started writing my next book, so I'm at the stage where I can't imagine that I'll ever get to the end of it. Assuming that I do, it will be published in February 2001. It's about revenge and injustice. It concerns an old murder, new evidence and an abandoned love affair, dangerously rekindled. The working title is *A Kind of Wild Justice*.

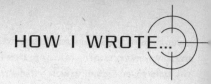

Crime Scribes Tell Us How...

HOW I WROTE
THE DIRECTOR'S CUT

Nicholas Royle

I wrote *The Director's Cut* (Sceptre) pretty much the same way I wrote my first three novels: by having one idea and holding on to it until another idea came along that I thought might react with it interestingly and produce something unexpected. The two ideas were basically these: 1) that amber and celluloid are very similar substances in lots of ways, both physically and metaphorically; and 2) if you've got a group of filmmakers shooting an underground movie of a man committing suicide, are they or are they not making a snuff movie? Because this book was commis-sioned (the first time I've had that experience with a novel), I had to produce an outline before I started. This I did, knowing that the finished book would bear very little resem-blance to the outline, because I simply cannot plan out a novel-length plot on its own. I have to write the book to find out what happens in it, to discover, also, what it's really about. So the plot I sketched out in the outline was only ever the barest guide for me. It changed a great deal in the writing. It has to be an organic process, otherwise I would get bored and give up. It took about eighteen months to

write, early in the morning before going to work, at weekends when not looking after my two children, on the way to work – that sort of thing. I've had to abandon the idea of waiting until I'm in the mood; instead I just pitch myself into it whenever there's half an hour going spare. I did, as I always do, a little bit every day, even Christmas Day. I have to do that or it would all start to trickle away.

As there is a whodunit element to the novel, I kept myself as much in the dark as I hoped the reader would be. For a long time even I didn't know whodunit. This kept it more interesting for me, and I hoped it would help make it more fun for the reader too. I did a lot of research, but my research rarely entails sitting in libraries and reading books or going through microfiches (although there was a bit of that, to dig into the history of the Franco-British Exhibition Halls and the White City, and to find out more about the disused cinemas of London). Mostly my research is

about breaking into abandoned buildings, which I use as locations in my fiction. I find disused spaces full of inspiration, as if they are packed with narrative in the form of memories and spectral traces of former lives. I get in and photograph them – or, increasingly, film them – then set my imagination free to see what it comes up with. I undertook three research trips out of London: 1) to visit the dissection rooms of the Bristol University Medical School Anatomy Department and get up close to dozens of cadavers; 2) to climb Ben More on the Isle of Mull; and 3) to visit my namesake, fellow writer and spirit double, Nicholas Royle, at the University of Stirling (he's now at the University of Sussex, where he's Professor of English). All these trips were in aid of getting one particular character right – Fraser Munro, an avant-garde filmmaker whose first victim in a series of murders is another filmmaker also called Fraser Munro. Otherwise, the book was researched and written in London between 1998 and 2000.

How I Wrote *Oxford Shift*
by Veronica Stallwood

December, 1998. Christ Church Cathedral, Oxford. On a cold, damp afternoon, the packed congregation has gathered for the Service of Nine Lessons and Carols. I am so tightly jammed into the middle of a row, facing towards the nave, that I can only stand, sit and kneel when the others do. The sound of the organ is rolling in the background. The Bishop of Oxford is wearing his most brilliant vestments. Choristers with scrubbed faces above burgundy cassocks and starched surplices are singing like proverbial angels. Representatives of City and University read the lessons. It's the kind of well-oiled ceremonial the English do so well.

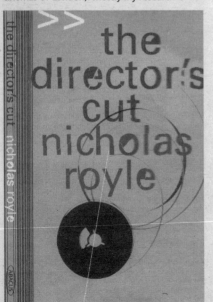

the director's cut
nicholas royle

Maybe it's my foreign upbringing, but I've never managed to feel part of this cosy English scene. I feel a sneaking desire to sabotage it – and so does my sleuth, Kate Ivory. We long to cause confusion, stir up some mayhem. But how?

The answer, to a crime novelist, is obvious. You place your murderer on one side of the cathedral – over *there*, I think, standing next to that column – and Kate Ivory sits on *this* side, trapped in the middle of a row of worshippers. Kate catches sight of the murderer. The murderer, spotting Kate, turns towards the door. Kate's spent the previous forty-one chapters tracking her down and so she's bound to follow. She escapes from her seat, using sharp elbows and boots, and sets off at a run – straight through the middle of the action, scattering mitre and crozier, upending choirboys and deflating city dignitaries as she goes.

If only.

So that's where it started – with the penultimate scene. The opening chapter, as it so often does, appeared some considerable time later. *Oxford Shift* is published by Headline.

How I Wrote *Fast Women*
by Maggie Hudson

It isn't always possible for me to determine the exact moment a novel is born. The process is usually too fragmentary, a collection of various threads that build into a skein without conscious effort, leaving me nonplussed as to the actual germination point. This, however, was not the case with *Fast Women*. The moment the book was born in its entirety was quite specific. It was nighttime and I was in Santa Teresa, a steeply high suburb of Rio de Janeiro, seated in the home of Ronnie Biggs. Ronnie was reminiscing with my companion, a friend of his from the 1950s

and 60s. At one period the two of them had served time together and lots of anecdotes and names of mutual acquaintances were being bandied about. "Fast women, slow horses," Ronnie said as the conversation turned to my companion's club-owning days in Soho. "That was the name of the game for young rascals like us, back then."

As a writer I would have been brain-dead if I'd failed to realise I was being given not only the title for my next book, but also the subject matter. Not Ronnie's story, of course – that is now the stuff of biography, though it reads like fiction. And not a literal account of my companion's story, though his graphic accounts of his bank robbery days – he served ten years in Parkhurst – were certainly grist to my mill. What intrigued me was how almost *historical* these reminiscences of forty years or

MAGGIE HUDSON

'Stunning – read this or we send the boys round'

Martina Cole

FAST WOMEN

so ago were. All the crimes under discussion were crimes carried out without guns. All were crimes with no drugs links whatsoever. Neither man had ever been involved in the dark side of crime – the Kray side of crime.

And that was the kind of first division criminal I wanted as my central character. Bryce Reece is a full-blown rascal, his anarchic tendencies first coming into play when, as the leader of a childhood gang, he pillages Bermondsey bombsites. Then follows his Teddy Boy years of the 1950s – and his years in prison when convicted of the manslaughter of his girlfriend's rapist. The 1960s see him as a Soho club-owner. The 1970s as a major bank robber. Throughout are his long-term feuds, his love affairs and his gob-smackingly impudent heists. It is the story of a life. The kind of life both Ronnie, and the friend who introduced me to

him, would instantly recognize. Which is why *Fast Women* starts with a funeral... or does it?

How I Wrote *A Chemical Prison* by Barbara Nadel

Few questions are simple. The one I frequently get asked is: why do you set your books in Turkey? Why an East End girl like myself should choose to wallow in such disordered exotica as exhibited in my books *Belshazzar's Daughter* and *A Chemical Prison* is, at face value, puzzling. True, I have a degree in psychology and have worked within institutions designed to accommodate those of differing perception... but why Turkey?

The answer, which Freud would have loved, is probably as much to do with formative erotic experience as it is with unusual states of mind. A moment in time involving a spectacular Turkish Marine, the dark alleyways of Istanbul and the dangerously charged political atmosphere of 1970s Turkey is as fresh in my mind today as it was then. So clichéd old hormones and death set somewhere hot then? Possibly. But then would I keep returning to Istanbul if I were not writing about it? And what of the spectacular Marine – a word I frequently employ to describe my detective protagonist?

Well... these are other questions that I may answer at another time. Possibly.
A Chemical Prison is published by Headline.

How I Wrote *Exile* by Denise Mina

Second novels are terrifying. Having used all the good ideas you've been building up through decades of observation, irritation and arguments in the first one, a second novel needs a professional attitude, consideration and planning. The worst of it is you can't pretend to yourself that no one's ever going to read it or spot the holes. My abiding memory of writing *Exile* was a panicked scream in my head like someone falling backwards off a cliff.

The book was written over four house moves: because of my partner's job we moved to Leicester for six months and because of my argumentative nature, we got evicted from the flat we took when we came back to Glasgow. Then we bought a house and had to move again. As unsettling as all the moving was, the foreign sales of *Garnethill* continued apace, I won the Creasey in Manchester that year and gave up my day job to write full time. Added to the panicked screaming was a deep sense of astonishment and gratitude at my good fortune.

Yearning to be settled somewhere – anywhere – I didn't think I'd look back on the time with any great affection, but I sometimes look at my hands and wonder where the calluses from the stacker boxes have gone. If you are in Leicester and happen to pass a solicitors called Kilty Goldfarb, pop in and say hello from me.

How I Wrote *School of the Night* by Judith Cook

The idea for *School of the Night* (Headline) arose in part because, some years back, I'd written a play (and book) about the murder of Christopher Marlowe. While researching him, I learned about the School of the Night, a secret society set up by Sir Walter Raleigh to discuss subjects considered deeply suspect, indeed dangerous. Needless to say it appealed to Marlowe and I considered it highly likely that it would have attracted my Elizabethan sleuth, Dr Simon Forman, who is based on a real life character. The other trigger was the

information given me by a market gardener in Suffolk; that around the time I'd set my book (the I590s) there was a tremendous vogue for the candied root of *eringo* (sea holly) which was grown there and was considered to be the sixteenth century equivalent of Viagra.

So what an excellent choice for both a poisoner, and a group of young bloods used to carrying out various experiments, who would leap at the chance of trying it out to see if it worked. Various uses came to mind: the young wife of an elderly, gross – and rich – man, who yearned to be a widow; the answer to a blackmailer; and a deeply unpleasant young man who would be no one's loss. The first Forman story was set in London, after which I took him further afield – on tour with the Lord Admiral's Men in the provinces, to the Scottish Borders and Edinburgh, and deep

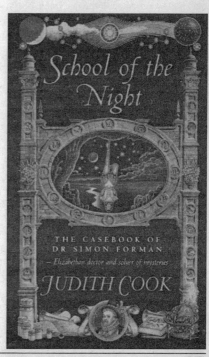

into rural witch-hunting country. (Apropos of *Blood on the Borders,* I am now an honorary member of the Armstrong clan, having made them the heroes of the story after using their splendid archive in Langholm. For four centuries they had been considered the bandits of the Borders.) *School of the Night* gave me the chance to bring Forman back to London again, to the alleys and stews of the Bankside and the traffic on the Thames. Not to mention the horrendous state of the Fleet River, graphically described by Ben Jonson in a long poem after he had been rowed from the Mermaid Inn to Holborn.

But there is a strange footnote to this. I was also commissioned to write a biography of the real Simon Forman for Chatto and Windus. I had read what was available on him before embarking on the fictional series, but now had to get down to the real thing: his diaries, case notes and other writings in the Bodleian Library and his medical books (with further notes) in King's College Library, Cambridge. The real Simon Forman is fascinating, if not exactly as dashing as his fictional counterpart, but it does seem as if he actually might have been a member of the School of the Night. He knew all the right people, was in the right place at the right time and was fascinated by the new scientists, as well as alchemy and astrology, and his diaries refer to meetings of some kind of secret circle, such references ceasing at about the same time Sir Robert Cecil set up an Inquisition to look into its activities. As to candied sea holly, from the extensive womanising described in his diaries, sometimes three in a day from 'Julia in Seething Lane up against the Cock' to Alice Blague, a Dean's wife, it doesn't look as if he had need of it!

How I Wrote *The Amorous Nightingale* by Edward Marston

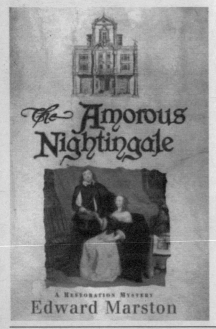

The Amorous Nightingale is the second in a series of Restoration mysteries, featuring Christopher Redmayne, an aspiring young architect, and Jonathan Bale, a Puritan constable. *The King's Evil* brought this unlikely pair together in a murder investigation and they made an effective team. The series examines the other restoration that took place – the rebuilding of London after the Great Fire of 1666. *The Amorous Nightingale* gave me the opportunity to combine three of my major obsessions: crime, theatre and architecture. Harriet Gow, the nightingale in question, is a talented actress whose performances on stage win her a starring role in the King's bed. When she is abducted, Charles II asks Redmayne and Bale to track her down. A tricky assignment is complicated by the fact that a husband and various lovers are soon uncovered. The nightingale has been excessively amorous. The murder of her maidservant adds a new desperation to the search.

Having written ten crime novels set in the Elizabethan theatre, I was eager to explore its Restoration counterpart. Actresses appeared on the English stage for the first time in 1660 but it was a dangerous profession, as Harriet Gow discovers. Two playhouses enjoyed a monopoly, giving Thomas Killigrew and Sir William Davenant, the respective managers, enormous power. These engaging rogues cried out for portrayal in a novel. Then, of course, there was theatre-loving Charles II, a man of many parts, the most notorious being aptly described in Rochester's satire on the King:

> Nor are his high desires above his strength
> His sceptre and his prick are of a length.

These real-life characters take their place alongside the fictional detectives and enrich the texture of the novel. Redmayne and Bale disagree violently over the importance of restoring a missing mistress to the royal collection but they battle their way through some of the darkest corners of the capital in pursuit of the kidnappers. The book is not over until the amorous nightingale sings.
The Amorous Nightingale is published by Headline.

How I Wrote *The Big Thaw* by Donald Harstad

This is a sequel to *The Known Dead*, which I wanted to build on. It continues the theme of the threat of the extreme right. It's an interesting challenge to use them as heavies, because, in actuality, I don't think these guys are really going to do anything major. Despite the amount of press they get, I think they're pretty marginalised. And even if America moves more to the right after the next presidential election, these guys would be mistaken if they felt that they'd find a sympathetic hearing – they are pariahs to all political persuasions. I had an unusual job at one time: I had to write the disaster scenarios for a riverboat company, in order that they might deal with emergencies. As a consequence, I know precisely how these things work, if the ship starts to sink, or catches fire or something. I thought: there's got to be a way I can use this. Tying this in with the dead of winter and extreme cold gave me my basic ingredients. There was also the challenge of a dual narrative, with both of my protagonists tackling different problems. Readers seem to be pleased with the results, so my hunches appear to have been right.

THE MERCURY'S RISING AND THE HEAT IS ON ...

THE BIG THAW
DONALD HARSTAD

How I Wrote *Hidden Evidence*
by David Owen

Writing *Hidden Evidence* (Time Life Books) was a very different commission from the norm. As a dedicated fan of realistic crime fiction, as opposed to the stylised body-in-the-library whodunit, I felt that forensic science played less than its full part, even in classics of the genre. All too often, the evidence of the pathologist, the fingerprint lab or the ballistics expert was inconclusive, to allow the main protagonist to solve the case without its help, by large amounts of intuition, experience and sometimes fortunate but unconvincing coincidences.

This is definitely a shame. Modern forensic science is an extremely powerful weapon against crime and criminals, provided it's deployed, aimed and used correctly. Different techniques can throw new light on otherwise insoluble crimes, where witnesses are not able to describe even the vaguest details of what they saw happen. So do writers of crime fiction play down its accomplishments to avoid detracting from the achievements of their creations? If so, their concern must surely be misplaced. Forensic scientists never solved a crime unaided. The range of true-life cases quoted in the book show a host of different ways in which they supported the detectives, rather than replaced them. For all the sophistication of present-day forensic science, it still takes a complex and fallible human being, the very core of high-quality crime fiction, to direct its revealing spotlight on to the right target.

How I Wrote *The Mermaids Feast*
by Janet Lawrence

I was inspired to write this book by a wonderful cruise my husband and I took last year up the Norwegian coast. I already knew something about Norwegian food, my mother was Swedish and I wrote a little Scandinavian cookbook some years ago, and I visited Sweden a number of times. But the furthest north I'd been in Norway was Lillehammer, just above Oslo. I was bowled over by the beauty of the countryside and warmth of the people. As we cruised into the Land of the Midnight Sun, the evenings were staying light later and later, and I became more and more fascinated by the floating world we inhabited, in which crew and passengers lived both together and apart – and I was intrigued by the business of feeding so many people so well. Soon, my mind was busy with a murder plot. The P&O personnel showed me behind the scenes, and I saw how the enormous amount of food that is required on every voyage is stored and prepared. Of course, none of the various exploits that take place in the book while Darina and William, her detective husband, enjoy the cruise could possibly happen in real-life!

The Mermaids Feast is published by Macmillan.

A Darina Lisle Mystery

THE Mermaid's Feast

JANET LAURENCE

TENDERLY – MAXIM JAKUBOWSKI

Apart from his regular column for CT, we asked the indefatigable Maxim to talk about his new book,
On Tenderness Express

*O*n *Tenderness Express* began as an exercise in writing a somewhat post-modern private eye story and, in the process, mutated into what now appears to be the final volume in a quartet, which I personally call *The Hotel Room Quartet* and might be reprinted in omnibus format as such, which brings to an end many of the preoccupations and strands of my previous two crime novels and the story collection *Life in the World of Women*. All about bad things happening to good people, bad people happening to good people, and people with cold hearts colliding with others of a softer disposition. Much of the action is set in America, on highways, in motels, a sort of desperate waltz into darkness juggling all my own regrets and obsessions.

Influences: all of crime fiction and much SF and fantasy, on the basis of you are what you eat. In random order: John Irving, Cornell Woolrich, J. G. Ballard, F. Scott Fitzgerald, James Crumley, David Goodis, Jim Thompson, Michael Perkins. Like a cocktail, really. Some influences are more apparent than others, others less so but no less important. As far as fledgling efforts, just the need to stand out at school when I was young and I was good at storytelling. Began writing at thirteen and published (efforts better now left buried) at sixteen.

I have very little unpublished stuff, apart from one embarassing novel I wrote at eighteen which had the whole weight of the world and deluded romanticism on its shoulders, encompassing reincarnation, the Wandering Jew and a bleak travelogue of south American brothels and decadence (at that age you write about what you don't know, then you learn to know better, and continue the embrassing process by writing about matters closer to reality, in my own case). In fact, a later science fiction novel which had many incarnations and was partly published in various places will finally be seeing the light of day next year from Toxic. Called *The Phosphorus War*, my homage and goodbye to the new wave of British speculative fiction, albeit with a year 2000 polish I'm applying right now.

What with Murder One and my Time Out and now Guardian column duties, I read a lot of crime and it's no secret my sympathies lean towards darkness and the USA, but I also try to read a lot outside the genre. And not just erotica! I still cast a fond eye on Golden Age locked room mysteries, knowing all too well I'd never be capable of writing one. Same names as the influences above, but I would rather not name contemporary names, as I live within the crime community and have already

angered P. D. James, Robert Crais and Andrew Vachss without really trying, and am amazed by how thin-skinned some people are. So: I love them all (not!).

Bloodshed is there, in the world outside our window and it would be hypocritical to ignore it. Violence hurts and too many books treat it as an exercise in style and prove incredibly unrealistic. On the other hand, it can also be caricatural and fun, viz Tarantino and Hiaasen and his whole school of camp grotesque followers. I assayed violence myself in *It's You That I Want to Kiss* and, in retrospect, maybe was too explicit, and went slightly over the top (although the fact that the major villain was called Mr Evil was, I thought, a sure sign of my intentions). Some people found it disturbing so some regrets there. But, it's like nudity in the movies, and should it advance the plot and have artistic merit, I'd be violent again.

Sex in my novels? The big question! Well, I plead guilty. It's there, it's in your face, it's anatomically realistic, it's crude, it's tender, it's about bodies and minds and the places in between. I write what I feel, and the sexuality of the characters and what they do about it is always paramount in my books. It is, I hope, what brings these people alive. Therefore, sexuality is unavoidable in what I write. You can't live without it; well, at any rate, I can't.

I often come up with titles first, sometimes characters, and I improvise a lot, particularly so in short stories. The novels are somewhat more structured, although in a loose way. I live with the idea and a rough approximation of the plot in my mind for up to a year before I actually put pen to paper and then I usually write the book in three months. But there's no preferred method. It's just what has worked for me over the last decade. In physical terms, I drink Coca-Cola from the bottle, eat chocolate and listen to rock music when I write fiction. Non-fiction, on the other hand, is more of a silent activity. But rock music (possibly a bigger influence on me than other writers) is fundamental and provides me with the right atmosphere for the book.

Films are a part of my life and always have been and I am heavily involved in various film festivals, including of course Crime Scene, and I would not be the person I am were it not for music. I still attend rock gigs even if, in some cases, I might happen to be the oldest person present, and I probably see over 150 films a year, so you might say I'm still a fan. Well, it's the only way to grow old disgracefully...

First for me in a novel? Always characters and places. I feel that if you get those right, the narrative just happens. It becomes an organic thing closely allied to the people and the places. There are only so many plots around and all have been used a thousand times. What is important is to spin the variations with elegance and get the reader involved in an emotional way even if he or she has already read the boy meets girl, or road chase or shoot-out or investigation canvas many times before.

I've enjoyed working with Jim Driver at the Do-Not Press and prefer working with small, independent publishers, but then I worked in big publishing myself for many years so I know the problems that face editors or people working in the conglomerates. It's a question of balance: you get marketed better at Pan or Headline or Hodder than you do at Robinson or Do-

Not, but then again I'm in the invidious position of not having to rely on my writing for the money, so I can afford to indulge. Often there is less choice.

I am of the world. I have somehow orbited towards the centre of the crime world what with Murder One, my reviewing, the festivals and all that, but somehow I don't think it has much bearing on what I actually write about. Personally I'd prefer splendid isolation, although not of the monastic variety, although my favourite poet and singer Leonard Cohen has now become a Zen seminarist (and no longer appears to write, though).

Having completed what turned out to be a quartet of books with many things in common (with a year's interruption in between for an erotic amuse gueule *The State of Montana*), I have now decided quite consciously that the form suits me and am planning another quartet of books. They will be crime, somewhat less erotic than my previous novels (although the characters will still have sex lives of course), many of the minor characters will reappear haphazardly from book to book, although not the main protagonists of the novels, and the emphasis will be on cities, one per book. The order will be London, New York, Paris and New Orleans. Foolishly, I'd be committing to this series for the next five years or so of my life and it is a bit daunting, but it's all brewing inside right now and the mental bubble is about to burst. The London book is called *Kiss Me Sadly* and I'm aiming at summer 2001 delivery. But then again, I might just write that time travel SF love story I've also been incubating for only twenty years. Ask me the question again next month.

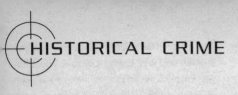

SON OF
HISTORICAL MAYHEM

*More **Michael Jecks** on his Knights Templar sequence...*

Some Knights Templar escaped execution by agreeing to go to a different religious order, others were deemed to be personally innocent and were released, but some simply faded away. It is thought that several joined the Knights of St John or the Teutonic Knights, where the Templars were still revered and the French King's more overblown accusations weren't believed. No doubt several Templars would have gone on to be mercenaries, but some would probably have returned to their old homes. My thinking was this far advanced when my wife and I got married. By sheer good fortune, on our honeymoon in Devon we came across Fursdon House in the countryside south of Tiverton. We were interested, we entered, and we enjoyed an hour or two being shown about the place. One thing caught my eye. On a wall was a family tree of the Fursdons, and it showed that the first of the family had appeared there in the late 1200s. While I stared at it, I idly wondered whether a Templar could have escaped to a place like this – perhaps because he had been raised here but his older brother inherited everything. He might have returned to find that his older brother had died and thus the whole shooting match was his. His name? Baldwin was common enough – Baldwin what? Fursdon? Fern sounded better. Furn – no, Furnshill. In this banal way Sir Baldwin de Furn-shill was born.

I immediately saw that Sir Baldwin would have wonderful attributes for a protagonist in a novel. He would be well travelled, experienced in fighting, experienced in business (especially banking), shrewd and open-minded. From his time in the Kingdom of Jerusalem he would have learned some wisdom from the Moors, and his outlook would certainly be different from the majority of the uneducated population. For one thing, he would surely have harboured a deep distrust of the Pope and French King, while possibly still believing in God. My Sir Baldwin feels strongly about certain matters; for example his crucial driving force is his despisal of injustice. Not a surprising trait in a man who has seen his friends tortured, condemned and burned at the stake simply to satisfy the personal greed of an avaricious King and a feeble Pope. A man like him would not unnaturally have shunned the limelight, preferring obscurity – but readers find that sort of thing dull, so I manipulated the poor devil's future and soon he became a Keeper of the King's Peace (the early form of Justice of the Peace). By this stage I was serious about writing a historical novel and Baldwin was so clear in my mind that I was already considering the plot. However I was sure that

there was little mileage in one protagonist. It is all very well having one man considering each move in the privacy of his own mind, but you only get a one-dimensional view of affairs if you see things through the same man's eyes. I needed to have a second man, one who was complementary to the first, but who would have his own firm opinions.

My first thought was of Holmes and Watson, but the good Doctor often tended towards utter gormlessness. I didn't want a second character to be like that. Mine should be complementary rather than a

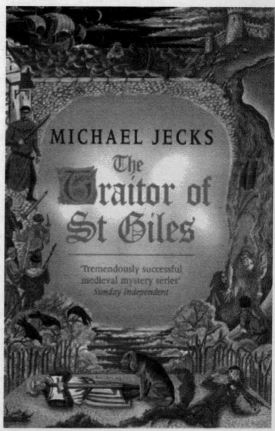

MICHAEL JECKS

The Traitor of St Giles

'Tremendously successful medieval mystery series' *Sunday Independent* mere idol-worshipper. It took some little time to figure out who that man would be. I spent many hours sitting at my desk and reading about the people of the time, but no one leaped out at me. What sort of man should it be? And then I learned of Stephen Puttock, Reeve on the Prior of Ely's manor of Sutton in Cambridgeshire. Stephen was a senior servant, even though he was a villein – effectively a slave who owed service to his master. However he was clearly a man of some importance. In ten years he acquired seven plots of land; he owned a flock of sheep and kept other men's sheep in his own fold. He was an example of a 'tenacious, resilient and enterprising' peasant, as described by Professor Colin Platt, who by dint of hard work advanced himself.

This gave me my second character: Simon Puttock would be the local Bailiff, I decided. He would be the officer in charge of Lydford Castle. A villein and son of a villein, he had nonetheless taken on this important position after hard work and would be a level-headed, stolid character. In retrospect choosing Simon as Baldwin's foil was extremely fortunate. Not only did I have two senior officers, one knight, one local man, who could sparkle during debates, who had totally different views of people and situations, but who could both respect each other for their strengths, I also had some other details I could throw into the mix. For example I decided early on that Baldwin would have little truck with superstition, while Simon would be wary of upsetting ghosts or goblins. Simon would be the man with more knowledge of local affairs and the people, while Baldwin could explain strange foreign ideas.

Simon would generally dislike dealing with corpses, while Baldwin would have less concern, having lived through the siege of Acre and seen plenty of dead bodies.

The truly fortunate part of the decision to base Simon in Lyford only occurred to me later: I had Sir Baldwin as the Keeper for Crediton, and that gave me a degree of latitude because I could have him looking into all kinds of odd felonies all over a wide area from Exeter up to Tiverton and west as far as I wanted, really – but then I learned more about the Stannaries of Devon, the ancient tin-mining industry, and realised that in Simon I had an officer who would be responsible for law enforcement on Dartmoor. Thus I have two characters who could legitimately be moved all over Devon. And I was delighted to move the pair of them to Tiverton for *The Traitor of St Giles* because ever since signing the Register of Marriages there, I had wanted to write something about it, incorporating the castle and making use of the land as it would have appeared.

The plot didn't come from Devon, though. I first had a glimpse of the plot while listening to a recital at Bletchingley Church in Surrey. It was a small local choir, and their repertoire has almost completely faded from my memory, but early in the evening they gave a rendition of 'The Three Ravens', a very old English song that tells of a knight lying dead under a tree while three ravens look on: his hounds and, for reasons which escape me, a hart mourn his passing. Presumably he was riding in chase of the hart and fell – you can guess at your own story, but *The Traitor of St Giles* is my take.

Some writers say that they get their inspiration from characters, then the story comes together; others say that their tales are plot-led and the characterisation is plastered onto people afterwards. In my case I start out with an initial idea. Sometimes it can be a murder, but sometimes it's far less ambitious. In this case it was the scene of the dead knight, but that was not enough. I wanted more colour to the tale. How do you manage that? In my case, I intertwined a dysfunctional family, a felon who had committed a rape and been forced to leave the country and who was found, beheaded, near the knight's corpse. But first, the location. Tiverton is an ancient market town that lies between two rivers: the Exe and the Lowman. The old town is up on a hill overlooking them both (the name comes apparently from 'Twyfyrde' which means two fords) and a castle which was sadly wrecked after the Civil War. This castle was one of several which the Courtenay family, the earls of Devon, owned and, as my book begins, Lord Hugh Courtenay is being spied on by several groups who would like his support.

The trouble was that the King was overly keen on his favourites. Historians have concluded that he was homosexual, and in an age where people settled disputes by donning heavy metalwork and slogging it out with war-axes, being known as a gay was not guaranteed to win you friends and Edward II's reign was characterised by a series of minor civil wars. After one group rose in arms he was forced to give up the Gascon Piers Gaveston – who was later beheaded by his enemies. It was a dramatic means of removing him, but effective. King Edward II's next close friend was

more dangerous. Hugh Despenser the Younger was an avaricious, jealous, grasping sort of man who would stop at nothing to fulfil his ambitions. And funnily enough, his ambition was to be extremely wealthy. He succeeded. He bullied, he threatened, he illegally imprisoned, he occasionally had recourse to open warfare, and eventually other more senior nobles grew more than a little alarmed. Working on the assumption that "If this fellow is prepared to steal from my neighbour, I could be next on his list", the lords from the Welsh Marches (the border lands) decided enough was enough. In 1321 they overran the Despenser lands and marched on London. Despenser was forced to run from the country and the King was forced to accept certain conditions. He reneged, of course, within a few months, but that wasn't the point (and will be the subject of one of my later books).

The Traitor of St Giles begins with this worrying position. Lord Hugh was trying to assess which way the wind was likely to blow, while assorted advisors suggested he should support the King and the Despensers, the Marcher Lords, or even the wily old Earl Thomas of Lancaster, who was always enthusiastic in his pursuit of King Edward II. Yet even a lord like Hugh can't call his advisors and knights to a meeting as war threatens the land without giving ammunition to suspicious enemies – or the King – so the pretext for their visit is the Feast of St Giles, at which the town has a great market.

Sir Baldwin, of course, as one of Lord Hugh's more intelligent advisors, was called to attend the feast and give off-the-record words of wisdom. Bailiff Puttock was also called because his father used to be a steward to Lord Hugh's father and because he could be a useful sounding board to test the views of his master, the Abbot of Tavistock. Thus the two are on hand when the dead body of Sir Gilbert, a renegade Templar, is found in a clearing south of the town. They accompany the coroner to investigate the murder and find that not only is Sir Gilbert dead, a felon called Philip Dyne has been decapitated nearby. Dyne, an apprentice, had been convicted of raping and murdering the daughter of Andrew Carter, a noted merchant; after gaining sanctuary at the local church, Dyne demanded the right to 'Abjure the Realm', which meant voluntary exile. He was given a prescribed route to the coast and once there must obtain passage abroad as quickly as possible or risk being caught again. However, if an abjurer was found more than a few feet from his road, he could be captured and beheaded on the spot. The coroner is satisfied that Dyne killed the knight and was then himself killed by some right-thinking people who witnessed it. It's happened before and no one should be convicted of homicide for executing an outlaw; it's justice if Dyne was killed.

But Sir Baldwin is uneasy at this explanation. Dyne was leaving the country wearing a penitent's clothing and carrying no weapon. Sir Baldwin knows that Sir Gilbert used to be a Templar, and that means he was a practised fighter, experienced with all weapons. To suggest that Dyne, an apprentice, could somehow have disarmed a Templar and then killed him with his own sword, and yet couldn't defend himself with that same weapon

against his own subsequent attacker, seems peculiar. And there is the curious matter of the dead hunting dog at Sir Gilbert's side. Did the murderer kill the dog first, in which case Sir Gilbert was surely on his guard – or did the man kill Sir Gilbert first, in which case why didn't the dog protect him?

It is all very odd, and Simon and Baldwin have to try to help the local coroner seek the murderer with a degree of caution since neither wishes to be caught up in the intrigues which necessarily revolve about Lord Hugh Courtenay, a man who has been a close advisor to the King and who more recently has been instrumental in curbing the royal powers. Except Simon and Baldwin are only too aware that the killer could have been motivated by the fact that Sir Gilbert was a messenger from the Despensers.

Writing I find great fun – and it is even more enjoyable to be able to earn money while doing what I've always enjoyed – reading about history. For this book I had to research Tiverton itself, criminal law and the rules for Abjuring the Realm, the laws concerning homicides outside of towns, and a whole range of other factors. So, as I said at the beginning, the great thing is that every day I indulge myself. I spend my time immersed in history. Occasionally it creates problems because when I consider the twentieth or, God help us, the twenty-first centuries, I am often confused. I exist in a perpetual state of mild confusion. To earn my crust I daydream absentmindedly – and claim it's a job!

And as Terry Pratchett says, no heavy lifting either!

JOHN FANTE:
BETWEEN TWO WORLDS

Woody Haut

The author of seven novels, two novellas, eleven screenplays and numerous short stories, John Fante's appeal belies his status as a cult writer. Born in 1909, he was one of the first to write realistically about low-life Los Angeles, and was a forerunner to a type of writing associated with Charles Willeford, Edward Bunker and Jim Thompson.

1933 WAS A BAD YEAR

JOHN FANTE

Moreover, Fante's fiction bridges the gap between real-life hardboilers and the likes of Charles Bukowski and Alexander Trocchi. Lauded by H. L. Mencken, as well as Bukowski, Fante appears to have gone out of his way to cultivate obscurity, first as an impoverished novelist whose early novels could barely find a publisher. This was despite his stories appearing, from 1932 when Fante was just twenty-three years old, in Mencken's *American Mercury* and White Burnett and Martha Foley's *Story* magazine, and despite the fact that he was a successful screenwriter who worked on such films as *Jeanne Eagels*, *Walk on the Wild Side*, *The Reluctant Saint* and *Full of Life* (adapted from his 1952 novel).

Too bad, because Fante's populist fiction revels in the urban diversity and chaos of Los Angeles. Concerning such perennials as love, sex, dope, drunkenness, writing, rejection and survival, it moves effortlessly between depictions of Italian-American culture and portrayals of fallen Angelinos, whether Mexican waitresses, Filipino dishwashers, Greek wrestlers, black itinerants and Jewish merchants and movie moguls.

After decades of literary neglect, Fante's resuscitation began in the 1980s thanks partly to Bukowski who, as a Fante fanatic, penned an introduction to a new edition of *Ask the Dust*. So devoted was Bukowski that, for a time, he took residence in Fante's old Bunker Hill hotel, visited the ailing writer in the hospital, and attended Fante's funeral. At Bukowski's urging, from the early 1980s onwards Black Sparrow Press would reprint virtually the entire Fante back catalogue, including two novels, *The Road to Los Angeles* from the 1930s, and *1933 Was a Bad Year* from the 1950s, which, up to that point, had gone unpublished. Around the same time, screenwriter-director Robert Towne helped convince Houghton Miflin to buy Fante's *Brotherhood of the Grape*. While in Britain, Granada reprinted *Wait Until Spring, Bandini* and *Ask the Dust*, both of which have recently gone through another print cycle courtesy of Canongate in Edinburgh, who published Stephen Cooper's biography of Fante, *Full of Life*, this year. Unfortunately, Fante did not live to witness the revival of his work. Diabetic since the mid-1950s, Fante lost his first leg in 1977 and his sight in 1975. Still he managed to write, dictating his work to his wife, Joyce, whom Fante met and married in 1937. Painstaking though the process of dictation must have been, Fante was able to produce *Dreams from Bunker Hill,* a classic tale concerning the ordeals of a young writer, and one of the great novels about Hollywood during the 1930s.

For a cult writer, Fante's books have sold remarkably well, Over 100,000 copies in the US since 1980. In France his sales have exceeded half a million, with much of his work having gone through a recent reprinting thanks to publishers 10/18. Articles have appeared in magazines like *Rolling Stone, American Film* and *Life*, who called Fante a national treasure. By the late 1980s, according to Joyce Fante, all of her husband's works but one had been optioned to film companies. And no wonder. Fante's autobiographical fiction, from *Journey to Los Angeles* to *Dreams from Bunker Hill*, constitutes a history of the city in an era when Bunker Hill rooming houses were populated by writers, actors, winos, and prostitutes; and when, during the Depression and war years, taxi-dance halls could be found along Main Street. By the time Fante's books were reprinted, LA had been overhauled. In 1964, Bunker Hill was cleared to make way for the Music Center, an event that heralded the arrival of the new Los Angeles.

Not only was Fante one of the great writers of the Depression, ranking alongside Steinbeck, Fitzgerald and Nathaniel West, but he was one of a handful of regional writers who burst upon the literary scene during the 1930s. While the likes of Sherwood Anderson, Dreiser, Ford Maddox Ford and Sinclair Lewis were lionised, and modernists – Dos Passos, Farrell and Fitzgerald – were the rage, Mencken in his magazine *American Mercury* and Foley in her journal *Story* went out of their way to promote and publish writers with a more hardboiled attitude towards their subject matter and the world in general.

These days, due to globalisation and the reduction of the world through mass communication, regionalism has lost much of its cutting edge. However, the regionalists of the 1930s — A. I. Bezzerides writing about Fresno, Edward Anderson and George Milburn writing about Texas, James Ross writing about North Carolina, Tom Kromer writing about hoboing through America, and John Fante writing about Los Angeles – came from the geographical and cultural margins. Not so much a literary movement as a reflection of Mencken's liberalism, his interest in regional language, and a general interest at that time in all things proletariat.

Surprisingly, Fante and Mencken never actually met. This even though Fante, like

a number of other young writers of the period, was Mencken's protégé early on, and, having carried on a twenty-year correspondence with the 'sage of Baltimore', dedicated two novels to him. It was on Mencken's advice that Fante, to subsidise his 'real writing', became a studio screenwriter. Although it earned him a great deal of money, scriptwriting, contrary to Mencken's belief, prevented Fante from doing much 'real writing'. Not initially enamoured with his new job, he wrote to his mother in 1935, saying, "In many ways I wish I had never worked for the movies. They have a tendency to spoil a good writer – particularly if he has not already published his first novel." Once ensconced in the studios, Fante, from the 1940s to the 1960s, produced little in the way of fiction. Still he harboured literary aspirations.

When future head of the writer's department at MGM, Ross B. Wills, said, "So you're another of those guys who are going to write the Great American Novel, are you?", Fante clenched his fists to the sky and mockingly proclaimed, "Ten! Twenty! Why I've got *forty* great books in me! All I want is time, a typewriter, and a sandwich now and then."

After arriving in California from Boulder, Colorado, in 1929, Fante immediately threw himself into writing, and, by 1932, was already on the fringe of Hollywood film and literary culture. Through fellow Italians Ernest and Jo Pagano, Fante was able to kick-start his career at MGM. From there he went to Warner, RKO, Columbia and Paramount. The Paganos played an important role in Fante's life, particularly Jo, who was author of *The Condemned*, an excellent Leopold and Loeb-type thriller (adapted for the screen by Cyril Endfield in 1950 and, with a script by Pagano, retitled *Try and Get Me*).

It was through Mencken that Fante secured a contract at Knopf for his first novel, *The Road to Los Angeles*. But Knopf eventually rejected the manuscript (as did Viking amongst others, where a humourless reader wrote the following: "Compensates for its feeling of inferiority and self-disgust induced by the habit of masturbation [...] in a parade of an undigested mass of fragments of Nietzsche, Schopenhauer, Spengler [...] together with self-advertisement as an important writer in quest of material for a magnum opus"), and that exquisite novel of 1930s Los Angeles would go unpublished for half a century. Four years after its rejection, Fante was finally able to publish his first novel,

when, in 1938, Stackpole and Sons, a small press that would soon be sued out of existence for its unauthorised edition of *Mein Kampf,* brought out *Wait Until Spring, Bandini*. In 1939, Stackpole also published *Ask the Dust*. In 1940, Fante finally broke into the big time when Viking published his collection of stories, entitled *Dago Red*.

It's the Bandini novels for which Fante is best known. Four novels whose protagonist is Arturo Bandini, a young romantic trapped within the confines of an immigrant Italian-American family and cultural tradition. Bandini's stonemason father is forever unemployed, behind on bills and on the verge of losing his temper: "Dio cane. Dio cane. It means God is a dog and Svevo Bandini was saying it to the snow. Why did Svevo lose ten dollars in a poker game tonight at the Imperial Poolhall? He was such a poor man, and he had three children, and the macaroni was not paid, nor was the house in which the three children and the macaroni were kept. God is a dog."

While his mother offsets her husband's violence with an oppressive and stubborn Catholicism, Arturo (Fante's alter ego) dreams of becoming a writer, and uses the confessional as a testing-ground for his future literary activities. With the same raw honesty and vulnerability, *Ask the Dust* portrays Arturo on the loose: drunk, libidinous, brash, ambitious, and swept away by the freedom that Los Angeles offers. At the time of publication, the novel did not receive the attention it deserved, perhaps because it was published in 1939, the same year as West's *Day of the Locust*, Steinbeck's *Grapes of Wrath* and Chandler's *The Big Sleep*. Still, it was talked up by the likes of

McWilliams, Adamic, Saroyan and Gene Fowler. There was even talk that Metro and then Paramount might adapt the novel for the screen, but nothing came of it, and the book took a back seat to other novels and films of the era.

As with the protagonist in *Ask the Dust*, Fante was unable to extricate himself from the studios. Though this meant encountering long spells when he wrote no fiction at all, neither his film work nor his eventual illness could entirely keep Fante from returning to his favourite genre, nor alter his style and subject matter, which remained unchanged throughout his career. Despite publishing in magazines and obtaining a handful of modest book contracts, Fante was never able to make much money from his fiction, nor find a substantial audience for his work. Yet he wasn't doing badly. In 1932, Mencken paid him $125 – roughly the equivalent of $1,000 at today's prices – for his story *Home Sweet Home*. And within the year there were four more stories paid at a similar rate. Even if it didn't compare with working for the studios, this was a period when writing for magazines could be a relatively lucrative occupation. In 1933 Knopf paid Fante $50 a month – a total of $600 in all – for the manuscript of *The Road to Los Angeles*.

After *Dago Red*, twelve years went by before Fante's next novel, the 1952 *Full of Life*. Following that book, Fante became one of literature's disappeared, not emerging until twenty-five years later with the publication of *Brotherhood of the Grape*, a novel in which Bandini returns to Colorado for his father's funeral, and mulls over the past. As usual it's an investigation

of guilt, lapsed Catholicism, drinking, sex, and the need to write. This against a backdrop of poverty, racism, and Bandini's need to prove himself. Two decades later, in an introduction to a new edition of *Ask the Dust,* Bukowski wrote: "[Fante] is a story of terrible luck and terrible fate and of a rare and natural courage." That could be slightly overstating his case. For Fante's lack of literary recognition was, in many ways, his own doing. Having been raised in poverty and needing the security that financial success can bring, Fante opted to write screenplays rather than pursue a career as a struggling novelist. Not that Fante's Hollywood work can be easily dismissed. He was, by all accounts, an excellent scriptwriter and rarely lacked work. Edward Dmytryk, who directed Fante scripts of *Walk on the Wild Side* and *The*

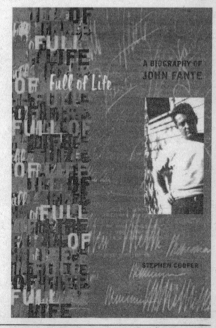

Reluctant Saint, and who was one of those indicted during the McCarthy era (only to end up giving names to the HUAC) said, "[Fante] was a great movie writer who wasn't understood by producers [...] He had a wonderful sense of contrast. To develop character. Not every writer has that [...] And Fante always had. Right from the very beginning."

Nevertheless, Fante always felt he had, to some degree, prostituted himself. According to friend and fellow scriptwriter A. I. Bezzerides (*Kiss Me Deadly, On Dangerous Ground*, etc) – another writer who chose a career in Hollywood rather than pursue his considerable talent as a novelist (*Thieves Market, They Drive by Night*) – "[Fante] knew he was a good writer. Even though he wasn't a successful writer [...] I think he was disappointed, because he wrote those things with all these feelings and nobody responded to him. And that they're responding to him today, like he wouldn't believe, is fantastic. But why so fucking late?"

Another reason Fante remained in the studios was because he had undoubtedly grown accustomed to a particular lifestyle. Soon he had a large house in Malibu, a family, and a mild gambling habit. Not to mention a taste for flashy convertibles, card playing and running up sizeable debts. Fortunately Fante, known for his eccentricity (at Metro, he shocked the secretaries by writing at his desk clad only in his underpants), quick temper and fondness for pinball machines (Saroyan modelled the pinball fanatic in *The Time of Your Life* on him) was able to collect a weekly salary in excess of four figures. But it wasn't all clear sailing for Fante in Hollywood. He had to contend with the political climate of the

1940s and 1950s. Certainly Fante believed his independent politics worked against him. Hardly rightwing – how could he have been when amongst his best friends were leftwing social critics McWilliams and Adamic (a former worker in a San Pedro pilot house who was found in his home dead from a gunshot wound at the height of the McCarthy era) – Fante did not fit into any political camp. Moreover, at that time, being a first generation Italian-American did not help matters. Often questioned by the FBI regarding his knowledge of Hollywood communism – standard procedure if one wanted a screenwriting job during the war – it's not inconceivable that Fante supplied them with enough information to keep him employed.

Ironically, Fante's greatest success as a novelist came during this period with the publication of his least hardboiled novel, *Full of Life* (1952). Made into a film starring Judy Holliday and Anthony Quinn, and directed by Richard Quine (1956), it concerns a couple's first child and their attempts to become upstanding middle-class citizens. After *Full of Life*, Fante went on to write scripts for Orson Welles, Harry Cohn, and Dino Di Laurentis, none of which would see the light of day. By the 1960s and the demise of the studio system, Fante, in poor health, had to scramble for work, a situation documented in his 1971 novella, and only work of fiction from that period, *My Dog Stupid*: "It was January, cold and dark and raining, and I was tired and wretched, and my windshield wipers weren't working, and I was hung over from a long evening of drinking and talking with a millionaire director who wanted ed me to write a film about the Tate

Murders 'in the manner of *Bonnie and Clyde*, with wit and style'. "We'll be partners, fifty-fifty." It was the third offer of that kind I'd had in six months, a very discouraging sign of the times."

Since arriving in California, Fante had been interested in Los Angeles Filipino culture and wanted to write a novel about it. With author Carlos Buscolan as his guide, he made the rounds of its nightclubs, restaurants and pool halls. As it turned out, Buscolan was a communist, and the subject of many of Fante's encounters with the FBI. Fante's novel was to be entitled *Little Brown Brothers*. Mentioned by the author as early as 1933, it was, by all accounts, an embarrassing affair and received a less than favourable reception at Viking. Intended to rival *The Grapes of Wrath* – Fante thought of it as James M. Cain crossed with Harriet Beecher Stowe – it was, unlike Fante's usual intuitive style, elaborately plotted and evidently dreadful. Thankfully, he abandoned the project in 1945.

Fante's career was given another boost in the early 1970s, when Robert Towne, while doing research for Polanski's *Chinatown,* came across *Ask the Dust,* and optioned the book, paying Fante $4,500, twice the amount that Fante received upon the book's initial publication. In a letter to McWilliams, Fante, in good humour, reflects on his fate as a novelist: "The combined revenue I have had from *Wait Until Spring, Bandini, Ask the Dust* and *Dago Red*...wouldn't purchase a lawnmower on today's market, and man, what I really need today is a good mower."

In the same letter, Fante mentions that he's begun *Brotherhood of the Grape,* "the story of four Italian wine drunks from Roseville, a tale revolving around my father and his friends". When, in 1975, Towne heard about the manuscript, he purchased an option on it even though it had yet to be published. Not only was Towne instrumental in getting it published, but he brought the book to the attention of Francis Ford Coppola who serialised it in his San Francisco magazine *City*. Invited to Coppola's home for dinner, Fante and his wife, after a screening of *Full of Life,* were told by Coppola that he intended to film *Brotherhood of the Grape* . With a script by Towne – "I don't think he is a very good screenwriter despite his reputation," said Fante in a letter to McWilliams – shooting was to commence after the completion of *Apocalypse Now*. Coppola also said he wanted Fante to write a script for him. But his studio, Zoetrope, would go bankrupt after *Apocalypse Now,*

JOHN FANTE

THE

BIG

HUN

GER

STORIES 1932-1959

Edited by Stephen Cooper

and *Brotherhood of the Grape* would never go into production. Nor would there be a Fante script. Though it is interesting to speculate on the result of such a collaboration, as well as the riches and reputation that might have come Fante's way.

While Fante's work remains more satisfying and realistic than any number of contemporary takes on Los Angeles, his son, Dan, carries on the family tradition, having written the excellent *Chump Change,* which contains material about his father. Suffice it to say that John Fante wrote some classic novels, as hardboiled as they come, about pre-war low-life Los Angeles. Certainly Bukowski was right when he said of Fante, "The way of his words and the way of his way are the same: strong and good and warm."

BIBLIOGRAPHY

Published by Black Sparrow Press *(distributed in the UK by Airlift):*

Wait Until Spring, Bandini

The Road to Los Angeles

Ask the Dust

Dreams from Bunker Hill

Dago Red (short stories)

Full of Life

The Brotherhood of the Grape

The Wine of Youth (stories)

1933 Was a Bad Year

West of Rome (novellas)

Selected Letters: Letters to H. L. Mencken

Published by Canongate:

Ask the Dust

Wait Until Spring, Bandini

Full of Life: A Biography of John Fante by Stephen Cooper

Chump Change by Dan Fante

THE MAN BEHIND MODESTY BLAISE

Mike Paterson on Peter O'Donnell

After last issue's illuminating piece by Peter O'Donnell on the genesis of his durable heroine, we asked Mike Paterson to tell us the whole Modesty story: her creator, the novels, the comic strips and the hardest thing Modesty ever survived: that dispiriting Monica Vitti movie.

When Quentin Tarantino's Midas touch supercharged the careers of forgotten cult figures in the mid 1990s, it was Modesty Blaise who was left behind. Despite the fact that it was a Modesty paperback featured in lurid close-up on the toilet floor splattered with the blood of John Travolta, her resurrection never matched those of Travolta, Dick Dale or Pam Grier. Yet it was Modesty Blaise who put the pulp fiction in *Pulp Fiction*.

Peter O'Donnell's creation featured in hundreds of newspaper comic strips around the world, thirteen novels spanning 1963 to 1996 and one curious jewel of a film. In a decade of high-kicking, haute couture heroines, Modesty out-spied, out-fought and out-quipped the competition.

Her spiritual sisters were Emma Peel and Pussy Galore, her ancestors the warrior queens of mythology and her children Buffy, Xena and Scully. But Modesty stands tall at the centre, protected by the domed vacuum of irony and instant camp. She knows it and she loves it. Yeah, Baby.

In 1942 Peter O'Donnell was a sergeant in charge of a mobile radio detachment in northern Persia protecting the oilfields from Nazi attack and overseeing the refugees evading the war in the Balkans. He describes one evening when a lone barefoot child, her belongings tied in a blanket, appeared carrying a crude weapon of a wooden club nailed with wire for protection. Carrying an air of someone who had seen atrocities but survived, she maintained a regal composure around her self-protective instincts. She sat to eat from the tins of food given to her by O'Donnell and, after carefully washing her utensils, stood to leave, giving him a smile at odds with her suffering. From this chance encounter a character was born.

The Comic Strip

Continuing his pre-war career of assorted journalism and newspaper strips, O'Donnell was given the brief by Beaverbrook Newspapers in 1962 of creating a new heroic character for a daily strip. Rather than recycling another square-jawed GI Joe or superhero he decided to create a more plausible alternative. Reflecting a fresh trend in altering gender roles at the cusp of the social revolution of the sixties, this character would be a strong woman. Rather than depicting a cat-walk model cowering until rescued by her hulking sidekick, this would be a fully rounded, independent and self-sufficient woman with a glamorous wardrobe *and* a karate kick. This would be Bond in reverse.

Ian Fleming had provided the template of the aspirational world of jet-set glamour and hyper-real espionage action. All it needed were some twists. Ditching the easy option of a one-dimensional helpless heroine, O'Donnell reached into historical mythology and took some classic precedents; Atalanta, the hunter of Calydon, who vowed to marry only a man who could beat her in a race; Hippolyta, Queen of the Amazons, possession of whose girdle was the ninth labour of Hercules; Boudicca, Queen of the Iceni, who slaughtered 70,000 Romans in battle during her campaigns. Like them, Modesty had to have a believable heroism bolstered by an authentic background 'born in the blood and the bone'.

Taking the bones of the character inspired by the feral child in the refugee camp, O'Donnell overlaid a history to make flesh a heroine authentic in her knowledge, experience and capabilities, but mysteriously exotic enough to maintain allure. Teamed with the artist Jim Holdaway, his collaborator on previous strips such as *Romeo Brown* in 1956, O'Donnell's *Modesty Blaise* made its debut in The Evening Standard on May 13th 1963.

The demands of the daily, three-frame strip were for instant action with little opportunity for scene-setting and enough of the crucial elements of sex, jeopardy, rescue and form-fitting catsuits to satisfy the page-skimmer. This was the newspaper version of channel-surfing avoidance. Teamed with her trusty, knife-throwing partner Willie Garvin (in a relationship of sexual tension that mirrors those of Steed and Mrs Peel and Mulder and Scully), Modesty high-kicked her way through countless capers with such heady titles as *The Vanishing Dollybirds, The Reluctant Chaperone* and *Gallows Bird*. The strip formula pitted Modesty and Willie (recruited from retirement from their underground organisation, The Network, by Sir Gerald Tarrant of British Intelligence) against a series of villainous groups and individuals, always using their skill and cunning to release each other from the jaws of death.

Jim Holdaway's artwork, despite the effort of daily creation, rises above the ordinary clichés. Modesty is a slightly dusky (foreign), slim but tall brunette depicted in stark black lines and imbued with a genuine sex appeal that manages to

MODESTY BLAISE
by PETER O'DONNELL

THAT'S GABRIEL ALL RIGHT, TAKE A LOOK AT 'IM, SAM... SEEMS LIKE HE'S GOT ALL 'IS TOP BRASS 'ERE

FOR A JOB?

ANNUAL GENERAL MEETING, MORE LIKELY... REPORTS AN' BRIEFING... THIS LOT'S MANAGEMENT, NOT WORKERS

VARLEY PHONED—SAYS THERE'S SOMETHING COME UP AT THE PHOENIX YOU OUGHT TO KNOW ABOUT

270

YOU RANG ME, VARLEY—WHY?

WELL, I-I GUESS MAYBE IT'S NOTHING AT ALL... BUT WE JUST RAN A *Cloud Nine* SESSION ON A WOMAN CALLED JANE LESTER

AND IT DIDN'T WORK! EVEN UNDER DEEP HYPNOSIS, THE ONLY THING WE DUG OUT WAS THAT HER REAL NAME IS *"MODESTY BLAISE"*

I DON'T KNOW IF THE NAME RINGS ANY BELL WITH YOU—

271

VARLEY... STOP TALKING, AND LISTEN

avoid sleaze. The action is efficiently dealt with in an economy of style that evokes the age of classic sixties pop art. This is pulp with attitude. Following Jim Holdaway's sudden death in 1970 the strips were illustrated by Enrique Badia Romero until 1979, then subsequently by John Burns, Pat Wright and Neville Colvin until, in 1986, Romero resumed work. That a daily strip can continue for so long is testament to the originality of vision and wealth of invention of its creator. For the general public, the legacy of Modesty Blaise in the memory is not from the strips but from one strange misconception of a film, a pop-art curiosity from an era of sometimes desperate cultural water-treading. To the genre aficionado, however, Modesty's true worth is in the paperback pulp of thirteen unpretentious, gloriously enjoyable books.

The Books

Following the success of the comic strips, it was inevitable that the Hollywood hyenas would begin to prowl. In 1964 O'Donnell was approached by Twentieth Century Fox to adapt the characters for the screen. In parallel to the screenplay a novel was written that enabled the characters to become much more fully rounded and properly realised. The first novel, *Modesty Blaise*, was published by Souvenir Press in 1965 in hardback and by Pan in 1966 in paperback.

The exotic mythology of the origins of the ass-kicking, sexually free Modesty is only fleetingly touched on in the comics. When we first meet Modesty and Willie they are already experienced professionals; world-weary, psychologically bonded and calculating killers when necessary. We start in the middle. Options are open either way immediately for scene-setting prequels and continuing adventures. Eventually, in rapid backstory to avoid delay to the action, we are given a taste of how Modesty became Modesty.

Like the classic characters from myth, Modesty's childhood was an apprenticeship of lone survival and learning through careful tutelage. After her parents were slaughtered in the village of an unnamed Balkan

Pan

Peter O'Donnell

DRAGON'S CLAW

Modesty Blaise

IN A NEW ADVENTURE...
THE SEVENTH AND PROBABLY THE BEST
Yorkshire Post

country, a young girl set out on a punch-drunk trek in an amnesiac haze. Suppressing the mental and physical pain inflicted on her during her journey she rapidly learns self-sufficiency and protection. After eventually ending up at a Persian camp for displaced persons she meets an academic named Lob who takes her as his pupil. He imparts an intense education in languages and culture as well as combat and, as she has arrived with no identity of her own, gives her the name Modesty and Blaise from Merlin the magician's mentor.

With her mind sharpened, her instinct tuned and her body toughened by endurance, Modesty steps into the world prepared. Seeking the security of money she organises a crime syndicate but with a moral base. When she has made a million she will retire. Picking up associates and contacts as she goes, she falls in with a broken man called Willie Garvin, an urchin from the East End of London with a deadly skill in knife throwing and a similar history of nefarious survival. She turns him into her right-hand man, they realise their ambition and they retire. She to her clothes, her jewels and her penthouse apartments: he to his pub on the Thames and the sexual conquests from his travels. But once they have had the taste of adventure and the adrenaline of combat, the sedentary lifestyle does not appeal. Retirement is just the beginning. This is the set-up for the real adventure.

Springing fully formed onto the page, the first novel blasts us with a familiar formula of sex, espionage, capture and escape with a verve, wit, pace and humour at odds with its cartoon origins. While the villains still have a larger-than-life cartoonish touch, the characters are far more rounded and maturely depicted than the majority of modern thrillers. Sex is suggested but not overtly depicted. The violence is lifelike: short, fast and brutal. The set-up is believable within the genre but open to flights of fantasy. Overall there is a lightness of tone that skates a middle ground between a more knowing Captain W. E. Johns and the research of Conan Doyle. Humour always comes to the rescue when hardware, weaponry and political intrigue look like taking over.

As obligatory arch-nemesis, Gabriel has a culture and a nice line in dry humour to go with his sadism: he watches Tom and Jerry cartoons and winces at the animated violence before killing a hapless agent. In Mrs Fothergill the novel provides one of the most gloriously outrageous villainous heavies in the genre: "Walking slowly towards him now – a man smoking a cigar – no, by God, a woman! She might have been forty. The face was heavily jowled and devoid of make-up except for a gash of carelessly applied lipstick. Her neck seemed to slope out almost directly from below the jaws to the broad shoulders. Mrs Fothergill, thought Grant, and felt his stomach twist with a stab of nameless fear."

"Have ye ever wondered about *Mister* Fothergill?" asks McWhirter, the comic relief sidekick of Gabriel. Such throwaway comic moments abound: heavies occupy themselves playing with piano wire and discuss mathematical probability over poker. Killers agonise over methods of despatch: Mrs Fothergill prefers being 'hands-on'. Hanging is not personal enough for her liking.

Eschewing the norm of agonisingly explaining everything, O'Donnell assumes an intelligence in the reader by giving his characters a culture and intelligence themselves. Compared to a recent by-the-num-bers blockbuster thriller (*The Devil's Teardrop* by Jeffrey Deaver) where an FBI agent (and, by patronising association, the reader) has to have the concept of anagrams explained to him, this is refreshingly different in a populist genre. Unlike such books that use throwaway cultural references as a facile shorthand, the impression is that O'Donnell has a love for his characters as well as a concern for their interests and expertise.

In keeping with the times (and anticipating the film) O'Donnell gives Modesty a glamorous entrance whenever she appears in each scene. Detailed descriptions of dress and bearing are given before moving on to the matter in hand: "Her hair was down, bound in a short club at the nape of her neck. She wore little make-up and her nails were unvarnished. A light nylon mac did much to hide the roll-neck sweater and black denim slacks she wore beneath it."

Yet Modesty is no mere clotheshorse. Her hand-to-hand combat skills are deadly, she can sword-fight with experts, she can repress pain through meditation and can induce unconsciousness by will. She is the 'Blondie doing the muscle stuff'. The fight sequences are described with such pacing and style as to be breathtaking. There's an authenticity and precision to them — the mark of an author who writes from experience rather than second-hand cinematic research.

With the discipline of a daily strip O'Donnell knows precisely how to pace the novel. Short scenes of action that acclimatise us to the skills of Modesty and Willie are interwoven with the plot-driving before building to a climax of escape from an island prison that is as inventive and exciting as anything in the genre.

By 1969 and the fourth title in the series, *A Taste for Death,* a formula had been found and characters established that were hard to beat. For sheer verve, excitement and humour this is a novel that stands up with the best examples of the thriller genre. It opens with a sequence where Willie, diving for pearls (to make a necklace for his 'princess'), sees a group of figures on a distant beach in chase, pursuit and eventually murder, that reads like a Hitchcock story-board. After establishing the scenario and introducing the villains (a chastened Gabriel and wise-cracking McWhirter amongst them) the story is distilled down to a simple hide, seek, capture and escape. In the mix are Delicata, a man-mountain of relentless immorality who happens to be unable to feel pain (a concept subsequently borrowed in the Bond movies), a blind empathic girl, a seemingly inescapable scenario involving Willie strapped to a chair with a bomb attached, and a sword-swishing criminal sidekick with designs on Modesty's honour.

By resisting the temptation of explicit-ness in terms of sex and violence O'Donnell is able to maintain a charm that alludes to a John Buchan swash-buckling quality while never being old-fashioned. Every element is perfectly judged: hardware is never Tom Clancy fetishistic, entry wounds never in Clive Barker close-up, psychopathic moti-vation stops short of Thomas Harris analy-sis. Throughout it all Modesty and Willie sustain a level of believable proficiency in their ability to escape the inescapable.

Following the success of the first book they continued their 'capers' in book form every few years until 1996 when a short story collection called *The Cobra Trap* brought them to a natural conclusion. In the

Modesty Blaise

books Peter O'Donnell displayed his true talent and gave voice to one of the great creations of genre fiction. Within the pages of the pulp novel Modesty was given her most flattering perspective. Despite the odd piece of cringingly accented dialogue or national stereotyping, there's little to date these books. Their adventures are escapism of a classic kind that exist outside fashion and, like Fleming's Bond, are written with such authority as to be immortal.

The Film

Inevitably, however, celluloid atrophies as it ages. The effect of Austin Powers has been cruel on the reputations of a swathe of hyperventilating 'happening' spy films of the sixties. Some have been immune due to their in-built sense of camp such as the Flint films (themselves parodies of Bond and his ilk of unlikely übermensch) or Dean Martin's Vegas swinger of a hero, Matt Helm. But for each of these there are any number of ill-conceived, eager to catch the flavour of a fleeting moment, circus tents of films crammed with a host of crimplene-suited spies among the lava-lamp scenery. One film that straddled the chasm between the two precipices was *Modesty Blaise*; not knowing enough to be truly camp, too competent to be genuinely awful, enough great character actors to balance the scenery-chewers and the showroom dummies, and too good a source to be short of a scenario. Imagine if the only filmed Bond was *Casino Royale* and you have the missed opportunity, botch-job that was *Modesty Blaise*.

After writing an initial screenplay in 1965, O'Donnell saw his treatment revised by five other writers until, by the time of filming, only one line of his original dialogue remained. In Joseph Losey, an American blueblood with a European sensibility and a pedigree in literary adaptations, there was a director with intellect and style. He was an émigré, blacklisted for refusing to testify at the Hollywood show trials, who settled in England in the 1950s and eventually established a reputation as a director famous for his moral scrutiny of class and the outsider. His breakthrough film, *The Servant* (1963), gave Dirk Bogarde one of his best escapes from a career of handsome leads and silly-ass doctors. As Gabriel, the bleach-blond fey villain and world-domination seeker, Bogarde took another step into the unknown. As director of a comic-strip adaptation with one stylistic eye on a Richard Lester kaleidoscope of Swinging London, Losey stepped out of his depth. He was helped by some inspired casting in the smaller roles. With Harry Andrews as Tarrant, Michael Craig as Hagan, Clive Revill as McWhirter and gifted comic character actors such as Joe Melia propping up the cast, a professionalism was assured.

For Willie Garvin, the knife-throwing cockney, there really was no other choice than to cast Terence Stamp. With his cool blue-eyed stare and insouciant swagger, Stamp is a delight of barely restrained pantomime. To see the mirror of his character in Stephen Soderbergh's *The Limey* is to imagine a franchise lost to history. Cast in the role of heroine, action babe and sexual-tension transmitter was Monica Vitti. Gorgeous, pouting Monica was a protégé of Michelangelo Antonioni (the King of Italian Neo-Realism) and spoke no English. An Austrian vocal coach was hired to teach her to speak the lines phonetically. In the end much of her

Modesty Blaise

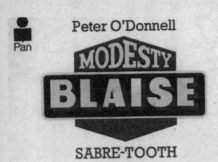

Peter O'Donnell

MODESTY BLAISE

SABRE-TOOTH

protection against the critics. It left us with one of the most memorable gags of sixties spy caper cinema where Bogarde, bound and staked-out under the desert sun, gasps in a voice parched from dehydration, "Champagne! Champagne!"

Peter O'Donnell says now of the film, "It makes my nose bleed just to think of it."

Rumours and Whispers:

In 1993 two British producers backed by Miramax Films bought an option on Modesty Blaise. Those expressing an interest in involvement at various times have been Neil Gaiman (MB fan and Nobel Laureate of graphic novels), Luc Besson (who has covered this ground in Modesty clone *La Femme Nikita*) and, most recently, Quentin Tarantino. Novelist Michael Marshall Smith is currently working on a version, and, according to producing partner Laurence Bender, an outline treatment has already been written based on *A Taste For Death* but, with

dialogue was dubbed. While certainly conveying the continental allure of Modesty in the costume budget-breaking sequences, she just didn't have the requisite athleticism for a believable action hero. Nevertheless its oddity is in some ways its strength, and by aiming for a camp sensibility it constructed a

Tarantino in the middle of his public backlash crisis of confidence, momentum is slow to build. "We just can't get a screenplay we like," says Bender. "When we do, it should be no problem casting it. Actresses will come out of the woodwork to play Modesty."

Let's hope Liz Hurley stays there.

Bibliography

Modesty Blaise (1965)

Sabre-Tooth (1966)

I, Lucifer (1967)

A Taste for Death (1969)

The Impossible Virgin (1971)

Pieces of Modesty (short stories) (1972)

The Silver Mistress (1973)

Last Days in Limbo (1976)

Dragon's Claw (1978)

Xanadu Talisman (1981)

Night of the Morningstar (1982)

Dead Man's Handle (1985)

Cobra Trap (1996)

NEWS FROM PLANET SPARKLE

Sparkle Hayter

Greetings Earthlings!

I apologise to those of you who tried to order the UK edition of *Chelsea Girls* through the Tart City All-Night Mall. We were told the mall would open by a certain date but there have been unforeseen bugs and unavoidable delays. I am very sorry about this. You can still order the UK edition through the indie online bookseller, The Big Bookshop (www.the-bigbookshop.co.uk) or through Amazon UK (www.amazon.co.uk). Big Bookshop takes MasterCard and Visa, Amazon takes Amex as well. The UK edition is superior and the UK reviews have been most kind. It pays to have your publisher sleep with the critics, so thanks Ion, and sorry about the rash! (Don't worry, they can cure that kind of thing now.) *Chelsea Girls* made the IMBA bestseller list for June and July. We blush, and thank the indie booksellers for this. The photos and negatives are in the mail...

Other news:

New web picks:
www.tartcity.com/sparkle/letter.htm
I am developing a media project, a lot of fun, and once it is set up I'll be creator and creative consultant and my workload will be much lighter. Also writing a non-mystery (third person for a change), and plan to write a sixth Robin Hudson down the line, for love more than money, and in my own time. This will likely be the final instalment, set in Paris, and I want it to be the best of all of them. Why Paris? It's the perfect place to look at media, men and women, love, sex and crime from a different, but not too overly foreign, PoV. Coincidentally, after I wrote *Chelsea Girls*, I ended up having two boyfriends in Paris (not simultaneously), so the omens seem to be pointing me there. Will probably go over for a month or two next year. Rents

are much cheaper there than New York and the food is far superior, and if you tell a guy in Paris you're a writer, it's like telling a guy in New York you're a model, so why not?

The Robin Hudson books are coming soon to Italy and Greece: Italy this year, Greece next. The first two books in French are being reprinted by a mass market house. Three books are out there now from Serpant a Plumes. The second book is now out in Sweden, and all five are out in Germany and the UK. Quebec reprint of the French version of *Cootie Girls* is due out this fall from Stanke.

Tart City: After launching tartcity.com, I turned over all editorial responsibilities to Katy and Lauren, so I'm semi-retired as a tart. I'm pretty much out of the Tart Noir thing now, and at forty-two am simply not as tarty as the rest of the gang (though still in the first half of my miniskirt years, thank you very much). Beth Tindall does most of the web work, and I am mainly looking after promotional and business things for tartcity.com now, with the occasional graphic or web page when Beth is too busy. There are new contributors on the site brought in by Lauren and Katy, and a lot of fresh material. By the end of the month, we hope to have a small version of our mall open to sell JJ Buch's incomparable *Dolls to Die For* as well as some other goodies.

www.tartcity.com

On my TBR: *Harry Potter and the Goblet of Fire*. Currently reading: *Harry Potter and the Prisoner of Azkaban*. I am completely hooked! Rowling – wow – managed to turn kids who are 'reluctant readers' away from TV and video games and take them into her realm. I hear the Potter books have done very well for the indie booksellers too. In Toronto, they are renting the Skydome for her reading to accommodate as many of the people who want to attend as possible. It's a miracle, and the books completely justify the response. If you haven't yet read them, don't wait.

That's about it. Thanks so much for all your support. Since the HarperCollins brouhaha last year, things have been tough, but it's going swimmingly now. Your emails, posts, free meals and beer have helped more than you know. If you want to 'send me an owl' check in to the (otherwise unadvertised) Robin Hudson forum at www.delphi.com/sparklehayter/start.

I remain,
Sparkle
A Goddamned Ray of Sunshine
All the Goddamned Time
http://www.tartcity.com/sparkle/

sparkle hayter
revenge of the cootie girls
'Feisty, sassy, sexy, wise-cracking and delightful' – *The Times*

READING TOO MUCH CRIME

Peter Robinson

In a Dry Season is the tenth Chief Inspector Banks novel, following immediately after *Dead Right*, and the first to be published by Macmillan. The book begins with the discovery of a skeleton found in a dried-up reservoir on the site of a village called Hobb's End in Yorkshire. Forensic examination and local records indicate that the body was probably buried there during the war. Interspersed with Banks's present-day investigation is a memoir or novella (the reader is never quite clear which) recounting the incidents leading up to the murder and giving a day-to-day picture of a Yorkshire village during the Second World War. As the writer of the memoir/novella comes to one conclusion about the killer, Banks, along with his sidekick and romantic interest Detective Sergeant Annie Cabbot, finds himself heading in another direction altogether.

I must say that when I was writing this book I thought I'd hit on a pretty original idea, which came to me when I visited Thrushcross Reservoir, near Otley, during the drought and saw the eerie remains of the village of West End. I was working on something else at the time and had to put off starting for a year or so. The day I finished *In a Dry Season*, I saw a blurb describing Reginald Hill's forthcoming book, *On Beulah Height,* in the Crime in Store catalogue. I was devastated. Hill has always been one of my heroes and here he was, pre-empting my story! Only when *In a Dry Season* was finally in print did I dare read *On Beulah Height* and, of course, I needn't have worried. The only thing the books have in common is the dried-up reservoir. I have since discovered other books that use the same sort of setting, so I'm now quite happy to be among the select 'Reservoir Noir' school!

In a Dry Season was first published in the USA by Avon and in Canada by Penguin. It got great reviews, was picked as one of the New York Time Book Review's 'notable books' of 1999, and has been nominated for an Edgar Award by the Mystery Writers of America.

I wrote poetry for many years before I started writing crime fiction, and my PhD dissertation was on 'The Sense of Place in Contemporary British Poetry'. I wrote about Ted Hughes, Philip Larkin, Basil Bunting, Geoffrey Hill and Seamus Heaney, in particular, so they were definite influences. Before that, like many people of my generation who hit their late teens to a soundtrack of Dylan, Hendrix, The Grateful Dead, Captain Beefheart, Jefferson Airplane and the rest, I first got excited by the major Beat writers: Ginsberg, Kerouac and Burroughs. I have also assimilated Hardy, Trollope and Graham Greene in relatively large doses, and when it comes to crime writers, it was reading Raymond Chandler and Georges Simenon that turned me on to the whole genre, and the Maigret books probably influenced me the most. Certainly Ruth Rendell and Reginald Hill were early influences, too.

I have numerous poems and about five unpublished novels in my bottom drawer (in the attic, actually), four of them written between about 1975 and 1980. The first is a sort of 'coming-of-age' novel with lots of sex, drugs and rock 'n' roll, and the next three are abortive attempts at a series featuring an unemployed university graduate in Leeds as the detective. There is also a fifth unpublished novel that I actually wrote in 1985 after *Gallows View*, the second Banks book. It's a private eye novel set in Toronto, called *Beginner's Luck*, and Penguin didn't want it because they'd already got the Banks series rolling. I suppose with a bit of work it *might* be publishable, but I can't seem to find the time or the inclination to go back and do it. On the whole, I think most authors produce a great deal of work that would be best left in the bottom drawer, but often success and public demand result in its being published. Sometimes, though, a writer might not get a series published until he's already written three or four books, so the earlier books are not necessarily bad.

The first Banks book I wrote was *A Dedicated Man* in the early eighties. I sent a sample chapter and an outline to Penguin Canada, who told me, six months later, that they liked it enough to want the whole

Photo: Clifford Robinson

manuscript. That took them another six months. But during that year I was waiting to hear their verdict, I wrote *Gallows View* and sent that along to them, too. It helped tip the balance in my favour. In the end, they said they wanted to publish *Gallows View* first because it had more sex and violence. I was just so happy I was getting published, I said fine, do whatever you want.

There are so many good writers in the genre today that it's impossible to keep up, but writers I never miss include Ruth Rendell (and Barbara Vine), Reginald Hill, Ian Rankin, Michael Connelly, Val McDermid, James Lee Burke, P. D. James, Ed McBain, Elmore Leonard, Cynthia Harrod-Eagles, Robert Barnard, Lawrence Block (the Matt Scudders), John Harvey, Minette Walters, Michelle Spring, Laurence Gough and Dennis Lehane. I read many others, of course, but these are the ones who first come to mind. I'm also constantly on the lookout for new writers. For example, I've just got onto my second book in J. Robert Janes's wonderful Kohler/St-Cyr series, set in occupied France, and I read Mo Hayder's excellent first novel *Birdman* a couple of weeks ago.

I have very broad tastes in crime fiction, and though I tend more towards hard-boiled private eye, psychological suspense and police procedurals, I don't dismiss cosies and amateur sleuths, or think that their authors should be boiled in oil. I've never had much time for those especially loud writers who seem to think that there can be only one *real* sort of crime writing (the sort they are writing, of course), and that everything else is crap. There is a lot of crap, but it runs the whole gamut of the genre and isn't confined to, say, cosies or

historicals.

I clearly spend far too much time reading crime fiction, and writing it, to read enough outside the field these days, but I try to keep up with the poetry – Seamus Heaney, Michael Longley, Geoffrey Hill, Tony Harrison and Charles Tomlinson in particular, along with anthologies of new work. I also try to read contemporary novels by the likes of Beryl Bainbridge, Melvyn Bragg, Ian McEwan, Julian Barnes, David Lodge, Pat Barker and Kate Atkinson. Then there's biography – Ross MacDonald, John Coltrane and Elvis Presley are the first three in line right now. This leaves me far less time for the classics I would love to revisit, and I intend to put a year aside soon to

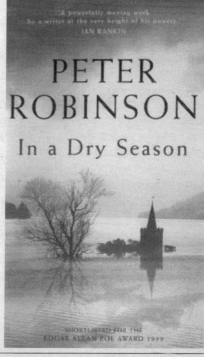

'A powerfully moving work
by a writer at the very height of his powers.'
IAN RANKIN

PETER
ROBINSON

In a Dry Season

SHORTLISTED FOR THE
EDGAR ALLAN POE AWARD 1999

reacquaint myself with Jane Austen, the Brontes, Hardy and Dickens.

I saw a lot of violence growing up on a Leeds council estate in the sixties, including fist-fights, knife-fights and razor-slashings. I also witnessed a shooting in Toronto some years ago. The thing about crime is that it often involves violence, and the thing about violence is that you rarely see it coming and it's over before you realise it. That's why I don't particularly go for books or movies that treat it in slow-motion and dwell on every grisly aspect. It's not that my stomach can't take it, but that it just isn't realistic. A good writer can make a little go a long way and make a much stronger impression with one small, telling detail than with pages and pages of gore. Most of the violence in my books takes place off-stage. Banks usually arrives when the deed's been done. I don't shirk the details of death, but I try not to dwell on them overmuch, either. That said, I've got no objection to a bit of gratuitous violence now and then. I did put Dennis Lehane and James Lee Burke on my list of favourites, after all!

Sex is rarely written about successfully. About the only book I can remember reading lately that does it well is Sebastian Faulks's *Birdsong*. In general, I'd go for the hint, the forbidden glimpse of skin or stocking-top that gives the erotic charge. There's no reason not to be frank about it – after all, we're all adults here – but being frank doesn't mean a writer has to write pages of grunting, moaning and sweaty prose to get the idea of sex across. There are books full of that sort of thing for those who want them, though in most cases I should imagine videos are more popular.

Another thing that irks me about sex writing is the flowery, metaphoric, clichéd language that so many writers use. You know the sort of thing – flowers opening, factory chimneys falling down and trains going into tunnels. If that's the best you can do, better not bother. Hitchcock did it well in *North by Northwest*. Monty Python did a great skit on it once. I believe there's also an annual award for the worst sex writing, which is giving the Bulwer Lytton worst opening lines contest a good run for its money. That sounds like a great idea.

What also bothers me is the idea of the political party package deal. You know, if you're left wing then you're pro choice, anti big corporations or whatever, and if you're right wing, you're pro fox hunting and anti gay rights. Nothing is that simple. I think you should be able to pick and choose your own pros and antis, and so what if there are inconsistencies? As Emerson wrote, "A foolish consistency is the hobgoblin of little minds, adored by little statesmen and philosophers and divines."

When I was a young wannabe writer, I read a book that left me thinking I couldn't be a writer if I wasn't an early riser. That put me right off. It was like the book about being a spy (another early ambition) that said I couldn't be a spy unless I could run up and down the stairs ten times, speak fifteen languages, swim five miles through an ocean of boiling… I'm sure you get the picture. Now I'd rank that bit about early rising up there with 'write what you know' as one of the worst pieces of advice you could give to an aspiring writer. Depending on what jobs I've had to do to make ends meet, I have written at practically every hour of the day and night, and the only thing I've found is that it doesn't make the slightest scrap of difference when you do it, as long as you do it.

Now that I'm fortunate to be writing full time, I find that my working methods are constantly changing. I try to write from about nine to three every day, some days just eating a sandwich at my desk and sometimes actually pausing for lunch. It depends. I still try to keep to those hours, but I find I'm moving more towards setting myself a number of pages to produce per day. The number varies, but five is a satisfying minimum for me. Of course, if you're writing that stichomythic Elmore Leonard dialogue, your day's work is done in half an hour. All you have to do then is spend the rest of the week polishing it!

I'm sure that using a computer has changed my working habits, but I've been using one for so long that I can't remember how. What's far more interesting to me is that even using the same method my habits have been changing. I used to rush through a first draft, without looking back, then spend ages on a second, third and fourth, first tinkering with the structure, then rewriting scenes, checking continuity, polishing the language. Now I find I revise and polish more as I go, and I'm likely to end up with a far more acceptable 'first' draft than I used to.

You hear so much about things like *Reservoir Dogs* and *Pulp Fiction* that in the end you have to go and see them just to find out what people are raving about. I'm lucky in that I've always been a film fan. When I was a kid there were several local cinemas – the Lyric, the Clifton, the Western, the Palace – all within walking distance. Most have now passed through the

bingo hall phase and become carpet warehouses. Anyway, they changed double bills and I went to as many as I could. I was also fortunate in that I could get in to X films at about twelve, so I got to see things like *Psycho*, *I Married a Monster from Outer Space* and *On the Waterfront* at a very early age. And you see how discriminating I was in my taste! If a film was banned in Leeds, as was *A Clockwork Orange*, then we'd go see it in Bradford. I don't go the cinema very often these days, but I do subscribe to the cable movie channels and own a VCR, so I still watch lots of films. TV series, too. *Homicide*'s been cancelled, but you know about the great HBO series, *The Sopranos*, which is beautifully written

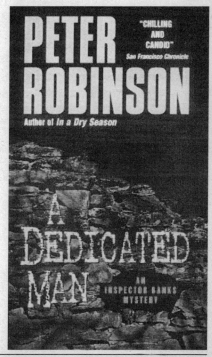

PETER ROBINSON

"CHILLING AND CANDID"
San Francisco Chronicle

Author of *In a Dry Season*

A DEDICATED MAN

AN INSPECTOR BANKS MYSTERY

and treats violence very realistically.

Music plays a big part in the books and their inspiration. When I first started writing Banks, the only fictional policeman I knew to whom music was important was early Morse, and he seemed almost exclusively a Wagnerian back then. I started Banks out on opera but gave him far more eclectic tastes over the series, so in one book he may be into English vocal music, in the next blues, and in another sixties rock. In *Past Reason Hated*, for example, a piece of music by Vivaldi left playing at the crime scene even provides a clue, and music often creates an atmosphere for scenes, or some sort of ironic counterpoint to the action or dialogue.

Editors have been invaluable to me over the years. We haven't always seen eye to eye on everything but that's okay. Sometimes the best relationships with editors tend to be when you're at each other's throat a bit, which at least means they give a damn. The unsatisfying relationships are when they just don't seem interested. I've had the latter experience with publishers, not with specific editors, both in the UK and the USA. My first UK publisher, Penguin, didn't seem to do a lot for me. I think they got the books in a box from Penguin Canada and stuck them in the corner of the warehouse. You could never find them in the shops. Constable did better, but they did small print runs and had no paperback line. They also wanted short books to keep down paper costs, and my books keep getting longer.

I was with Berkley for a while in the US, until they dropped me just *before* they published the second book of a two-book contract, a year or so after my first Edgar nomination. That book happened to be *Innocent Graves,* which was picked as *People* magazine 'page-turner of the week', one of *Publishers Weekly*'s 'books of the year', and was nominated for a Hammett Award by the International Association of Crime Writers. I had to finance my own book tour, and John Harvey very kindly let me join him for readings/signings in San Francisco, Los Angeles, Scottsdale and Madison as part of his *Easy Meat* tour. We had a great time, and his publicist at Henry Holt was very good to me, but it was all a bit embarrassing.

Editors from different houses seldom agree with one another, and problems can arise because of that. The Canadian version of *In a Dry Season* is slightly different from the American version, for example, because I got caught in the middle of an editorial disagreement and let myself be pushed into making cuts. Luckily, the Macmillan version is the complete one.

The next book is called *Cold is the Grave*. It has come out from Avon/HarperCollins in the US and from Penguin in Canada, and is due to be published by Macmillan in the UK in April 2001. It was tough to do a follow-up to *In a Dry Season*, with its two time frames and alternating narrative, so I didn't try. *Cold is the Grave* is a much bleaker, harder-edged book. It begins with Chief Constable Riddle seeing pictures of his runaway daughter naked on the Internet. For various reasons, he sends Banks to look for her and hush things up, promising him a smoother career track if he succeeds. Banks goes to London and tracks her down through the porn world, but it isn't until he finds her that his troubles really begin.

I AM NOT
A NUMBER

Mike Paterson on The Prisoner...

We've already looked at the DVD issue of episodes one to four of The Prisoner (from Carlton Video), but we make no apologies for noting the release of the entire series on five unmissable DVDs. The excellence of Patrick McGoohan's groundbreaking series needs no rehearsing here – if you haven't discovered it yet, you're doing yourself a grave disservice... And here's the perfect medium – the astonishing clarity of the DVD transfers belies the age of the series (was this really made in the Sixties?), and there are the usual tempting extras – including material on all the various actors who played the tormenting Number Two. The much-contested sequence of episodes (on its last TV outing, Channel 4 showed them in the wrong order) is solved here by the best possible options – there is, of course, no definitive numbering. As the company has delayed further releases in the equally unmissable Danger Man series (Number Six when he was still John Drake), this will

do to be going on with_and if you want more…

Aside from a few isolated exceptions, the truly original, inventive and daring is absent from current television. Risk has been largely eliminated. Individual control is rare. Catching the advertiser's demographic is paramount. When something new does rise to the surface it is eventually starved of air by an uncomprehending network. The last great work of TV nonconformity, *Twin Peaks*, initially thrived then petered out through lack of support by a puzzled television company. Even now David Lynch has seen *Mullholland Drive*, his 1998 noir drama, dumped by ABC in the United States without being broadcast. Shows that shine with originality are perceived by the mass public and television companies as flaming meteors blazing across the sky then disappearing into dust.

In the sixties, the decade of artistic boundary-stretching, the archetypal TV cult was *The Prisoner*. We are familiar now with the elements that constitute its puzzle; a spy drama rising from the ashes of another, an allegory of individual identity amongst conformity, numbers replacing names. The literary and artistic influence is also unusual for the time; the language of Orwell, the bureaucratic nightmare of Kafka, the inverted logic of Lewis Carroll, the surreal landscape of Magritte and Delvaux. How could such a thing possibly work?

Its existence is due to the success of *Dangerman,* the persistence of its star, Patrick McGoohan, and the hunch of the man in control of the company that made it, Lew Grade. How it has managed to sustain its cult appeal is something less tangible. Patrick McGoohan, famously reluctant to discuss the show and prickly in inter-

views, once retorted, "If one gives answers to a conundrum it is no longer a conundrum." We are hardwired to seek order and meaning from confusion. When we see a puzzle we must solve it. Nobody could solve *The Prisoner.* Not even its creator.

In seventeen episodes, mostly made on a tight schedule, quickly written and filmed, a man imprisoned by unknown authorities (possibly secret service ex-employers) is in the process of being brainwashed or debriefed while all the time trying to escape. Within this straightforward formula the possibility to extend the drama into flights of fancy was large. Using the generous budget of ITC and with the good luck to have the oddity of Clough William-Ellis' Portmeirion village for location shooting, each episode played with a James Bond psychodrama of paranoid cat and mouse. Its opening sequence is one seared into our consciousness and has become a classic emblem of the art of television. While Ron Grainer's theme thunderstrikes out, a story unfolds in rapid edits; a dashing man driving a sports car, a *Point Blank* corridor march to a dark office, a desk-thumping resignation, a gassed bedroom and drugged awakening into a strange wonderland. This is one of the great set-ups of genre drama. A Gulag Priory for a Bond with a nervous breakdown.

McGoohan (once a Bond candidate himself) had already made a conventional spy drama with *Dangerman* and was now taking it into a more hallucinogenic arena. Perfect for 1967. Given the initial idea by *Dangerman* writer George Markstein and hiring director Don Chaffey (responsible for *Jason & The Argonauts* and many of the best *Avengers* episodes) McGoohan set up his own production company to oversee the series. Using a family of cast and crew, a singularity of vision was able to be preserved. McGoohan wrote and directed many episodes himself and rarely had to bow to outside pressure.

Viewing it now, one is struck by many things: McGoohan has a presence and authentic intelligence lacking in most leading actors of genre drama. His single-minded drive to create such a thought-provoking series while maintaining artistic control is in perfect parallel to the struggle of his character. The look of the series, like the toy-box architecture of Portmeirion, is a mix of the familiar and the jarring; the fantasy element of Number Two's control room allows a science fiction flavour, the costumes are uniforms outside of fashion never betraying a particular time or place. The freedom ITC allowed him to produce episodes as unconventional as the penultimate one – effectively a theatrical two-hander between McGoohan and Leo McKern as Number Two – is remarkable. Few high profile shows would have such courage today.

Some of the fantasy episodes (such as the saloon bar westerns or Kenneth Griffith's Napoleon) recall *The Avengers* without evoking the same sense of fun. Occasionally it takes itself too seriously and the studied oddness becomes tedious. Amongst the many great character actors lending it a gravitas (Eric Portman, Leo McKern, Kenneth Griffith) are some who provoke sniggers of camp recognition (Peter Wyngarde, Darren Nesbitt, Patrick Cargill, Donald Sinden). The final episode, written and directed by McGoohan under pressure, was intended to provide a final revelation behind the struggle. In the rush to finish, the symbolism of the concepts behind the show reached critical mass causing a confusing mess that satisfied few people and clarified little. It did, however, maintain the conundrum and stay true to the bravery of McGoohan's vision.

Before video there was little opportunity to digest and review a series such as *The Prisoner*. Only word of mouth and a repeat run every few years allowed its underground popularity to snowball. By the time Channel Four showed it as a showcase for a new channel in the Eighties, it was becoming a cult for the cognoscenti. Video releases added to this. Books, societies for people who like to meet up and dress up and web sites have made it the ultimate clique for the literate fan boy and girl. Now we have the limited edition box set DVD with which to revel in the enigma of one of the most discussed television programmes of all time.

It now takes its place amongst a satellite-beamed plethora of programmes, jostling for space on the video shelves with *The Twilight Zone* and *Outer Limits, The Avengers* and *The Champions*. In the last ten years most of the great ideas and all of the best writing in TV has been in cop dramas (*Homicide*) and comedy (*Frasier*). Occasionally a mid season *X Files* will astonish or a *Star Trek Next Generation* will impress, but few fantasy programmes have the ability to approach the invention or verve of *The Prisoner*. That's why it is still a cult.

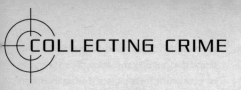

THE PULPS:
TERROR AND SPICE

Mike Ashley

Mike Ashley has written and/or compiled nearly sixty books covering a wide range of subjects, from science fiction and fantasy, to mystery and horror and to ancient history. He has a keen interest in the history and development of genre fiction, particularly in magazines, and has a collection of over 15,000 books and magazines. Amongst his mystery anthologies are The Mammoth Book of Historical Whodunnits, The Mammoth Book of Historical Detectives, Shakespearean Whodunnits, Shakespearean Detectives, Classical Whodunnits, The Mammoth Book of New Sherlock Holmes Adventures, Royal Whodunnits *and* The Mammoth Book of Impossible Crimes. *He is also working on a biography of Algernon Blackwood.*

Seeing those Prion postcards reviewed elsewhere in this issue made me think of the real sleaze magazines, back in the 1930s – pulps like *Terror Tales* and *Horror Stories* and *Dime Mystery*. These must rate as the least subtle of all pulps – and that's saying something. These weren't straight sex stories or stories of honest lust: these were the nadir of pulp fiction – utterly mindless mayhem and depravity. So, needless to say, they are very collectable, and since they were almost all crime magazines (assuming they fit into any category at all) they seem just right for this issue of *Crime Time*.

So let's journey back to the days when pulps were pulps, when men were animals, and when women were just there to be tortured, maimed and mutilated.

It all began with Henry Steeger who, still in his twenties, set up Popular Publications in East 42nd Street, New York in the summer of 1930, and issued a batch of pulps – *Battle Aces, Gang World, Western Rangers* and *Detective Action Stories*. They did moderately well, *Battle Aces* being the money-spinner. Other titles were added, but Steeger still didn't feel things were shifting sufficiently. "We made enough money to keep going", he remarked in an interview in 1977", but it was not until we started *Dime Detective* that the profits really began rolling in." *Dime Detective*'s first issue is dated November 1931. Its featured authors included Frederick Nebel, T. T. Flynn and Erle Stanley Gardner. It delivered a diet of fast action, often violent stories where crimes were solved by brute force and bravado rather than by footwork and deduction. Steeger and his partner, Harry Goldsmith, discovered that what the readers seemed to like most were stories of dark and lurid menace. It took the hard-boiled school of fiction, which had emerged in *Black Mask* during the twenties, and opened the valve on violence. Sales began to rocket. *Dime Detective* went from a monthly to a twice-a-month schedule and Steeger brought in as his right-hand man Rogers Terrill, formerly the managing editor at Fiction House, which was laying off staff because of financial difficulties in the Depression.

Realizing that the readers liked the weird menace stories in *Dime Detective*, and being a fan of the Grand Guignol Theatre in Paris, Steeger decided to concentrate in that area. In December 1932 he launched a new magazine which would soon revolutionize the field of terror tales – *Dime Mystery Book*. Compared to later issues this first issue was a bit tame. Although the cover story was "Bride's House Horror" by Beldon Duff (who? – almost certainly a pseudonym, but I don't know whose), the other stories bore such tame titles as "The Poetical Policeman" (by Edgar Wallace, believe it or not) and "Thirteen Hours". The public weren't that overwhelmed by this and it was down to Rogers Terrill to push the magazine in the direction the public wanted. With the issue for October 1933 it became *Dime Mystery Magazine* and shifted fully armed into the terror market. Here were such knee-trembling titles as "The Dance of the Skeletons", "The Graveless Dead", "The Monster in the Dark" and "Gate of the Two Coffins." In fact the titles are part of the fun of the Popular weird-menace magazines. Here's just a sampling from later issues:

They Feed at Midnight

The Tongueless Horror

Court of the Grave Creatures

Girl for the Torture God

Music for the Lusting Dead

Murder Dyed Their Lips

Brides of the Dust Demon

Master of the Legless Ones

Well, I'm sure we all know a few people who fit the last title. Hugh B. Cave, who was a regular contributor to the magazines, reflected about these titles. "Most of them [had] such words as 'dark', 'devil' or 'devils', 'unholy', 'death', 'night', 'lost', 'pain', 'terror' or 'shadow' in their titles. Those titles were really out of this world! As I remember it, Harry Steeger or his editors made most of mine up, or at least added to my originals to heighten their allure."

The most common formula for the title would be along the lines of "The House of the Living Dead" or "The Mistress of the Grinning Corpse" or "Prey for the Creeping Death". It didn't really matter if the title described the story or not. The plots were so formulaic and stereotyped that one description could fit all. The standard plot was as follows. A girl, always beautiful, usually a fiancée and sometimes an heiress, would be

abducted by some revenge-mad homicidal maniac. This maniac usually had a house hidden away in the woods/swamps/mountains equipped with a fully functional torture chamber. His henchmen were nearly always deformed in some way – hunchbacks, dwarves, giants, none with an IQ in double figures. Our hero would usually bungle his way into trying to rescue the girl. One or other of them (or both) would be tortured, often by suspension over vats of revolting things, or menaced by some giant knife or buzz-saw which would make the Spanish Inquisition proud, until either our hero breaks free and gives the villain a good thrashing, or the villain falls victim to his own fiendish devices, or the villain escapes to return another day. And as for other beasts – well, name your animal. Apes were the most common, or dogs, or alligators.

Well, nothing new there then. It's a formula that's been around since the gothic horrors of the late eighteenth and nineteenth centuries, and was used time and again in the horror movies of the thirties and forties, missed the fifties, but was back with Hammer in the sixties, and so on to date. The *Pan Book of Horror Stories* series thrived on this kind of story for years. We can all name a book/film/TV series that's used this basic plot.

The challenge to the writers was to try and better themselves every time. They had to come up with more and more weird and fiendish tortures, more lurid scenes of violence and depravity, and throw in as much titillation as could be allowed. In fact *Dime Mystery* was pretty tame on sex. It was the later magazines that spiced things up. What *Dime Mystery* wanted was menace, thrills, violence and heroics. No political correctness here. Villains were usually deformed and sometimes foreign (or both). Chinese or Russians were often good villains, or South Americans, though many were just mad Americans or British. Blacks were never villains – least ways, I don't remember any. They were always victims – either forced to do the torturing or the first in the vat to test it.

Besides the formulaic plots and the alluring titles, what also grabbed readers were the covers. Boy did these magazines have covers! The original cover artist for *Dime Mystery* was Walter Baumhofer, better remembered today, mercifully, for his covers for *Doc Savage*. Baumhofer was an excellent artist and his covers emphasized the menace without over-egging the sadism. But in his wake came Norman Saunders, H. J. Ward and, above all, John Newton Howitt. Ward and Saunders could depict beautiful women who positively glowed with femininity, but Howitt was the one for homicidal maniacs, torture chambers and women in terror. Howitt was a former landscape painter forced to produce these covers during the Depression. Apparently he later burned all his pulp paintings because he hated them so much, yet they are all he's remembered for today, even though he went on to paint many covers for the slicks in the forties. I hope some of the covers I've selected reproduce well enough for you to see the mayhem and madness. It's these covers that make the magazines so collectable. You can pay anywhere between £10 and £20 for an issue of *Dime Mystery*, *Terror Tales* and *Horror Stories* and £30 or more for the various *Spicy* magazines.

But I'm getting ahead of myself as usual. What about the stories themselves? Well, take the August 1935 *Dime Mystery*. Here's the full line-up complete with the blood-curdling story summaries written to ensnare the reader:

"Death's Bridal Coffin" by George Edson.

Madness claimed the leading lady on the opening night of the play that had been called accursed. Unholy lust stalked the boards of that old theatre, and laid a fleshless hand on the fiancée of Mark Baldwin, in that dank crypt where Death had prepared a bridal coffin for two!

"Death Tells a Fairy Tale" by Robert Howard Norton
One by one little Alice's playmates vanished down that long, dark hall.

"The Devil's Music Box" by Wyatt Blassingame
Evelyn Drew knew what was necessary to produce the weird, evil music that came from that uncanny vase – for the fearsome figure at her side had told her. Must the blood of herself and her lover mingle to produce the next tune?

"Dead Man's Darling" by Arthur J. Burks
Delie Traynor, alone with her dying father, thought of the curse put upon them long ago.

Was Bascom Lieth waiting somewhere in the wind and rain of that awful night, ready to seize her with arms that writhed with evil lust?

"Dream Monster" by Robert Treat Sperry
Baron St Germain struggled with the scaly thing that had been his lovely Valerie!

"A Wife for Bluebeard" by Winston Bouvé
Mathias Logan wooed Molly Devlin – so that she might bear him a son to change the evil, tainted strain of his accursed line.

"The Swamp God's Mistress" by Paul Ernst
Could the love of her young husband reach out into that dread swamp and pluck Josephine Faynor from the grip of a nameless thing about whose den lay scattered the whitening bones of three young brides?

"Ghost Crosses" by Rex Grahame
Would the thing in the lake force John Gowers to surrender his own daughter?

All good gut-rousing stuff. The stories did not always live up to these blurbs, though in this issue, Paul Ernst's "The Swamp God's Mistress" is good fun. In almost all cases the stories had natural solutions. It was rare for *Dime Mystery* or its many imitators to run stories that were wholly supernatural, though sometimes a mystery might be left in the air. Unless the author was very clever, the more bizarre the mystery, the more disappointing was the natural solution. Apes were sometimes revealed to be a man in a rubber suit; strange apparitions were usually someone playing tricks with the lighting; sometimes you'd even have the 'only a dream' ending or the ramblings of a madman. But you have to remember that in the early 1930s few readers of the pulps had encountered stories like this before. If ever a story played out to a macho sex-starved juvenile fantasy, these did. And the magazine sold in its hundreds of thousands.

And who were the writers who could produce this formula-riddled fodder? They were all regular pulpsters who could turn a hand to any standard material for the magazines – not just pulps. Several of them like Hugh B. Cave and Paul Ernst also wrote for the slick magazines. Regulars included Wyatt Blassingame, one of the better and more original writers, John H. Knox, Nathan Schachner, Arthur Leo Zagat, G. T. Fleming Roberts, Chandler H. Whipple, Donald Barr Chidsey, Wayne Rogers, Ray Cummings, Norvell Page, Arthur J. Burks. Some are better known for their science fiction, others for their westerns, others were just capable all-rounders. Arthur J. Burks, known as the 'Speed Merchant of the Pulps', could produce up to 18,000 words a day. All were capable of producing a million words of copy a year. But there is the odd surprise in *Dime Mystery*. I've already mentioned Edgar Wallace, who turned up in several issues, as did Cornell Woolrich, starting with "Dark Melody of Madness" (July 1935). John Dickson Carr appeared with "The Man Who Was Dead" in the May 1935 issue.

Success soon begat imitators. Steeger himself was keen to breed companions. Within a year of the success of *Dime Mystery* came *Terror Tales* (first issue September 1934) followed by *Horror Stories* (January 1935). Both these magazines ran the same material as *Dime Mystery*, although, as the titles suggest, the emphasis was on pure menace and violence. There was very little mystery. *Terror Tales* contained some great story titles: "The Curse of the Swollen Ones", "Death Lives at Our House" (I know the feeling), "School for Satan's Show Girls" and "Messiah of the Maimed" (that title has something). *Horror Stories* had such gems as: "The Well of Suicides", "Priestess of Writhing Death", "The Chair Where Terror Sat". But it was easy to get a bit repetitive. "Things That Once Were Men" (*Horror Stories*, October 1935) was fine, but "Things That Once Were Girls" (*Horror Stories*, August/September 1938) lost the edge a little. And there were clearly off days. "Horror in the Cornfield" doesn't set me alight, nor does "Water Madness" or "The Last Horror", and "A Night in Camberwell" seems to miss the point entirely! The titles of *Terror Tales* and *Horror Stories* may suggest an attempt to imitate *Weird Tales*, but in fact Steeger's pulps were ploughing their own furrow. If anything, Farnsworth Wright, editor of the unique *Weird Tales*, felt the urge to try and copy the competition: in the mid-thirties he started to run some weird-menace stories but, thankfully, did not resort to the torture covers – *Weird Tales* was doing just fine with

the sexy nudes painted by Margaret Brundage. But it showed that the impact of Popular's magazine was being felt.

The whole point, though, was that these were not supernatural stories but horror stories with a bizarre and sadistic bent. In the mid-thirties there was a sudden eruption of these magazines, rather like boils. Some of them burst instantly after just a few scratches. Others festered for years before eventually morphing into more traditional crime and mystery magazines in the forties. The longest lived rival to *Dime Mystery* was *Thrilling Mystery* from Ned Pines's Standard Magazines. This began in October 1935, soon after Ned Pines had threatened Henry Steeger with court action when Steeger published a new magazine, *Thrilling Mysteries*, in April 1935. Just as *Dime* in the title had become Popular's trademark, so *Thrilling* had become Standard's. Pines's *Thrilling Detective* had been a

success since its first issue in November 1931. *Thrilling Mystery* was pretty much an exact copy of *Dime Mystery*. Most of the authors were the same. There were different cover artists, but the image was the same – some hapless damsel in mortal distress. The story titles were similar – "City of Creeping Death", "Slaves of the Dancing Death", "Vengeance of the Moldering Dead" – though they didn't have quite the verve of Popular's. Also the stories tended to be tamer. There was virtually no sex or nudity and the violence was toned down. Neither Ned Pines nor his editorial director Leo Margulies had much interest in the weird menace field. They were just cashing in on a vogue. Although they used many of the same writers they brought in some of their own, including many well known science fiction writers like Jack Williamson, Henry Kuttner, Edmond Hamilton. Their presence has tended to draw attention to *Thrilling Mystery*, but it isn't really that interesting. It's more a curiosity with the occasional sparkle.

If we leave the *Spicy* titles aside for a while, the next competition was *Ace Mystery*, published by Aaron Wyn, the same publisher who would launch Ace Books in the 1950s. Wyn's editor was Harry Widmer, one of the lesser-known but longer surviving magazine editors – he was still editing mystery magazines well into the fifties. *Ace Mystery* only saw three bi-monthly issues, from May to September 1936. Wyn's heart wasn't really in it and when sales proved only average he converted the magazine into the more conventional *Detective Romances*. The stories – with such titles as "Satan's Faceless Henchmen", "Mistress of Snarling Death", "Bride for the Half-Dead" and "Blade of the Doomed" – weren't quite as maniacal as those in *Dime Mystery* or its companions, even though they were mostly by the same authors (Frederick C. Davis, Hugh B. Cave, Paul Ernst, John H. Knox). Indeed the contents contained a higher than average number of genuine supernatural stories of which the best is almost certainly "Coyote Woman" by Charles Marquis Warren, a cowboy vampire story. It's still a fairly easy magazine to find as it isn't avidly collected, and prices are seldom more than £15-£20 an issue. It's probably most interesting because of the work by Davis, a great pulp author who was churning out the *Operator #5* novels at this time and went on to be a regular crime novelist. Steve Fisher was another useful contributor in the days before he became a Hollywood scriptwriter. Wyn made two other half-hearted attempts to launch a weird-menace magazine. There was a one-shot *Eerie Stories* in August 1937 and four issues of *Eerie Mysteries* in 1938-39. It didn't look like Wyn was buying new stories though. Most of these were stories he already had in his inventory or were reprinted from other magazines with new titles pepped up for the occasion, and newly created pen names. So, "The Murder Masterpiece" by G. T. Fleming-Roberts from *Secret Agent X* (September 1934) became "The Pain Master's Bride" by Rexton Archer. These magazines are slightly harder to find, *Eerie Stories* especially, which is fancied for its alluring Norman Saunders good-girl-art cover. Copies may fetch as high as £20-£25.

If you wanted violence, the place to turn to was the Red Circle magazines. These were run by Martin and Abraham Goodman, the same people who launched Marvel Comics. Goodman didn't care what he published if he could cash in on something profitable. His early success had come with western magazines, which is why his main pulp subsidiary was called Western Fiction. He had been edging towards the weird-menace pulps with *Star Detective*. Launched in May 1935 this featured the usual tortured damsel cover and sported titles such as "Death Stalks the Night" and "Brains for Sale", though these were mostly conventional hard-boiled crime stories with the emphasis on violence. Then, in March 1938, they launched *Mystery Tales*, an all-screaming all-writhing terror magazine, followed by *Uncanny Tales* (April 1939). Goodman never invested much money in his pulps so they seldom appeared on a regular schedule. An issue went out once the previous one had sold. So there are only nine issues of *Mystery Tales* and five of *Uncanny Tales* even though both lasted till May 1940. Unfortunately someone must have got worked up into a frenzy as my copy of that March 1938 *Mystery Tales* is missing both the cover and the contents page. But I can still give you an idea of what the issue is like. It's all rather bloodthirsty, with a preponderance of headless horrors. Take the opening of "Heads, I Lose" by Harvey Jackson: *All of a sudden it happened, and my uncle's decapitated head crashed off the white wall. It dropped onto a bridge table, then to the floor. The wall was blotched with blood where it bounced, the gory, bleeding strands of the neck left gelatinous gore on the playing cards. It doesn't even seem funny now, in retrospect.* No, I don't suppose it does. The story goes on to describe this house of horror with the uncle's death followed by the aunt's, who tumbles down the stairs, cracking her head open, and then the cousin's, who is almost decapitated by a knife. The police are stumped, thinking it "the work of a fiend". In the end the narrator confesses to having

done them in because he didn't like them.

"Haunt Me No More!" by J. Louis Quinn (I'm sure this is the same as James L. Quinn who launched *If Science Fiction* in 1952) is the story of another crazed murderer, the basic plot being one of possession. The introductory blurb says: "Is there some unearthly power from the dread netherlands that moulds our every action?" Well, quite likely. The illustration to "Queen of the Blood Brigade" by James F. Henderson shows a near-naked woman fleeing from a mob with her head blasted from her neck and the caption, "Her scream of tortured horror rang in my ears… and then her head left her body in a blast of

HEADS, I LOSE
by Harvey Jackson

There's murder in the air—and a fiendish monster lifts his nostrils to sniff its weird compelling message… and kills … and kills again!

ALL of a sudden it happened, and my uncle's decapitated head crashed off the white wall. It dropped onto a bridge table, then to the floor. The wall was blotched with blood where it bounced, the gory, bleeding strands of the neck left gelatinous gore on the playing cards. It doesn't even seem funny now, in retrospect. Although I hated my uncle; God, how I hated him!

We just looked at the head on the floor. The eyes looked out rather stupidly, like a doll's. They were not even surprised eyes. They said nothing. But all the time the blood ran out of the neck. That was what they all crimson!" This story is about a gang called the Black Company that menaces a small American town. At one point the narrator tells us, "My mind was a chamber of horrors in which headless bodies, bodiless heads, and black-clothed, skull-faced figures gyrated in a nightmare kaleidoscope", adding, "It was incredible, unbelievable that these things could have happened in twentieth century United States." I can't think why.

"Terror Wears a Leopard Skin" by Leslie B. Lueck is more straightforward. A man keeps a near-naked woman in a lion's cage and terrorizes her with a whip. "Creep Shadow" by John Leslie isn't a rewrite of Abraham Merritt's classic, but it is a more conventional

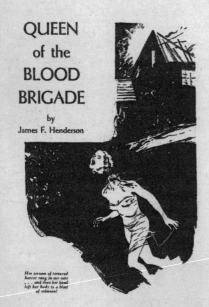

QUEEN
of the
BLOOD
BRIGADE

by
James F. Henderson

*Her scream of tortured
horror rang in my ears
... and then her head
left her body in a blast
of crimson!*

A Novelette of Bizarre Horror and Chilling Fear
That Will Keep You Quaking at Its Eerie Menace!

weird-menace story about a fiancée trapped in a house of terror. The villain of the piece is the unlikely named Shaster Sneeds, the fiancée's guardian who fits the usual description: "His great misshapen body and shaggy beetle-browed head filled me with distrust."

The stalwarts of the weird menace brigade were present. Wayne Rogers produced "Murder is a Merry Maid", a rather mild title for a story about a woman whose body is mutilated in order to live beneath the sea, so that a half-crazed scientist can take over the world. Ah yes, that plot. Wyatt Blassingame had a genuine ghost story, "Tryst With the Unknown". And Henry Treat Sperry, amongst the most prolific of the weird-menace mob until his early death in 1939, and one-time editor of *Dime Mystery*, wrote the lead story, "Listen to the Devil's Drums", where so-called witchcraft and hellspawn are rife in Pennsylvania. This is fairly representative of the stuff churned out by *Mystery Tales*. A heavy emphasis on violence and mutilation with a lot of titillation. These magazines are not that highly collected, though they round out the collection if you want the extremes. But issues in good condition aren't easy to find. I suspect covers were ripped off to adorn walls, or issues were rolled up to beat people with. So finding a copy in really good condition may set you back £20-£30.

If you wanted all out titillation with a modicum of violence, then the magazines for you were the *Spicy* brigade, particularly *Spicy Detective Stories* (first issue April 1934) and *Spicy Mystery Stories* (July 1934). These came from Frank Anmar's Culture Publications, and are highly collectable, mostly because of the covers by H. J. Ward. The *Spicy* magazines liked to mix plenty of sex with just enough violence. Provided our hero got eyeballs full of flesh and plenty to grunt about, Anmar and Co. were happy. Take this snippet from "Mansion of Monsters" by Charles R. Allen in the March 1936 *Spicy Mystery Stories*:

Cramer recoiled automatically. His staggering feet reached the center of the inky-black room, struck against something soft and yielding. He toppled over. Almost instantly he was on his knees, lashing out with hard fists at the thing on the floor. His knuckles smashed home into soft yielding flesh, warm and resilient. He gasped in amazement, opened his fingers, prodded the inert form before him. His exploring hand passed over smooth, warm flesh, touched lightly two proud hillocks of girl-flesh: satin-soft breasts. His other hand probed and found the girl's head-curling ringlets of silky hair. "Doris!" he gasped. "Doris! Are you all right?" Probably not!

A lot of well known writers (of the day) produced reams for the *Spicy*s, mostly under pen names. E. Hoffmann Price, Wyatt Blassingame, Victor Rousseau, Hugh B. Cave (where he used his inspired alias, Justin Case), Norvell W. Page, Laurence Donovan were all regulars, though the major wordsmith was Robert Leslie Bellem. Bellem became best known for his stories about Dan Turner, Hollywood detective, though he spent his last years writing TV scripts for *Perry Mason* and *77 Sunset Strip*. I suspect no-one knows now just how many stories he wrote for the pulps, since so many were under pen names, and he could easily write the whole issue of any of the *Spicy* magazines. He's become something of a cult author, adding to the collectability of these magazines. Bellem usually wrote in a clipped Chandleresque style, but sometimes he would get carried away. Here's an example of Bellem at his most loquacious, from the

June 1940 *Private Detective*, which featured Bellem's "Drunk, Disorderly, and Dead" on the cover. This showed a scantily clad woman (drawn by Jerome Rozen for once) being tattooed all over her chest!

I leaped over his sprawled bulk; took to the staircase. An upstairs door opened and Dahlia Mannerling said: "What's all the commotion?"

"The name is Turner and I'm about to raise the lid off hell", I told her. I put my two palms on her chest and shoved. She staggered backward into her rose-tinted boudoir. She was wearing a nightie and a negligee, both thinner than the tissue of a Christmas present; and what I saw through gossamer silk made me forget the pain in my bruised chest. How could a guy think of his own bosom when he had a chance to cop a swivel at Dahlia's?

Subtle, eh? Well, I suppose it's better than all those heads being chopped off, although even Bellem got into that in "The Executioner" (*Spicy Mystery,* August 1935) where a mad Nazi executioner beheads his victims even as they proclaim their innocence. Issues of any of the *Spicy* magazines – there were also *Spicy Adventure Stories* and *Spicy Western Stories* – are getting harder to find at anything much under £30 an issue in good condition.

By the end of the 1930s the weird-menace boil had well and truly burst. By the early 1940s the horrors of World War II were far worse than anything the pulpsters could depict. The magazines either folded or changed their policy to more conventional fiction. *Terror Tales* and *Horror Stories* folded in March and April 1941. The Red Circle magazines had given up by May 1940. The *Spicy*s tamed themselves down and became *Speed Mystery* (and so on) after December 1942. Even as early as 1938 both *Dime Mystery* and

Thrilling Mystery had started to shift to more traditional detective stories and this change was complete by the end of 1941. There was one last magazine to enter the fray. This was *Mystery Novels and Short Stories* from Louis Silberkleit's Double Action Magazines. This first appeared in September 1939 but was very erratic and only saw six issues before folding in September 1941. It offered just the same old fare, much of it by authors hidden under house names, but including Arthur J. Burks, Frank Belknap Long, G. T. Fleming-Roberts and Harold Ward. By now titles like "Mistress of the Murder Madmen", "Maidens for Bondage" and "Death Mates for the Lust Lost" were starting to pall. Hardly anyone collects *Mystery Novels* these days, even though it's fiendishly difficult to find. It's only in the last few years that it's been clear just how many issues were published since it actually started with issue number four! Even so it's difficult to get issues for less than £10, and more likely £20 for good issues. That's assuming, of course, anyone wants a full set of these magazines. *Dime Mystery* is the best to collect, since it was the forerunner, and had the more original and inventive stories (well, on a scale running from 1 to 2). *Terror Tales* and *Horror Stories* are also worth tracking down, and if you want great fun covers, *Spicy Mystery*. But getting all of these (over 300 issues for just these four titles) will set you back a few thousand pounds.

This wasn't the end of the weird menace magazines. In the very early sixties a few digest magazines erupted along the same lines – *Shock* and *Web Terror Stories* being the best known. But I think we've had enough of all this mindless mayhem. The following is a list of the main magazines with the total number of issues.

Dime Mystery Magazine,
December 1932-December 1949 (154 issues) [continued for 5 more issues to October 1950 as *15 Mystery Stories*]

Spicy Detective Stories,
April 1934-December 1942 (104 issues)

Spicy Mystery Stories,
July 1934-December 1942 (73 issues)

Terror Tales,
September 1934-March/April 1941 (51 issues)

Horror Stories, January 1935-April 1941 (41 issues)

Thrilling Mysteries, April 1935 (1 issue)

Thrilling Mystery,
October 1935-May 1947 (74 issues) [continued for 14 more issues to Winter 1951 as *Detective Mystery Novel Magazine*]

Ace Mystery,
May-September 1936 (3 issues) [continued for 2 more issues to January 1937 as *Detective Romances*]

Eerie Stories, August 1937 (1 issue)

Mystery Tales, March 1938-May 1940 (9 issues)

Eerie Mysteries,
August 1938-April/May 1939 (4 issues)

Uncanny Tales,
April/May 1939-May 1940 (5 issues) [this was really a continuation of *Star Detective*]

Mystery Novels and Short Stories,
September 1939-September 1941 (6 issues)

BULLETS

Adrian Muller

- **Conventions**

Three of Britain's biggest crime fiction conventions have announced dates for next year.

Crime Scene will be back from 12-15 July at London's National Film Theatre. A highlight of Crime Scene 2001 will be a celebration of the works of Agatha Christie.

Oxford's St Hilda's College has its annual **Mystery Weekend** 17-19 August featuring the theme 'Scene of the Crime: Location in Crime Fiction'.

Dead on Deansgate also returns in 2001: 12-14 October are the dates for the Manchester based convention.

- **The CWA Daggers Shortlists**

THE MACALLAN GOLD AND SILVER DAGGERS FOR FICTION

- Martin Cruz Smith for *Havana Bay* (Macmillan)

- James Lee Burke for *Purple Cane Road* (Orion)
- Jonathan Lethem for *Motherless Brooklyn* (Faber & Faber)
- Donna Leon for *Friends in High Places* (William Heinemann)
- Eliot Pattison for *The Skull Mantra* (Century)
- Lucy Wadham for *Lost* (Faber & Faber)

THE MACALLAN GOLD DAGGER FOR NON-FICTION

- Tony Barnes, Richard Elias and Peter Walsh for *Cocky* (Milo Books)
- Edward Bunker for *Mr Blue* (No Exit Press)
- Andrew Motion for *Wainewright the Poisoner* (Faber & Faber)
- Tony Thompson for *Bloggs 19* (Warner Books)
- Errol Trzebinski for *The Life and Death of Lord Errol* (Fourth Estate)

THE MACALLAN SHORT-STORY DAGGER

- Doug Allyn for *Bad Boyz Klub* (Penguin)
- Gillian Linscott for *For All the Saints*
  (Headline)
- Denise Mina for *Helena and the Babies*
  (The Do Not Press)
- James Sallis for *Blue Devils*
  (Toxic Publishing)

THE JOHN CREASEY MEMORIAL DAGGER

(For best crime novel by a debuting author;
  sponsored by Chivers Press)

- Joolz Denby for *Stone Baby*
  (HarperCollins)
- Andrew Pyper for *Lost Girls*
  (Macmillan)
- Boston Teran for *God Is a Bullet*
  (Macmillan)

The annual Dagger Awards are the most prestigious British awards in the field of crime writing. The winner of the John Creasey Memorial Dagger will be announced after the Gala Dinner at Dead on Deansgate on 28 October. The winners in the Macallan Daggers will announced, and be presented with their award at the Award Lunch on Friday, the 10th of November at the Cafe Royal in London.

• **Other Award News**

ANTHONY AWARDS
(BOUCHERCON 2000)

Best Novel:
Peter Robinson for *In a Dry Season*
Best First Novel:
Donna Andrews for *Murder With Peacocks*
Best Paperback Original:
Laura Lippman for *In Big Trouble*

Best Short Story:
Noir Lite by Meg Chittenden
Best Critical Non-Fiction:
Wiletta Heising for *Detecting Women*
(3rd edition)
Best Series Of The Century:
Agatha Christie's Hercule Poirot
Best Writer Of The Century: Agatha Christie
Best Novel Of The Century:
Daphne Du Maurier for *Rebecca*

MACAVITY AWARDS 2000

(The Macavity Awards are nominated and voted on by members of Mystery Readers International. Membership is open to all fans, readers, writers, editors and publishers. Mystery Readers International publishes the *Mystery Readers Journal*.)
Best Mystery Novel:
The Flower Master by Sujata Massey
Best First Mystery Novel:
Inner City Blues by Paula L. Woods
Best Non-Fiction:
Ross Macdonald by Tom Nolan
Best Short Story:
Maubi and the Jumbies by Kate Grilley

• **New British Crime Titles**
(Author – *Title* (series): Publisher, price)

October
Ted Allbeury – *The Assets*: Hodder &
Stoughton, £16.99
Keith Baker – *Lunenburg*: Headline, £17.99
Lawrence Block – *Hit List* (Matt Scudder):
Orion, £16.99
Anthony Bourdain – *Gone Bamboo*:
Canongate, £10.00
Jan Burke – *Bones* (Irene Kelly): Robert
Hale, £17.99

W. J. Burley – *Wycliffe and the Guild of Nine* (Wycliffe): Victor Gollancz, £16.99

Gwendoline Butler – *A Coffin for Christmas* (John Coffin): HarperCollins, £16.99

Caleb Carr – *Killing Time*: Little, Brown, £9.99

Whitney Chadwick – *Framed* (debut crime novel): Pan, £5.99

Kate Charles – *Cruel Habitations*: Little, Brown, £15.99

Jon Cleary – *Bear Pit* (Scobie Malone): HarperCollins, £16.99

Anthea Cohen – *Angel and the French Widow* (Agnes Turner): Constable, £16.99.

Robin Cook – *Shock*: Macmillan, £16.99

Gareth Creer – *Big Sky*: Anchor, £9.99

Clive Cussler – *Blue Gold* (Numa series): Simon & Schuster, £10.99

Diana Diamond – *The Trophy Wife*: Robert Hale, £17.99

Dexter Dias – *Power of Attorney*: Hodder & Stoughton, £12.99

Michael Dibdin – *Thanksgiving*: Faber & Faber, £12.99

Paul Doherty – *The Anubis Slaying* (Egyptian series): Headline, £9.99/£17.99

Ruth Dudley Edwards – *The Anglo-Irish Murders* (Amiss & Troutbeck): HarperCollins, £16.99

Alan Dunn – *Die Cast*: Piatkus

Marjorie Eccles – *Echoes of Silence* (Tom Richmond): Constable, £16.99

Clive Egleton – *The Honey Trap*: Hodder & Stoughton, £16.99

Janet Evanovich – *Hot Six* (Stephanie Plum): Macmillan, £14.99

John Farrow – *Ice Lake* (Emile Cinq-Mars): Century, £16.99

Alma Fritchley – *Chicken Shack* (Letty Campbell): The Women's Press, £6.99

Sylvian Hamilton – *The Bone-Pedlar* (new series): Orion, £9.99

Stuart Harrison – *Still Water*: HarperCollins, £9.99

Tony Hillerman – *Hunting Badger* (Chee & Leaphorn): HarperCollins, £16.99

Philip Hook – *An Innocent Eye*. Hodder & Stoughton, £16.99

Maggie Hudson – *Fast Women*: HarperCollins, £5.99/£16.99

Deryn Lake – *Death at the Apothecaries' Hall* (John Rawlington): Hodder & Stoughton, £16.99

Stephen Leather – *Stretch*: Hodder & Stoughton, £16.99

Roy Lewis – *A Form of Death* (Eric Ward): Allison & Busby, £16.99

Laura Lippman – *The Sugar House* (debut crime novel): Orion, £9.99/£16.99

John D. MacDonald – *The Empty Trap*: Robert Hale, £16.99

Hannah March – *Death Be My Theme* (Robert Fairfax): Headline, £17.99

Viviane Moore – *A Black Romance*: Victor Gollancz, £9.99

Marcia Muller – *Listen to the Silence* (Sharon McCone): The Women's Press, £6.99

Michael Palmer – *Flashback*: Century, £16.99

Una-Mary Parker – *Sweet Vengeance*: Headline, £17.99

James Patterson – *Roses are Red* (Alex Cross): Headline, £16.99

Elizabeth Peters – *The Falcon at the Portal* (Amelia Peabody): Robinson, £6.99

Elizabeth Peters – *The Mummy Case* (Amelia Peabody): Robinson, £6.99

Peter Prince – *Bubbles*: Bloomsbury, £15.99

Robert Rankin – *Waiting for Godalming*:
  Doubleday, £16.99
Julian Rathbone – *Accidents Will Happen*:
  Severn House, 17.99
Elizabeth Redfern – *The Music of Spheres*
  (debut crime novel): Century, £15.99
Steven Saylor – *Last Seen in Massilia*
  (Gordianus): Robinson, £15.99
Manda Scott – *No Good Deed*:
  Headline, £9.99/£17.99
Lisa See – *Dragon Bones*: Century, £10.00
Michael Shea – *A Cold Conspiracy*:
  Severn House, £17.99
Sydney Sheldon – *The Sky is Falling*:
  HarperCollins, £16.99
Sarah Smith – *The Knowledge of Water*:
  Arrow, £5.99
CJ Songer – *Bait* (debut crime novel):
  Robert Hale, £17.99
Sally Spencer – *The Dark Lady*:
  Severn House, £17.99
Kate Stacey – *The Canary Thief*:
  Piatkus, £6.99
Leah Stewart – *Body of a Girl*:
  Piatkus, £16.99
Scarlett Thomas – *Bright Young Things*:
  Flame, £10.00
Mark Timlin – *All the Empty Places*:
  No Exit Press, £14.99
Peter Tonkin – *High Water*:
  Headline, £17.99
Rececca Tope – *Grave Concerns*:
  Piatkus, £17.99
Minette Walters – *The Shape of Snakes*:
  Macmillan, £16.99
Donald E. Westlake – *Corkscrew*:
  Robert Hale, £17.99
Margaret Yorke – *A Case to Answer*:
  Little, Brown, £15.99

November

Kenneth Abel – *Cold Steel Rain*:
  Orion, £9.99/£16.99
Geoffrey Archer – *Double Eagle*:
  Century, £10.00
Reed Arvin – *The Will*: Simon & Schuster,
  £9.99
Martina Cole – *Broken*: Headline,
  £9.99/£16.99
Thomas H. Cook – *Places in the Dark*:
  Victor Gollancz, £9.99/£16.99
Brian Cooper – *The Norfolk Triangle*
  (Tench & Lubbock): Constable, £16.99
Peter Moir Fotheringham – *Death of a
  Fading Beauty*: Robert Hale, £17.99
John Francome – *Lifeline*:
  Headline, £9.99/£17.99
John Gilstrap – *Even Steven*:
  Michael Joseph, £9.99
Robert Goddard – *Sea Change*:
  Bantam, £16.99
Peter Guttridge – *Foiled Again*
  (Nick Madrid): Headline, £17.99
H. R. F. Keating – *Breaking and Entering*
  (the last(?) Inspector Ghote):
  Macmillan, £16.99
Joe R. Lansdale – *The Bottoms*:
  Victor Gollancz, £9.99/£16.99
David Liss – *A Conspiracy of Paper*: Abacus,
  £10.99
Peter Millar – *Bleak Midwinter*:
  Bloomsbury, £16.99
Fidelis Morgan – *Unnatural Fire* (debut
  crime novel): HarperCollins, £9.99
Scott Phillips – *The Ice Harvest*:
  Picador, £10.00
Candace Robb – *A Trust Betrayed* (Margaret
  Kerr – new series): Heinemann, £10.00
Linden Salter – *The Major's Minion*:
  Robert Hale, £16.99

Danzy Senna – *From Caucasia, With Love*:
Bloomsbury, £16.99
Robert Tanebaum – *True Justice*:
Simon & Schuster, £10.00
Alison Taylor – *Child's Play*:
William Heineman, £15.99
June Thomson – *The Unquiet Grave*
(Inspector Finch): Constable, £16.99
Barry Troy – *Dirty Money*: Piatkus, £17.99

December

William Bernhardt – *Silent Justice*:
Robert Hale. £17.99
John Burke – *Stalking Widow*:
Robert Hale, £16.99
Christopher Cook – *Robbers* (debut crime
novel): No Exit Press, £10.00
Michael Jecks – *The Boy Bishop's
Glovemaker* (Furnshill & Puttock):
Headline, £17.99
Edward Marston – *The Elephant's of
Norwich* (Domesday series):
Headline, £17.99

Peter May – *The Killing Room*
(Li Yan & Margaret Campbell):
Hodder & Stoughton, £16.99
Rory McCormac – *Malpractice*
(Frank Samson): Arrow, £5.99
George P. Pelecanos – *Right as Rain*:
Victor Gollancz, £9.99/£16.99
Anne Perry – *Slaves and Obsession*
(Hester & Monk): Headline, £17.99
Norman Russell – *The Devereaux
Inheritance*: Robert Hale, £17.99
Jean Saunders – *Illusion* (Alex Best):
Robert Hale, £17.99
Jenny Siler – *Iced*: Orion, £9.99/£16.99
Veronica Stallwood – *Oxford Shadows*
(Kate Ivory): Headline, £17.99
Sebastian Stuart – *The Mentor*:
Piatkus, £9.99
Hwee Hwee Tan – *Generica*: Michael
Joseph, £9.99
MJ Trow – *Maxwell's Curse* (Peter Maxwell):
Hodder & Stoughton, £16.99

For further information on the above titles, or to order books, contact:

Crime in Store, 14 Bedford Street, Covent Garden, London WC2E 9HE
Tel: +44 (0)20 7379 3795, fax: +44 (0)20 7379 8988
Email: CrimeBks@aol.com
Website: http://www.crimeinstore.co.uk

Murder One, 71-73 Charing Cross Road, London WC2H 0AA
Tel: +44 (0)20 7734 3483, fax: +44 (0)20 7734 3429
Email: 106562.2021@compuserve.com
Website: http://www.murderone.co.uk

Post Mortem Books, 58 Stanford Avenue, Hassocks, Sussex BN6 8JH
Tel: +44 (0)1273 843066, fax: +44 (0)1273 845090
Email: ralph@pmbooks.demon.co.uk
Website: http://www.postmortembooks.co.uk

AUDIOCRIME

Brian Ritterspak

Wasp's Nest and Other Stories/
Four-and-Twenty Blackbirds/
Miss Marple's Final Cases
by Agatha Christie, HarperCollins
These tapes benefit immeasurably from their
readers: actors closely associated with Christie
adaptations on TV, and sounding exactly the
right note in the recreation of her hermetic
world. Hugh Fraser's readings of such stories
as *Wasps Nest*, *The Veiled Lady* and *The Lost
Mine* are perfectly judged, with a subtle dif-
ferentiation made between the tone of the
various stories. Perhaps *The Dream* in *Four-
and-Twenty Blackbirds* is the most disturbing-
ly realised tale in the various Fraser
collections. Joan Hickson, of course, was many
people's idea of the definitive Miss Marple,
and the reading of *Miss Marple's Final Cases* is
exemplary. There's a curious dislocation
between her use of a narrative voice and the
sudden switch to Christie's elderly sleuth, but
this is soon overcome. No one immune to
Christie's world (and there are just as many
who dislike her books as who love them) will
be converted by these tapes, but for those
prepared to enter into this ordered universe,
these are singularly diverting readings.

The Seventh Sinner
by Elizabeth Peters, Isis
For a group of students enjoying the pleasures of a fellowship in Rome, life is good, and
Peters' heroine Jean considers herself luckier
still in her enjoyable world. But when the
unprepossessing student Albert attempts to
join in, they try their best keep him at bay.

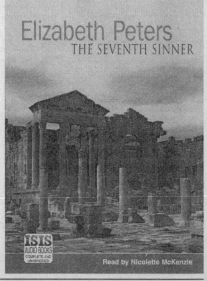

Elizabeth Peters
THE SEVENTH SINNER

ISIS
AUDIO BOOKS
COMPLETE AND
UNABRIDGED

Read by Nicolette McKenzie

But when the group (who call themselves the Seven Sinners) explore a Roman temple, they find him with his throat slashed. This sharp and engaging mystery is sympathetically read.

Piranha to Scurfy and Other Stories

by Ruth Rendell, Random House

The short story is, in many ways, the perfect medium for the audiobook, and Ruth Rendell continues to be a passionate supporter of the form, providing some vintage entries in her latest collection, *Piranha to Scurfy and Other Stories*. In Penelope Wilton, Rendell has the perfect reader for this beguilingly disparate selection of tales, united by the usual cold-eyed Rendell narrative voice. Wilton has long been one of this country's finest actresses, equally adroit at comedy and the most demanding drama. Here, she finds a neutral, dispassionate voice that is the perfect conduit

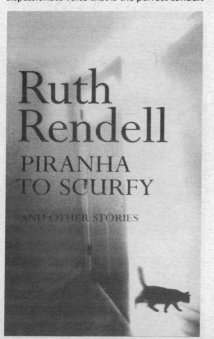

for Rendell's understated prose. The title story (the longest in the book, and a reference to an encyclopaedia entry) is something of a departure for Rendell: although her work has always been rich in elements of the macabre, this is her first full-scale horror tale, and a curious concoction it is. Taking equal parts of Stephen King (of whom a suave surrogate appears in the piece), the great English ghost story writer M. R. James and Rendell's own individual ground of twisted psychology, the tale is ostensibly an atmospheric study in burgeoning mental terror, as a lonely and socially maladroit man finds himself driven to the point of madness when the demon of a best-selling horror tale appears to infiltrate itself into his daily life. Wilton's reading never lays on the horrors with a trowel, allowing the steady accumulation of detail to make its telling effect. The characterisation, perfectly delineated by the actress, has all the dark fascination of Rendell's best work, and if that final shiver of horror isn't quite delivered, Rendell enthusiasts will be more than diverted. The other tales are equally compelling, with *The Professional* and *The Astronomical Scarf* being particularly well turned. There is also a pleasingly steady progression of mood throughout the tales, and Wilton finds the dark humour of such pieces as *High Mysterious Union* as acutely as the fatalistic menace of the other tales.

Death Is Now My Neighbour

by Colin Dexter, Macmillan

One of Dexter's more intriguing whodunnits is capably abridged in this beguiling adaptation (which still runs to three hours). Kevin Whately handles the narrative chores well, even though he's probably a curious choice for the task, given his identification with Lewis.

Underneath Every Stone

by Paula Gosling, Isis

Election time has rolled around in Blackwater Bay, but the corpse in Cotter's Cut has sheriff Matt Gabriel arresting the unprepossessing Frog Bartlett. But one person believes Bartlett innocent, and finances a strong defence. And when somebody else is killed, Gabriel finds himself a suspect. As usual with Gosling, quirky characterisation and overripe atmosphere creates a truly heady mix. Hayward Morse is just the right reader for this, characterising everything with wit and sympathy.

The Fortune Teller

by Donald James, Isis

Does it matter that James borrowed his basic concept (dogged rugged Russian cop solves murders in frigid landscape) from Martin Cruz Smith? Not really. James is able to infuse his narratives with more than enough of his own invention and atmosphere. Konstantin Vadim is back in his own hometown after an unhappy sojourn in Moscow. But when his young wife answers an emergency medical call and doesn't return, he is increasingly desperate. Investigations lead to a second woman who was abducted on the same night. Tudor Bonham has a nicely dispassionate tone that suits this particularly well, and he has the measure of James striking descriptive passages.

Cold Heart

by Linda La Plante, Macmillan

Glenys Barber's career as an actress may have reached its apogee with *Dempsey and Makepeace*, but she proves an adroit narrator for La Plante's glossy and involving tale. Ex-lieutenant Lorraine Page is well characterised, and the plotting is skilful.

*Macmillan, HarperCollins and Random House audiotapes are available from all good bookshops; Isis and Soundings tapes are available by mail order from Isis Publishing on Freephone **0800 731 5637** or from Soundings on **0191 253 4155**.*

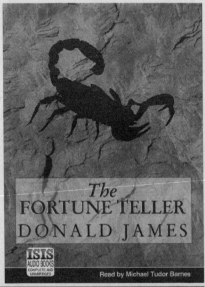

CRIME AND HISTORY

Gwendoline Butler

While writing her own highly acclaimed crime novels for HarperCollins and CT Publishing, we're glad to say that Gwendoline Butler finds time to take her regular look at recent historical crime novels for CT...

As all readers of crime fiction know, it is addictive. This is especially true of historical crime. Once you get a taste for it, you want to go on. Dipping into ancient Egypt, Imperial Rome, a gory scene with Genghis Khan, or crime in a medieval nunnery, or death before the battle of Waterloo. Fortunately there is a great deal of historical canvas to enjoy in the genre.

The Horus Killings by Paul Docherty (Headline, £5.99). The civilisation of ancient Egypt is fascinating to us today, although the servile labour on which it rested probably found it oppressive and dull enough. Paul Docherty, an accomplished historian, sets the scene with skill, engaging the reader from the moment we see Hatusu, Queen and Pharaoh, arriving at the Temple of Horus dressed like a goddess. She is one of the most important of the Egyptian women rulers, like Nefertiti and Cleopatra. A series of vicious killings cause

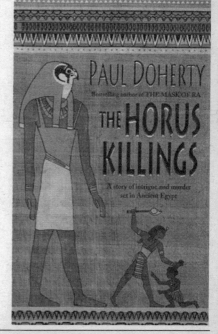

the priests of Horus to question whether she should be Queen and Pharaoh instead of her stepson. The Queen engages a distinguished judge (Egyptian society was very legalistic) to find out who and what is behind the killing, a mystery he solves at some cost to himself. How can we know what it was like to live in ancient Egypt? We cannot. But suspend judgement, accept this picture of a distant world and enjoy yourself.

A big step forward in time to *The Foxes of Warwick* by Edward Marston (Headline, £5.99). This shows us a much less sophisticated world than ancient Egypt, but just as violent. A body is flushed up by the hounds of Henry Beaumont, Constable of Warwick Castle, who have lost a fox but found a dead man. Norman and Saxon march across the stage together in a strong story in which justice is done by a pair of Domesday Commissioners, Ralph Delchard and Gervase Bret, lawyers and rivals – although whether the Domesday Commissioners, interested as they were in boundaries and tax obligations, would have had time and energy to undertake a murder investigation is unclear. Law keeping was more usually the responsibility of the men of the Frankpledge. However, Marston has Ralph and Gervase do so and do it well. It is interesting to be reminded that the Commissioners were married men who took their wives on tour with them (the Domesday Book is silent on this). When William the Norman came to England to claim what he regarded as his inheritance, he had no idea what was there. The purpose of the Domesday Survey was to find out from every estate and village who was there, their status, free or unfree, their obligations to the king and to write them down, which was done with great skill. I doubt if a real Commissioner would have wanted to do much investigation. Or would have got much help from the villagers. They were not welcome figures on most estates, either. All the same, the style and verve of the writing makes it a book to commend.

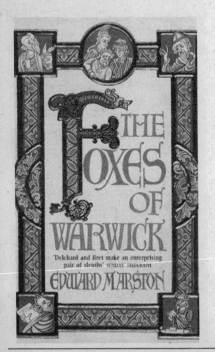

Fortune Like The Moon by Alys Clare (New English Library, £5.99) Here we have moved in time to Plantagenet England in the time of King Richard, son of Henry II and Eleanor of Aquitaine, formidable parents. Richard is shown as concerned about the murder and rape of a young nun, something which is hard to believe of that redoubtable warrior (not always a man of good judgement, either), but it introduces us to a vivid picture of twelfth century society and to two attractive detectives: Josse, once a soldier and a brave one, and Abbess Helewise of Hawkenlye, a clever, sharp minded woman. So forget King Richard, this is an enjoyable read with a family background.

The Treason of the Ghosts by Paul Docherty (Headline, £9.99). A gripping title. With this book, we are another step forward in time to the thirteenth century, the reign of King Edward I. This is a striking medieval serial killing piece, or indeed, two. The first is a series of murders of young women, garroted and raped, while at the same time another killer is murdering the jurors who had passed judgement on the Lord of the Manor as killer of the first group of young women. The first group? Yes, because even after the hanging of Sir Roger, more murders take place. This is an enjoyable novel by a professional writer who takes recreating the past with great seriousness. And Sir Hugh Corbett, together with

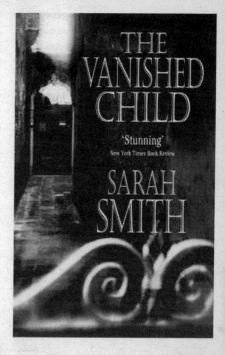

his servants Ranulf and Chanson, makes a convincing investigator of a series of terrible crimes. (They always hunt in couples or threes, don't they, these investigators?).

There is a big jump forward in time to *Half Moon Street* by Anne Perry, (Headline, £17.99). Here we are in one of her Victorian mysteries and thus we have moved into another world. The detective is a professional, a policeman, Inspector Thomas Pitt, a successful and dedicated detective officer, complete with wife, children and maidservant in the basement. But since this is written with a contemporary readership in mind, the wife is an upper class lady with a mother now married to an actor, one much younger than she is, but after all, this is romance. It is a romance, not a picture of Victorian society as it was. Perry is never very sure-footed about the shadings of Victorian classes and how the system worked, but it is all very enjoyable. And it begins with a stunningly gruesome killing and moves on with style. This is one of Anne Perry's most entertaining books. The theatrical background, with more than a hint of Oscar Wilde, helps here. Read on.

With *The Vanished Child* by Sarah Smith (Arrow Books, £5.99), we are in the early twentieth century. This is in many ways the cleverest and most sophisticated book here reviewed, being more than a mystery and murder story (although it is all these too), but a serious, thoughtful novel as well. Set in New England and Switzerland it is a story of a missing child and a man with no memory. It is a book to be read carefully because the plot is complex and the telling of it complicated.

Alison Joseph
The night **watch**

'Sister Agnes is a mordant and energetic heroine' *The Times*

Take your eyes off the page and you may get lost.

The Night Watch by Alison Joseph (Headline, £17.99) takes us back to the world of today. Interestingly, the investigator is a young nun, Sister Agnes Bourdillon. She is assisted by her close friend, Father Julius, who is himself part of the puzzle. Sister Agnes is a delightful figure to whose own questionings and unhappiness we respond with sympathy. This is more than a detective story; it is a tale about men and women trying to do what is right.

Finally, back to where we came in (the Middle Ages) in *The St John's Fern* by Kate Sedley (Headline, £17.99) I found this a happy and involving mystery, and one told in the first person by Roger the Chapman. He tells it as an old man, looking back. A chapman was a travelling salesman but Roger, as well as having once taken his vows at Glastonbury, is also a travelling detective. He feels that God called him to the task. Feeling restless and wanting to go on his travels again, he takes a lift with a carter who is going to visit his daughter, Joanna. Her neighbour, Master Capstick, has been beaten to death. The chief suspect vanishes and the locals blame St John's Fern, which is said to help people vanish completely. Witchcraft is suspected also. Just the sort of case to attract Roger as it might have done Sherlock Holmes. The practical Roger investigates to find the true murderer. Roger the restless Chapman, always on the move, always working on crime, must have been a tiresome husband but he is a delight to read about. And at a time when all crime fiction seems to have a sad or at least a bittersweet ending, this book has ends happily.

pocket essential noir...

almost everything you need to know for just £2.99

FILM NOIR - The laconic private eye...the corrupt cop...the heist that goes wrong...the femme fatale with the rich husband and dim lover...These are the trademark characters of the movement known as film noir. 1940 to 1958 was the heyday of film noir, that allusive mixture of stark lighting and even starker emotions. Noir explored the dark side of post-war society - gangsters, hoodlums, prostitutes and killers - and showed how it corrupted the good and the beautiful.

Many of these films are now touchstones of what we regard as 'classic' Hollywood - The Maltese Falcon, The Big Sleep, Double Indemnity and The Postman Always Rings Twice.

The Pocket Essential Film Noir charts the progression of the noir style as a vehicle for film-makers who wanted to record the darkness at the heart of American society as it emerged from World War to the Cold War. As well as an introductory essay on the origins of noir, a variety of subjects are explained by a more detailed examination of specific noir films.

NOIR FICTION - The murky history of noir fiction both influenced and influenced by its cinematic equivalent, film noir. - from the 30s to the present day.

Both movements document the adventures of hard-boiled detectives and double-crossing dames, often against a backdrop of corruption and twisted storylines that leave the characters stranded in a morally bankrupt underworld. Yet while film noir has been reclaimed as a rich period in American film-making, noir fiction, despite being the precursor, remains critically under-appreciated. In the Noir Fiction Pocket Essential Paul Duncan charts the rise of film noir's neglected sibling, from 30s pulps to the 90s bestsellers lists. This is the first survey of its kind to cover both American and British figures, featuring quintessential noir authors James M Cain and James Ellroy, alongside such lesser known British innovators as Gerald Kersh and Derek Raymond. In all, nine of the most significant authors in the history of noir fiction are profiled in depth and the book includes a reference section for those who wish to venture deeper into literature's neglected dark side.

Paul Duncan is co-founder of Crime Time magazine, and editor of The Third Degree: Crime Writers In Conversation.

available from bookshops or ring 020 7430 1021 or log on at **www.pocketessentials.com**

COLUMN

A PERSONAL VIEW

Mark Timlin

The creator of Nick Sharman (and crime reviewer for The Independent on Sunday*) gives CT the unvarnished truth (if he can just remember what happened last night)...*

This year saw the first in what I hope is going to be an annual event at the National Film Theatre in London. A three-day crime fest of panels, interviews, readings and films called *Crime Scene*. It's organised by Adrian Wooton and Maxim Jakubowski. I was there for all three days, and thoroughly enjoyed myself. Not only did I get to meet and greet my buds on the British crime writing front, but I also ran into a quartet of top US crime writers, namely George Pelecanos, Dennis Lehane, Jeffrey Deaver and Robert Crais.

The week before the event opened I'd reviewed Robert Crais' latest novel, *Demolition Angel* in the *Independent on Sunday*, and gave it a jolly good (and well deserved, I might add) review. So being up for a bit of bribery and corruption, I telephoned Helen Richardson at Orion and asked innocently if there was going to be a bit of a do for Robert. On being informed in the negative, she promptly invited me for lunch at a top Covent Garden eatery, which I also thoroughly enjoyed, digging into the leek and potato soup, scallops with a pea sauce on a potato cake, mucho glasses of white wine, cappuccino and brandy. Boy, how we reviewers live.

So what was Mr Crais like? I hear you ask.

And did we get on? In short, did I like the bloke. What's not to like? He's young, rich, successful. Happily married to a beautiful woman. We never met, but I imagine she's a bit of a stunner. He's well dressed, handsome, tanned, with a full head of black hair. His book's just hit the top ten best hardback sellers over here, and in the States he's been a top author for many years. I imagine Orion flew him business class to London and back to LA where (and here I'm inventing) he has a top of the range Mercedes or BMW waiting in the long-term car park to whisk him and his wife home to a comfortable house or apartment. *Demolition Angel* has been optioned for a film, possibly starring Julia Roberts, and in the past he's worked with Michael Mann and Steven Bochko. Own up, I should have hated the geezer. In fact he was charming, and our two and a half hours together flew by.

I quizzed him about working on *Hill Street Blues* and *Miami Vice* and he was a fount of funny and interesting stories – one in particular, which I'll recount with his permission in a bit. After we'd parted and gone our separate ways, I wandered back to the railway station and, whilst travelling home on the tube and

DLR, my thoughts turned to the difference in perceptions, ambitions and aspirations of American and British crime writers. And the rewards of course.

Now, I've been pretty lucky. Every book and short story I've written up to the present has been published. And that's a lot. But I had to use seven names to do it. I had five TV shows on ITV, and I review stuff for a number of outlets which gets me enough free books to stock a library. But compared to someone like Crais, I'm nowhere. And nor are most of my contemporaries on the British scene. We may strut around London doing the do, but how many of us actually earn a living from our major work source, i.e. novel writing? Not many, I'll bet. Husbands, wives, families, all help. Some are happy to support us, I imagine many are not. And there are awards and various arts grants to help the struggling author survive. But you've got to jump through hoops to get them, and beware if your face doesn't fit. I know, because I've been there and never received one yet. The UK is a third world country for authors and don't ever forget it.

And as for that story… Well, are you sitting comfortably? You are? Then I'll begin. Robert Crais made his name with his Elvis Cole novels. Stories of the wisecracking LA PI and his buddy Joe Pike. The books were made to be filmed, and eventually a famous Hollywood actress (whose name I've been asked not to disclose) had her people contact Crais. She was looking for a movie project to direct and his novels were top of her list. He declined to make the meet. Eventually she offered to fly out from New York to LA to see him. He still wasn't keen, but having seen some of her films and thinking she looked pretty hot, he agreed. She jetted in, he drove over to a hotel by the airport. She still looked OK, but he refused to sell.

Now what's the moral of this story? Let's take a moment, as they might say in *NYPD Blue*. The moral is simply that, if a similar thing had happened to a British crime writer – say for instance Elizabeth Hurley's people had been on the blower – blimey, there'd've been dancing in the streets. Notwithstanding how Hurley is perceived as an actress, a human being, or for that matter a director. Who would give a damn? Not me pal! All I would think of is that if someone of that kind of status wanted to direct, produce or appear in one of my novels on the screen, then there'd be loads of money washing about the project and I could probably pick up as much cash for writing a dozen lines of dialogue that never made the final script as I could get in advances for a couple of books.

And yet Crais turned the woman down. And the reason? He didn't actually say it in so many words, but I imagine that he simply didn't need the dough. That writing successful novels in the States, even genre novels, pays the rent and lots more. But over here it doesn't – not unless you're really lucky. A sad fact but a true one.

Why wasn't I born in Mobile, Alabama?

TIMLIN'S TOP TIPS
FOR DAYS OF MIST AND MELLOW FRIGHTFULNESS

Hot Springs by Stephen Hunter (Century)
Cardiff Dead by John Williams (Bloomsbury)
Power of Attorney by Dexter Dias (Hodder)
On Writing by Stephen King (Hodder)

Stalker by Faye Kellerman (Hodder)
Narrowback by Michael Ledwidge (Warner)
The Big Blowdown by George P. Pelecanos (Serpent's Tail)

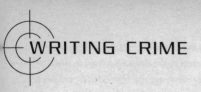

BEING BORED BY SERIAL KILLERS

Natasha Cooper

CT prides itself on the number of top crime writers who are happy to write for these pages – and here's Natasha Cooper (aka Clare Layton), regularly to be found as reviewee at the back of CT for her HarperCollins Trish Maguire crime treats, talking about the crime writer's life...

Looking back, it's hard to remember quite why serial killer novels once seemed so exciting. The first I read was *Rules of Prey* by John Sandford, quickly followed by *The Silence of the Lambs*, which, as far as I can remember, was published in the UK in the same summer. I was bowled over by both. The mixture of shock and pace was unlike anything I had found in any other crime novel until then.

In those days, like just about everyone else, I was fascinated. The idea of the anti-hero moving undiscovered through towns and cities, selecting his (usually female) victims, stalking them, kidnapping and killing them, is the stuff of nightmares, which made it easy to identify with the investigator. The race between the killer, longing to satisfy his mad craving one more time, and the detective, desperate to save the last victim, could be mouth-dryingly exciting.

Now it all seems so wearyingly familiar that excitement is the last thing I feel. I know, of course, that the detective will get there in time. But I also know that on the way, as the full horror of the killer's evil brilliance is revealed, the detective will probably make all kinds of dark discoveries about his or her own psyche. Somewhere in the depths of the unconscious there will be a point of contact with the killer's mind. And I know that the serial killer will be an eccentric loner, sociopath, psychopath, and so on. He will probably have been abused in childhood, and is likely to be wreaking his revenge on an uncaring society by terrorising and killing. If not that, then he will be taking sexual satisfaction from mutilation and murder because that is the only way he can relate to women.

The Anatomy of Motive by John Douglas and Mark Olshaker (Simon & Schuster, £16.99, 0-684-86081-3) uncovers the reality that gave rise to the plethora of serial killer novels. Described on the jacket flap as 'the model for Special Agent Jack Crawford in *The Silence of the Lambs*', Douglas probably knows more about mass murderers than anyone else. He came to the UK in 1996 and writes that he was 'really pumped up by the Brits' fascination with the subject [...] killers, rapists, bombers [...] men whose evil and depraved acts challenge the bounds of the human imagination.' I wonder whether that level of enthusiasm will persist much longer.

The book opens with an account of a television interview Douglas gave on the morning of the Dunblane shootings. Having shown how he correctly identified many of the characteristics that would be discovered in the perpetrator, he goes on to explain the difference between the typical mass murderer, spree killer, and serial killer. Only serial killers, it seems, are sexually motivated, which may be why far more fiction is written about them

than the other types of multi-murderer. I have come to believe that the pleasure offered to readers of serial killer thrillers is not far removed from that provided by the traditional romance. The one may be full of four-letter words and explicit sex and violence, while the other brims over with euphemism and froth, but there are fundamental similarities – and therefore limitations.

A man, powerful (at least in his own mind), charismatic, and dangerous – probably with a secret sorrow – is drawn to select one particular innocent woman for his very own because something about her appearance and manner makes her appeal to him above all other women he sees. In a traditional romance his

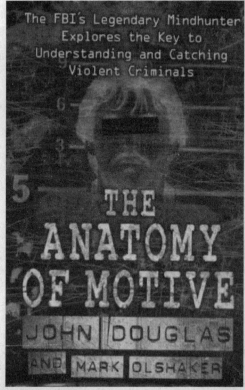

The FBI's Legendary Mindhunter Explores the Key to Understanding and Catching Violent Criminals

THE ANATOMY OF MOTIVE

JOHN DOUGLAS AND MARK OLSHAKER

aim is to marry, deflower and keep her from any other man. In a serial killer thriller he wants to rape, torment, and kill her, ensuring that no other man will get his hands on her.

There seems to be no way of developing the basic plot in either genre. In serial killer thrillers the only novelty lies in ever-more stomach-churningly explicit description of what the villain does to his victims before, during, and after killing them. As far as I can tell, there really isn't much further to go, at least I hope there isn't. I was interested to hear recently from the assistant manager of a major chain bookseller that several customers brought back one of this year's most graphically unpleasant hardbacks because they simply couldn't bear to read it. If punters are beginning to rebel, writers should pay attention. The traditional romance is all but dead. Serial killer thrillers are likely to go the same way. Of course some novelists can create characters of such originality – or appeal – that they turn even the stalest sub-genre into something that seems fresh and different. And some can use even grossly explicit violence to good effect. But there are not many of them.

For me a more interesting variation on the powerful, charismatic alpha male character comes with Patrick Redmond's second novel, *The Puppet Show* (Hodder & Stoughton, £10.00, 0-340-74819-2). There is no serial killer here, only a staggeringly effective businessman, who may or may not be malevolent. Max Somerton has the classic tragic past, but his interest in the young innocent is not sexual. Recognising his younger self in Michael, a City lawyer who was reared in children's homes and then with foster parents, Max takes him up. With influence and material help Michael could become successful and powerful as Max himself. Michael's fiancée, Rebecca, is convinced Max is sinister, but for Michael, he is the longed-for father, who will heal all past wounds. If I couldn't entirely believe in Max, I found the novel really gripping. Redmond's picture of twenty-something London professionals under stress is very effective. The tensions between Michael and Rebecca, and the rest of her family, are particularly well executed, and his portrait of children in care is achingly painful.

The exploration of the characters' battles with their own – and other people's – demons in a psychological thriller like this are much more interesting to me than any number of anguished sleuths chasing sexually-dysfunctional psychopaths through the entrails of their mutilated victims.

Author of THE WISHING GAME

Patrick Redmond

THE PUPPET SHOW

'Other writers may be hailed as the new Patrick Redmond in years to come'
Daily Mirror

TO THE MAX

Maxim Jakubowski

His own books have earned him the sobriquet King of the Erotic Thriller; he's one of the genre's premier editors... Mr Maxim Jakubowski.

Following the recent onslaught of darker-than-dark American crime fabulists, the British sleuths are back in force to reclaim familiar territory, with the investigative pack in brilliant form. Darling of the Scottish best-seller lists already, Ian Rankin should crack the national ones this time around – if there is any justice in the world of crime – with his eleventh Inspector John Rebus novel, *Set in Darkness* (Orion, £16.99). This is a series that has been growing in assurance and gravitas for over a decade now and its time has come

with a television adaptation featuring John Hannah in the can. And we all know what television did for Inspector Morse! As a central figure, Rebus is both deeply flawed, invariably pig-headed, but harbours a strong moral centre which is often at awkward odds with the cases he is called on to examine. The charm is to watch how this hard-drinking policeman juggles and solves crimes and dilemmas. Edinburgh is his patch and few authors have dug as deep as Rankin in unveiling the secret heart of the city. It's a bumpy ride but always well worth it. The new Scottish parliament at Queensberry House is the setting for a bizarre series of murders and Rebus' intervention soon charts a new map of the psyche of modern Scotland, a country torn between past and present in the wake of devolution. Complex, humane and gripping.

Journalist Stephen Larkin is one of the most interesting of the new wave of British amateur detectives and his third appearance in Martyn Waites' *Candleland* (Allison & Busby, £16.99) is cause for celebration as it bears witness to the flowering of a major new talent. A cynical loner with a distinct Chandler noir side to his character, Larkin is asked by a policeman from his native Newcastle to hunt down his lost, HIV positive daughter amongst the murky London underworld. Warring drug dealers, child prostitution, born-again Christian gangsters, a vicious gang leader and a guest appearance by Paul Charles' Camden Town Inspector Christy Kennedy all punctuate a white-knuckle ride of a case.

Some British thriller writers prefer to set their books in America and Rob Ryan is an undoubted leader of the pack. His *Underdogs* has already become the Seattle crime novel par excellence and *Nine Mil* (Headline, £9.99) confirms the Sunday Times and GQ travel journalist as a unique exponent of rough and gutsy US-set tales where anything that can go wrong necessarily does for its low life characters. Atlantic City taxi driver Ed Behr's horizons are shrinking faster than his waistline is expanding, and memories of prison and the girl who got away pepper his nightmares. Then a face from the past reappears and a mad plan forms in his disturbed brain. Fast, violent and a delight. On the opposite American coast, psychologist Dr Alex Delaware and

cop Milo Sturgis team up in Jonathan Kellerman's *Monster* (Little, Brown, £15.99) to investigate a murder in a hospital for the criminally insane. Kellerman has long been the master of the US psychological thriller and plots like a Swiss clockmaker with the twists coming fast and furious. Maybe not his best, but a fast, professional read, with strong insights into the quirks of human nature, this will not disappoint the many Kellerman fans.

Hailed by Muriel Spark, *Corpsing* by Toby Litt (Hamish Hamilton, £9.99) sees a young British mainstream novelist try his hand at the criminal and pull off a remarkable achievement. Following the path of a bullet in two directions – one into the body it enters and the other back into the gun barrel into the motivation of the person who fired it, *Corpsing* manages to be both suspense-filled and full of literary conceits. Fetishistic à la Cornwell in its systematic analysis of bullet penetration and autopsy, and hard-edged in its x-ray of modern relationships, this has all the hallmarks of a future cult book. The boy done good. While Toby Litt ingeniously reinvents the crime genre, Reginald Hill is a comfortable veteran of the traditional British police procedural with a sting in the tail, and the latest Dalziel and Pascoe, *Arms and the Women* (HarperCollins, £16.99), focuses on Ellie, Pascoe's wife, and an attempt to kidnap her. As ever, the roots of the case lie in the past and Hill orchestrates the whole thing with inch-like precision and sly wit. Maybe not his best, but Dalziel and Pascoe are always great company.

There must definitely be something in the water in Florida to inspire local crime and mystery writers to evoke such heights of bizarre villainy in their books. Or maybe the unremitting sunshine does something to the brain and inspires the most convoluted, absurd plots! At any rate, following in the gonzo footsteps of Elmore Leonard, James Hall, Les Standiford, Lawrence Shames and, of course, Carl Hiaasen, another columnist for the Miami Herald now hits the fiction trail with all guns blazing and grotesques on parade. Dave Barry's *Big Trouble* (Piatkus, £9.99) is a spectacular and hilarious debut from a journalist until now better known for his humorous columns and books. In Coconut Grove, strange things are happening. A group of teenagers embark on a silly prank to embarrass their school friend Jenny Herk. Little do they know that her father Arthur has been embezzling money from his company and that his employers have become overly keen to provide him with a terminal golden handshake, more like a concrete overcoat in fact. So, in come the hit men from New Jersey. Add to the mix bizarre Russian arm dealers, Eliot Arnold, a struggling ad man whose son leads the eponymous squirtmaster gang, the Miami police and a very strange toad and you have the perfect recipe for a day of sheer mayhem. This is crime fiction which brings a wide smile to one's lips in a unique, outrageously warped and cheerfully depraved manner. Wonderful entertainment. Equally hip and full of belly laughs is Doug Swanson's *Umbrella Man* (No Exit Press, £6.99) in which Jack Flippo, a Texas sleuth now on his fourth outing, stumbles across a few frames from a black and white film that just might show a second gunman firing at President Kennedy from the notorious Grassy Knoll. This proves a deadly introduction to the zany world of conspiracy theorists and soon, an unholy mess of a comic caper in which no Dallas low life is left untouched. A gossamer light look into a murky case.

Some books grab you by the collar or the privates from their opening page onwards and never let go. Untputdownable becomes a cliché in the case of Douglas Winter's *Run* (Canongate, £9.99); let's just say this novel is irresistible. Imagine reading Elmore Leonard for the first time and add a zest of Quentin Tarantino and John Woo's combined large screen pyrotechnics and you might get an idea of the flavour of this unique novel which transcends the hardboiled genre by a meaty mile and leaves the reader gasping from beginning to end. Breathless stuff indeed. Burdon Lane looks like an unassuming traditional Washington DC businessman, with his picket fence house, his conservative car and attire, his barmaid girlfriend, but the appearance is skin-deep. Lane is a professional arms dealer, cool, calm and collected, ruthless and deadly when crossed. His weekend gun run should be busi-

RANKIN AND REBUS –
NUMBER ONE BESTSELLERS

Ian
Rankin
Set in Darkness

ness as usual, riding the Iron Highway from Dirty City to Manhattan with his usual crew of friendly psychopaths, but once in New York all hell is set loose in an orgy of gunfire and flames and Lane soon has to hunt down the reasons and the men responsible as he himself is forced to go on the run with the most improbable rap gangsta companion from the opposing team. Winter's prose is colloquial, street smart and creates an unrelenting pace criss-crossed by an unerring touch for gun fetishism and popular culture.

It has been almost twenty years since screenwriter Marc Behm made a similarly awesome impact with his *The Eye of the Beholder* (recently reissued by No Exit Press at £6.99). Having retired to France, the eight novels he had written since had only appeared locally in translation. *Afraid to Death* (No Exit Press, £6.99) is the first to surface in his native language and is a fascinating counterpart to his earlier masterpiece. Whereas the private eye of the earlier, twice-filmed novel, was obsessed by a younger woman and pursued her across the vast American continent, the protagonist is, this time around, a teenage boy who becomes similarly captivated by a mysterious young woman he observes on the other side of the lake in his hometown. Every sighting of the woman is followed by a death and soon he has convinced himself she is none other than the angel of death. At the first opportunity, he leaves his home and goes on the run to avoid a future meeting with her that could prove fatal. As he grows older, he finds himself unable to settle anywhere, convinced she is about to find him again and his whole life is taken over by the fear of the reappearance of this beautiful young woman who somehow never seems to grow older. Darkly obses-

sive, gripping and poetic, this is the sort of book which, with its supernatural overtones, betrays all the ground rules of traditional crime writing and lurks, like the stuff of nightmares, in the memory thereafter. Wonderfully disturbing.

On a more cheerful note, the return of the effervescent TV newswoman Robin Hudson is cause for rejoicing in Sparkle Hayter's *The Chelsea Girl Murders* (No Exit Press, £14.99). A fire forces this New York version of Bridget Jones with added spunk and wit to vacate her apartment and move into the legendary Chelsea Hotel, with her cat Louise Bryant. Suffice to say the unlikely-named Sparkle, ex-TV reporter and Canadian of this parish, has also lived in the legendary Bohemian hotel for some years. Naturally, chaos ensues as the bodies begin to pile up in rooms, stairs and all nooks and crannies of the hostelry. Will Robin solve the fiendish crimes? Will Robin get the bad guy? The good guy? Both? A usual it's a fun ride with enough jokes to fill a hotel room and a splendid cast of bizarre New Yorkers and confirms Miss Hayter as the comic queen of all she surveys. Another highly popular series reaches its ninth instalment in Donna Leon's *Friends in High Places* (Macmillan, £15.99) featuring the engaging Commissario Guido Brunetti, of the Venice police force. Once again, Donna Leon offers a bitter-sweet view of her adoptive city through the investigations of her dogged policeman walking a dodgy tightrope between crime fighting and local politics.

There is a distinct paucity of black writers in crime fiction. America has given us Chester Himes, Walter Mosley and a handful of lesser-known authors, but apart from the school of X-Press 'Yardie' entertainers, the only one who comes to mind in Britain is Mike Phillips. All the more pity as Phillips is one those rare mystery mavens who insists on using the thriller form to question social reality in the guise of entertainment. A *Shadow of Myself* (HarperCollins, £16.99) is his most accomplished, bravura performance in subverting genre to pose many relevant and poignant questions about race, history and identity. A black British filmmaker attending a festival in Prague comes face to face with a hitherto unknown half brother, sired by his Ghanaian father during his studies in Eastern Europe. Much to his surprise, this encounter soon pulls him into a violent maelstrom of intrigue in the Sargasso sea of post cold war Europe. The opposition between Western-educated and Iron Curtain-bred Third World descendants proves a compelling background for a fast-paced meditation on how politics shape personal lives and a bittersweet reflection on the past, through the eyes of their once idealistic father.

Another of our most vibrant mystery authors is Val McDermid who improves impressively from book to book. Her new thriller *Killing the Shadows* (HarperCollins, £16.99) is as disturbing and compelling as her just paperbacked *A Place of Execution* (HarperCollins, £6.99). McDermid has become our leading specialist in the unrelenting autopsy of everyday evil and abnormal psychopathology and both thrills and scares as she dissects the sheer creepiness of British crime at both its most sordid as well as fiendishly clever, in this tale of celebrity stalking with a difference, in which the Internet and new technologies take on a most sinister colouring. The subtle orchestration in the rise of terror is masterful and puts American experts like the much-overrated Patricia Cornwell and Kathy Reichs to shame. Should by justice be adorning the bestseller list!

Mary Scott is the author of the award-winning literary novel *Not in Newbury* and the splendidly-titled collection *Nudists May Be Encountered*. Her debut crime novel, *Murder on Wheels* (Allison & Busby, £16.99) sees her tackling genre fiction with gusto and spinning witty variations on its tropes. For over a decade already Lindsey Davis has been regaling readers with the tales of Marcus Didius Falco, an Imperial Rome sleuth whose style affectionately mirrors the romantic side of Philip Marlow down those mean cobbled Roman streets. *Ode to a Banker* (Century, £16.99) is the twelfth Falco romp and a witty satire of publishing and banking with striking contemporary resonance when it comes to greed and patronage. The belly laughs come tumbling along amongst the shenanigans and Rome is brought to uproarious life, hot, noisy and smelly and full of unforgettable characters.

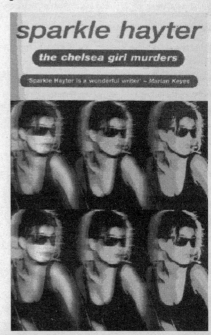

sparkle hayter

the chelsea girl murders

'Sparkle Hayter is a wonderful writer' – Marian Keyes

FILM BOOK REVIEWS

Michael Carlson

Thelma & Louise by Marita Sturken (BFI Modern Classics, £8.99, ISBN 0-85170-809-9)

Pulp Fiction by Dana Polan (BFI Modern Classics, £8.99, ISBN 0-85170-808-0)

Taxi Driver by Amy Taubin (BFI Film Classics, £8.99, ISBN 0-85170-393-3)

M by Anton Kaes (BFI Film Classics, £8.99, ISBN 0-85170-370-4)

Film Noir by Paul Duncan (Pocket Essentials, £2.99, ISBN 1-903047-08-0)

Sam Peckinpah by Richard Luck (Pocket Essentials, £2.99, ISBN 1-903047-20-X)

Steve McQueen by Richard Luck (Pocket Essentials, £2.99, ISBN 1-903047-23-4)

Sergio Leone by Christopher Frayling (Faber and Faber, £20.00, ISBN 0-571-16438-2)

Easy Riders, Raging Bulls by Peter Biskind (Bloomsbury, £8.99, ISBN 0-7475-4421-2)

The BFI's Modern Classics series takes some risks, especially when they jump on to the latest passing fancy and attempt to, well, turn a hula hoop into a cyclotron. The series went nuclear with two of last summer's releases. Dana Polan, author of the volume on *Pulp Fiction,* teaches in the Critical Studies programme at USC, and dedicates his book to Marita Sturken, who helps him "see the fun and beauty of life". Marita Sturken, author of the volume on *Thelma & Louise,* teaches at the Annenburg School for Communication at USC and thanks Dana Polen for his "advice support and love".

It is sweet of the BFI to provide professors with the academic equivalent of reading the banns, but it would be sweeter still if the published analysis could get beyond the solipsistic nature of its provenance. Sturken is both better and worse than Polen. She actually sees most of the weaknesses of *Thelma & Louise,* but ignores them in order to make her analysis. The key point being that Harlan, the redneck who attacks Thelma, is not murdered for attempting to rape her: Louise shoots him because he of his attitude – he won't apologise for his behaviour. Sturken recognises this, but then ignores her own analysis, referring back to the 'violent rape' with a Catharine MacKinnon-like belief that the idea is the same as the event. Ridley Scott made a number of successful genre movies, inserting women into traditional male roles, and made the cash registers ring as a result. The cynical nature of this enterprise is most obvious in *T&L* when a spliff-sucking rastaman appears out of nowhere in the Oklahoma desert, in order to generate a cheap laugh from an audience unworried about conventional genre suspension of disbelief. Sturken, to her credit, recognises this. *T&L* was lifted above the existing genre of 'female revenge' films, and this was the key to its success. But in the end, her analysis of the film boils down to the idea that she still wears her *Thelma & Louise* T-shirt, and that friends she had never heard utter a word at the movies were impelled to say 'yeah!' while they watched *T&L*. Believe that as you will, this is criticism along the lines of "a good book is a book that does good", by which standard *Uncle Tom's Cabin* becomes the greatest book ever written.

Polen, on the other hand, is just as fascinated by *Pulp Fiction's* cult following. The 'fun and beauty' of life appears to consist of using all that free internet time that professors get, to surf all the saddo Tarantinorantulas out there. Think about it. Video nerds combing through films packed with references by another video nerd post their revelations on the internet, and we need a professor to tell us this is a 'phenomenon'. One thing QT's films do is empower nerds, fans and critics alike (all those who can't walk the walk) to at least talk the talk. Every time they do, Polen will quote them. In fact, the biggest selling point of this book is that you don't have to follow its footnotes to the internet and elsewhere, because all the chaff and dross has been assembled for you, if not culled. Both Polen and Sturken bring a postmodern sensibility to their analysis; to wit, one doesn't look for meanings, one experiences the film. This gives meaning to any cultural (preferably pop cultural) reference

dropped into a film, whether coherently or not; it also makes a list of FAQs from websites as valid as criticism. Which is fine and dandy, but why take up space in this series when you could be out experiencing instead? One for series editor Rob White to ponder, while he funds the writers' honeymoon.

The BFI's Film Classics ('Film' as opposed to 'Modern'?… hmmm) continues on more solid ground with Amy Taubin's analysis of *Taxi Driver*. Taubin does a far better job of getting her readers into the film's background and milieu. She has the luxury of time's passage to help her, but she also writes as if meaning is not a dirty word. Context is essential to experience, and Taubin explores the audience context: a time when, with a war raging in the US, society being stretched at its limits by social change, the film industry itself was being transformed by a new frankness on the key matters of sex and violence. She also follows the film-making context of scripter Paul

Thelma & Louise
Marita Sturken

Schrader and director Martin Scorsese, analysing influences as things that produce or effect meaning, form being an extension of content. Taubin also points out that Tarantino's *Reservoir Dogs* was the first US independent film to "blatantly display the influence of *Taxi Driver*'s kinetic and visceral punch". At least here the reference has some point, at least in reverse. Even recognising that today's equivalent of John Hinckley would probably be at home locked in a Uma Thurman chat room, rather than stalking her, the Hinckley references bring a sense of cause and effect that extends beyond the professorial office.

A more traditional academic approach to the series is presented by Anton Kaes in his analysis of Fritz Lang's *M*, which is valuable for its information about variant versions, and its addition of a missing scene deleted by the German censors. Kaes also provides important background about Germany after the Great War, including references to Lang's culture that would be missed today (imagine the writer of the *Pulp Fiction* volume in a series similar to this one, working seventy years from now) and to German serial killers at the time. Kaes is also sharp on Lang's visuals, how they build a sense of modern community, through shots of isolation. This is something Lang would return to throughout his career. This is a essential text for anyone interested in the roots of film noir, and of serial killers.

The Pocket Essentials series is less ambitious than the BFI's Film and Modern Classics, and thus the idiosyncratic nature of Paul Duncan's *Film Noir: Films of Trust and Betrayal* makes it a welcome addition. For completists, there is a comprehensive list of films noirs, from *Abandoned* to *The Wronged Man*, with useful supplements on pre- and post-noir. But the core of the book is Duncan's own analysis of the eponymous theme, which isolates an important cornerstone of noir, the man torn between two women: the beautiful and the dutiful. Noir films play on variations, they take different points of view, but that triangle is an essential part of the genre. The films Duncan chooses to illustrate his idea are an interesting mix, mainly because most of them fail to follow the formula easily, and thus he gets to prove his point by indirection, as it were. Thus, although *The Killers* presents the audience with both beautiful and dutiful women, no one in the film is forced to choose between them. Instead, in Kubrick's film, people are betrayed by themselves, their own worst instincts. It's a fascinating, off-beat take on the genre, and a valuable addition to the literature of noir.

POCKET ESSENTIALS FILM

High Sierra   Vertigo   Double Indemnity

Farewell, My Lovely   **Paul Duncan**

The Killing   Night of the Hunter   Touch of Evil

Leave Her to Heaven   Build My Gallows High

Shadow of a Doubt

The Third Man

Night and the City

Film

Noir

Richard Luck's two entries into the series follow more conventional pathways. His *Sam Peckinpah* is the more interesting of the two, though he has a tendency to not allow Sam his more serious moments. For example, I've always read the quotation from Lao Tzu which preceeds *Straw Dogs* as a challenge to the critics of his violence, to see the meaning beneath the bloody surface, that this is something which lurks in all of us and presents its own satisfactions when it is indulged. This, to me, is the reason he lingers on shots of children indulging in cruelty for fun: not to show that "children are bastards" as Luck says, but to remind us of how early and how deep the roots of violent behaviour run. Similarly, while *The Getaway* isn't the greatest of Peckinpah movies, it is one of the clearest statements of many of his basic themes, particularly the one which divides women into madonnas and whores, a division made not by their sexual behaviour but by their possession of manly virtues of loyalty and competence. In this he's very much like Howard Hawks, and it may be why at least part of that theme, allowing Kim Basinger lots of competence, made it into the remake of the film. But basically Luck's takes on the film are sound, his analysis of the available bibliography is solid, and one can never have too much information about the director of two of the five greatest westerns ever made.

For some reason, Luck apologises for not having 'much' (i.e. any) screen acting experience before tackling his volume on Steve McQueen (he didn't apologise for a similar shortage of directing experience before tackling Sam). But it points out a problem in that McQueen's iconic stature today, his value as an advertising image, stems mostly from a few classic performances in which he invested characters in good but not necessarily great movies with a certain 'cool' presence. Which is why *The Getaway*, with the combination of his passion for Ali MacGraw and the direction of Peckinpah, drove him out of that cool shell. But it was their previous effort, *Junior Bonner,* which Luck rightly sees as the high point of McQueen's career (I'm not sure he doesn't overvalue it in terms of the greatest of all time – I'm also still trying to figure out his analogy to Kurt Vonnegut). I also have more fondness for *Tom Horn* than Luck has, while admitting that, on the small screen especially, it can be hard to watch. But as a dying performance, it takes some beating.

Sergio Leone only made one crime movie, per se, and it was his last feature, but *Once Upon A Time In America* is a great one (Adrian Martin's BFI Modern Classic volume is one

of the best of that series, and is still available: see Crime Time 2.2 for my enthusiastic review) and that would be enough to recommend Christopher Frayling's monumental biography *Sergio Leone: Something To Do With Death* even if it weren't a fascinating combination of biography, history, and criticism. Frayling, an authority on spaghetti westerns, has done prodigious research, and provides necessary background into the film career of Leone's father, Roberto Roberti, which was a huge influence on his own work, as well as valuable information about the Italian film industry which spawned Leone in the 1950s. It puts the grand taste and visual ambition of this landmark director into a sort of mighty perspective: it's just the kind of widescreen close-up volume Leone deserves and is recommended without hesitation.

SERGIO LEONE

Something To Do With Death
Christopher Frayling

Peter Biskind's story is subtitled "how the sex 'n' drugs 'n' rock 'n' roll generation saved Hollywood", though in that context 'transformed' might be a better word than 'saved'. This is the history of a sea-change in Hollywood films, which he sees starting with *Bonnie and Clyde* and which reaches its apotheosis with *Heaven's Gate*. What happened was a convergence of two things: first, the 1960s generation gap, which Hollywood moguls had some trouble understanding and exploiting so they looked to younger people to show them the way, and second, the influence of 'auteur theory' in the film industry: the effect of people realising the importance of directors. In both cases, the result was not what might have been anticipated. The fact that the director may be the creative force behind a film did not necessarily mean he was the person best positioned to get that film made. The apprenticeships served in the studio system, and the structured environment, were already under threat as the economics of the film business were changed by television. Television, and later film schools, would serve as the apprentice ground for fledgling directors, who would be given a control early in their careers that a Howard Hawks or a Joseph H. Lewis would have been stunned to receive.

In terms of the generation gap, what Biskind makes most clear is the way the sex, drugs, and rock 'n' roll people turned out to be not that very different from what had gone before them, only presented with more opportunity and fewer restraints on their own self-indulgent behaviour. The new moguls weren't interested in assimilating as much as taking over, a generation of would-be Bugsy Siegels with cinema as their Vegas. Many of these younger people were, in effect, children of the industry, and they were either born with or soon learned that money was really the only way they could measure their success. Of course, one of the blind spots of 'auteur' theory was that, although the personal vision of directors might be spotted in all the various movies they turned out in the studio system, it couldn't turn the vast number of run-of-the-mill works, or even clunkers, into either art or box office gold. Using Europe as a model was hardly better: how many foreign films had anyone actually seen besides the classics of Bergman, Truffaut, Fellini and so on. Europe produced levels of schlock Hollywood could hardly conceive of, as anyone who follows British cinema surely knows. Directors convinced of their own genius had huge critical blind spots. Billy Friedkin brought in various Europeans to help him, made a disastrous remake of *The Wages of Fear*, and finally, since he couldn't marry his idols, married Jeanne Moreau. Eventually everyone falls prey to the reality of Hollywood, which is that virtually no one out there can ever predict what the public is or isn't going to like, and why. Which is why so much money is spent by the marketing departments, and why the place is such a creative echo-chamber of copy-catting and stolen ideas.

Biskind does a deft job of switching between the business and the personal sides of his characters. The most telling of these, to me, is Paul Schrader, who comes out of a critical, intellectual background (drawing on his famous fundamentalist childhood) to become a scriptwriter and director who will repeatedly screw his brother out of both credit and money. It helps make the point as well that Hollywood is fantasy land: reality is what name is on the credit, not who actually did the work. Success has many fathers and failure is an orphan, goes the old saying. In Hollywood, success breeds patricide and fratricide. The Schrader brothers' relationship is a dark echo perhaps of that between Warren Beatty and Robert Towne. Beatty is a key figure in this book, the ultimate Hollywood player, and really the one person who has been able to work the system to do what HE wants to do, as producer, actor, and director. Towne tried to move on the same path and the result was first *Personal Best,* which may be the ultimate fetish film (not that I mind it from that point of view) and then *The Two Jakes,* whose failure somehow shows just how

far things had slid since *Chinatown*.

At the centre of *ERRB* are the movie brats, Coppola, Lucas, Spielberg. The first two had dreams of setting up counter-studios: Coppola has been reduced to hackwork and Lucas to recapitulating *Star Wars*. Spielberg, meanwhile, paying off a huge divorce settlement to Amy Irvine, creates the sort of Disney TV dramas he watched as a boy in the 1950s, but on a larger and more obviously moral stage. What are *Schindler's List* or *Armistead* or *Saving Private Ryan* if not *Davy Crockett* or *Johnny Tremain* on a wider scale? At their peak they were trading percentage points in each other's movies like they were trading cards (and when John Milius' epic *Big Wednesday* flopped George Lucas asked for his *Star Wars* points back).

And what has been the result of Hollywood's sea change? With the final collapse of the 'creative' producer system, control of what remained of the studios passed to corporate money men, from outside the system,

Pulp Fiction
Dana Polan

and the structuring of films passed on to the bankable talents, the actors, and thus to their agents. Whatever you may think about the 1968-1980 era, you have to admit there was a steady stream of great, almost great, and flawed but fascinating films. What have we had since? One of the things the Crime Time Millennial Film Poll suggests is that the 1970s were indeed a Golden Age for crime films.

If anything, the book is so crammed with gripping anecdote that you sometimes have to force yourself to stay with the plot. Biskind makes the transition from drug-crazed personal lives to ego-crazed corporate bloodletting with ease, meaning this is as fascinating a look at Hollywood as you'll find anywhere. There are a few problems with some of the stories, often self-contradictory, which go with the territory of Hollywood mythmaking. Nowadays, when Dennis Hopper can play sneaker pitch-man and respected artist, you have to take what you can get. Hopper stands in stark contrast to Hal Ashby, whose story at one point appears to be taking centre stage, but Biskind finally moves away from dwelling on its telling tragedy. Ashby might be our moral figure, but I'm not sure that Brian de Palma might not have been more telling as a bookend. Although his career covers the same dates as Coppola and Scorsese, he's mainly on the periphery of the main tale. Given his penchant for remakes that may be rightly so, but he also seems to have cruised along within the system, however it changed, for thirty years. I think DePalma's *Scarface* may be the absolute best metaphor for Hollywood in this era which Biskind describes so well. Think about it. When Tony Montana buries his face in a mountain of coke, who does he resemble more, Al Capone or Dennis Hopper?

MIKE HODGES
INTERVIEWED

Charles Waring

By his own admission, British movie direc-tor Mike Hodges likes to make intelligent and thought-provoking films. So it comes as something of a surprise that America, the home of Hollywood and formulaic, escapist filmmaking, should embrace the director's lat-est film, *Croupier*. *Croupier* is a tenebrous, cerebral thriller which focuses on the double life of Jack Manfred, a writer by day and a casino croupier by night. The film was com-pleted some three years ago and represents only Hodges's eighth cinema feature film in a directorial career that spans almost thirty years and began with *Get Carter* back in 1971. Despite an eclectic, though relatively slim body of work – which includes films as varied (and reviled) as *Morons From Out of Space* and *Prayer for the Dying* – to date, *Get Carter* has eclipsed, in terms of its appeal and influence, everything else the director has done. *Croupier*, however, may change all

that, having been vociferously championed by many American critics as the director's finest cinematic offering. In the wake of *Croupier's* phenomenal stateside success, *CT* spoke to Hodges to not only ascertain his own perspective regarding the film's achieve-ments but also outline any future plans.

Speaking from his country retreat in deep-est Dorset, Hodges is understandably euphor-ic about *Croupier's* good fortune at the American box office. I quote to him figures from a recent article in *The Sunday Times*, which estimates that the film has taken more than two million dollars in just thirteen weeks. As our interview later reveals, Hodges is not a film maker driven by monetary con-siderations, but he's keen to update me about the film's financial state of play. "It's now up to four and a half million. It's not *Gladiator* style but it's the art film of the year, certainly. It's a very considerable achievement and I'm absolutely delighted, of course, and somewhat astonished."

A propos of critical reaction to the film, Mike Hodges is keen to correct a widely held but erroneous perception that *Croupier* fared badly at the hands of UK film pundits. From perusing recent UK press coverage of the movie prior to our telephone interview, I, too, had wrongly assumed that *Croupier's* reception by critics here was less than favourable. This was not so, as Hodges took pains to explain. "It didn't have lukewarm reviews in the UK. No, we had good reviews and a marvellous review from Peter Preston in *The Guardian*. It's very funny. People say this and it's not true at all, actually. It had very good reviews. It's absolutely typical. Somehow these rumours get out and they sort of become fact."

In fact, the film's low (some would say non-existent) profile here in Britain was due to a patent lack of enthusiasm on the part of British co-sponsors, Film Four, who were involved in the production work along with a German investment company. Hodges elucidated me on the problems, which threatened to leave *Croupier* languishing in obscurity. "What happened was that Film Four were not particularly interested in the film. There was a change of management there. The previous head of production was a man called David Aukin, who had commissioned the script from Paul Mayersberg but didn't like the film. When he saw the final cut and dub, he actually said that the only thing he liked about it were the end credits. So, basically, he then left to go on to other things. Anyway, Film Four – as is usual with new management in these situations – was lukewarm about it. It went into the Berlin marketplace (that was like running in a funeral parlour, practically)

so the overseas sales were minimal because nobody was very enthusiastic about the film. If the people that make the film aren't enthusiastic, it's highly likely that nobody else is going to be. I managed to get the British film industry to distribute it in England to save it from the ignominy of going straight to video or onto television. Despite fantastic reviews, the BFI didn't have any money, of course, to distribute it properly. So there were only two prints, a small poster – not a full size poster – and no useable trailer. The film limped round the BFI circuit through the National Film Theatres in the usual major cities. But where the audiences saw it, they liked it. It took £30,000 in six months, or something like that. Hardly anyone saw it – hardly anyone knew about it. And these days you cannot expect a film to go out without some form of publicity. But there was practically none. So it wasn't anything to do with the audiences and wasn't anything to do with the critical reviews. It was basically total apathy on the part of Film Four. Making a film is tough. If you then get that kind of treatment, it's discouraging. So of course I feel vindicated in a very big way because the American reviews went through the roof. But the American reviews, much to my surprise, were across America, not just the major cities. We had great reviews everywhere and that really surprised me."

Did it strike him as somewhat ironic that America has embraced an independent film that is the antithesis of the cliché-ridden, pyrotechnical film that Hollywood churns out week-in week-out for mass-consumption? "Absolutely. I think that's probably the reason for its success. But nobody can quite say what it is that has attracted this kind of attention. I think it's a collection of things and it's probably because it's not a formulaic film that it vindicates not just my belief in this film but it vindicates my belief that audiences are screaming for intelligent films. And whether you like the film or not, it's a complex and interesting existentialist film. It's not a particularly hopeful film: it's a film for anyone who has a beady eye on life itself. And it's interesting in that respect. So it vindicates anybody who wants to make intelligent films".

In Britain, Hodges is regarded as something of a one-hit wonder, the man who made the seminal British gangster movie *Get Carter* but little else. Many Americans, though, are certainly more cognisant of the film director's other work and as a result hold his canon in high esteem. Indeed, last year, Hodges's career was honoured by a film retrospective in California. "In Los Angeles they ran ten of my films including the first two television films I made before *Get Carter* – one was called *Suspect* and one was called *Rumour*. In fact this was really the launch pad for *Croupier* because I'd never seen it with an audience apart from a crew and cast showing and they ran it over the weekend alternating with *Get Carter*. The audience reaction was just terrific: there was a standing ovation at the end on Saturday night. And I knew then that *Croupier* might work in America – I wasn't sure whether it was going to extend beyond the likes of LA, so it was then that I had the first intimation that 1) it works with audiences and 2) it might take off in America. But never did I dream that it would do what it's done." As a result of *Croupier's* appeal to American audiences, has he experienced Hollywood producers and studios beating a path to his door? "Yes, there's been a lot of interest. It amuses me, to be honest with you, because I haven't changed as a director and I haven't changed as a person."

Croupier is Hodges' first feature since 1989's ill-fated *Black Rainbow*, a macabre supernatural tale about a medium starring Rosanna Arquette and Jason Robards. But, as Hodges told *CT*, although filmmaking is an important aspect of his life, he has other interests as well, which include writing plays and performing music (Hodges is a keen pianist). However, the reason for his protracted hiatus from filmmaking was partly disillusionment with the treatment meted out to *Black Rainbow* by its less-than-sympathetic distributors. "Well, I think *Black Rainbow* suffered terribly from bad distribution. Here, it ran, I think, for seven weeks in the Curzon and again had fantastic reviews. But because Palace Pictures were going to the wall financially, they sold it to video for a quick sale, and then in America Miramax had it and they too were in financial difficulties. And having had the film for a year, they then put it straight onto cable television without any distribution at all. And it's very discouraging, and also I want to make films that are different and interesting and if you don't get those scripts and you can't get that kind of interest then you may as well not make any films. It isn't from choice but that's the way it is."

Our conversation inevitably returns to *Croupier*, which its director describes as "the antithesis of concept movies". Indeed, the film is a profound, modern day allegory, examining power and control in the context of human relationships. "It's very complex and very multi-layered. When the script was sent to me it was very different – obviously it had the same story line and the same characters there, but Paul [Mayersberg] and I worked on it for quite a long time. When I first read it before we got to work on it, it seemed to me the most appropriate subject for our times. I felt that it encompassed just about everything that was happening on many levels, political as well as personal. It's very complex in so far as that whilst it's not overtly political it is representative of what the French call 'capitalism sauvage'. It is a world where money has become the predominant talking point." I concur and suggest that filthy lucre has become the *raison d'être* for everything. Hodges agrees. "Absolutely. It's really interesting that in the 1960s and in the whole of my younger life, people never talked about money. It was actually *de rigueur* not to talk about it. No one ever discussed their salary, no one ever showed off about the amount of money they had and no one flaunted it. It was such a subtle world where money, though important, was not, the *raison d'être*: we all had a dream that there were other virtues and values. But that has vanished. It was so rapid during the Thatcher years, of course. So *Croupier* seems particularly relevant at that level. Also, I think it was relevant in terms of an age where gambling has become a virtue – we now have the lottery here. Gambling has become a national pastime at such an extensive level that even our arts depend upon it. Another level at which the film attracted me was that Jack Manfred, the main character, is a control freak. He tries to control his life and I think that we all have the illusion, particularly again nowadays, that we think that we can control our lives: we have filofaxes and our days are filled up, our time is occupied, we have mobile phones, we have life insurance, health insurance, we insure our houses, holidays and everything. We have the whole accoutrements of a life we feel we control."

I interject by saying that what he's just described is all a form of gambling. "It is and it's all an illusion. And that's what the film's also about. It says you think that you have control over everything but it is actually an illusion. My objective with the casino and the whole gambling element of the picture was that whilst it is a sort of Mecca, when you start taking the sounds of the ball going round and the sounds of the casino and start spreading it into Jack's personal life, then you see that everything else is a gamble. However much he thinks he controls it, it's not so. And he recognises that."

I then explain to Hodges that for me personally, the key example in the film of arbitrary events taking away control and changing lives is best illustrated when Jack's girlfriend, Marion, is killed by a hit and run driver. He's intrigued by this example. "It's very interesting. People ask why. When I was doing it, one morning we woke up and Princess Diana had been killed in a car crash. I mean it was exactly the same – I think we were editing the film when it happened. Her number was up, literally." For myself, I regard that scene as one of the most poignant moments in the film, revealing to Jack that however much he wanted control in life, he could not really have it. Only as a writer, maybe, could he achieve that kind of detached, God-like control. Hodges avers and adds, "He knows he's not a good writer, too."

One aspect of Jack Manfred's character which particularly intrigued me is the broad-brimmed hat he wears. I asked Hodges about the thinking behind this idiosyncrasy, which he attributed to the movie's scriptwriter, Paul Mayersberg. The director found the idea intriguing because of its association with some of his favourite movies, including Jean-Pierre Melville's *Le Samourai* with Alain Delon. "Paul put it in and I extended it – at first I was nervous about the idea: it seemed so corny in some ways. Then I decided, in fact, I should take the bull by the horns. The very first time you see it, it's sat on his desk next to a cigarette burning. So the image of a noir film is there. He puts it on when he's writing: it's almost like a thinking cap. Then I extended it. There was one moment when Marion came in and she wanted him to be a writer. She would keep him as long as when they went out to meet friends or whatever, she could say he was a writer – not a croupier. Jack being a croupier really upsets her. And there's a moment when he's writing and she comes in and puts the hat on him. And it's a very significant moment because the hat may well have come from her – and the hat is her image of what a writer is. But he's too smart to know that all writers wear hats! But it became kind of emblematic for him, the hat." Does he think it represents the romantic ideal of the writer that Marion wanted? "Yes, and when Jack returns from the weekend in the country and he thinks she's left him and he goes to the fridge to get his usual vodka, there's a package in there. When he unwraps the package, it's a present from her: it's an ugly, horrible gold chain with a book on it. Again it underlines her romantic view of him. In fact, the first thing he ever says about Marion is that she's a romantic and he's not. So that, really, is part of what the hat's about. And of course, there's a lot of humour in *Croupier* – Americans laughed with it a lot. It's not just all very po-faced. So it is kind of tongue in cheek and the hat is part of that, I think."

Initially, Jack cultivates an almost scientific detachment as he observes life in the casino. Does Hodges, as a filmmaker, share Jack's voyeuristic detachment? "Yes, I think every filmmaker is probably voyeuristic but I think we're all voyeuristic in many ways. I don't know anybody who doesn't love sitting in a cafe watching other people. We all love watching each other, I think." Hodges is more hesitant when I enquire of him whether filmmakers need to be more observant than other people. He ponders for a few moments before eventually answering. "Well, ideally, but I'm not sure that's always the case. I've known a lot of filmmakers, who, like politicians, don't actually see ordinary people. They lose contact observing people. A lot of them live in Beverley Hills and don't get to watch people. Maybe that's what accounts for the kind of films that come out of Los Angeles."

As the centrepiece of the film's action, the casino in *Croupier* is an impressive setting – it's an opulent subterranean dungeon festooned with wall-to-wall mirrors. For all its glitz, it could almost be a vision of hell, the croupier dealing out cards either of damnation or salvation to the lost souls at the gaming tables. It wasn't, however, filmed at a real casino but constructed especially for the film. Did they contemplate using a genuine casino? "No. We'd never have got in. Well, I wouldn't want to actually, because it's too restrictive in regard of the hours you would've had to work. The casino is so important that I wanted to create our own, so we built it in a studio in Germany – over half the money was German and had to be spent there. I wanted the casino to be built for my purposes. All the mirrors, for example, I wanted because I liked the idea of Jack's image being broken up. It gave it a quality which underlined the deceit of everything really. Nobody knows who's doing what to whom in *Croupier*. Nobody knows what the other person's thinking and the mirrors, in a sense, reflect that kind of deceit. And there's also an element of narcissism as well." Much time was also expended on background research to achieve the film's authenticity. "I went to casinos, obviously. But I went to two or three, that's all. Other people who know casinos very well find it extraordinarily accurate. A lot of people have commented on it and the casting of the manager, for example (Alexander Morton). They thought he was just brilliant and terribly accurate. But the key to it really was that Clive Owen (Jack) and Kate Hardie (Bella) went to croupier school. They trained to be croupiers. All the actors who were croupiers went there. Then I supplemented them with real croupiers and I had a croupier advisor. So we had people who were skilled with all the details."

Hodges is effusive in his praise for scriptwriter, Paul Mayersberg and describes an almost symbiotic working relationship. He was less than complimentary, however, regarding Croupier's sponsors, Film Four. "The editing was a nightmare at Film Four. I don't think they understood the film at all, which made it difficult to hang on to the film as I thought it should be." Did he have to stand his ground resolutely on some issues? "Absolutely. You have to fight tooth and nail. We'd finished filming and the film was very near to completion and someone would say they'd got some extra money and could we re-shoot the whole of the beginning. They could never understand that the beginning is the end: the whole film's a flashback. They just didn't comprehend it. It was a grim editing experience for me: if you are editing for people that don't understand the film it's just painful." In answer to my question about whether this particular aspect of filmmaking has put him off working in Hollywood again,

Hodges was diplomatic. "I think you have to be extremely careful who you work with. You have to work with people who share your view. The really interesting thing about films is the number of times one goes to make a film and you find out you're making a different film to what everybody else is. And that's when the trouble starts. So you try desperately to make sure that everybody knows the film that you're making before you start. And it's better you pull out before that stage happens when patently people don't share your vision."

On the ever-moving roulette wheel of life, what goes around comes around. Mike Hodges – modest, unassuming man that he is – may have thought his number was up as a film director but Croupier dealt him a winning hand and has given him a new lease of life. He's still not sure what he's going to do next – some people would like him to do a thriller, of course, but Hodges, like the iconoclastic filmmaker he undoubtedly is, doesn't back certainties and contemplates something radically different and unusual: a screen treatment of Thomas Mann's novel Mario the Magician. Having graduated from being perceived as a cult director to achieving veteran status, Hodges, admits that at sixty-eight years old the sands of time are inexorably running down regarding the making of another film. But like an inveterate gambler with the lure of another big win, Hodges is adamant that another movie is within his sights: "I'm sure I will make another film." Some might think that with a recent track record that rivals Stanley Kubrick's for intervals between films, the odds are not on his side. But I, for one, would not like to bet against him.

CRIME IN STORE

LONDON'S CRIME AND MYSTERY STORE

CATALOGUE NUMBER 17 SUMMER 2000

THE crime writer's bookshop is now open seven days a week – Summer Sundays run throughout September. Come and see us or write to us to be on the free mailing list – our catalogue is out six times a year. We stock signed first editions, US import paperbacks and hardbacks, audio books, Sherlockiana, reference, adventure and second hand – first editions and paperbacks. Many author events and signings. Past signings have included Patricia Cornwell, Dick Francis, Michael Connelly and Ian Rankin.

Crime in Store
14 Bedford St, Covent Garden
London WC2E 9HE

Telephone: 020 7379 3795
Fax: 020 7379 8988
e-mail: CrimeBks@AOL.com
www.crimeinstore.co.uk

Monday–Saturday 10.30 – 6.30
Sunday (June–Sept) 12 – 5

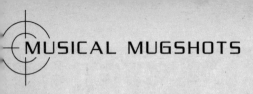

ROY BUDD

Charles Waring

In a world where everything has become commodified, only a fool would doubt the power of advertising. Although in the medium of television, visual appearance remains the be-and-end-all of everything, an advert's soundtrack has become an equally important component of the copywriter's hard-sell policy and has been able to inject hipness into the most mundane of products. These days, advertising agencies harbour a propensity for using pre-existing music rather than commission new pieces, a policy that often works for the mutual benefit of the product and the composer or performer. The combination of Steve McQueen's presence (albeit computer enhanced) and Lalo Schifrin's classic jazz-tinged score to *Bullitt* succeeded in not only giving an aura of hipness to the Ford Puma motor car but reawakened public interest in Peter Yates's original 1968 movie and its soundtrack. Similarly, the British musician, Roy Budd, was largely a forgotten man until the theme he wrote for the British gangster movie *Get Carter* starring Michael Caine, resurfaced as the soundtrack for a sleek Campari advert in 1997. Almost overnight, Budd's music became highly sought after, prompting a reissue programme by Castle Music of the composer's impressive back catalogue of movie scores. *Get Carter*, like Schifrin's *Bullitt*

theme, was also remixed by hepcat DJs for the dance market and issued as a commercially successful single. Interest in Mike Hodges's cult 1971 film, which was recently brought to video format, helped to further enhance Budd's rapidly escalating reputation amongst both pundits and punters. With a new batch of Budd reissues about to hit the shops, the crime cognoscenti at CT thought it was about time that one of this sceptred isle's most talented and underrated musicians was profiled in the ongoing CT series, Musical Mugshots.

Sadly, Roy Budd is no longer around to appreciate the rekindled interest in his work -- he died some seven years ago, back in 1993 at the age of forty-six. He was born in Croydon, Surrey, on 14th March 1947. Young Roy was interested in music from an early age and could pick out tunes on the piano at just four years old. By the time he had reached twelve, Budd was regarded as something of a precocious child prodigy and sought after by radio and TV programmes to showcase his musical abilities. Budd actually made his debut on the small screen as long ago as 1959 (he was twelve) when he appeared on ITV's entertainment flagship, *Saturday Night At The London Palladium*, broadcast live and compered by a relatively youthful Bruce Forsyth (this variety show has recently been revived with Forsyth reprising his role as host). Performing at the piano and accompanied by the house orchestra, apparently the twelve-year-old Budd was so nerve-racked and pumped with adrenaline that he reeled off his piece at break-neck pace and concluded the instrumental at least a minute in front of the lagging orchestra! However, undeterred by this mishap and somewhat unpropitious entry into the cut-throat entertainment arena, Budd eventually conquered a nervous disposition to the point that he was beginning to perform regularly in public and could be seen as leader of small ensembles at the capital's hippest jazz hang-outs. He led the Roy Budd Quartet and garnered such a good response from the public that he decided to pursue a professional career in music.

After leaving school, Budd came to the attention of Jack Fishman, a successful songwriter and first beneficiary of the Ivor Novello songwriter award (he'd written hit tunes for artists like Petula Clark). Through his association with Fishman, Budd signed to the music publisher, MCA Music, for three years. However, after twelve months had elapsed and with little to show for his tenure at the company, Budd was allowed to leave MCA and was promptly snapped up by Pye Records in 1966, who added him as an artist to a roster presided over by an A&R executive in the guise of one Tony Hatch, no mean songwriter himself (also responsible for the theme to the 1970's Midlands-based soap opera, Crossroads). Under Hatch's expert guidance, Budd cut Birth of the Budd as a single, following it up with the 1967 parent album, Pick Yourself Up. Both were well received and paved the way for a prolific series of releases which totaled an astonishing thirteen albums in his eleven year residence at the Pye company (his contract was terminated in 1976).

Budd's undoubted forte was jazz, but he also dabbled with the popular easy listening format, recording lounge covers of popular songs (he recorded a whole album of Gilbert O'Sullivan tunes), show tunes (including a funked up rendering of Jesus Christ Superstar), and even classical music themes (notable examples being Fauré's Pavane and Rodrigo's Concerto for Guitar).

By the early 70s, Budd's musical attention had focused on film music, something that he patently knew little about when he blagged his way into providing the score for the controversial, bloodthirsty US Western picture, Soldier Blue, in 1970. Legend has it that the film's director, Ralph Nelson, was in need of an English composer and that Budd solicited him with a tape, which he declared contained original material: it was, in fact, a compilation of orchestral music by the film composer Jerry Goldsmith (Planet Of The Apes and Alien) and the renowned, Academy Award-winning veteran Hollywood film scorer, Dimitri Tiomkin (High Noon and Gunfight at the OK Corral). Fortunately for Budd, Nelson was not familiar with the works or the composers in question and, obviously impressed by what he heard (but who wouldn't be?), signed Budd to provide Soldier Blue's score. For the first time in his career, Budd was confronted with scoring music for a large orchestra and, in desperation to learn about the craft, consulted many a weighty tome on the art of orchestration. Miraculously, his temerity paid off and the composer produced a memorable film score debut resulting in offers of more work which included the crime films Get Carter (1971), Fear is the Key (1972), The Stone Killer (1973), The Black Windmill (1974) and Diamonds (1975). Although Budd's predilection for large orchestral ensembles supplemented by sinewy electric bass lines and wah-wah guitars resulted in a heavy symphonic jazz-funk sound well-suited to the thriller genre, he was a versatile composer equally adept at scoring light comedic drama like *Steptoe and Son Ride Again* (1973), Westerns in the form of *Catlow* (1971) and fantasy films such as *Sinbad and the Eye of the Tiger* (1977).

Despite being kept busy by a glut of film work in the 1970s, Budd played jazz when he could in some of London's prestigious jazz venues like Ronnie Scott's and was often in demand for live work accompanying a musical megastar or two who happened to show up in town.

At the time of his premature death in August 1993, Roy Budd had been working on a grandiose orchestral piece to complement the silent movie version of *The Phantom of the Opera* starring Lon Chaney Sr. Indeed the world premiere of Budd's ambitious score was already scheduled to take place at the Barbican cinema in London. But only a month before the proposed unveiling of Budd's magnum opus, the composer died.

Roy Budd may no longer be with us but his music is finally garnering the attention and plaudits it undoubtedly deserves. What follows is a critical evaluation of the best of the Budd canon currently available on CD.

Roy Budd on CD

Get Carter

(Cinephile CINCD001) Initially misunderstood and undervalued by domestic film critics, Mike Hodges' bleak fable of gangland payback starring Michael Caine as a man seeking retribution for his brother's death accrued a cult following over the years and is now widely regarded as a classic movie. At the time of *Get Carter*'s release in 1971, the film's complete soundtrack album was only released in Japan (now a highly-prized collectors' album valued at £1,500!) although a single featuring the main theme briefly appeared in Britain on the defunct Pye label. *Get Carter* represents Roy Budd's most famous soundtrack and was only the second film he scored. Budget limitations (a meagre £450 was allocated for the film's music) resulted in a small ensemble recording featuring Budd's own jazz trio supplemented by a percussionist and guitar player. Some of the material was co-written with Budd's mentor, Jack Fishman. The film's haunting main theme (played on a harpsichord and which reappears in various guises throughout the movie) blends minimalist electric jazz-funk with Indian tabla

---

Filmography

Soldier Blue (1970)
The Magnificent Seven Deadly Sins (1971)
Kidnapped (1971)
Flight of the Doves (1971)
Zeppelin (1971)
Get Carter (1971)
Catlow (1971)
Something To Hide (1972) (aka Shattered)
Fear is the Key (1972)
The Carey Treatment (1972) (aka Emergency Ward)

Steptoe and Son Ride Again (1973)
Man at the Top (1973)
The Stone Killer (1973)
The Internecine Project (1974)
The Black Windmill (1974)
The Destructors (1974) (aka The Marseille Contract UK)
Diamonds (1975)
Paper Tiger (1975)
Welcome To Blood City (1977)

(aka Blood City)
Sinbad and the Eye of the Tiger (1977) (aka Sinbad at the World's End)
Tomorrow Never Comes (1978)
The Wild Geese (1978)
The Sea Wolves (1980)
Mama Dracula (1980)
The Final Option (1982) (aka Who Dares Wins)
Field Of Honor (1984)
Wild Geese II (1985)

percussion and expertly captures the film's thematic bleakness. The other incidental music Budd contributes is more overtly pop-influenced and has dated a tad, but overall, this is a great package which is enhanced by nuggets of memorable film dialogue.

The Stone Killer

(Cinephile CINCD006) Most critics agree that this brutal movie directed by Michael Winner and starring Charles Bronson as a hard-nosed LA cop single-handedly taking on the Mafia was an absolute dud. However, one of its redeeming features was Budd's exciting soundtrack, characterised by the composer's penchant for throbbing bass parts and propulsive, muscular rhythms and the occasional foray into lounge territory. Lots of rasping moog synth and stirring symphonic funk.

Fear is the Key (Cinephile CINCD002) Based on an Alistair MacLean thriller, Barry Newman (best remembered as the TV lawyer Petrocelli in the early 1970s) hatches a cunning (though somewhat convoluted) plan to get even with the dastardly fiends who killed his wife and child in a plane crash. An above average, reasonably exciting thriller is enhanced by Budd's savvy blend of jazz, grandiose symphonic themes and blistering ass-crack funk (the latter particularly evident on the ten minute car chase sequence which features the legendary jazz horn man Tubby Hayes on sax).

Diamonds (Cinephile CINCD003) Starring Richard 'Shaft' Roundtree, Robert Shaw and Shelley Winters and filmed in Israel, *Diamonds* is a rip-roaring heist movie about a scheming, corrupt London jewel merchant who masterminds a daring raid on the Tel Aviv diamond repository. Regarded by many as Budd's best soundtrack, *Diamonds* features unusual, exotic instrumentation for its atmospheric Middle Eastern inspired themes (Tel Aviv and Marketplace) and, in musical terms, covers many different bases: there's an easy-listening bossa nova tune (Beauty and the Bass), some jazz (Party Piece), a succulent slice of uncut bass-driven prime funk (The Thief) plus a soul-tinged song sung by the Philly female vocal trio, The Three Degrees, called Hearts and Diamonds. Classy stuff.

The Birth of the Budd

(Sequel NEMCD927) This excellent, value-for-money, twenty-five-track compilation is essential for a wider appreciation of Roy Budd's unique talents. Its eclectic selection of material ranges from Budd's dynamic film themes (*Get Carter*, *Soldier Blue* and *Fear is the Key*) through self-penned jazz workouts (Birth Of The Budd) to cheesy easy listening moments (a louche rendering of a couple of Gilbert O'Sullivan tunes) and Jack Loussier style renditions of well-known classical music themes. A well-rounded musical portrait of one of Britain's most undervalued film composers and which serves as a useful introduction to the man's work.

Also available on Cinephile Records:
The Black Windmill (CINCD004)
Sinbad and the Eye of the Tiger (CINCD005)
Marseille Contract (CINCD009)
Paper Tiger (CINCD012)
The Wild Geese (CINCD014)
Kidnapped (CINCD015)
Something To Hide, Foxbat and The
    Internecine Project (CINCD0019)
Tomorrow Never Comes (CINCD020)

CTTV

Charles Waring

Although I confess to being a bit of a nocturnal creature, I've yet to achieve bona fide insomniac status. However, those poor souls amongst CT readers who have difficulty in sleeping at night will rejoice in the fact that, at last, there is a decent crime show broadcast on terrestrial TV after midnight that is definitely worth staying up for: namely *Brooklyn South*. However, if you're like me and can't be bothered with propping up heavy eyelids with matchsticks, you'll much prefer programming the video to record the show and view the results at a more civilized hour.

This issue of CTTV, we'll be supplying all the information you'll ever need to know about BBC2's superlative late-night cop show Brooklyn South.

Brooklyn South

On Saturday May 7th at 12.05am, BBC2 transmitted the ninety-minute pilot episode of Brooklyn South, a show created by that great impresario of gritty American television drama, Steven Bochco.

The show's opening eight-minute sequence was one of the most tense, exciting and dramatic scenes I have ever witnessed on a mainstream cop programme. If perchance you didn't see it, let me recreate it for you. Imagine the interior of the 74th Precinct Police Station in Brooklyn off Flatbush Avenue. It's around seven in the morning and a handful of uniformed beat cops arrive for the day shift, ready to attend roll call and be given their daily assignments. The duty sergeant shows a poster of an African-American called DeShawn Hopkins, wanted for a recent bank robbery homicide. He's also a crack head and one bad mutha. Cut to an exterior shot. Just outside the station a minor car accident occurs. A passing cop car stops and asks the drivers to pull over. Cut to another shot of a tall, gangly African-American walking briskly down the street a block away from the station. The face matches the poster mugshot of DeShawn Hopkins. There's a fierce determina-

tion in his demeanour. A businessman accidentally bumps into him and is thumped full in the face for his troubles. Hopkins strides on, apparently indifferent to the world about him. He walks straight out into the road without looking and cars screech to a halt to let him pass. Hopkins continues walking towards the cops attending the traffic accident and pulls a handgun from behind his back, firing off some rounds and downing both police and civilians. His rampage continues when he guns down more cops. The shots are heard from within the station and Hopkins, who is leaving a trail of bloody mayhem in his wake, is pursued on foot by a posse of police officers. There's an exchange of shots between parked cars and a plain clothes cop is hit in the leg. Then the sharp, high-pitched crack of a second gun is heard echoing from the rooftops and the wounded cop has the top of his head blown off, his skull bursting like a pulverized grapefruit. Hopkins is wounded in another exchange of gunfire and temporarily disappears only to re-emerge from a shop door holding a woman hostage. But this time, his luck's run out and he's pistol-whipped to the ground before being arrested. The rooftop sniper, however, cannot be located. Fade to black followed by the opening credits and Mike Post's (yes, it's that man again!) stirring theme tune.

At this juncture I was hooked. *Brooklyn South* had me by the short and curlies and wouldn't let go. Since that opening first episode, the BBC has shown two episodes back to back each Friday night/Saturday morning and I still can't get enough of it. But it also got me to wondering: why isn't this excellent show on a couple of hours earlier, like, say, *NYPD Blue*? It was an enigma, certainly, and one which I endeavoured to investigate.

The Mystery Deepens

Steven Bochco is a name synonymous with success. His track record in the television industry speaks for itself. Bochco, of course, was the man responsible for bringing pathfinding cop shows like *Hill Street Blues* and *NYPD Blue* to our TV screens. He also gave the world the marvellous courtroom epic *Murder One* and popular series like *LA Law*. In fact, despite the serious adult themes of his shows, Bochco is in essence a primetime specialist, so it came as something of a surprise to find his latest opus being consigned to the after-hours ghetto usually reserved for embarrassingly God-awful shows like *Nash Bridges* and *Renegade*. Indeed, Bochco programmes are customarily greeted with a fanfare of publicity, but for this one there was a muted, strangely reticent response from the media. Actually, the show only came to my attention by accident, and the fact that my CT duties prompt me to scour the pages of TV guides in search of fresh cop food to devour. As regards *Brooklyn South*, there was scant information to be gleaned from perusing the Radio Times and such like. Even the BBC publicity department had precious little knowledge to divulge about the background of *Brooklyn South*. CBS television was listed as co-producers of the show, but nothing was forthcoming from probing their website. Then, after ploughing through pages and pages of mostly irrelevant text procured by the sedulous efforts of a resourceful internet search engine, I discovered a website called 'Remembering Brooklyn South'. The penny dropped, so to speak, and everything then fell into place.

Brooklyn South: The Death of a Cop Show

The mystery surrounding *Brooklyn South* is

now solved. It had the potential to be one of the best police dramas ever. It could have been, in the memorable words of one Marlon Brando, a contender, but was gunned down in its prime. The perpetrator? CBS, no less, who cited poor audience ratings as the reason for the show's cancellation after a promising first season. A joint venture by Bochco Productions and CBS Television, with Steven Bochco, David Milch, Bill Finkelstein and Bill Clark (all of *NYPD Blue* fame) on board as executive producers, *Brooklyn South*, debuted in September 1997, and lasted for twenty-one hour-long episodes until April 1998.

Steven Bochco is not a man inured to failure and was understandably dismayed by CBS's decision to axe the show in May 1998. Ironically, the show garnered a prestigious Emmy Award for Mark Tinker's direction of its feature-length pilot episode while it also triumphed in the Best New Drama category at the People's Choice Awards in the US. Ratings analysts in the States actually believed that the show's audience figures weren't that bad for a fledgling series. Indeed, *Brooklyn South* prompted generally favourable reviews by America's TV critics, some of whom believed that the show, like, say, *Hill Street Blues* or *The X-Files*, would attract a larger audience if it was allowed to continue for a second season. Champions of the show (a proportion of whom instigated a campaign to save the show) blamed CBS's programming strategy for hastening the series' demise – aired on a Monday night in the States, *Brooklyn South* certainly was up against stiff competition in the shape of live American football games and *Ally McBeal*. The programme's cancellation came as a shock to many in the TV industry and prompted much speculation in the American broadcasting media about the real reasons why the show was scrapped. The consensus of journalistic opinion on the matter gravitated towards the contemplation of an ulterior motive behind CBS's decision: that hoary old chestnut, money.

Apparently, CBS had to pay Bochco Productions for episodes of *Brooklyn South*, and, in an effort to cut costs and promote their own self-produced shows, they opted to ditch it. Other shows bit the dust too, as the big American networks purged themselves of programmes devised by outside production companies in an attempt to make bigger profits. Ultimately, ratings didn't come into the equation: that old devil, Mammon, was up to his nefarious shenanigans again!

Regarded as a failure in terms of ratings and the fact that CBS pulled the plug on it, it's possible that the Beeb bought it cheap and decided to transmit it at an unreasonably late hour because they thought *Brooklyn South* might prove itself a primetime turkey over here. That's the only rationale I can perceive for its after midnight slot.

The Background

Set at the fictionalised 74th Station Precinct in the heart of Brooklyn in New York, *Brooklyn South* depicts the professional and personal lives of a group of uniformed street cops pounding the beat in one of the Big Apple's most racially diverse areas. It is therefore a highly volatile and potentially explosive location for the police, requiring diplomacy, prudence and self-conscious community policing. Subjects tackled in the first season included drug dealers, domestic violence, police brutality, homophobia and racism, family feuds, robbery, assault and more bizarre issues (a clown orgy occurs in one memorable episode!), all handled with an efficacious blend of pathos, humanity and humour. Indeed, as with Steven Bochco's other impressive works (*Hill Street Blues*, *LA Law* and *NYPD Blue*), *Brooklyn South* expertly combines intense and poignant dramatic scenes with moments of low-brow, bizarre humour. The contrast doesn't so much jar as reflect the perverse complexities and ironies of real life.

Like Bochco's previous police dramas, *Brooklyn South* boasts a prodigious ensemble cast and features believable characters, strong storylines, taut dialogue, a sizzling dramatic tension achieved by short, juxtaposed scenes, crisp editing and a probing, perpetually moving camera which brings a documentary feel to the proceedings. Likened to a modern *Hill Street Blues* by its co-creator, David Milch, he described Brooklyn South thus: "*Brooklyn South* is about cops [...] who engage with crime [...] just before it's about to occur, prevent a crime that's occurring, manage to keep it from getting worse – as opposed to detectives who are reactive and trying to solve a crime."

Courting Controversy

Prior to the transmission of *Brooklyn South*'s pilot episode, CBS ran a dramatic advertising trailer which incurred the wrath of the ever-vigilant American Family Association, a right-wing, Christian morality watchdog, due to what they perceived as its graphic violence. They insisted that CBS abort the show's premiere, which with its violence and strong language earned the distinction of a TV-MA rating in America (indicating that the show's content is designated for adults only). After the hullabaloo engendered by the pilot, the show was toned down and carried a TV-14 rating for future episodes.

Brooklyn South endured further controver-sy when the outspoken President of Brooklyn Borough, Howard Golden, berated the show's producer, Steven Bochco, for what he perceived as the programme's 'perpetuation of a myth' in its delineation of the area's inhabitants as people predisposed to violence and crime. Not content with firing a salvo at Bochco, an irate Golden implored New York's Mayor, Rudolph Giuliani, not to co-operate with *Brooklyn South*'s makers as regards location filming in the city, though the Mayor declined to get involved in what he regarded as an imposition of censorship. Ethnic groups also joined the fray and were deeply critical of *Brooklyn South*'s dearth of roles for actors from minority groups, a fact that was not lost on the programme makers given the alacrity with which African-American actor, Richard T. Jones, was introduced to the cast.

The Cast

Sgt Francis X. Donovan (Jon Tenney)
Handsome and fiercely intelligent, the station's popular duty sergeant is renowned for being tough but fair. He's genuinely concerned about the well-being of his fellow officers. A natural leader, Donovan sets standards by his unimpeachable behaviour. His consoling of Ann-Marie Kersey regarding the death of her detective boyfriend results in a nascent romantic entanglement. Significantly, the fact that Donovan is a reluctant informant of the IAB, recruited out of the Academy, adds a frisson of moral ambivalence to his identity.

Officer Jimmy Doyle (Dylan Walsh)
Boasting a muscular frame and chiselled features, Doyle is everyone's idea of a stand-up guy. Immensely likeable, pragmatic, resource-

ful, resilient and loyal, he's an idealist who really wants to make the world a better place. He attempts to let some criminals see their failings by teaching them a lesson they won't forget in a hurry (however the case of converting to the straight and narrow a teenage African-American boy who does drug-running for dope dealers ends in tragedy). Doyle will do what it takes to get the job done. He's paired with the mouthy Phil Rousakoff and hopes his shining example will transform an opinionated troublemaker into a decent cop. Doyle turned down a gold shield in order to keep patrolling the street.

Terry Doyle (Patrick McGaw)
Jimmy's younger brother who is following big brother's footsteps by studying at the Police Academy. However, Jimmy is compromised by an association with Irish mobsters via a moonlighting taxi-driving job he has taken up. He goes undercover to help secure the arrest of the gang and almost gets killed in a bank heist.

IAB Lieutenant Stan Jonas (James Sikking)
When the suspect, DeShawn Hopkins dies in custody in the pilot episode, the wily, po-faced Jonas (who's blessed with the visage of the grim reaper) arrives to investigate the death which has stirred up accusations of police brutality in the sensitive local African-American community. All the precinct's cops are wary of Jonas until he leaves the IAB to take up the post of station captain. Actor, James Sikking, who plays Jonas, was also a regular of *Hill Street Blues* (he played Lt Howard Hunter).

Officer Ann-Marie Kersey (Yancy Butler)
The girlfriend of one of officers downed in the DeShawn Hopkins incident who finds it increasingly difficult to cope with the demands of the job. In coming to terms with her loss, she is comforted by Donovan and confesses to him that she feels responsible for the death in custody of DeShawn Hopkins: apparently, she kicked Hopkins in the back when the unconscious gunman was left alone in a holding room awaiting medical care (the station coroner revealed that Hopkins was possible killed by a kick to the lumbar area).

Officer Jack Lowry (Titus Welliver)
Initially accused of inflicting a fatal blow to DeShawn Hopkins in custody but later exonerated by a tribunal. Lowry is experiencing traumatic marital problems – his wife, Yvonne, wants to live the highlife but her lifestyle incurs the burden of crippling financial debts. Things are compounded when Lowry also discovers his wife has been having an affair with another man. A coke-snorting, trampish nymphomaniac, Yvonne tries to exploit Lowry's troubles for financial gain by setting him up to confess to beating DeShawn Hopkins in front of a covert surveillance man from the media. Fortunately for Lowry, she becomes the victim of a RTA.

Officer Phil Roussakoff (Michael De Luise)
An arrogant new transfer to the station and teamed with Doyle: Roussakoff has problems with knowing when to shut up but settles in well and gets on fine with Doyle to the extent that Doyle sanctions the dating of his own sister.

Sgt Richard Santoro (Gary Basaraba)
The programme's most likeable character. He's tall, beefy and, in short, an imposing physical presence. Sure, Santoro can get tough when the job demands it, but more often than not he's a patient listener of

other's troubles and boasts a flair for diplomacy in sensitive situations. His jerk of a brother-in-law puts Santoro under suspicion by the IAB (Santoro was a guarantor for his brother-in-law's business premises which, unknown to him, has been a repository for stolen property).

Officer Nona Valentine (Klea Scott)
African-American female officer and Jack Lowry's partner.

Officer Hector Villanueva (Adam Rodriguez)
Young hispanic beat officer and partner of Clement Johnson.

Officer Clement Johnson (Richard T. Jones)
African-American officer who is often harassed by the black community for his joining the police force.

Cop Speak – An NYPD Lexicon

DOA: dead on arrival

hump: 1) your ass (He's gonna bust my hump over this petty crap?) or 2) a moron (That stupid hump scratched my car!)

juice: influence, i.e. some cops have lots of juice at other precincts when their friends get in trouble

reaching out: to provide help or contact

lawyering up: a suspect's decision to stop answering questions and ask for legal counsel

the house: station house

up/catching: baseball metaphors used to describe the system in which cases are assigned (Simone caught that murder in Chinatown because he was up)

bus: ambulance

BROOKLYN SOUTH: EPISODE GUIDE

1-1: 22 September 1997: Feature Length Pilot

1-2: 29 September 1997: Life Under Castro

1-3: 6 October 1997: Why Can't Even a Couple of Us Get Along

1-4: 13 October 1997: Touched by a Checkered Cab

1-5: 20 October 1997: Clown Without Pity

1-6: 3 November 1997: A Reverend Runs Through It

1-7: 10 November 1997: Love Hurts

1-8: 17 November 1997: Wild Irish Woahs

1-9: 24 November 1997: McMurder One

1-10: 8 December 1997: Dublin or Nuthin'

1-11: 12 January 1998:Gay Avec

1-12: 19 January 1998: Exposing Johnson

1-13: 26 January 1998: Tears On My Willow

1-14: 2 February 1998: Violet Inviolate

1-15: 23 February 1998: Fisticuffs

1-16: 2 March 1998: Don't Be My Valentine

1-17: 9 March 1998: Dead Man Sleeping

1-18: 16 March 1998: Fools Russian

1-19: 23 March 1998: Doggonit

1-20: 13 April 1998: Cinnamon Buns

1-21: 20 April 1998: Skells in a Cell

1-22: 27 April 1998: Queens for a Day

CCRB: Civilian Complaint Review Board

CSU: Crime Scene Unit

Dee Wee: phonetic for DWI, driving while intoxicated

DT: street slang for detective

EDP: emotionally disturbed person (politically correct version of 'psycho')

EMS: Emergency Medical Services, aka 'every minute sucks', underpaid, overworked and under-appreciated!

ESU: Emergency Services Unit

mope/mutt: unauthorised term for a 'perp'

Red Menace: unofficial term for City Fire Department

Rat Squad: Internal Affairs Bureau (IAB)

FAT: NYPD's Fugitive Apprehension Team

five-O: slang for cops

flying/to fly:
leaving one's usual precinct to fill in a shortage of manpower somewhere else

fudge-packer: homosexual male

(to) go down: getting arrested

good people:
NYPD compliment meaning kosher, nice, reliable (irrespective of race, sexual orientation)

gun run: search for a weapon reported sighted in the hands of a 'perp'

hit: tactical assault on a criminal location

MOS: member of the service (police officer), used on the radio

OC: organized crime

One PP: One Police Plaza, NYPD headquarters in downtown Manhattan

open carrier:
officer or police vehicle with open radio

package: escorted prisoner or VIP

paying the rent:
handing out a certain number of traffic summonses and moving violationsz

perp: perpetrator/criminal

Puzzle Palace: officer's term for OPP

rabbi: an individual's guide and guardian angel in the dept

rip: loss in pay due to disciplinary infraction such as unauthorised moonlighting.

RMP: Radio Mobile Patrol, the NYPD blue and white 'sector' car

sector: subdivision within a precinct, which covers several blocks (a sector car is assigned to patrol the area)

skel: police slang, short for skeleton, and describing what most drug users end up looking like:
also a derogatory term for lowlifes and vagrants:
also, according to *The City In Slang, New York Life and Popular Speech* by Irving Lewis Allen (1993), William Safire believes 'skell' is 'a shortening of skellum meaning rascal or thief', and akin to 'skelder' which means 'to beg on the streets and is now used in popular speech to denote the homeless'

SNAG: Special Narcotics and Guns Unit

SNEU: Special Narcotics Enforcement Unit

SOD: Special Operations Division

squad: short for Detective Squad, attached to specific precinct

TARU: Technical and Research Unit

tune up: describes rough treatment meted out by cops to a 'perp'

tunnel rats:
NYPD Transit Bureau (subway cops)

white shirts: lieutenants, who wear white uniform shirts

Sources

http://www.rememberingbrooklynsouth.com

http://home.akos.net/ kamala/bk-south.htm

http://annie.simplenet.com/bs.htm/

CRIME ON VIDEO

Barry Forshaw

Many would call it the most significant experiment in popular television ever made. Certainly, *The Prisoner* mystified audiences on its initial showing, but the influence of Patrick McGoohan's remarkable brainchild has continued to grow and grow, with a new Hollywood movie version in the offing. Ostensibly a sequel to McGoohan's taut and intelligent secret agent series *Danger Man*, the new series dealt with the same agent (never identified as *Danger Man's* John Drake, but audiences were allowed to draw their own conclusions) now called – against his will – Number Six, and finding himself in a surrealistic village, all false bonhomie, where a succession of sinister authority figures (always known as Number Two) endeavoured to find out why Number Six had tended his resignation. On the level of a brilliantly made adventure series, *The Prisoner* was non-pareil, but it was the surrealistic setting (the village

of Portmeirion made to look like something out of a science fiction nightmare) and the serious issues (identity, human relations) tackled within the series that gave it the reputation it quickly acquired – and which has grown ever since. Carlton Video's DVD reissue of the entire series begins very promisingly, with first-rate transfers presenting this classic TV venture in the best possible format. Carlton has also begun to issue *The Prisoner's* predecessor, *Danger Man*, but so far only the half-hour episodes. One can only hope that it isn't too long before they get around to the hour-long episodes of the latter, as these prefigure the later work in tone and intelligence. A very warm welcome for a much needed enterprise, and further proof that the DVD medium will soon have VHS on the run.

Warner Home Video continues to do sterling service for the crime genre – but as this is one of the mainstays of the cinema, it isn't too difficult to come up with some splendid movies. As Agatha Christie's reputation is recaptured from the doldrums into which it sank (critically rather than commercially, of course), Warner has come up with a batch of Christie movies. This is an interestingly varied bunch, from one of the best adaptations, the star-studded *Murder on the Orient Express*, to several of the charming Margaret Rutherford vehicles such as *Murder at the Gallop* (too much emphasis on comedy, but Rutherford is always eminently watchable). And there is Angela Lansbury's celebrated incarnation of Miss Marple in *The Mirror Crack'd*, with Peter Ustinov's eccentric Poirot represented by *Death on the Nile* and *Thirteen at Dinner*. But perhaps the most intriguing entry in this feast of Christie is *Agatha* with Dustin Hoffman and Vanessa Redgrave giving a possible solution to the author's famous brief disappearance. It's a shame that the very best film ever made from the author's work, Billy Wilder's *Witness for the Prosecution* (with the wonderful double act of Charles Laughton and Elsa Lanchester) isn't here to set the seal on a beguiling collection.

The career of controversial director Abel Ferrara has produced some extremely interesting work, as well as some seriously misconceived movies. Ferrara has tremendous energy, but little discipline, and his films work best when the former quality is able to sustain them. *Fear City* (MIA) is not among his most impressive work, but this strange and compelling film still commands the attention. Tom Berenger and

Melanie Griffiths rise above their recent indifferent performances to produce some remarkable work in this grim tale of a psychopath who mutilates his victims.

A considerable furore was created by the low-budget 'sleeper' *Henry: Portrait of a Serial Killer*, and the version that most people saw in this country was trimmed of its most disturbing elements (probably leading people to wonder what the fuss was all about). This was an intelligent, well-made movie dealing with a provocative subject, and if the sequel, *Henry: Portrait of a Serial Killer 2: Mask of Sanity* (Mosaic) is less likely to create a similar

AGATHA CHRISTIE'S
MURDER ON THE ORIENT EXPRESS

storm, that's probably due to the more relaxed climate we are currently enjoying (although such things are cyclical, and no doubt there's a newspaper or politician anxious to move us back to more censorious days). While this is a more straightforward film than the original, it is still a tense and powerfully acted work that cleverly plays on our expectations from the first film. The creative team is different to that of the earlier film, and this is, of course, accounts for the more fitful success of the sequel.

Talk about riding for a fall. When Mel Gib-

son remade the classic John Boorman/Lee Marvin movie *Point Blank* as *Payback*, it was inevitable that most critics would unite in saying how far superior the original movie was. But would anyone be foolish enough to remake the finest gangster movie ever made in this country, Mike Hodges' *Get Carter*, with Michael Caine at his very best as the cold-hearted anti-hero? Well, Sylvester Stallone has done it, and Caine has even lent his approval by appearing in the movie. But we hear that Stallone has given Carter a kind of redemption – and the whole point of the original movie is the bleakness of Carter's world: at the centre of which is its heartless hero. If you wish to remind yourself just how good the original was, here is the perfect opportunity: Warner have finally issued the movie on DVD (in the correct widescreen ratio, of course) and it is one of the most superlative transfers of a seventies movie yet to get the DVD treatment. The picture is crystal clear, the sound has a resonance and body that no previous incarnation of the film has had, and there is a host of extras for the DVD issue: an audio commentary from Mike Hodges and cinematographer Wolfgang Suschitzky, three trailers, Michael Caine's personal introduction to the film and Roy Budd's celebrated score. As audiences grow increasingly tired of the jokey approach to the British gangster film inaugurated by *Lock, Stock and Two Smoking Barrels*, it's time to remind ourselves just how good this movie was. Don't wait for Sylvester Stallone.

It's a cause for genuine regret that the Warner animated series of *Batman* has never been treated with any kind of respect in this country. Chopped up and shown in braindead Kiddie TV shows, it's clear that no producer has ever looked at how adult and intelligent these episodes are (far more, for instance, than the last Batman live-action movie), and only the Cartoon Network has shown many of the episodes uncut. The follow-up series, *Batman of the Future* (Warner), lacks the dark and brooding quality of the earlier series (which clearly showed the influence of the grim Tim Burton movie vision, even re-using Danny Elfman's pounding symphonic theme from the first film), but this series is still well worthwhile. Featuring a young protege of Bruce Wayne's in a superpowered suit (sans cape), the series is still rich with invention and wit. But quite its cleverest coup is featuring an ageing and crusty Bruce Wayne, directing his impetuous young follower electronically from the dark confines of Wayne mansion. The contrast between the old guru and the inexperienced acolyte (the latter inevitably inclined to screw things up) is always a safe theme in fiction, and so it proves here. The latest volume, *Spellbound*, features episodes of varying quality, but at its best it is highly diverting, even if *Batman: The Animated Series* remains the finest achievement in this field.

How long will it last? The current liberalisation of film censorship is very welcome, and who could argue if fewer restrictions for adults mean a few more for children? The new climate has inspired one distributor, Tartan Video, to initiate a unique offer: they are planning to replace censored copies of the films at half price. Welcoming the BBFC's move to liberalise classification standards for 18-category films, they applaud that fact that over eighteens will finally be treated as responsible adults with free choice over what they want to watch. But as Tartan is a company with a real knowledge of the products they sell, they are keen to be able to offer films in versions the director intended. To this end, they have asked the BBFC to re-classify all their previously censored films. Under more realistic guidelines, the uncut versions will be available for the first time ever in the UK. Owners of previously censored Tartan video films will be able to send the tapes to the company's offices and receive the new uncut versions for half price, as they become available. The returned tapes will be donated to charities promoting civil liberties. We'll report in this column when the offer begins. Pessimist that I am, though, I'm sure a politician wishing to make a name for himself will soon step into the arena and plead for greater censorship. After all, neither of the main political parties has shown anything but a nanny-ish attitude to what adults may watch.

While Carlton TV may not be exactly a byword for the very best the medium has to offer, its video arm is a repository for some really interesting material, such as the simultaneous DVD and VHS release of *The Remorseful Day*, the final film in Colin Dexter's long-running (and highly successful) Inspector Morse series. This has all the authority and interest of the series at its very best (not to mention John Thaw's definitive portrayal of the morose, opera-loving cop), and, of course, there is something about it which makes it different from all other episodes in the series. If you haven't seen it, it would be a shame to remind you of that.

THE VERDICT

Cry of the Panther by Adam Armstrong
Bantam, £9.99, 0-5930-4682-X

One of the most stimulating aspects of Adam Armstrong's début novel *Cry of the Panther* is the impossibility of fitting the book into any genre. This is a tale at once epic and personal, stunningly realistic and magical, literary and popular in style. At the centre are two brilliantly drawn protagonists, struggling with their unfulfilled lives, who we follow from childhood to the adventure and the relationship that they find themselves in as adults. Imogen is eight years old when she offers to guide the rescue searchers looking for her lost brother – even though she is unable to comprehend her mysterious vision of the search that leads into the heart of the American wilderness. Her brother's best friend, Connla, also joins the group, but when they find the lost boy he has been drowned. Thirty years later in Scotland, Imogen is still attempting to come to terms with the strange mystery of her brother's death. Unable to enjoy relationships, she finds solace in the beauty of the Scottish landscape, so different from the America of her youth, but equally stunning. Connla, too, has been unable to adjust to the world of men and lives in a Thoreau-like solitude in a cabin in the wilderness. His way of recording the natural beauty

of the world (as Imogen does through paintings) is with a camera. Newspaper reports that a rare wild beast – the eponymous panther –, has been seen results in a massive odyssey that will bring the two together – as well as finally resolving the truth about their mutual childhood tragedy. There are elements of Latin American magic realism here, but Armstrong's evocative narrative is princi-

A passionate novel of love, hope
and the power of nature

CRY OF THE
PANTHER
ADAM ARMSTRONG

pally a voyage of self-discovery for his two tormented protagonists. Rarely does the author put a foot wrong in marrying his intensely physical epic with the seething inner lives of his characters.

Eve Tan Gee

The Chinese Girl by John Baker
Gollancz, £9.99, 0-575-07016-1
Slowly but surely, John Baker's series featuring the tenacious Sam Turner has acquired much favourable word-of-mouth, with *Poet in the Gutter* and *Death Minus Zero* nosing ahead in the popularity stakes. Baker strikes out at a tangent in *The Chinese Girl*, with a narrative so rich with menace and atmosphere that we don't miss Turner. Released from jail, Stone Lewis is trying to change his

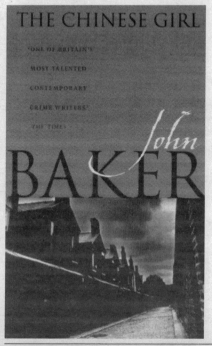

wasted life into something positive. Ill-advised tattoos on his face have people shying away from him as he wanders the outside world, and when he finds a battered Asian girl in the doorway of his insalubrious basement room, it isn't long before he's firmly back in the dangerous morass that he'd try to escape. We've read a million versions of the ex-con pulled back unwillingly into the criminal world before, but rarely delivered with the exuberance that Baker demonstrates here. He's also particularly skilful at marrying the disparate worlds of the American tough-guy thriller with the English novel of cold-eyed social observation. The cleverest trick here is making the non-tattooed reader identify so closely with the hapless Lewis, and we follow his dangerous odyssey with total attention. The danger is offset with Baker's trademark wit, and many readers will be more than happy with this accomplished break from the Sam Turner series.

Brian Ritterspak

Afraid to Death by Marc Behm
No Exit Press, £6.99, 1-901982-65-3
The French loved American pulp fiction and film noir because they felt it reflected, usually unwittingly (which pleased their aesthetic prejudices) their own Existential world-view. This got refined into the French new wave (novels and films by the likes of Robbe-Grillet and Goddard) which took many of the elements of American genre fiction and stripped it of everything but its bare narration. We can argue the relative artistic success of such work until the semioticians come home to roost, but in *Afraid To Death* what we have is the next step, the existential novel reduced to thriller motifs. Originally published in French in 1991, this is Marc Behm's companion piece

to *Eye of the Beholder*, which lent itself famously to a stylish, substance-free neo-cultish mini-hit movie, so cool it had a sketch of an eye instead of 'eye' in the title. Like *Eye of the Beholder*, *Afraid to Death* is primarily a road story, where the same danger keeps recurring, with the protagonist helpless to stop it, at least in part because he seems to be bringing it on himself. Life is like that, as Sartre might have said if he were a contestant in Big Brother. If you've a fondness for your metaphors big and your style worn upfront, you'll like Behm a lot. Even if you don't, you might enjoy the trip anyway.

Michael Carlson

Nark by John Burns
Pan, £5.99, 0-330-37247-5

With so many hard-bitten heroes vying for readers' attention, John Burns' Max Chard series has formidable obstacles to overcome. But the reason this witty and inventive sequence works so well is that Burns' tabloid hack is such a fully rounded anti-hero. Packing his books with highly credible Fleet Street background and mixing this into pleasingly skewed thriller plots is a formula that is paying dividends. When Max learns that his newspaper has decided to buy the story of a woman and her boyfriend who are hiding in protective custody, Max finds himself having to deal with the gang involved, who have netted £5 million from a safe deposit robbery. But soon bodies begin to fall, and Max is sent to the couple's secret hideaway to get the low-down on them. Needless to say, there are elements (such as the sexually available blonde Cindy Reilly) that convince Max that nothing is as it seems. A particular pleasure of Burns' books is the way the humour arises from the always plausible plotting: however

outrageous, the authenticity of the hack's life always persuades us to accept the unlikely goings-on. Max remains a character that the reader is more than happy to spend time with: we wouldn't want to be him, but we enjoy every moment of his at-the-edge lifestyle with relish. The pacing, too, is handled with the skill of a master, and as Max comes closer and closer to the solution, there is subtly concealed acceleration – no set-pieces, but solidly realised tension.

Judith Gray

Spike by John Burns
Macmillan, £16.99, 0-333-77951-7

Max Shard is back, and it's a real pleasure to reacquaint ourselves with John Burns' cynical Fleet Street hack. As before, the authenticity

JOHN BURNS

'A sharp and snappy plot keeps action at the forefront of this lively novel.'

THE TIMES

of the writing makes the plots really leap off the page, and Max is the perfect guide through a dark and blackly comic world. Max Chard finds himself doing what a Chief Crime Correspondent is rarely expected to do: spy on a young woman through her bedroom window. But his editor has received a tabloid tip that a Labour MP (with a previously unblemished reputation) is enjoying a little extra-conjugal pleasure. Max is mentally composing his headline when he sees the MP leave the mews house in the early hours, and he spots a mysterious figure dressed in black also loitering. Soon Max has a whole suitcase of questions: why is his editor reluctant to run the scoop? Why is the MP's mistress reported missing the next day? And who is the figure in black? When the body of the young woman is found at the bottom of nearby cliffs in the MP's constituency, Max starts to realise that adultery is only one part of the story. Again, the impressive trick of marrying the investigative reporter detail with a solid crime narrative is brought off with aplomb. Of course, Max is more than a simple hack: questions of honour and commitment are subtly mixed into the murky brew here, but never at the expense of a powerful piece of storytelling. But the emphasis is always satisfyingly on the steadily unfolding revelations – and there are some choice ones on offer here.

Judith Gray

The Stollenberg Legacy by Brian Callison
HarperCollins, £16.99, 0-00-225972-9
While his name may not yet possess the currency of more familiar practitioners, many readers now recognise Brian Callison as one of the most accomplished adventure writers this country can boast, with his fellow scribes happy to present laurels. The jacket of this new book may suggest a dotty tome on Egyptian mysticism, but this is a riveting piece of maritime action with a fifty-year-old mystery at its centre. Among the legends of the Second World War, the myth of the Stollenberg Convoy was one of the most memorable. Orders were sent out as the Third Reich collapsed to disperse the countless looted treasures across the globe, with the most valued (and mysterious) item entrusted to SS Colonel Manfred Stollenberg. It never arrived. Merchant sailor Michael Kyle becomes interested in the case via his historian flatmate David McDonald. But McDonald dies in a strange accident, and Kyle's reluctance to accept the official explanation soon embroils him in a highly dangerous situation with the eponymous legacy at its centre. Kyle is strongly characterised, and the pacing has all the energy we expect from this author. It goes

without saying that the nautical detail has all the requisite salty authenticity.

Barry Forshaw

The Big Squeeze by Jim Cirni
Soho Crime, £7.99, 1-569470-58-8
Jim Cirni has brought the language and the feel of the pulp novels of the early 1960s to life in this tale of small-time hood 'Dip' Dippolito, who wants to get out of the rackets for a peaceful life with his girlfriend, but finds himself caught in the centre of mob warfare after he takes a bullet meant for his boss's son.

The fact that the son is a no-good, who lacks respect for his father, merely complicates matters, as turf wars reminiscent of the legendary Gallo/Profaci feud break out and threaten to catch Dip smack dab in the middle. Throw in a test of loyalty to his best friend, and you've got a classic film noir scenario, written in prose lean enough to remind you of Dan Marlowe or Day Keene. That's pretty high praise these days, when everyone's trying to capture the magic of pulp fiction without understanding the spareness which is at its very centre. Cirni understands. He builds the story carefully, he tells it in the tone of the characters themselves, and it works. He catches the contradictions, the weaknesses and doubts below the surface, the pettiness and the ever-present randomness of violence which grow out of small time dreams. This is a strong novel, and would be a natural for development as a screenplay. In Hollywood they'd be lining up to play Dip.

Michael Carlson

Broken by Martina Cole
Headline, £9.99, 0-7472-7752-4
The amazing success of all Martina Cole's crime novels must be a source of despair to those writers who have struggled for years. Right from the start, she has enjoyed unqualified approval for her distinctive and powerfully written fiction. Even the workaday TV adaptations of *Dangerous Lady* and *The Jump* merely brought more kudos her way (she's been less lucky than Colin Dexter in her transfer to the screen – but she should worry). A child is abandoned in a deserted stretch of woodland and another on the top of a derelict building. DI Kate Burrows makes the inevitable connections, and when one child dies, she finds herself up against a killer utterly without scruples. Her lover Patrick offers support in this troubling case, but he is under pressure himself. A body is found in his Soho club, and Patrick himself is on the line as a suspect. And Kate begins to doubt him... In prose that is always expressive and trenchant, Cole weaves her spell throughout this lengthy

and ambitious narrative. Kate is an exuberantly characterised heroine, and the sardonic Patrick enjoys equally felicitous handling from the author. Another winner for Cole.

Brain Ritterspak

Blood Mud by K. C. Constantine
No Exit Press, £6.99, 1-901982-81-5
Mario Balzic has retired as police chief of Rockburg, Pennsylvania. He's working part-time as an insurance investigator, and, while investigating a theft from a gun shop, he has a 'cardiac episode'. As he recovers, and pursues his investigation, he finds that he is no longer in a position to accomplish everything he thinks should be accomplished, and he has to come to terms with that. Oh, you think, another character dealing with age, and as far as that thought goes, you would be right. But *Blood Mud* is also about the way times

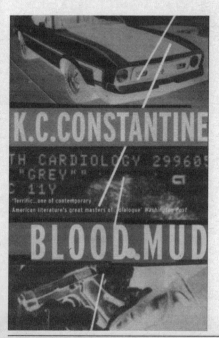

have changed, the way our profit- and media-driven society has let the corruptions which always existed but were kept in check by unwritten laws and common agreement, simply take over and do what they will. In that it reminds me of George Higgins' *A Change of Gravity*, although Constantine's focus is more intensely personal than Higgins'. Constantine makes Balzic face the very real fear of aging and death, and the key to the novel is the way he has to adjust both to his own mortality and its effect on the rest of his family, maybe for the first time in his life. The various strands of the theft, which lead to murder, are resolved (in a fashion) but the point is made clearly that their resolution is somehow less important to the life of a man, even a retired police chief, than his coming to terms with himself. It's a bravura bit of writing, maybe the best of a fine series.

Michael Carlson

Demolition Angel by Robert Crais
Orion, £12.99, 0-752-83217-4
About three-quarters of the way through this novel, I felt my reading slowing down. The plot was beginning to change gears as things moved toward resolution, but I was enjoying things so much I was in no hurry to get to the end. I confess this without embarrassment, because in his first non-Elvis Cole, close on the heels of *LA Requiem* (which was the best of the Cole books), Robert Crais has delivered. Crais once wrote on *Cagney & Lacey,* but there's little of either cop in his bomb squad officer, Carol Starkey. She's a cop whose toughness masks a basic fear inside herself, and she has to overcome that fear in order to cope with Mr Red the bomber's bomber. She also has to cope with the LA police bureaucracy, and, as a part of it, isn't free to Elvis Cole

'We can now add the name Crais to the pantheon of great American writers' SUNDAY TIMES

Black. Let's hope that character survives intact when the film, which Crais is scripting, appears. Read the book. See the movie. Hope it doesn't bomb. (Sorry about that one.)

Michael Carlson

Into the Fire by Linda Davies
HarperCollins, £6.99, 0-00-651188-0
It doesn't take too much work to imagine the film rights for Linda Davies' third novel becoming hot property: exotic locations, high finance scams and a powerful, attractive female lead. Helen Jencks is the City high-flyer turned into a Nick Leeson figure behind her back. Aided by an ageing security services spook, she flees to Peru, leading in turn to more danger and a dangerous liaison in the jungles and shanty towns. As her vengeance

and wisecrack her way around it. The story is built carefully, with a second, shadow plot moving beneath the chase for Mr Red, and in the process Crais delivers a fascinating slice of life cut from the internet world of bomb freaks. It's not a pleasant sight, but it's one which sets the tone for all the characters on both sides of the law, what the professors out there on their edu computers might celebrate as a 'sub-culture'. Crais would put the emphasis firmly on the 'sub'. Is it some sort of coincidence that the best of the LA series detective writers, Michael Connelly and Crais, have both produced non-series books with strong female leads? If so we can only be thankful. It is interesting that, in the same sense that a Hollywood star might prefer to play Elvis Cole rather than tackle the darker side of Harry Bosch, Carol Starkey's upfront aggression might be more of a challenge than Cassie

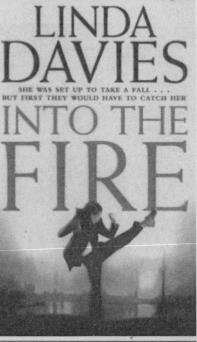

LINDA DAVIES

SHE WAS SET UP TO TAKE A FALL . . .
BUT FIRST THEY WOULD HAVE TO CATCH HER

INTO THE FIRE

is sweetly dished out to sleazy traders, extracting herself from the clutches of the charming yet sinister Maldonado proves more difficult. Indeed, Maldonado's very presence provides a key to one of the book's recurrent themes, that of the sins of the father – real or imagined – being continually revisited on the present. The novel has a peculiarly uneven feel to it. Its Peruvian scenes seem staid and predictable, despite the three years spent there by the author. Likewise, the secretive shenanigans conducted within British Intelligence owe more to sub-Bond action adventures than to Le Carré's business-like observations of 'the Firm' at work. Such chapters unfold side by side with sharp insights into the financial markets, including a comprehensible crash-course in the workings of derivatives markets. Here the characters are finely drawn, from shady maths genius Hugh Wallace to security guru Michael Freyn, despite the occasional lapse into Bridget Jones-style dinner party moans and culinary product placement. A riveting and frustrating beach read.

Graham Barnfield

The Empty Chair by Jeffery Deaver
Hodder and Stoughton, £10.00, 0-340-76748-0
The Empty Chair is Deaver's latest novel concerning Lincoln Rhyme, a renowned criminologist whose quadriplegia does nothing to confine his brilliant mind and somewhat abrasive personality. Figuratively kicking his heels in North Carolina awaiting experimental surgery to restore some of his lost mobility, Rhyme is asked by a local sheriff to help in tracking down a disturbed youngster named Garrett Hanlon. Hanlon, known to the locals as the Insect Boy and already suspected of involvement in two suspicious deaths, has

apparently murdered a promising young student and abducted two women, disappearing into the depths of the treacherous swamps. Rhyme brings to the case both his exceptional talent for the analysis of physical evidence, and his equally brilliant partner and sometime lover, Detective Amelia Sachs. Rhyme and Sachs track the fugitive boy through the swamps whilst avoiding the murderous attention of an unofficial posse, but things go dangerously wrong when Sachs abruptly switches sides and becomes the hunted. She is convinced that the Insect Boy is innocent of the crimes, but Rhyme must reluctantly turn his investigative gaze on his erstwhile partner. One theme running through the novel is that Rhyme and Sachs are 'fishes out of water' away from their usual New York haunts, and ironically Deaver also seems a little unsure of

THE NEW LINCOLN RHYME THRILLER

The EMPTY CHAIR

Jeffery DEAVER

'The best psychological thriller writer around'
THE TIMES

himself in the North Carolina setting. Although he has a superb feel for the geography and unique terrain of the Tar Heel State, he trades a little too much on Southern stereotypes, from vicious rednecks to shady good ol' boy businessmen. For instance, the local cops are suitably hostile to the Yankee outsiders, and range from mildly incompetent at best to corrupt and dangerous. The plot sometimes seems a little predictable and wrapped up a little neatly at the end, although *The Empty Chair* certainly contains some terrific plot twists and moments of uncertainty for the reader. Rhyme can appear a little too omniscient at times, and the character of Amelia, former model, brilliant detective and crack-shot, tends to grate occasionally. That having been said, Deaver certainly still knows how to crank up the tension and certainly delivers the goods. Although not one of Deaver's best, *The Empty Chair* is still an extremely entertaining read and fans of Deaver will find much to enjoy here.

Dan Staines

Thanksgiving by Michael Dibdin
Faber and Faber, £12.99, 0-571-20484-8
Versatility is vital in all the arts. The badge (or logo) of Thalia the Muse of Theatre is the masks of Comedy and Tragedy. The most prolific crime writers, Christie, Carr, Gardner, Simenon and my esteemed colleague Gwendoline Butler, have all created several detectives, and in comedy P. G. Wodehouse created a galaxy of strong characters. The first books of Dibdin were clever pastiches. The ingenious *A Rich Full Death* has Robert Browning as a sleuth, *The Dying of the Light* was almost a Christie look-alike. Then came the much-acclaimed Aurelio Zen series. Now this book, *Thanksgiving*, is a short volume of 178 pages

divided into sections: Lucy in the Sky (shades of the Beatles), Not Here, Window or Aisle?, Here Comes the Night, Thanksgiving Day. The narrator is a journalist – we are not told a great deal about his literary gifts, but judging from his mental attitude, they don't amount to much. His wife dies, he is heartbroken, so he goes to see her unpleasant first husband in Nevada, a two-faced individual. On the way back he nearly gets mixed up with a grubby, tough prostitute. First husband found shot with narrator's gun. Police and family enquiries. Chapters of flashback memories. Killer apparently untraced. What are the influences for this oddly compelling story? Russian writers of gloom are mentioned, so they might be partly to blame: there are echoes of the 1940s American and 1960s French films, with dream sequences, joined

(or separated) by a Joycean 'stream of consciousness'. Not really a crime or mystery, just a weak man behaving weakly. Apply the Hitchcock syndromes. First, what will happen to the characters three weeks after the finish? The narrator will be living in his parents' home in France, doing nothing. Secondly, the icebox syndrome. Half an hour after you finish reading the book, start wondering how the end was contrived. Did he kill the first husband, and not include this in his disjointed reminiscences? Who inherits the two estates? Does his family trust him or not? Dibdin presumably wrote this to prove he could, and readers will be keen to see if he's brought off the trick.

John Kennedy Melling

Noir Fiction: Dark Highways
by Paul Duncan
Pocket Essentials, £2.99, 1-903047-11-0
One of the problems in dealing with the world of noir is trying to define it: in the past decade the terms pulp and hard-boiled have been used as if all three were interchangeable, and used to cover everything from stylistic exercises in cheap laddish violence to standard works that might be defined by that awful British term 'tec. Paul Duncan is a noir purist: he traces the dark highways of the genre of gloom back through the French, heavily influenced by existentialism in their perceptions of fictions that mix American heroes with Europe's gothic sensibility. He's better at tracing the European roots, the 'emotionally untouchable' American hero predates cowboys, as D. H. Lawrence noted in his analysis of Cooper's Deerslayer. Likewise he misses Hemingway's earliest work (eg *In Our Time)*, which is heavily influenced by Gertrude Stein and by journalism, and pre-

dates even Hammett. This is not a major problem, because the path Duncan follows, which leads us from Dostoyevsky and Conrad (again, without reference to their work being predated by Hawthorne, Melville, and Poe) to Ellroy and Derek Raymond, is an idiosyncratic one: if we might want to argue the nature of the absurdity in the theatre of the absurd, it is instructive to see Nathanael West linked with Cain and McCoy, or Camus with Bardin and Woolrich. It's also valuable to have re-evaluations of important but now ignored figures like Gerald Kersh, and, in my case, to be introduced to Boris Vian or Shane Stevens. A major reference for Duncan was Charles Willeford's *New Forms of Ugly*, a master's thesis published only in a small press limited edition. From the summary, Willeford's definition of the classic noir protagonist ('the Immobilised Man') would suggest that Ralph Ellison's *Invisible Man* be considered as a noir classic. This book represents the best of what the Pocket Essentials series can be: concise, coherent, and provocative, without getting lost in theory or rhetoric; a starting point for further debate and research. Now it's time to make Willeford's thesis available again, what better place than in this series?

Michael Carlson

Shattered by Dick Francis
Michael Joseph, £16.99, 0-7181-4453-8
Few writers can lay claim to having made a genre entirely their own, but the racing thriller remains unassailably Dick Francis territory. And with *Shattered*, as smoothly crafted a piece of entertainment as anything he has produced, we're reminded that despite various pretenders to the throne (several being ex-jockeys like Francis), he retains his crown – even the recent kerfuffle regarding the

authorship of his books (his wife having apparently lent a hand at times) has only increased his profile, with readers seemingly indifferent to this revelation. What is his secret? Actually, the Francis phenomenon is based on several elements: primarily, of course, it's the author's finely honed narrative skills that immediately marked him out as a master entertainer – thrillers such as *Rat Race*, *Smokescreen* and *Trail Run* bristled with an energy and momentum that made most UK thriller writers seem workaday by comparison. But Francis' ace in the hole, of course, is the sense he conveys to the reader that his books are the perfect entrée into the world of racing: that satisfying sense of insider knowledge gives the plot, however implausible (as they often are), a shining patina of authenticity. *Shattered* once again conveys that the equestrian world is quite as dangerous as Colin Dexter's Groves of Academe: jockey

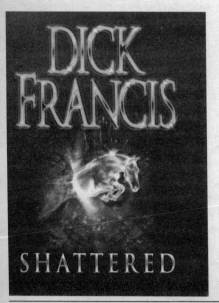

Martin Stukely dies after a fall in a steeplechase at Cheltenham races, and his friend, artist Gerald Logan, finds that the dead man has a connection to a stolen videotape with mysterious (and highly valuable) contents. Logan is more familiar with the problems of glass-blowing than violence and extortion, but he is soon undergoing a crash course in survival techniques as some very malignant heavies target him. Francis has broadened his canvas with this one (his protagonist being only peripherally connected with the racing world), and this has resulted in a signal recharging of the batteries. The lean, unfussy narrative has the customary race-to-the-tape motion, but Logan is a nicely judged semi-hero, convincingly at sea (as most of us would be) in very dangerous waters.

Eve Tan Gee

The Mile High Club by Kinky Friedman
Faber & Faber, £5.99, 0-571-20379-5
Friedman remains one of the quirkiest and most original writers working in what might loosely be called the crime genre. His unorthodox plotting, unique characters and (most of all) cheerfully black humour mark out his work as quite unlike that of any other practitioner. This latest opus is his most demented yet, with his protagonist (curiously, also called Kinky) up against a series of mystifying problems. Meeting a beautiful woman on a plane, Kinky finds himself holding her pink imitation leather suitcase when she suddenly disappears. But is he fated to meet the beguiling Khadija Kejela again? Soon, Friedman's bemused hero finds himself mixed up with Arab terrorists, Israeli counter-agents and sinister State Department officials all mixing it in Kinky's Vandam Street loft in search of passports missing from that pink leather

suitcase. And the one area in which Friedman pays tribute to his illustrious literary predecessors is in his treatment of his alluring *femme fatale*: Khadija is (of course) not what she seems to be, and Kinky is fated to rue the day he met her – not least when he's abducted by ruthless Islamic terrorists. As usual, the first-person narration is impeccably handled, with the one-liners delivered with customary aplomb. If the freshness of earlier Kinkster outings isn't present, there's the pleasure of spending time with an old friend – and Friedman is someone it's always good to meet up with again. Best of all, he's still able to juxtapose the laughs and the thrills with a masterly hand – an area in which so many writers come unstuck.

Brian Ritterspak

The Kingdom of Shadows by Alan Furst
Orion, £16.99, 0-575-06837-X

Told with Ambler-like precision, *Kingdom of Shadows* is the sixth installment of Furst's set of spy novels covering the years leading up to and during World War Two. This time we're in bohemian Paris prior to the occupation, where we follow the clandestine life of former Hungarian cavalry officer Nicholas Morath. Moving between Parisian bars and restaurants and travelling by train and car to Juan-des-Pins, Slovakia, Sudetenland and Hungary, where he rescues an assortment of misfits, Morath is employed by his mysterious uncle, Polanyi. While Nicholas does the thankless legwork, his uncle hobnobs with SS renegades seeking to overthrow Hitler who they believe cannot win the war, Abwehr intelligence officers, British politicians of various political persuasions and an assortment of defectors. Kept in the dark about the nature of his work, Morath finds that every shadow casts another shadow, and every plot has yet another twist to it. As usual in a Furst novel, the story unfolds in a series of vignettes. One is reminded of not only Ambler and Graham Greene, but those haunting 1940s spy movies about an era when people suddenly realised that, to cite a quotation in the book by novelist Joseph Roth, "We overestimated the world." The reader, like the protagonist, is kept in the dark regarding what is happening, which only adds to the mystery. Scrupulously researched with some wonderfully drawn characters, Furst knows his subject, and, as a writer, is easily the equal of Kerr, Harris and Le Carré. Read these novels and hear the clash of ideologies at a time when everyday life was often filled with acts of heroism. This is Euro-espionage-noir at its best.

Woody Haut

And another view...

It must be daunting for an author to be compared Graham Greene, John Le Carré and Robert Harris, but Alan Furst's much acclaimed sequence of novels set during the 1930s and World War Two unquestionably demonstrate the virtues of his predecessors: brilliantly detailed backgrounds in which the periods involved are faultlessly conjured up; highly impressive plotting and (his ace in the hole) characterisation that has all the richness and complexity of the very best writers. With *Kingdom of Shadows*, Furst moves his writing on to yet another level: the sense of danger and foreboding that informs this tale of intrigue and betrayal brings back for the reader the all too rare rush of excitement that only the finest novels in this field can convey. It's 1938, and a sinister tide of Fascism is growing in strength throughout Europe. Ex-cavalry officer Nicholas Morath (originally from Hungary) returns to his young mistress in Paris' Seventh Arrondisement. He has been helping his uncle Count Janos Polanyi, a diplomat, in his attempt to stop Hungary drifting into an allegiance with Nazi Germany. But this is a very dangerous game for Morath and his uncle, involving double dealing between defectors, SS renegades and British politicians. And as Hitler marches into Prague, Morath's foolhardy country-hopping endeavours grow ever more dangerous. On the level of a highly intelligent espionage tale, Furst demonstrates a masterly command of the idiom, with Polanyi's dangerous odysseys between the Czech fortresses of the Sudeten mountains and the villas of Budapest handled in an utterly authoritative fashion. From the author of *Night Soldiers* and *Dark Star* we have come to expect no less than a definitive treatment of the apparatus of the adventure novel. But (of course) there is much more to Furst's achievement than this, considerable though it is. The driving force behind his narrative is always the struggles within the souls of his characters, and the way the human spirit can survive under the most appalling conditions. Morath, in particular, is drawn with all the complexity and insight that has become Furst's trademark, and we follow his journeys with ever mounting concern.

Brain Ritterspak

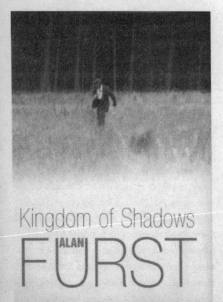

Kingdom of Shadows
ALAN
FURST

Undercurrents by Frances Fyfield
Little, Brown & Co., £9.99, 0-316-85387-9
Frances Fyfield is now universally acclaimed as one of this country's finest crime writers, with a depth of psychological understanding quite the equal of the previously unassailable duo of P. D. James and Ruth Rendell. The intense and expressive quality of her prose illumi-

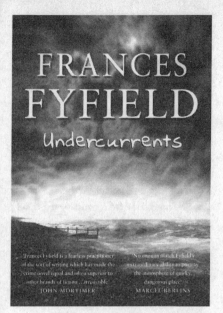

FRANCES
FYFIELD

Undercurrents

'Frances Fyfield is a fearless practitioner of the sort of writing which has made the crime novel equal and often superior to other brands of fiction ... irresistible'
JOHN MORTIMER

'No one can match Fyfield's extraordinary ability to portray the atmosphere of quirky, dangerous place.'
MARCEL BERLINS

nates narratives that both celebrate traditional storytelling values and explode them. With such books as *Shadows in the Mirror* and *Staring at the Light*, she has consolidated an already distinctive reputation. But her latest book, *Undercurrents*, may well be the most disturbing yet. In the past, some male readers may have been discomforted by her recurring preoccupation with male violence against women, but Henry Evans, the protagonist of this novel, is the perfect conduit for both the male and female reader into a truly mesmerising narrative. When Henry was backpacking around India some twenty years before, he encountered the beguiling Francesca Chisholm. Francesca's father died, and Henry's reluctance to alter his travel plans obliged her to leave without him. For all of his adult life, he has regretted this decision with a keen sense of loss, and finally resolves to travel to the English coastal town of War-

bling (the name is the book's only miscalculation) to track her down. But Henry is in for a shock. It's a very wet February, and his hotel is flooded, so he is obliged to stay at a strange alternative hostel called, inappropriately, The House of Enchantment. The solicitor who knew Francesca suggests that he regard her as dead, but Henry persists. He discovers that Francesca has confessed to killing her five-year-old son, drowning him in the sea (hence the dual meaning of the title). She is imprisoned, and the case appears to be closed. But is it? Henry decides to find out precisely what happened. And his scarifying odyssey into the dark night of the soul – both his and hers – is something he finds himself unprepared for. Like all of the finest crime novels, Fyfield adroitly presents her protagonist (and the reader) with an implacable mystery – but the solving of this mystery is no mechanical trick, as it so often was in the golden age of crime fiction. The journey Henry undertakes will change him forever, and the insights into the troubled Francesca's psyche are as rich and profound as anything in literary fiction. As always with this author, the characters are fastidiously created, and the taut structure of the plot is accentuated by the relative brevity of her narrative. Some may wish for a longer book, but there isn't a wasted word here, and anyone in doubt as to Fyfield's position in the pantheon of English crime writing should not hesitate.

Ralph Travis

That Sleep Of Death by Philip Gooden
Constable Robinson, £6.99, 1-84119-146-9
Have you read *Hamlet*? If so, you should enjoy this novel set in the world of Shakespeare's players. If not, then you may struggle to pick up references scattered liberally

That
Sleep of Death
Philip Gooden

An Elizabethan murder mystery
featuring Shakespearean player Nick Revill

the main story, narrated by Revill. There are also echoes of Dickens, particularly in a boat chase on the Thames which has suggestions of Magwitch's flight in *Great Expectations*. Philip Gooden obviously intends to develop a series character and has made a promising start here. By confining Shakespeare to a walk-on role he produces a greater degree of authenticity in his setting. He also includes many little details of a player's life (such as only having your own part written down) showing he has researched Elizabethan theatre. The one false note is struck by the character of Nell the whore – perhaps he should follow Dickens in disposing of little Nell before she becomes too nauseating!

Anne Curry

Gravedigger by Joseph Hansen
No Exit Press, £4.99, 1-874061-83-1
The tough, witty and idiomatic writing of Joseph Hansen has made his Brandstetter series of detective novels among the most cherishable in the genre. In swift-moving and concise narratives, Hansen takes us through brightly-lit Californian backdrops of ritzy seaside resorts and snowbound mountain camps, where evil deeds are done. Here, Charles Westover, a disbarred lawyer, files an insurance claim after he alleges that his missing teenage daughter has been murdered. But tenacious claims investigator Dave Brandstetter is soon applying his well-honed skills, and finds that young women appear to have been murdered by the fanatical guru of a sinister cult. Perhaps this is what happened to Serenity, Westover's daughter. But Dave finds it isn't quite that simple. While the plot may echo a situation in Ross MacDonald's masterly *The Moving Target* – and we've met an awful lot of frightening cult leaders, (both on the

throughout the book. Nick Revill, a young actor, is hired by the Chamberlain's Men – whose playwright is William Shakespeare. After helping to prevent an injustice, Nick is recruited to observe the Eliot household where a young man's father has recently died and his mother has swiftly married her husband's brother. Notice any parallels yet? Nick is soon trying to juggle his duties as a minor member of the players with his suspicions of the most mysterious of that company – a certain Mr W. S. The book has much in common with the film *Shakespeare in Love* – full of colourful stock characters such as boatmen with foul language, creepy apothecary and tart with a heart who provides her services free to Revill. Despite these dramatic stereotypes, the book has an underlying darkness which is emphasised by the narrative device of the murderer interjecting his thoughts into printed page and off), Hansen is, as always, his own man. Many novels three or four times as long as this are unable to cram in as many colourfully drawn characters and sharply delineated situations, while Brandstetter remains a memorable protagonist, and a worthy heir to Spade and Marlowe. As always, the witty dialogue is a particular plus, and the powerfully orchestrated finale is brought off with real aplomb.

Judith Gray

The Big Thaw by Donald Harstad
Fourth Estate, £9.99, 1-84115-394-X
Having served as a sheriff in north-eastern Iowa for twenty-six years, Harstad used his accumulated experience of the darker side of human experience to create the remarkable *Eleven Days*. And, pleasingly, he has broken

the Second Novel Curse to produce another thriller shot through with the intensity and power of its predecessor. This time, Nation County is suffering as the dead of winter exerts a paralysing grip. Deputy Sheriff Carl Houseman is dealing with the usual criminal fraternity of Iowa, while his partner and friend Hester Gorse has undertaken security duty on the floating casino Colonel Beauregard. Both will find themselves fighting for their lives when a ruthless group of men attempt a million-dollar siege of the economic assets of the state. Harstad's unerring tactics here involve a carefully orchestrated double jeopardy for his beleaguered protagonists: while Carl fights for control of the investigation, and find himself at the extremes of his survival skills, Hester is trapped on the Beauregard, firmly in the eye

A BRANDSTETTER MYSTERY

JOSEPH HANSEN
Gravedigger

'After 40 years, Hammett has a worthy successor' *The Times* of the storm. We've read the 'conflict between lawmen' scenario before, but rarely as adroitly handled as here – this is down to a combination of economical but rounded characterisation, and a sense of verisimilitude that no doubt results from Harstad's long experience as law officer. Hester, too, is a highly plausible creation – and her more direct experience of dangerous situations in the narrative means that she must carry the weight. That Harstad pulls this off as convincingly as Houseman's clashes with his fellow law enforcers is an index of his considerable skill.

Carol Yornstrand

Hunting Badger by Tony Hillerman
HarperCollins, £16.99, 0-00-226199-5
Once again, Navaho Tribal Police Sergeant. Jim Chee is teamed with (now retired) Lieutenant Joe Leaphorn, as they both find themselves drawn into a robbery/murder at the

Ute tribal casino. It's a low-key sort of story, as the contrasts between Chee and Leaphorn are emphasised before they eventually come to recognise their own similarities. This is fascinating for those who've followed the series, since Chee is the more traditional Navaho, who has studied tribal rites in an effort to become a healer. He is also more of a loner, and relieved to be back in his rank of sergeant, after a temporary promotion to lieutenant forced too much American-style bureaucracy on him. Leaphorn, in contrast, is the more assimilated, a man fascinated with police work, who studied police science in the big cities but is feeling deeply the loss of his wife, whose own Navaho sensibilities kept him in touch with that part of himself. Now retired, and beginning a new relationship, he finds surprises in the certainties he always felt about himself. For those coming to Hillerman for the first time, this background is not so much filled in as revealed while the story proceeds, and if the investigation itself is low-key, that allows both characters their free reign, and the novel is the better for it. An impressive piece of writing from one of America's best crime writers, it is also interesting to compare Leaphorn's struggle with retirement to Mario Balzic's in K. C. Constantine's *Blood Mud*. Is a generation of crime writers finding retirement a crucial issue? I find this realism preferable to thinking of Spenser, the Korean War veteran, still knocking out the ladies and kayo'ing the villains as he and Hawk approach seventy. Would they do it with Leaphorn's grace?

Dust to Dust by Tami Hoag
Orion, £9.99, 0-752-81432-X
Thomas Harris and *Silence of the Lambs* provided the prototype for Hoag's previous spell-

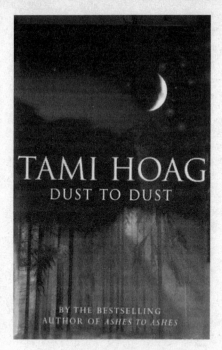

intrigue when he begins his investigation, and (as is par for the course for all police thrillers) heavy pressure is soon coming down from on high to terminate the case. Hoag has demonstrated in such intelligent novels as *A Thin Dark Line* and *Guilty as Sin* an effortless command of thriller technique, adroitly juggling the twin demands of character and plot. This is a cooler and more restrained book than its predecessor, but no less dynamic for all that. The set-piece confrontations will ensure that it will take quite a lot to distract the reader from Hoag's narrative, and the use of short, idiosyncratic paragraphs in the closing chapters is an innovative touch.

Vic Buckner

Sleeping Partner by James Humphreys
Macmillan, £16.99, 0-333-90107-X
There has been a positive avalanche of début crime novels recently, and it's a formidable

binder, *Ashes to Ashes*, in which FBI agent Kate Conlan and her former lover hunted the Cremator, a serial killer with the grim modus operandi of burning his female victims alive. *Ashes to Ashes* was not a book for the squeamish, and neither is the equally impressive *Dust to Dust*. But, as before, grisly tension is not the only commodity on offer here – the internal politics of the police investigations are handled with genuine panache, and Hoag's protagonists Kovac and his partner Tinks Liska are very solidly drawn. When internal affairs investigator Andy Fallon appears to take his own life, a metaphorical time bomb is set for the Minneapolis police department. Fallon (who was gay) was looking into the possible police connection in the death of another gay officer. The laconic Sam Kovac finds a labyrinth of deception and

Boys like Damian make girls like Bridget write diaries . . .

Humphreys delivers a tale that both grips with its elegant plotting and offers insights into character rarely found in the genre. Humphreys works at 10 Downing Street as an advisor in the Prime Minister's office, but there is none of the studied artificiality of most thrillers written by politicians. One is tempted to say that Humphreys should give up the day job forthwith and continue to turn out novels with this degree of authoritative storytelling nous.

Ralph Travis

E-Males by Allen Jarvis
Pan, £5.99, 0-330-37387-0
This geezer, right, desk job, likes blow jobs, that sort of thing. Split up with his girl, time for big changes, early retirement, that kind of thing. Wants to change his life for keeps, as easy as his Photoshop software can change the faces of mates in an old student picture.

task sorting the wheat from the chaff. James Humphreys' *Sleeping Partner* instantly announces itself as one of the more provocative and intelligent first novels in some time, even without the enthusiastic imprimatur of Colin Dexter (creator of Morse) on the jacket. Clarissa Morland is a shy and attractive twenty-seven-year-old who is on trial for the murder of a man with whom she once had a relationship. John Grant was murdered at his lonely farmhouse – but Clarissa can only remember being extracted from the wreckage of a car crash that morning. Did she kill Grant? And why does the car crash bear all the signs of a frenzied getaway? As Humphreys' lucidly detailed narrative unfolds, the reader is led into the darker corners of the human soul. While skilfully utilising the standard apparatus of the courtroom thriller,

One big E deal, through mate's brother or brother's mate, that ought to set them up. Sorted. Only thing is, right, what if he doesn't really like his mates? You get the picture. Bored twenty-somethings yak about nights out, angst and consumer durables. Swap their trainspotters' observations over best pin-up (Jo Guest) and best Russ Meyer movie (probably *Ultra-Vixens*). The list-making and morbid obsessing over past relationships fall well short of *High Fidelity*. Their crimes are incidental, their hedonism not so much undermining the big deal's execution as preventing them from really planning it. Whereas bunches of anti-social lads can get the right treatment from a skilled author – see Kevin Sampson's *Awaydays* – this lot are too mediocre for the reader to care. Neither nice guys nor Mr Nice-style drug dealers, we remain largely indifferent to their collective fate. Tired and derivative: *This Life* and *Lock, Stock* have a lot to answer for.

Graham Barnfield

Sleeping Cruelty by Lynda La Plante
Macmillan, £16.99, 0-333-73653-2
La Plante has achieved considerable success with a canny balancing act between genres. Initially, her thrillers may appear to be simple, non-reflective blockbusters with strong women characters, but she is a far more subtle writer than this might initially suggest. It takes real skill to produce popular writing as sophisticated as this, however pungent the narratives might seem. And if the sex, extravagance and revenge she deals in may be the stuff of lesser novels (particularly the airport blockbuster), her books treat the subjects in a head-on, vigorous fashion that guarantees high interest. The central character in *Sleeping Cruelty* represents a departure for her. Sir William Benedict is enjoying all the glittering prizes that his wealth and position have granted him. Relishing his reputation as a self-made man (with his own island in the Caribbean), he is particularly keen that his political protégé Andrew Maynard should succeed, and he has been bankrolling Maynard's campaign heavily. But Maynard, who was gay, commits suicide, and Benedict soon finds his reputation falling apart as swiftly as his ordered world. The hellish existence he finds himself in is rendered even more painful by the people who were closest to him. But Benedict is marshalling his forces, and begins to dream of an uncompromising revenge. In such books as *The Legacy*, *Bella Mafia* and *Cold Blood*, La Plante demonstrated a sure grasp in her delineation of larger-than-life characters. But she has replaced her powerful

DENNIS
GONE, BABY, GONE
LEHANE

'STUNNINGLY GOOD'
JAMES PATTERSON

female protagonists with a richly-drawn anti-hero in Benedict. The details of his lifestyle and the cold-blooded betrayals by his nearest and dearest are handled in the usual confident fashion, but it's the characterisation of Benedict that really grips the attention. Initial fears that that he may be a broadly-drawn, one-dimensional creation are quickly allayed, and the reader is cast adrift when La Plante pulls off her principal coup: thoroughly involving us in Benedict's highly dubious activities.

Ingrid Rains

Gone, Baby, Gone by Dennis Lehane
Bantam, £5.99, 0-553-81220-3
This is the fourth of Lehane's Boston-based series featuring private eyes Patrick Kenzie and Angela Gennaro, and to my mind it is the best. This is partially because the relationship between the two partners has resolved itself, thus taking the distracting, Cheers-style 'will they, won't they' element out of the equation, while opening it up for further conflict. And it is that latter possibility which Lehane brings to the fore in this tale of betrayal, kidnapping and child abuse. This book addresses ambiguities which are not usually visited by writers walking down those particularly contemporary mean streets, and they provide a number of telling twists. One problem with this series has been the distance between the sensitive characters of Kenzie and Gennaro, as revealed through Patrick's narration, and the rather less-sensitive persona they are required to be by the demands of the story, if not their profession. The presence of their deus-ex-machina sidekick Bubba, a kind of less-challenging uber-Hawk, makes this contrast all the more apparent. The closest parallel I can think of for this is Elvis Cole, but Robert Crais makes the harder edges of Cole's

background clearer. This is an on-going problem which Lehane evidently tackles book by book. In the meantime, *Gone, Baby, Gone* moves at a pace which accelerates throughout, until the moment when the resolutions come, with their inevitable let-downs. A first-rate piece of writing.

Michael Carlson

The Blind In Darkness by Stephen Lewis
Berkley Prime Crime, $5.99, 0-425-17466-2
The town of Newbury is a harsh place – especially if you are an outsider to the suspicious English community. However, Stephen Lewis's novel is set in Newbury in New England rather than Berkshire and the time is the seventeenth century. The outsider is called Massaquoit, an Indian servant of the midwife Catherine

A Mystery of Colonial Times

THE BLIND IN DARKNESS

STEPHEN LEWIS
AUTHOR OF *THE DUMB SHALL SING*

Williams; and when an old man is murdered, the people turn on him as the obvious suspect. Stephen Lewis evokes the atmosphere of a Puritan town rather successfully, perhaps inspired by the superb reconstructions at Old Sturbridge and Plimoth Plantation in New England. Unfortunately his main characters of Catherine and Massaquoit are simply not strong enough to carry the story. Massaquoit in particular is almost a caricature of political correctness; the 'good Indian' persecuted by the white men. Lewis uses the character of another Indian who works for the white men in an attempt to contrast this behaviour with the 'noble savage' nature of Massaquoit but only succeeds in creating a messy and confusing story line. The central mystery solution is glaringly obvious to a reader with twentieth century experiences, therefore it is frustrating that none of the seventeenth century characters figure out the puzzle. It seems that the mystery of the death is solved almost by accident, and although Lewis tries to slip in a twist on the final page, it is too late to perk up the lassitude of the rest of the book.

Anne Curry

Death Knock by Frederic Lindsay
Hodder & Stoughton, £17.99, 0-340-76570-4
Frederic Lindsay's *Idle Hands* was a particularly powerful entry in the impressive Lindsay canon, and it's good to report that this fourth thriller featuring Edinburgh detective Jim Meldrum is well up-to-par. The city is suffering through a heatwave, and Meldrum finds himself taking a shortcut through a housing development experiment. Caught up in the ambush of firemen by vicious twelve-year-olds, he arrives at a murder scene with a chunk out of his skull and mild concussion. His confusion isn't helped when the murdered redheaded woman in an evening gown is revealed to be a man, celebrated business figure Brian Ashton. And soon he is uncovering even more bizarre secrets, with the aid of crime profiler and academic Henry Stanley. Lindsay's Edinburgh is a less malevolent place than the city of some of his crime-writing confreres, but it's still a sinister trail Jim Meldrum is forced to tread as he uncovers corruption and dark sexual secrets. Plotting is as skilfully wrought as in earlier Meldrum novels such as *A Kind of Dying* and *Kissing Judas*, while the tenacious Jim is as sharply characterised as ever. The relationship with crime profiler Henry Stanley, too, is strikingly handled, with just the right astringent tone, and the revelations are spun out in a perfectly measured fashion.

Judith Gray

back\slash

a cyber thriller

william h. lovejoy

Back\slash – A Cyber Thriller
by William H. Lovejoy
Pinnacle, £5.99, 0-78600-437-1

Published a few years ago when Millennium Bug phobia was all the rage, this is a long, plodding, unconvincing and finally disappointing tale. Cyber terrorism is on the loose; all the terrible things they say will happen, but never do, come to pass. The experts and authorities are clueless and FBI Agent Luanne Russell turns to Kirk Conrad, a renegade computer genius she once jailed to find the prankster. A cast list is given at the beginning, like a play. We have the FBI; the Committee set up by the American government; its international counterpart; and 'Globenet', a private company that has set up an alternative network. It is like keeping track of four families, some members of which play such minor roles they could have been omitted. You don't have to know how a computer works to type a letter or a car to drive it. When explaining the packet switching network, that is the basis of computer networks, lecturers usually draw a 'T' for a terminal that attaches to a big cloud with other terminals attached to its edges. What goes on inside the cloud nobody cares about – you only need to know the packets will go from one terminal to another. The main problem with this book is that it is overburdened with exposition. People, who in real life would know all about it, are carefully told the details so the reader will know. Another failing is that giving the specification of a state of the art computer is soon going to be outdated. Worst of all, at the end it almost seems as if you finish the book without finding out who the 'frowning face' villain is. For a writer

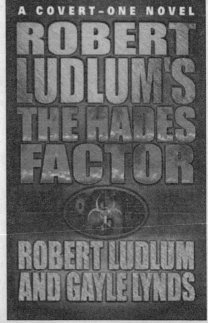

A COVERT-ONE NOVEL

ROBERT LUDLUM'S THE HADES FACTOR

ROBERT LUDLUM AND GAYLE LYNDS

of over a dozen books, Lovejoy should put writing over technical expertise because it is the quality of the writing readers want not technical knowledge.

Martin Spellman

The Hades Factor
by Robert Ludlum & Gayle Lynds
HarperCollins, £9.99, 0-00-710166-X
There was a time when Robert Ludlum had the blockbuster thriller genre absolutely sewn up: his massive, swiftly moving narratives of suspense provided kinetically charged bouts of action and beguilingly convoluted plotting that more than made up for any lack of subtlety. But other writers wrested the crown from Ludlum, and his star was eclipsed. This new book bids fair to make him a player again, even if the reader might be apprehensive at a co-author's name being given equal prominence on the jacket (few authors, from Arthur C. Clarke down, have benefited from this kind of collaborative process). Nevertheless, *The Hades Factor* moves with all the swiftness of vintage Ludlum, and stirs in many of the customary ingredients: government subterfuge, dangerous scientific secrets up for grabs, and espionage flamboyantly conducted over several continents. When a young girl in Atlanta, a soldier in California and a vagrant in Boston all die hideous deaths, a team of scientists in a US government laboratory is given the task of nailing a possible doomsday virus. The leading researcher from the lab, Lt. Col. Jonathan Smith, finds himself the victim of several attempts on his life as he returns from overseas, and he is devastated to find that the fourth victim of the virus is his own fiancée. And as Smith tracks the virus to the darkest corners of government, massive violence is directed against him and his team, while the clock ticks ominously on. Few will spot where Ludlum ends and Lynds begins in this outrageously entertaining piece.

Vic Buckner

The Servant by Robin Maugham
Dr Strangelove by Peter George
Prion, £5.99, 1-853753-89-0 / 1-853753-10-6
Having always disliked 'film' books in the past, I was won over by Neville Smith's *Gumshoe*, which is brilliant. Turning scripts into books can be a great addition to a great film. The problem with *Dr Strangelove*, for example, is 'why bother?' It is so familiar – great fun and so on – but having seen the film several times you end up questioning the book's purpose. Robin Maugham's *The Servant*, on the other hand, gives us an opportunity to discover afresh a compelling narrative which, at the very least, has you

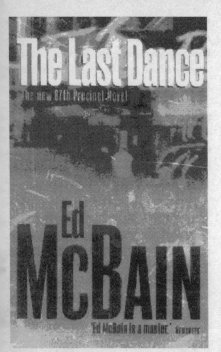

The Last Dance by Ed McBain
Hodder & Stoughton, £5.99, 0-340-72806-X
This book pushes the genre as there is more than the criminal to find. The theme is about conscience, informing and racial conflict against the usual background of urban decay. It begins when an old man is found dead in bed but it is soon discovered that he had been drugged with rohypnol and hung from the bathroom door. *The Last Dance* is the last dance of the evening or at the end of a rope. What did a penniless old man have to be killed for? Apparently this is how Ed McBain starts his books – with the crime – and then he works away from there. He considers the 87th Precinct books to be like chapters in one vast work, and someday maybe they will all be published in that way. There has already been one book surveying the series – *The Boys from Grover Avenue* by George Dove

reassessing one of the key British films of the 1960s. It also draws our attention to Maugham's writing. Neil Bartlet's excellent introduction highlights its pivotal role in gay fiction, and the fact that Maugham thought the film a travesty makes the book worth reading. At times clumsy and heavy handed it makes for a compelling read. One of the enduring images of *Dr Strangelove* is the start of a nuclear war over General Ripper's vital fluids. Maugham's haunting novella meanwhile helps to debunk all those myths about safe and normal relationships. With the US still testing Star Wars and Clause 28 still alive and well in middle England, these two books serve as a timely reminder – if you need it – that nothing is safe and normal – if it ever was.

Peter Walker

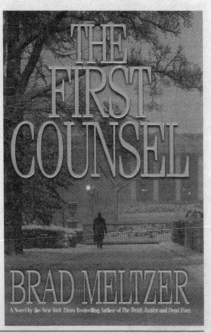

(1985, Bowling Green University Press). McBain has published eighty fiction books and this is the fiftieth in the old faithful 87th Precinct series. Their popularity is due to the fact that he knows how to tell a story and, while some are better than others, none are disappointing. This one is set in the theatre and publishing worlds like the 'Cats' book – *Romance* published in 1995. Cynthia Keating, the old man's daughter, is the first suspect as she called 911. But it is not that simple – there are some other strands to unravel. One failing is the use of the old ploy of 'the ambiguous name', but this does not spoil it. McBain has been to this country and there is a connection in the book, but it is overdrawn and won't convince the English reader.

Martin Spellman

The First Counsel by Brad Meltzer
Hodder & Stoughton, £10.00, 0-340-46937-8
Since the success of *Primary Colours*, White House-connected *romans à clef* have become a hot item, but this is the first time the concept has been successfully welded onto the thriller format. Actually, though, the real-life references are less important than Meltzer's smooth handling of an ingenious plot. 'Shadow' is the Secret Service code name for the President's daughter, Nora Hartson. Young White House lawyer Michael Garrick finds that there are side effects to dating the First Daughter, and they are not all desirable. On one of their dates, Nora and Michael witness something that they shouldn't see. In order to protect her, Michael begins a process of cover-up that soon plunges him into nightmare. And the reader is in familiar territory: the hero who can turn to no-one for aid. Meltzer is another lawyer/novelist, with all that implies – but the pacy writing and well-turned characterisation lift this one well out of the rut, and the relationship between Michael and the unhappy Nora is treated intelligently, adding another cachet of quality.

Vic Buckner

Killers on the Loose: Unsolved Cases of Serial Murder by Antonio Mendoza
Virgin, £6.99, 0-7535-0442-1
According to Mendoza, there are currently between thirty-five and fifty serial killers working in North America, while up to four may be operating in the UK. "Once a rare phenomenon, serial killing has become increasingly frequent with dozens of maniacs terrorising different cities simultaneously." However, while for Mendoza the serial killer is "an uncomfortably unfathomable reality of modern life", he doesn't attempt to fathom

the serial killer, nor to define for the reader what serial killing actually is. Mark Seltzer, on the other hand, in *Serial Killers: Death and Life in America's Wound Culture* (London: Routledge, 1998) notes that the term was coined by FBI's Robert Ressler in the mid-1970s, and Seltzer offers the FBI's definition of serial killing: "the killing of at least four victims, over a period greater than seventy-two hours." The major shortcoming of Mendoza's survey is that it makes no reference to any other work on the subject. It's not that Mendoza hasn't carried out any research – clearly he has – but he provides no references to substantiate what appears to be a paper-bound version of the case studies on his website. The book abounds with unsourced quotes from various law enforcement officials that might be from newspapers, television

news or from interviews, but the sources are never stated (in fact the only reference Mendoza provides in the whole 240 pages is to his own website). So while the cover tells us that "this is the first look at serial killers at large, from one of the world's foremost authorities", this claim appears to be no more than an unsupported assertion on the part of the blurb-writer. *Killers on the Loose* is superficially alluring but ultimately unsatisfying – the paperback equivalent of a salacious American television documentary. According to the ads in the back of the book, this is one of a series of true crime titles published by Virgin, including books on the Dunblane killings and Harold Shipman. One can only hope these are rather more substantial and purposeful than Mendoza's offering: if they are not, then someone at Virgin ought to look more closely at quality control in the publishing division, unless these endeavours are meant simply to provide hot air to help fuel Richard Branson's ballooning expeditions.

Eddie Duggan

Dead at Daybreak by Deon Meyer
Hodder & Stoughton, £16.99, 0-340-73942-8
Deon Meyer's *Dead Before Dying* was an impressive debut, suggesting real talent but raising a question about the quality of the original writing, which is translated from Afrikaans. With this book, Meyer confirms the talent his first book showed, and, if in the end he again builds a plot which requires a major break in the pace and tone in order to be resolved, he has established that tone with such panache that he can get away with it. Meyer tells two stories simultaneously. One is the tale of former cop Van Heerden, now investigating an unusual robbery/murder on

From the author of DEAD BEFORE DYING

DEON MEYER

DEAD AT DAYBREAK

THE PAST IS NEVER DEAD

behalf of a lawyer friend. The other, narrated in alternate chapters, traces Van Heerden's life story, and eventually the story of his exit from the police force. Just as those two tales turns out to be intertwined, the narration itself turns out to be an integral part of the plot. Meyer's transformation of some relatively standard elements into literary conceits is accompanied by a use of language which suggests Van Heerden's own difficulty in finding expression. As Meyer showed in his first book, his best writing deals with his characters' expression and sexuality. The sensitivity of Van Heerden's story also contrasts with the character he reveals as he fights his way through the story. That story takes us back to the 'glory' days of South Africa as a major player in the CIA's efforts in Africa, and if the novel's fulcrum is the unlikely tale of a rugby match between Soviet soldiers and ANC guerrillas at a base near Kazakhstan, well (strange as it seems) it works – as does this book. Meyer is a writer to take seriously – the best crime writer out of South Africa since James McClure.

Michael Carlson

Exile by Denise Mina
Bantam, £16.99, 0-593-04653-6
Thriller writers such as Ian Rankin have heaped praise upon the shoulders of Denise Mina, who won the John Creasey Best First Crime Novel prize for her remarkable *Garnethill*. But high reader expectations can be a heavy cross to bear, and more than one writer has come to grief attempting to recreate earlier triumphs. On the evidence of *Exile*, however, Mina is a writer up for the long haul: this is every bit as atmospheric and idiosyncratic as the earlier novel, with an increased sharpness in characterisation that makes for a highly compelling read. Whether or not Scottish crime writers such as Mina and Rankin do their country any service by presenting it as a highly dangerous place matters not a damn – the Glasgow setting of this piece is rendered with a gritty authority that might not please the Scottish Tourist Board, but is perfect for the reader. Mina's protagonist Maureen O'Donnell is working in the Glasgow Women's Shelter when she encounters Anne Harris, suffering from two broken ribs and fighting the effects of a crippling descent into alcoholism. But a fortnight later, Anne's body turns up in the Thames, grotesquely mutilated and embedded in a mattress. Is Anne's husband the murderer, as he so clearly seems to be? But he has four kids to bring up alone, and closer examination makes him look a less likely suspect. Maureen and her friend Leslie

DENISE
MINA

AUTHOR OF *GARNETHILL*, WINNER OF THE
JOHN CREASEY AWARD FOR BEST FIRST CRIME NOVEL

EXILE

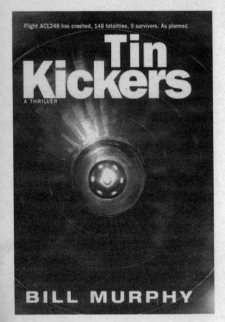

Flight ACL248 has crashed, 148 fatalities, 0 survivors. As planned.

Tin Kickers

A THRILLER

BILL MURPHY

try to penetrate the indifference surrounding Anne's death, but Leslie is curiously close-mouthed about what she knows. Attempting to escape from the turmoil of her own life, Maureen travels to London, but she is soon immersed in a dangerous world of violence and drug abuse. Utilising the classic structure of the thriller (the investigator in danger of encountering the same fate as the victim) Mina brings a level of compassion and understanding to her grim tale that ensures a remarkable experience for the reader. She is unblushing in confronting the darker side of life, and her conflicted heroine is satisfyingly embroiled in the revelations she is forced to confront. The final effect of this idiosyncratic and dark thriller is both life-affirming and exhilarating, and though we may all soon need a holiday from the criminal alleys of Scotland, it isn't time yet.

Carol Yornstrand

Tin Kickers by Bill Murphy
Hodder & Stoughton, £16.99, 0-340-76598-4
More cynical crap designed to part the gullible from their hard-earned, launched at the height of the summer season to catch the dump-bin reader speeding through passport control. Maybe not at airports so much though, seeing as how it starts with a Los Angeles International to Mexico City ditching with all hands. Want to pretend we care? Okay, Ron Carter is a 'Tin Kicker' (gotta love that jargon), an air accident investigator. Nancy Kronziac works for the FBI Counter Intelligence Group. Together this poverty row Mulder and Scully must sift through the wreckage and piece together the far-reaching criminal conspiracy that "takes the reader from the sweating jungles of Mexico to the hallowed halls of Washington DC itself." This is ugly, silly mind pollutant, showcasing writing that scales the dizzy heights of the mediocre, and reads like it was plotted on (if not by) a Speak 'n' Spell. From the reassuringly butch cover to the obvious page count (and garish Dick & Jane typeface), it doesn't have an ironic bone in its stultifyingly inadequate body. Expect to see cricketers and ex-Tory Cabinet Ministers salivating from those 'My Media' columns in The Guardian any day.

Gerald Houghton

A Chemical Prison by Barbara Nadel
Headline, £17.99, 0-747-22344-0
Nadel made a considerable impact with her first novel, *Belshazzar's Daughter*. With its brilliantly realised Istanbul setting, highly unusual plotting and innovative protagonist, Inspector Cetin Ikmen, it was clearly going to be a hard act to follow. But *A Chemical Prison* pulls off the trick triumphantly, with our knowledge of Ikmen being satisfyingly broad-

ened in a new brainteaser. Ikmen and forensic pathologist Arto Sarkissian are childhood friends, and, despite differences, still work together within the confines of Istanbul's criminal justice system. When both attend the possible murder of a twenty-year-old boy in an apartment near the Topkapi Museum, their friendship is tested when the case proves to have some extremely strange ramifications. As before, Istanbul itself remains a key player in this distinguished and evocative novel. But it's the characterisation that makes it really hum, and Nadel bids fair to be a bright particular star in the crime-writing firmament.

Barry Forshaw

Hugger Mugger by Robert B. Parker
John Murray, £16.99, 0-71955-669-4
When Boston private eye Spenser first appeared some thirty novels ago, he was, like Raymond Chandler's Marlowe, a former

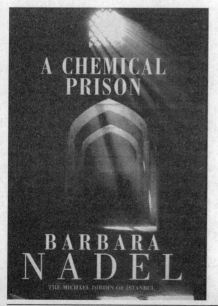

insubordinate cop. But he had a sensitive side. The ex-pugilist could also put down his pistol, pick up a pestle, and prepare a perfect pesto pronto. Helped by his therapist girlfriend, Susan Silverman, Spenser grows ever more sensitive, and embarrassingly self-referential. Susan thinks they resemble Nick and Nora Charles, but Hammett's Nora was always more Clara Bow than Susie Orbach. When Spenser arrives in Lamarr, Georgia to investigate shots fired at racehorse Hugger Mugger, Susan tells him he's trapped in a Tennessee Williams play. If *King Lear* played as *Falconcrest* qualifies as Tennessee Williams, I'm Stanley Kowalski. Dropping Spenser into the midst of the over-julepped and over-sexed Clive family gives our hero plenty of opportunity to prove his moral superiority with both punches and punch-lines. Parker builds his story through quick scenes which flow beautifully, in which Spenser eats an inordinate number of doughnuts and lands enough ironic one-liners to keep the pages turning. This formula works so well, Parker's added another two series characters to his repertoire: Sunny Randall, a female Spenser, and Jesse Stone, an alcoholic police chief who is Spenser's id made real. Whoever the star, the formula makes sidekicks essential, since every hero needs to have his world view reflected, and every comic needs straight-men. Spenser's usual alter ego, Hawk, is on vacation, but in Georgia you must be able to look up sidekicks in the yellow pages. Our hero bonds immediately with a slow but sly black cop who also provides junk food, then finds the world's toughest gay man, Teddy Sapp, to, er, back him up. Can you tell Hawk from a handsaw? Although it's entertaining, reliance on formula finds *Hugger Mugger* flopping in the final furlongs. Spenser's need to always have the

last word means Parker's femme fatale fails to convince, and the spider-woman's actual victim isn't allowed enough of his own character to let her display her venom properly. Parker gets to close with a classic film noir line, but without the build-up it fizzles rather than sizzles.

Michael Carlson

Trouble In Paradise by Robert B. Parker
No Exit Press, £5.99, 1-901982-73-4
Robert B. Parker's fame as a crime writer rests largely with his popular Spenser novels, a series of books which adhere firmly to the first-person private eye narrative in the tradition established by Raymond Chandler in the 1940s. Recently, however, Parker has rested Spenser and invented a new crime-fighting hero, Jesse Stone, who debuted in the book *Night Passage*. Stone is a former Golden State police officer who renounced the LA's mean

streets and has relocated to a small Massachusetts coastal town on America's eastern seaboard. That town is called Paradise (hence the title of this new novel) and Stone is installed as its Chief of Police. Paradise seems a quiet town with quiet people, a hicky backwater where not much happens. Recalcitrant teenagers with bumptious parents seem to pose the biggest criminal conundrum for Stone until the arrival of ex-con Jimmy Macklin who puts a specialist crew together to ransack the small, adjoining island of Stiles. Linked by a single bridge to the mainland and patrolled by officious rent-a-cops, Stiles Island is an exclusive, upmarket repository for the rich and well-heeled. Macklin plans to take control of the island, rob its inhabitants, boost the local bank and leave it a millionaire several times over. But, of course, he didn't count on a savvy, resourceful local cop like Jesse Stone. Stone is a strong, thoughtful, taciturn man whose complex romantic entanglements cause him more heartache and grief than the prospect of confronting ruthless and violent criminals. A pacy page-turner of a novel with strong characters, zippy dialogue and visceral action scenes, *Trouble In Paradise* is an eminently entertaining read which attests to Robert B. Parker's god-like status among contemporary crime writers.

Charles Waring

A Cold Touch of Ice by Michael Pearce
HarperCollins, £16.99, 0-00-232697-3
One of the most sheerly entertaining sequences in crime fiction is Michael Pearce's ingenious Mamur Zapt mysteries. His protagonist, who has been granted the title Mamur Zapt, is a Welsh captain serving in Edwardian Cairo, ostensibly answering to the Khedive (the chief of the Cairo secret police), but ulti-

mately to his English masters. As usual Gareth Owen's Welshness grants him an anti-establishment sympathy with the Egyptian natives, and the greatest possible use is made of richly delineated local colour. In fact, the cosmopolitan setting, with its heady mix of religions and social divisions, always affords even more pleasure than the convoluted plots (here initiated by a heated political discussion followed by a brutal murder, with Owen obliged to balance the demands of natural justice and political expediency). In a series as long-running as this, refreshing the customary ingredients must be a Herculean task, but such is Pearce's understated professionalism that we are never conscious of having encountered these particular situations before. We have observed Owen's inner struggle over his duties on many occasions, but they are han-

dled in the new book with a sharply observed and satisfying skill, set against a colourful new cast of characters.

Judith Gray

No Witnesses by Ridley Pearson
Island Publishing
Pearson sometimes does five redrafts of his books because he likes them 'intricate and tight'. *No Witnesses* is so called because someone is poisoning people by contaminating food products. Extortion is also demanded and collected from automatic teller machines, sight unseen. The idea of the book came from the Heinz Baby Food tampering case (which Pearson refers to here), in which ATMs were also used to collect the ransom. He supposedly developed the idea while at Oxford for a year on a Chandler Fellowship. This was set up for six years by Graham Greene's nephew in memory of crime writer Raymond Chandler. Three British writers, including Ian Rankin, went to the States and three Americans came to Oxford. Homicide Sergeant Lou Boldt and police psychologist Daphne Matthews are on this case. The villain is soon christened the 'Tin Man' as he tampers with tinned produce. Although this is a long novel (469 pages) it is one book and not two, as books of this length so often are. Tension is kept going all the way through. His research is thorough, including the software used to slow down the ATM machines to allow the police time to intercept the ransom withdrawals. But it never becomes overbearing or boring as is sometimes the case when a lot of detailed explanation is needed – the plot is kept in sight. That said, Pearson admits to occasionally inventing some items and blending them in with the truth. There is a long interview with him on

MICHAEL PEARCE
A COLD TOUCH OF ICE
SHEER FUN Marcel Berlins, *The Times*

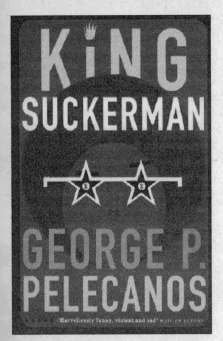

movie boom that reached its mainstream acme in *Shaft*. *King Suckerman* forms the second part of the DC Quartet, and its characters reappear in the other three books, each highlighting a different take on the sleazy, drug-filled underbelly of black American crime. *King Suckerman* is the book Quentin Tarantino would have written had he not ventured into filmmaking. It is engorged with so many 1970s film references – real and imagined – that it's hard to know whether you're reading a straight story or a parody. Each character's dialogue is hipper than a very hip Huggy Bear, and a honky like me (this means a white person – I learnt it from *Live and Let Die*) is probably not going to get the full picture. Violence and humour sit side by side, in a style well honed in such diverse fare as *Lock, Stock...* and *Reservoir Dogs* (Tarantino's second mention this review) – although the surfeit of characters, and their similar attributes, can make the plot a little hard to follow. And

www.mysteryguide.com for anyone interested. Pearson was originally a musician who started writing screenplays and moved on to novels. The care he takes in reading other books plus the research and writing of his own pays off in a riveting read. Despite all the painstaking work, he has published several others including *Undercurrents*, *Beyond Recognition* and *The Angel Maker*.

Martin Spellman

King Suckerman by George P. Pelecanos
Serpent's Tail, £5.99, 1-852427-34-5
Nowadays you can't move for programmes about the 1970s. It's official – the decade of *Starsky and Hutch* and Spangles is more fashionable now than it ever was. Fresh on the heels of this retro conveyor belt comes George Pelecanos' *King Suckerman*, a book clearly influenced by the 70s blaxploitation

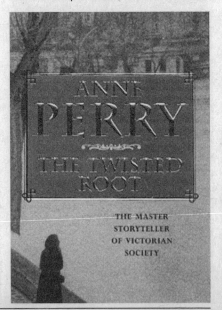

some of the motivation is so cryptic you can easily blink and miss it. But the dialogue is where Pelecanos really scores, delivering an engaging stream of street patois direct from the ghettos of Harlem (the second *Live and Let Die* reference this review). So if you yearn for the days of *Easy Rider* and Jimi Hendrix, this is the book for you. It may be hard work, but then so was riding a space hopper.

Mark Campbell

The Twisted Root by Anne Perry
Headline, £5.99, 0-7472-6323-X
Miriam Gardner has disappeared, fleeing from a party to celebrate her betrothal to Lucius Stourbridge. Lucius asks William Monk, an investigative agent, and an ex-police officer, for help. Although not normally given to sentimentality, Monk has recently married Hester, and his happiness is complete: he feels for the young man's distress and determines to do all he can to find Miriam. The Stourbridge family's coachman is also missing, along with a coach and horses, and this provides the starting point for Monk's investigation. Concern for Miriam's safety grows when the coachman is found murdered. The answer to the puzzle lies in Miriam's past: and someone is willing to kill, rather than have it revealed. Hester has her own problems to worry about: medicines are missing from the hospital where she is struggling to improve standards and provide proper training for nurses and more professional care for the sick. Hester fears that one of the nurses in her charge may be the culprit. Matters are further complicated when it seems there could be some connection between the disappearance of the medicines and Monk's case. The relationship between Hester and Monk is lively and interesting, with enough spikiness to pre-vent their evident delight in each other descending into mawkishness, and the conundrum of Miriam's past is genuinely baffling. However, the historical detail is given too much prominence for my taste, as, for example, when old Mr Robb tells Hester about his time on the battleships at Waterloo. There is too much re-evaluation and recapping of the various elements of the case in the earlier chapters; with a little less repetition the tension could be heightened. The final chapters go at a fair clip, however, building the suspense well, and the revelation of Miriam's childhood trauma is a real surprise.

Margaret Murphy

The Hit List by Chris Ryan
Century, £15.99, 0-7126-8411-5
Did you know that Robert Maxwell's final dip in the sea was not an act of suicide but assassination? According to Chris Ryan's tough and

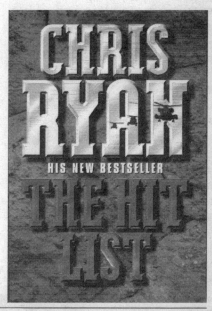

SIMON SHAW

KILLING GRACE

SIMON SHAW IS ONE OF THE VERY BEST OF OUR CRIME-FICTION WRITERS *Sunday Telegraph*

energetic thriller, the shadowy agency behind the tycoon's death is at the heart of a major conspiracy in the British establishment. But Ryan has ex-SAS man Neil Slater involved in the plot when terrorists try to kidnap one of his pupils (Neil has left the army to take up a new life as a teacher). Dismissed from school after the violence he demonstrates in the incident, he is soon drawn back into the covert world when Radovan Karadjic is captured to face a trial for war crimes at The Hague. Slater finds himself assigned to kill the arms salesman involved in the Karadjic operation, and soon a very nasty can of worms is opened up. Others tackle the pared-down SAS novel but few do it as energetically as Ryan. All the expected technical detail is on hand to facilitate the action, and few of the psychological niceties that Ryan knows would slow things down. The phrase 'a cracking good read' has

lost some of its currency, but it was coined for this high-octane piece. The characterisation of Slater may break no new ground, but few readers caught up in this outrageous narrative will have cause for complaint.

Ingrid Rains

Killing Grace by Simon Shaw
HarperCollins, £9.99, 0-00-710009-4
In books such as *Bloody Instructions* and *Dead for a Ducat* the talented Simon Shaw has been doing considerably more than carving out a nice line in Shakespearian titles. Marrying the cold-eyed psychological intensity of Ruth Rendell to a scalpel-sharp observation of the social scene, Shaw's speciality has been a series of elaborately choreographed *danses macabres* between his characters. In *Killing Grace*, he adds a new dimension to his devious art: the motives of his three central characters unfold in a continually disorientating fashion, constantly inviting the reader to think he/she has all the necessary bearings, only to throw the compass away. The charismatic Lewis has an irresistible fascination for women, and, as he works as a builder, he is fully able to avail himself of the houses, beds and sexual charms of his clients' wives. But his pleasant philandering is starting to lose its charm: he has no money, and he's finding it more difficult to observe his primary rule – never get involved. But the captivating Julie forces him to break his code, and he is still seeing her long after he has finished the job on her house. Peter McGovern could not be more different. He's rich, and as unprepossessing as Lewis is attractive. But Julie is his wife, and when the two men meet by chance over a game of pool, all three lives will shortly be changed irrevocably. Mixed into this dangerous brew is the deceptively angelic

Grace, whose fragile good looks conceal a ruthless sensibility and an acerbic tongue. When she becomes involved with both men, the outcome for one or more of the characters will have bloody consequences. Quite the most striking thing about Shaw's smoothly amoral tale is its dispassionate telling: Shaw never nudges the reader but guides him inexorably through a narrative that becomes ever more sinister. And however reptilian his characters, we remain transfixed. He's even good at freshening up situations we've heard before.

Vic Buckner

Chain of Fools: A Donald Strachey Mystery, by Richard Stevenson
St Martins Press, £7.95, 0-312-16796-2
It is good that there are still writers of short (under 200 page) crime novels around. Gay PI, Donald Strachey, and his buddy Tim Callahan

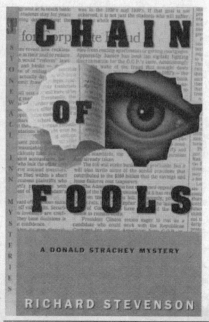

look into the months-old death of Eric Osborne after his sister survives a murder attempt. The background is the forthcoming takeover by rival buyers of a crusading American newspaper called the Edensburg Herald, which the Osborne family own. From the start, the premise of killing off board members to secure the sale for one of the groups seems unlikely, especially as neither of them ever put in an appearance. The plot seems too stagy with unnatural and forced dialogue. Writers like Horace McCoy, say in *Kiss Tomorrow Goodbye*, manage to weave the background in as the main character acts, without the reader noticing. In the first half of this book there is little action as page after page of talking heads explain the background of the paper and the characteristics of the large Osborne clan. The difficulty with family matters; business organisations and computer technology is that, apart from those closely involved, most people find them boring. Also, while there are probably more gay people around than most people realise, too many gay relationships are included. The late Eric and his sister are both gay, as are Donald and Timmy, of course, and even the police detective's son, who plays no part in the book. However, it does get going halfway through, but this never overcomes the weaknesses at the outset. Stevenson has written a series of Strachey books, which are generally highly regarded. They are hard to find in the shops, which is usually a good sign. Amazon.co.uk can get them. This one is not the best.

Martin Spellman

All The Empty Places by Mark Timlin
No Exit Press, £14.99, 1-901982-88-2
Sometimes a book just clicks. Pick it up, start

All the Empty Places
MARK TIMLIN

reading and before you know it you've missed *Corrie*, putting the kids to bed and a goodnight kiss from the missus (mine showed an almost Sharmanesque propensity toward violence when her patience finally ran out around midnight: "Will you stop reading that f***ing book!"). And so it is with this one, the sixteenth in the Nick Sharman series. I read it in one go (almost) and loved it. The plot involves... well, what the plot always involves: women, two-timing women, a great double-cross (prizes for those who, like me, spotted it coming!), money, violence and small furry animals. But before you can say "they're all the same" the conclusion involves a tunnel, rats and a pair of handcuff's. (For possibly only the third time in the series I went "oooh, yuk!"). On top of all this there's also a very neat bank robbery, some serious

GBH and loads of action all lovingly done in that inimitable Timlin style. Hell, what more do you want? You either love it or want to write to the Daily Mail about it. (If I was to add a bit of weighty 'analysis' to this review I'd point out that Sharman is way out on the edge of legality here and reading this makes you wonder where he's heading and the tunnel theme revisits the 'dark' themes of recent books – but in reality that sounds boring even to me.) Anyway, it's all great fun and probably one of the best of all the books in the series. Obviously the swap to No Exit has been a good one, as this follows the equally wonderful *Quick Before They Catch Us*. Long may it continue.

Peter Walker

Charles Willeford Omnibus
No Exit Press, £9.99, 1-874061-39-4
Although his Hoke Mosely detective novels made him a reputation in the last years of his life (and *Miami Blues* was made into an underrated movie) Charles Willeford was, in some ways, the last of the 1950s pulp writers. The three novels collected here were published between 1967 and 1972, and demonstrate Willeford at his pulpy best. *Pick-Up* starts with a scene that could be Edward Hopper's *Nighthawks*, only the woman is a drunk, and she drags the counterman with her in an inevitable, downward spiral. *The Burnt Orange Heresy* may be the best crime novel ever set in the milieu of the art world, while *Cockfighter* is the book that spawned the Monte Hellman-Warren Oates film classic of the same name. Do I really need to tell you more? These books aren't the easiest to find individually, and now you can pick them up in one volume. Do it.

Michael Carlson

SERENDIPITY

John Kennedy Melling

I discussed before in this column that excellent French weekly magazine *Le Nouveau Detective*, a true crime account of most recent international murders and crimes, and some historic examples. Founded in 1928, one of the early contributors in the 1930s was Jean Cocteau. When I was in Nice recently, researching on French crime writer Boileau-Narcejac I found another French crime magazine, *Dossiers Criminels*, a fairly new bi-monthly publication. The issue I bought contained an up-to-date survey of Marylin Monroe's(sic) murder, some other recent world crimes, including the disappearance of Doctor Godard.

Self-publishing – again I have commented on this previously. There are some crime writers who have achieved success, and I know at first hand of others. Michael J. Burrell published a book on Piers, *A Walk Across the Waves* in 1998, to which I contributed, and this is now making a profit for him. His second book is *Cliffhangers*, about Cliff Lifts, to which I contributed the Foreword. I belong to the Marylebone Rifle and Pistol Club and the Chairman's wife, Madeline Macdonald, published *The Last Year of the Gang* through Book Guild, who tell me their books are in every good bookshop.

Crime writers express great joy in joining various organisation – but what do many of them do to help? Not only the CWA, but I have seen writers elected to the originally prestigious Detection Club with whoops of joy and pride – and some of them don't bother to turn up ever again to the three meetings a year. What a good idea if members who missed a certain number of meetings were forced to drop out as happens in several older organisations. Fifty years ago an American magazine published 20 rules for members – two of them were, never to join a committee, and criticise those who do, either for not doing the job properly or alternatively for doing the job well for their own glory!

Where Are the Giants of Yesteryear?

On the CWA Committee from 1985 to 1988, I tried, as a non-fiction writer, to suggest workable ideas. One was to present a prestige award to outstanding crime writers, rather like the MWA Grand Master. The Committee agreed. Chairman Lady Antonia Fraser asked for my nomination, but, when I put forward the greatest living author Georges Simenon, replied, "But John, he isn't English". Furious, I was about to resign, when fellow columnist Gwendoline Butler saw my reaction, and quickly put forward Eric Ambler, for his services to espionage crime writing. We agreed. I was delighted that the night he received it at the CWA dinner at Armoury House, the BBC televised the event, so the three faces most seen were Ambler, Antonia's and mine, as toastmaster.

The award was taken over by a commercial jeweller, became an annual event, but only one or two names have significantly enriched and enlarged the genre. Apart from Ambler, Leslie Charteris, whose books, short stories, magazines, films and TV series of *The Saint* did more good than anyone save Christie, and American Ed McBain for the police procedural, have been outstanding. The award seems to have degenerated into an Annual Good Conduct Prize, often to past chairmen of the CWA, which wasn't my original thought. I am told one crime writer was heard to ask if it wasn't time they received an award!

A similar problem, perhaps, is coming to the Detection Club, founded in 1931 by the great names of Chesterton, Bentley, Berkeley, Christie and Sayers, with its own premises, library and publication of classics like *The Floating Admiral* and *Ask a Policeman*. Chesterton served as president for four years, Bentley for thirteen, Sayers for ten, Christie for eighteen (with the amazing Lord Gorell as co-president for five years till his death, as Christie was notoriously unable to speak in public, a great disadvantage for a president), the taciturn Symons for nine years, and the present, Harry Keating, completing his fifteen years – so presumably a new president may soon come up for consideration for election. The duties are not onerous – only three dinner meetings a year, with short speeches, a casual election procedure that was perhaps more striking in the 1930s with the great names clustered round. But who are the great names now – most have either died or, like the charming and erudite Michael Gilbert, rather retired from public life. We shall see what we shall see, as the French say.

Party Time(d) Right

There are several good reasons for a successful book launch. First it is to introduce the book and the author to the media, the trade and his professional colleagues. Second to let him and the guests know that the publisher is efficient, successful and caring for both writers and the trade. Lastly, to make all the guests feel welcome. When Susan Herbert is hostess at an Allison & Busby party, she invariably succeeds on all counts. Immaculately dressed, she, Rod (the director) and the staff were indefatigable, and no-one was left standing in the corner. The first hardcover crime book from the company is *Candleland* by Martyn Waites, an amiable giant of a young man, who, as an actor, read the short excerpt from his book quietly and convincingly; a scene in the Newcastle I know well. I am not reviewing his book, so I shall merely say it is a strong, bitter, harrowing *noir* canvas. An interesting guest list, including a Conservative politician! I spent some time with Priscilla Masters, a slimmer, elegant, amusing Priscilla, in an eye-catching red and black suit that became her well. Her brother was with her, and Rod joined us to talk animatedly about the problems of selling books, not to readers, but to booksellers. We shared anecdotes about our shooting skills. Geoffrey Bailey, from Crime in Store, in a tuxedo and on his way to a birthday party, gave me the lowdown on bookselling problems with which I sympathised, because I have attended, and spoken, at the functions he holds regularly. Patricia Hall I met; she is now at A & B, following some rather casual-sounding treatment from her previous publishers. Harry Keating and Sheila, en route to Harrogate, were in the homogenous gathering. I left feeling I had benefited from my attendance and enjoyed myself in this friendly, yet sophisticated, evening.